W9-CBX-121

COLD CITY

ALSO BY F. PAUL WILSON

Repairman Jack*

The Tomb
Legacies
Conspiracies
All the Rage
Hosts
The Haunted Air
Gateways
Crisscross
Infernal
Harbingers
Bloodline
By the Sword
Ground Zero
Fatal Error
The Dark at the End

Teen Jack*

Jack: Secret Histories
Jack: Secret Circles
Jack: Secret Vengeance

The Adversary Cycle*

The Keep
The Tomb
The Touch
Reborn
Reprisal
Nightworld

Other Novels

Healer
Wheels Within Wheels
An Enemy of the State
*Black Wind**
Dydeetown World
The Tery
*Sibs**
The Select
Virgin
Implant
Deep as the Marrow
Mirage (with Matthew J. Costello)
Nightkill (with Steven Spruill)
Masque (with Matthew J. Costello)
The Christmas Thingy
Sims
The Fifth Harmonic
Midnight Mass

Short Fiction

Soft and Others
*The Barrens and Others**
*Aftershock & Others**
*The Peabody-Ozymandias Traveling Circus & Oddity Emporium**
*Quick Fixes**

Editor

Freak Show
Diagnosis: Terminal

* See "The Secret History of the World" (page 367).

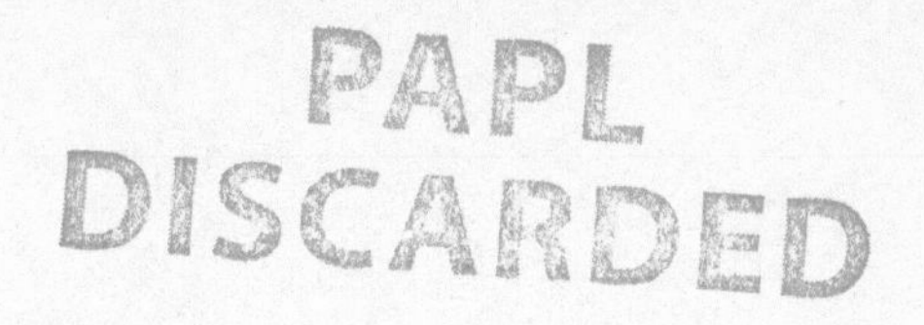

COLD CITY

A Repairman Jack Novel

THE EARLY YEARS TRILOGY: BOOK ONE

F. PAUL WILSON

A TOM DOHERTY ASSOCIATES BOOK • NEW YORK

This is a work of fiction. All of the characters, organizations, and events portrayed in this novel are either products of the author's imagination or are used fictitiously.

COLD CITY

A Tor Book
Published by Tom Doherty Associates, LLC
175 Fifth Avenue
New York, NY 10010

www.tor-forge.com

Library of Congress Cataloging-in-Publication Data

Wilson, F. Paul (Francis Paul)
Cold city / F. Paul Wilson. — 1st ed.
p. cm.
"A Tom Doherty Associates Book."
ISBN 978-0-7653-3014-7 (hardcover)
ISBN 978-1-4299-4833-3 (e-book)
1. Repairman Jack (Fictitious character)—Fiction. 2. New York (N.Y.)—Fiction.
I. Title.
PS3573.I45695C65 2012
813'.54—dc23

2012024852

First Edition: November 2012

Printed in the United States of America

0 9 8 7 6 5 4 3 2 1

ACKNOWLEDGMENTS

Thanks to the usual crew for their efforts: my wife, Mary; my editor, David Hartwell; Steven Spruill; Elizabeth Monteleone; Heather Graham; Kathy Love; plus Becky Maines, Blake Dollens, Dannielle Romeo; and my agent, Albert Zuckerman.

AUTHOR'S NOTE

If you've never read a Repairman Jack novel, *Cold City* is a good place to start. It kicks off the Early Years Trilogy, which begins in 1990 and recounts how Jack arrived in New York City as a callow twenty-one-year-old and made the city his home.

NYC was a different place then. The Disneyfication of Times Square was still years away. A national recession was on, the crime rate was high, and 42nd Street was still Grindhouse Row.

Jack was different too. He didn't know the ropes yet—hell, he didn't even know where to find the ropes. But he's a quick learner, adaptable, and choosy about who he'll call a friend. In other words, a natural-born survivor.

Meet the new Jack, not the same as the old Jack—but all the ingredients are there to brew up the guy people will come to know as the Repairman.

—F. Paul Wilson,
the Jersey Shore

THURSDAY

1

Jack might have reacted differently if he'd seen the punch coming. He might have been able to hold back a little. But he was caught off guard, and what followed shocked everyone. Jack most of all.

No surprise where it came from. Rico had been riding him since the summer, and pushing especially hard today.

The morning had started as usual. Giovanni Pastorelli, boss and owner of Two Paisanos Landscaping, had picked him up at a predesignated subway stop in Brooklyn—Jack lived in Manhattan and trained out—and then picked up the four Dominicans who made up the rest of the crew. The Dominicans all lived together in a crowded apartment in Bushwick but Giovanni refused to drive through there. He made the "wetbacks"—his not-unaffectionate term for them when they weren't around—train to a safer neighborhood.

Jack had arrived in the city in June and came across the Two Paisanos boss in July at a nursery. His landscaping business had started with two paisanos but now had only one, Giovanni, who almost laughed Jack off when he'd asked if he needed an extra hand. He was a twenty-one-year-old who looked younger. But he'd worked with a number of landscapers in high school and college, and ten minutes of talk convinced the boss he'd be taking on experienced help.

But Jack's knowledge of Spanish, rudimentary though it was, clinched the hire. The boss had come over from Sicily with his folks at age eight and had lived in Bath Beach forever. He spoke Italian and English but little Spanish. Jack had taken Spanish in high school and some at Rutgers. The

Dominicans who made up the rest of Giovanni's crew spoke next to no English.

Giovanni worked them all like dogs seven days a week but no harder than he worked himself. He liked to say, "You'll get plenty of days off—in the winter." He paid cash, four bucks an hour—twenty cents above minimum wage—with no overtime but also no deductions.

Though a newcomer, Jack quickly became Giovanni's go-to guy. He could understand the Dominicans if they spoke slowly, and was able to relay the boss's work orders to them.

Before Jack, that had been Rico's job. He spoke little English, but enough to act as go-between. He probably felt demoted. Plus, Giovanni loved to talk and would launch long, rambling monologues about wine, women, and Italy at Jack, something never possible with Rico. That had to gall him. He'd been with Giovanni—or *jefe*, as he called him—for years, then Jack strolls in and becomes right-hand man within weeks of his arrival.

Jack had come to like Giovanni. He was something of a peacock with his pompadour hair and waxed mustache, and could be a harsh taskmaster when they were running late or weather put him behind schedule. But he was unfailingly fair, paying on time and to the dime.

He liked his "wetbacks" and respected how hard they worked. But his old-country values didn't allow much respect for his clients.

"A man who won't work his own land don't deserve it."

Jack had lost count of how many times he'd heard him mutter that as they'd unload the mowers and blowers and weed whackers from the trailer. Giovanni charged jaw-dropping lawn maintenance fees, but people paid him. He had the quality homeowners wanted most in their gardener: He showed up. On top of that, he and his crew did good work.

On this otherwise unremarkable late October day, the Two Paisanos crew was in Forest Hills performing a fall cleanup around a two-story Tudor in the shadow of the West Side Tennis Club stadium. Last month they'd worked at the club itself, planting mums for the fall. His dad was a big tennis fan and Jack remembered seeing the place on TV when the US Open was held here.

Carlos, Juan, and Ramon were happy-go-lucky sorts who loved having a job and money to spend in the midst of a recession. But Rico had a chip on his shoulder. Today he'd started in the moment he got in the truck. Childish stuff. He was seated behind Jack so he began jabbing his knees against Jack's seat back. Jack seethed. The months of bad 'tude and verbal abuse were getting to him. But he did his best to ignore the guy. Rico never seemed to be playing with a full deck anyway, and appeared to be missing more cards than usual today.

When they reached the work site Rico started with the name-calling in Spanish. One thing lacking in his Spanish classes in Rutgers had been vernacular obscenities. But Jack had picked up quite a few since July. Rico was using them all. Usually the comments were directed at Jack, but today Rico had expanded into Jack's ancestry, particularly his parents. With Jack's mother buried less than a year now, the guy was stomping on hallowed ground. But he didn't know that. Jack set his jaw, tamped the fire rising within, and put on his headphones. He started UB40's latest spinning in his Discman. The easy, mid-tempo reggae of *Labour of Love II* offered a peaceful break from Rico's rants.

Rico must have become royally pissed that he couldn't get a rise. So pissed he hauled off and sucker-punched Jack in the face.

As his headphones went flying and pain exploded in his cheek, Jack felt something snap. Not physically, but mentally, emotionally. A darkness enveloped him. He'd felt it surge up in him before, but never like this. He took martial arts classes but whatever he'd learned was lost in an explosive rush of uncontrollable rage. Usually he fought it, but this time he embraced it. A dark joy filled him as he leaped at Rico with an animal howl.

He pounded his face, feeling his nose snap beneath his knuckles, his lips shred against his teeth. Rico reeled back, and Jack quarter-spun his body as he aimed a kick at his left knee. His boot heel connected with the outside of the knee, caving it inward. Even over the roaring in his ears he could hear the ligaments snap. As Rico went down, Jack stomped on the knee, then kicked him in the ribs, once, twice. As Rico clutched his chest and rolled onto his side, Jack picked up a bowling-ball-size rock from the garden border and raised it to smash his head.

A pair of powerful arms encircled him and wrenched him around. He lost his grip on the rock and it landed on the grass, denting the turf. Giovanni's voice was shouting close behind his left ear.

"Enough! He's down! He's finished! Stop it, for fuck's sake!"

The darkness receded, Jack's vision cleared, and he saw Rico on the ground, his face bloodied, wailing as one arm clutched his ribs and another his knee.

"All right," Jack said, relaxing as he stared in wonder at Rico. "All right."

What just happened?

Maybe five seconds had passed. So little time, so much damage.

Carlos, Juan, and Ramon stood in a semicircle behind Rico, their gazes shifting from Jack to their fallen roommate, their expressions alternating between fear and anger.

Giovanni released him from behind and spun him around. He looked frightened, upset.

"What were you gonna do? Kill him?"

"I don't know. I mean, no. I guess I lost it."

"Lost it! Damn right, you lost it!" He looked over Jack's shoulder at where Rico lay. "Christ, I never seen anything like it." His expression darkened. "You better get outta here."

"What?"

"You can catch an E or an F back into the city over on Seventy-first Avenue."

Jack felt a new surge of anger, but nothing like before. "Hey, aren't we forgetting something here? I was the guy who was minding his own business when he—"

"I know all about it, but you're still upright and moving. He ain't walking anywhere after the way you fucked up his knee."

"So—"

"So nothing. I know these guys. They're thick like brothers. You stick around you're gonna find some hedge trimmers chewing up your face. Or a shovel flattening the back of your head. Git. They'll cool down if you're not around."

The heat surged again. He was ready to take on the remaining three right now.

"*They'll* cool down? What about me?"

"Don't be a jerk. You're outnumbered. Move. I'll call you later."

"Yeah?" Jack said, resisting the urge to take a swing at Giovanni. "Don't bother."

Railing silently at the unfairness of it all, he picked up his Discman and started walking.

2

He got off the F at the 42nd Street stop with his cheek throbbing, his right hand swollen and tender, the knuckles scraped and purpling.

He'd cooled off but was still angry at Giovanni for sending him home. Yeah, well, what else was new? He'd spent most of the year angry at something.

He'd got off a good ways from what he called home these days—a tiny apartment he'd found over a flower shop down in the West Twenties. But he didn't want to go there. He didn't hate the place, but didn't much like it either. Two rooms, good for sleeping and reading and little else. Except maybe watching TV—if he'd had a TV.

He was feeling pretty low, and sitting in that drafty, empty box would only push him lower.

He didn't know what to do with himself. Free time? What was that? Here it was October and he hadn't had a day off since hiring on with Two Paisanos back in July.

He came up to street level in front of Bryant Park, which wasn't much of a park at the moment. The city had rimmed it with boards and a high chain-link fence, closing it for "renovation," whatever that meant. A black guy in a crisp blue Windbreaker and jeans saw him looking and stopped.

"Yeah, used to be a great place to get high."

"So I hear," Jack said.

As he'd heard someone put it: "Home to the three H's—hookers, heroin, and homeless."

"Speakin' of gettin' high, you lookin'?"

Jack glanced at him. Didn't look like a dealer. Had to admit, a little oblivion might ease the pain, but he'd never got into that. Tried weed in Rutgers but found beer more to his liking. Sure as hell tasted better.

"Nah."

A preferred form of oblivion waited farther down the Deuce.

"You have a nice day, then," the guy said and strolled on.

Jack looked around. He saw the back of the New York Public Library. He could walk up to Fifth Avenue, pass between the stone lions guarding the entrance, find a book, and read.

But the siren call of the grindhouses beckoned.

He crossed Sixth and started walking west on 42nd. Halfway along the block the porn shops began to appear. Not exclusively. The XXX peep shows competed with delis and a pizza place and an electronics shop, and of course the ever-present souvenir stores offering the tacky cast-metal Empire State Buildings, World Trade Center towers, and sickly green Statues of Liberty. All made in China.

Dinkins had been mayor for close to a year now and was threatening to clean up the Times Square area. Jack didn't know how he felt about that. Sure, it would be great for tourists who wanted to bring their kids here, but . . . West 42nd was the Deuce, and it wouldn't—*couldn't* be the Deuce without the sleaze factor.

But so far, no cleanup, no change.

The Deuceland *uber alles.*

He crossed Seventh and entered Grindhouse Row—the stretch of the Deuce between Seventh and Eighth, a cheek-by-jowl parade of glittering movie marquees, each trying to outblaze the next along the length of the block.

A back alley of heaven.

Some of the theaters showed first-run hits from the majors—*Goodfellas* had come out last month and was still going strong here, as was *Arachnophobia*—but most offered either reruns or low-budget exploitation films. Choices ranged from *Zapped Again* and *10 Violent Women* to ancient oldies like *The Immoral Mr. Teas* and *The Orgy at Lil's Place.* None of those appealed. But then he came to a Sonny Chiba triple feature: *The Streetfighter, Return of the Streetfighter,* and *The Streetfighter's Last Revenge.* He'd seen these on videotape but never on the big screen.

Yes!

He checked the twenty-four-hour timetable on the box office glass and saw he had about twenty minutes before the next feature began. So he walked back up to Times Square and hit the Roy Rogers there for some roast beef—or was that Trigger?—on a bun with extra horse—see?—radish sauce.

He wandered as he ate. The newspaper that gave the square its name was published half a block down 43rd. The *Light* had offices here too. An Armed Forces recruiting station sat on the downtown end of the triangle formed by Broadway's angled path across Seventh. Not much activity there. With all the saber-rattling since Iraq's invasion of Kuwait a few months ago, enlistment was essentially a nonstop ticket to the desert.

Speaking of tickets—a big crowd was gathered around the TKTS booth on the same triangle. With the recession in full swing, discount Broadway tickets seemed in greater demand than ever. *Cats* and *Les Mis* were still going strong, and *The Phantom* was somewhere down one of these side streets. Jack hadn't seen any of them, and had no desire to. Well, *The Phantom* might be okay if it weren't a musical.

A pang stole through his chest as he remembered how his mother would buy all the Broadway soundtracks as soon as they'd come out. Broadway was the Muzak of his childhood. That had been one thing he hadn't missed when he'd moved out to live at school.

He shook his head. Still couldn't believe she was gone.

He tucked the memories away and covered the still-open wound. Yeah, he really needed an afternoon of chop-socky.

Might even stay and see the trilogy a second time.

3

Vinny Donato stood back and let Tommy do the talking. Tommy Totaro loved to talk. He was known as "Tommy Ten-thumbs" because he had the goddamnedest thickest, shortest fingers anyone had ever seen. Like little Genoa salamis . . . like, well, like eight extra thumbs. But these days he should have been known as "Tommy the Snorter," on account of how he liked the powder. And once he had a snootful, he became "Tommy the Talker" and never shut up.

Vinny preferred eating to talking. And the only white powder he liked was the sugar on his zeppoles. He pulled one from a grease-stained sack from his favorite bakery in Bensonhurst and popped it into his mouth. He offered the sack to Aldo D'Amico standing next to him, but Aldo shook his head and took a drag on his Camel instead. That was why he was so skinny—he preferred smoking to eating. Anyways, he only had eyes for Tommy and the guy seated beside him.

Vinny almost felt sorry for Harry Detrick. Almost. Some guys never learn.

"So Harry," Tommy was saying, waving and wiggling those salamis in the air. His left nostril was rimmed with white. "You and me we got this . . . this connection, y'know. It's a very complex thing. It's cosmic, it's karmic, it's . . . money. It binds us. It flows between us like . . . like love. I love people and you love the ponies but you can't love the ponies the way you'd like to love them without money, and so money has flowed between us to facilitate that love. But lately, Harry, the love has been flowing only one way, and that hurts me." He placed a hand over his heart, or at least where it was supposed to be. "It hurts me in here, and it hurts me deeply."

Harry Detrick squirmed in his wrinkled suit. Vinny guessed he was about forty, maybe five years older than Tommy; no guessing about him being overweight—his gut was as big as Vinny's. His comb-over had got messed up when Vinny and Aldo dragged him into this West Side garage; its sweat-soaked strands were plastered down every which way, exposing his pink scalp.

His lower lip trembled. "Look, Tommy, I can—"

Tommy grabbed his wrist, almost gently. "Shh, my brother. The love not only connects us, it binds. But that's not all that binds us. Our karmas are intertwined, and binding us as well. And yet, with all that, there's still *more* that binds us."

The *click* of the handcuff closing around Harry's right wrist echoed off the bare concrete walls.

Harry jumped. "What—?"

Here we go with the cuffs again, Vinny thought.

The cuffs were part of Tommy's act. The coke he used before he braced losers brought out not only his inner blabbermouth but his inner drama queen as well. Pretty soon the little black book would appear.

"Hush now," Tommy said softly as he clicked the other half of the pair around his own left wrist. "We now have a more tangible bond, one that will remain in place until I feel a little of that love reversing its course and flowing toward me."

Harry got this panicky look and started twisting in his chair, pushing at the cuff as if he was going to slip out of it. Whimpering, he jumped up from the chair and began shaking his arm which, of course, shook Tommy's arm.

Vinny knew what was coming next. Because Tommy didn't like the customers shaking his arm.

Tommy gave him the look. "Vinny?"

Vinny swallowed his zeppole and reached into his jacket pocket. The Taser was all charged and ready to go. He whipped it out, jammed it against Harry's upper arm, and hit the button. Harry stiffened, then dropped to the floor where he did a little twitching. Vinny had hit him with a short zap. By the time he'd pocketed the Taser and put down his donuts, Harry was quiet and limp, breathing hard, eyes staring.

Vinny and Aldo hauled him up and draped him back into the chair where he dangled like overcooked linguine. In a little bit he got control of his muscles again and straightened.

"Tommy . . ." His voice sounded strangled. "Tommy, please . . ."

Tommy motioned to the donut bag and removed a zeppole when Vinny held it out to him.

"Harry, Harry, Harry." He bit into the zeppole. "I need love, Harry. You gonna give me love?"

"Tommy, please. After all these years, ain't I always been good for it?"

"You know the expression, Harry: Yeah, but what have you done for me lately?"

"I been sick, and business has been slow. Maybe you don't feel it in your business, but there's a recession going on out there."

"Yeah, I'm hearing that a lot lately, Harry, and I sympathize, I really do, but it's not like I'm in this alone, you know. If it was just me, I'd give you a break. But I got Vinny and Ali-D here to worry about."

He noticed Aldo shift on his feet. He hated that name. Only Tommy Ten-thumbs called him Ali-D. No one else dared. To everyone else he was Aldo. *Al-doe.* The whole name. Forget Paul Simon—you did not call this guy "Al." Aldo. Nothing else.

"Yeah, they don't look it, but my guys need love too. But even then, considering our karmic connection, I might even be able to let them go without love. But let me ask you, Harry. You ever hear that expression, 'The buck stops here'? Hmmm, Harry?"

Harry nodded. "Tommy . . ."

"Just listen. The problem is that the buck don't stop here, it don't stop with me. It's gotta go beyond me. And you know who that buck goes to, don't you, Harry."

Harry shuddered and nodded again. "Tony Cannon."

"Righto. Tony 'the Cannon' Campisi. And Tony ain't got no love connection with you, Harry. Tony's all about the money. Now, the money I loaned you comes from him. He wants it back—with his interest. And if he can't get the principal, he wants the vig, he wants his juice."

Tommy finished the zeppole and reached into his back pocket with his free hand. Out it came: the little black book.

"Let's see, Harry. I got you bookmarked here and it says . . . it says you're late—way late—with principal and vig."

"Ten percent a week." Harry groaned. "I can't keep doing it. Can he give me a break on the rate?"

"He already did, Harry. It's been twelve for a while now. He let you have the old rate because you were a return customer. Now you've made him regret that. I mean, you're backed up three weeks, Harry, and that's not good because now not only are you paying ten percent on the principal, you're paying ten percent on the vig as well."

"You couldn't ask him? Please?"

"And get my balls cut off with a butter knife? We're bonded, Harry, but not that close. Tony wanted me to deliver a message."

Which was bullshit. Tony Cannon had said, "See that he catches up." Nothing more. All this drama was Tommy's idea. At times like this Vinny felt like he was in the cast of some sort of traveling troupe. The Ten-Thumbs Theater.

Harry sobbed and blubbered as Aldo began to pull on black leather gloves.

"I don't want you to take this personal, Harry, because it's not. I like you, I really do, but I ain't got a choice. Really, I feel so bonded to you that I'm going to let Ali-D deliver Tony's message. You know why I call him Ali-D, don't you? Because he's got a punch like Muhammad Ali. And what's more, he *likes* to punch. Me, I've got no taste for it. Especially when a karmic pal like you is involved." He motioned Aldo forward. "Harry, meet Ali-D."

. . . he's got a punch like Muhammad Ali . . .

That was what pissed off Aldo so much about the name. He didn't want to be connected to no *moulinyan*, even if he'd been world champ.

Aldo landed a right jab into the center of Harry's face, rocking his head back. He groaned as blood began to trickle from his nose.

"Body shots, Ali!" Tommy cried, holding up his cuffed wrist and dragging Harry's with it. "Body shots! We're connected here, and I don't want no splatter!"

So Aldo worked Harry's ribs and gut, which wasn't so easy on a guy in a chair. Harry pleaded at first, tried to protect himself with his free hand, but Aldo was quick and strong and landed one solid shot after another. Vinny offered Tommy another zeppole but he passed. He was too involved in watching Harry receive his "message."

Vinny popped another into his mouth and wandered away. He didn't approve of beat-downs like this—not on someone who owed you money. Someone who'd ratted you out, *that* was a different story. You wanted to do major damage then. You wanted to inflict major hurt before you put them down. Because you wanted their body found and its condition to send a message loud and clear.

But someone who owed you money, someone you were doing business with, like Harry, you didn't need this shit. When Vinny was sent out to encourage a loanee in arrears to catch up, all he took along was a pair of pliers, or maybe a ball-peen hammer. A dislocated or broken finger was ninety-five percent effective. For the other five percent, you brought out the artillery and asked Aldo along.

Harry stopped begging. Vinny turned back toward the others in time to see him slump forward and slide to the floor.

"Hey, what gives?" Tommy said. "You give him another head shot?"

Aldo shook his head. "Not even close."

Vinny stepped up for a closer look. He watched Harry's chest, waiting to see him take a breath. His gut clenched when he didn't.

"Hey, he ain't breathin'!"

"Oh, shit!" Aldo knelt and lifted Harry's head. Unblinking baby blues stared ceilingward.

"He's gone!" Vinny said.

"Whatta y'mean, 'gone'?"

"Gone as in *dead*."

"Christ!" Tommy cried, pawing at his pockets "I'm cuffed to a fuckin' dead man! Get him offa me!"

"Where's the key?" Aldo said.

As Tommy continued to search his pockets, Vinny thought about what deep shit they were in. Tony Cannon always warned about getting too rough with a loanee. If the guy was completely tapped out, a through-and-through deadbeat who was never gonna pay, then yeah, mess him up and make him disappear. But you did not want to lose a guy with assets of any kind, because that was a guy with paying potential.

"Dead guys don't pay no vig." How many times had he heard the Cannon say that?

Looked like he'd be hearing it again. Real soon. That would be the least of it. Because the Cannon—who more correctly should have been called Tony "Penny-pincher" Campisi—would be pissed to beat all hell.

Tommy finally produced the key but his shaky fat fingers couldn't work it into the keyhole. After a half dozen tries, he threw it at Aldo.

"Unlock it!" His voice was rising toward girly levels. "Get this dead fucker offa me!"

Vinny turned away. Pathetic.

4

Jack found a note slipped under his door when he got back to his apartment.

Your boss called.

The movies had siphoned off some of his anger, leaving him strangely relaxed. But he felt himself tensing up again as he plunked coins in the hallway pay phone. He recognized Giovanni's voice when he answered.

"It's Jack. You rang?"

"Why don't you have a goddamn phone?"

"Because nobody calls me."

And because the phone company wanted all sorts of ID.

"I do."

"Yeah, well . . ."

Jack usually called Giovanni so he'd know where to meet up the next morning.

"Anyways, you messed up Rico pretty bad. His knee's swole up like a cantaloupe."

"Really."

Jack rubbed his swollen cheek. Couldn't dredge up much sympathy for the guy. All he felt was bewilderment about how much damage he'd inflicted so quickly.

"Yeah. Really. He can't work. Which means I've got a short crew."

"The four of us can handle—"

"Ain't no four of you. Only three. You can't come back."

Jack tightened his grip on the receiver. "What?"

"They'll kill you, Jack. You show up, you're gonna get cut up."

Jack swallowed. "You're kidding, right?"

"I wish."

"They didn't look all crazy mad when I left."

"That's 'cause they was in shock. Me too. None of us ever seen anything like that. You was like—I don't know what you was like. Like a psycho. But after you left and they figured out what kinda shape Rico was in, they was gonna go after you. I told them they leave the job, don't come back."

"You don't think they'll cool off?"

"No way. They're super pissed because Rico's down and won't be bringing in his rent and food money and they'll have to stake him that until he's back on his feet. You know my Spanish ain't that good, but I heard them talking about some new gang—'day-day-pay' or something like that. They want to sic 'em on you."

D-D-P?

"Never heard of it."

He'd heard of Bloods and Crips and Latin Kings, but knew next to nothing about New York's gang culture.

"You know those machetes they like to use to clear brush? Well, they was swinging them around and talking about looking you up. They don't know where you live—neither do I, for that matter—but they see you, they gonna cut you up in little pieces."

"Jeez."

"Yeah. Jeez."

The realization hit him. "So I'm out of a job."

"No way you can come back, man. Season's coming to a close anyway. I can send what I owe you."

Jack gave him the address of the mailbox he rented over on Tenth Avenue.

"Hey, Jack—good luck and . . . get yourself a gun."

"What?"

"I'm serious. Somebody brings a knife, you bring a machete. Somebody brings a machete—like these guys—you better bring a gun."

A gun . . . jeez.

"Well, it was good knowing you, Giovanni."

"Yeah, me too. You're a good worker, Jack. Sorry to lose you. Remember what I said."

"Giovanni . . . just one thing."

"What?"

"Fuck you."

He slammed the phone down and, as soon as it hit the cradle, thought, Why'd I say that?

Really . . . what was the matter with him? Giovanni was a good guy. He'd just warned him about a possible threat to his life.

What's wrong with me?

Jack returned to his apartment and stepped to his window. One floor below, Sixth Avenue churned in the growing darkness. Bumper-to-bumper cars and people heading home from their jobs.

He shook his head. He'd started the day with a job and not an enemy in the world. Now he was out of work and had a bunch of Dominicans out for his blood. But the worst of it, he was having trouble remembering the fight. Fight? Could he call it a fight? Rico had landed the first shot and became a punching/kicking bag after that. Jack remembered the dark surge swelling within, and then something else had seemed in control. The rock was the scariest part of it all. Would he have really crushed Rico's skull if Giovanni hadn't stopped him?

Wouldn't be the first time he'd killed someone.

He'd given into that darkness once before, but he'd had some control then and remembered every detail about that time.

Giovanni's words came back to him.

You was like—I don't know what you was like. Like a psycho.

He guessed he'd just snapped. The combination of Rico's riding him day after day, week after week, had built up a charge and the punch had hit the detonator. Never happened before. Hoped it never happened again. He didn't like being out of control.

. . . Get yourself a gun.

Maybe not a bad idea. He'd wanted one since he was a kid but his father would never allow a gun in the house. No longer a matter of want. Now it appeared he *needed* one.

But where to find one? He'd have to get on the radar to buy one legally, and he didn't want to do that. So he'd have to go black market. And if he did find one, how much would it cost? He was out of a job and his life savings were in a Ziploc bag behind the floor molding in his bedroom. He had monthly rent to pay and food to buy and jobs of any kind were scarce—especially jobs that paid cash.

He realized the middle of a recession had not been the best time to drop off the map. But he hadn't thought about that in June when he'd packed up his stuff, emptied his bank account, and hopped on his Harley. He'd left a note saying he'd be on the road and not to worry.

Impulse had nothing to do with it.

Whoever Jack had been during the first twenty-one years of his life had begun to fade months earlier when, on a snowy night back in February, he'd let the darkness take over. But instead of today's blinding black heat, he'd fallen under the sway of a fury as icy as the wind ripping along the turnpike that night. He'd hung a man by his feet from an overpass, made him a human piñata that the racing southbound traffic battered to an unrecognizable pulp.

After that, the world changed—or at least the way it looked to him. Maybe cold-blooded murder does that. Killing Ed hadn't eased the rage. Instead, it seemed to become a part of him, coloring all his perceptions. His grades at Rutgers plummeted. He was going to fail out so he dropped out. School, grades, they didn't seem to matter.

Nothing mattered and everything—every goddamn thing—annoyed the hell out of him. His older brother Tom had always been an ass, and good thing he wasn't around much because he might have ended up like Rico, or worse. Much as he loved his sister Kate, her marital bliss set his teeth on edge. And Dad . . . Dad was the worst. He hadn't done anything about Mom's murder beyond bugging the cops about finding her killer. Couldn't he see she was just another statistic to them? He kept waiting for someone else to handle it. So many times Jack had wanted to grab him and shake him and scream in his face that he'd be waiting forever because the cops weren't going to find the guy because Jack had already found him and fixed it so the fucker would never again throw another cinder block off another overpass. Ever. In fact he'd never do *anything* again. EVER!

Finally he couldn't take it anymore. He couldn't stand being Jack from Johnson another day. He needed to be Jack from nowhere. No family, no history, no last name except the one he'd chosen for the day or the week or the month or maybe just the moment.

And why the hell not? He was fed up with *belonging*, had it up to here with *participating*. He wanted out and goddammit he was getting out. No woman in his life—Karina had left for Berkeley and no one knew what she was into these days, probably Karina least of all. He had no one new he cared about or who cared about him. With Weezy and Eddie off to their respective schools and out of touch, he had no close friends. He was born before a Social Security number was mandatory and had never bothered to apply for one. No one had ever paid him on the books so officialdom had no tax records on him. Didn't even have a driver's license. He'd bought the Harley used from a newspaper ad and had never bothered to register it.

Beyond a name on the Rutgers University class of '91 student rolls, he had no official existence.

Why not keep it that way?

So he dropped out.

Probably caused a lot of consternation and confusion at home, but he'd spent his whole life being the good son. No more. He was now a killer. And not by accident. He'd murdered someone in cold blood. That case was still open. The cops had expended tons more effort trying to solve Ed's murder than his mother's. After all, Ed's death had made the national press, blurry photos of his battered body swinging from the overpass appeared in every major paper, while Mom had never been more than a footnote.

Earlier today on the turnpike, some lady riding along with her husband and son had the life crushed out of her by a cinder block dropped from an overpass. And in other news . . .

Subsequent details of Ed's unsavory past had dimmed the hue and cry for justice. Eight months now and no announcement of a suspect. That didn't mean they couldn't get a break. Jack didn't want to be around if they did.

Committing cold-blooded murder, even if no one else knew about it, seemed to have drawn a line in the sand between him and everyone he knew.

So far, so good. The building owner didn't care who he was, only that he paid his rent on time. The rent included utilities. Jack paid cash. He worked for cash. The only tax he paid—at least knowingly—was sales tax.

The invisible man.

Well, not really. If truly invisible he wouldn't need a gun.

Again . . . where to find one? No clue. But he had an idea of a guy who might point him in the right direction.

5

Jack was relieved to see the OPEN sign in the door to the Isher Sports Shop. A bell dinged as he opened it.

Down a narrow aisle a heavyset man looked up from behind the rear counter where he perched next to a dusty cash register. His eyes fixed on Jack over the wire rims of his half-frame reading glasses.

"It's the boychick from Jersey. I find him an apartment and what does he do? Does he call? Does he write? Never. Deaf, mute, and illiterate he becomes."

Jack felt bad about that. He'd first met Abraham Grossman maybe seven or eight years ago as a kid while working at Mr. Rosen's store. He'd come into USED one day and—without saying he was the owner's nephew—tried to game Jack into gypping his boss. When that didn't work, he'd left his card, saying anytime Jack was in town to look him up: *"You got a friend in the big city, kid."* He never visited USED again but Jack kept the card and took him up on the offer as soon as he'd found a garage for his Harley.

The man he'd found had less hair and a bigger waistline than he remembered, but the staccato patter was the same. Jack visited the Isher Sports Shop maybe a half dozen times in the first month he'd been here, and each time Abe was dressed the same: a half-sleeve white shirt with a black tie over black pants, sometimes belted, sometimes not. He stood maybe five-five or -six; he had twenty or so years and at least twice that many pounds on Jack.

He needed either a bigger store or lots less stock. Bicycles hung upside down from the ceiling like bats; floor level was a post-tornado rat's nest of rods and reels and clubs and racquets, hoops and nets and bats and balls of every imaginable size, color, and consistency.

"Hey, sorry, Mister Grossman," he said, approaching through the maze. "I got this job and—"

"Job, schmob. And it's *Abe.* I told you that. Mister Grossman was my father, *alev ha-sholem.*"

Abe was always throwing weird expressions about.

"What's that mean?" Jack said as he arrived safely at the scarred counter.

Close up now he could see that today was a *not* day for a belt. But Abe had accessorized instead with a rainbow of stains. Jack had seen the yellow of mustard and the red of catsup before, and those were in evidence today, but he'd somehow added green to the mix. Guacamole? The white specks that dusted his black pants might have been dandruff, but dandruff didn't smear. Powdered sugar, no doubt.

"What's what mean?" Abe said.

"*Alev* . . . something."

"*Alev ha-sholem.* If you grew up in Brooklyn you'd know already. But you had a deprived childhood in the wilds of New Jersey, so you're forgiven. I know my uncle Jake had a tough life, but what made him settle there I'll never know."

"I think he liked being alone. And I still don't know what that *alev* thing means."

"It's the Yiddish equivalent of 'rest in peace.'"

"Oh. Sorry."

"Don't be. He's long gone." He fixed Jack again with a hard stare. "Nu? You got no phone?"

"No."

He looked genuinely shocked. "Who doesn't have a phone?"

"Me?"

"Well, you ought to get one of those new ones you carry around with you in a bag. What do they call them?"

"Um, bag phones."

"No-no. Something else. They're smaller now. Like a brick with a straw sticking out. I've seen them."

"Mobile phone?"

"That's it!" he said, pointing at Jack. "A mobile phone you should get so you can call your uncle Abe and let him know how you are doing out there in the world."

Uncle Abe? When did that happen?

"Mostly getting fired."

He frowned. "Uncle Jake always said you were such a good worker. A *nar* you work for!"

Jack explained the circumstances.

"He told you to buy a gun?"

Jack nodded. "So I came to you."

Abe seemed to freeze. Not that he ever moved much, but he'd suddenly become a statue.

"Do I look like a gun dealer?" He gestured at the crowded aisles. "Do you see guns here?"

"No. But that's just it. I don't really want to go to a gun dealer. I'm looking for someone with a gun to sell. You know, a private deal."

"Why on earth would you come to me for a black market gun?"

Jack noticed the Yiddishisms had disappeared and the accent had flattened into everyday New Yorkese.

Jack wondered if he'd said something wrong. "I didn't—"

"Did someone say I could sell you one?"

Was that it? Did Abe think that Jack thought he was a gunrunner? No way.

"No-no. Nothing like that. It's just that you've lived in the city all your life and I figured you might have heard something and could point me in the right direction."

He seemed to relax. "Ah, so you mean during my lifetime of shmoozing I should have maybe come across at least one person who might be in that line of merchandise."

The accent was back.

"Exactly."

He took off his reading glasses and, without looking, began to clean them with his tie. Jack noticed a bit of what appeared to be dried egg yolk on the tie smearing across the lenses but said nothing.

"Let me ask you first: Are you experienced?"

Jack had to smile. "Are you Jimi Hendrix?"

"What?"

"Sorry. If you mean with guns, no. Back in high school I plinked at cans in the Pines with a friend's twenty-two rifle, but that's about it."

"All right then. I'm not promising, but let's just say I do find someone who can help you out, you must first promise me something."

Jack thought he was ahead of him. "To use it only for defense? Sure. I—"

"No-no." He wagged a finger. "If I can deliver, you must promise to go to a certain person—whose name I'll give—who will teach you how to safely use your purchase."

He put the glasses back on, tried to see through the egg smear, frowned, and reached for a tissue.

"Won't he want to know if the gun's registered?"

"He won't want to know from nothing except if you've got the hundred dollars he'll charge for his course in pistolry."

"A *hundred*?"

"Yes, and this is a deal breaker. I don't want you out and about with a weapon you can't field strip and keep clean and in perfect working order. So, you promise?"

A hundred bucks . . . he had limited funds and nothing coming in, but could see the wisdom of knowing the proper care and feeding of something that could kill with a finger twitch.

"I promise. But speaking of bucks, what can I expect to pay?"

"Not that I have much experience with this, but for something used of good manufacture and in good working order, I'd say you'll need three hundred American."

"'American'?"

He seemed momentarily flustered. "Well, as opposed to gold."

"Gold?"

What was he talking about?

"Oy. Enough with the parrot act. Three hundred already. And you'd better give it to me in advance, because I'll need cash in hand to bring the price down. Like an Arab rug dealer he haggles."

Obviously Abe already had someone in mind, and Jack got the feeling the cash in advance was more a test of trust than anything else. Well, he'd brought cash in case Abe sent him somewhere, and for some reason he couldn't fully fathom, he trusted this odd man, so . . .

He counted out three hundred and handed it over.

"When can I expect—?"

"Stay home tomorrow. All day. A package will arrive—"

"Mail?"

"Don't be a shmuck. Just be home and ready to sign." He snapped his fingers. "I don't recall your last name."

He'd never asked so Jack had never told him. He gave him the pseudonym he'd used on the apartment mailbox. Might as well be consistent, especially if he was going to get a delivery there.

"Moore." He spelled it.

Shortly before renting the place he'd passed a dinky little playground over on Tenth Avenue dedicated to Clement Clarke Moore. He doubted any of the kids playing there—or their folks, for that matter—knew its namesake was the guy who wrote "The Night Before Christmas."

"Okay. Remember, stay home and—"

"Don't worry. Like a hermit I'll be."

Abe looked at him, then laughed.

"Kid, you're all right."

6

Nasser al-Thani was surprised when a dark-haired young—very young—woman opened the door.

"Ooh, look at you," she said in a seductive tone, her gaze wandering up and down his long gray thobe. "I've never done one of you guys."

"I'm sorry." He checked the number on the door—yes, suite 1201. "I was expecting—"

"I bet you could teach me things. You know, like secrets of the harem and all that."

What was she talking about?

"Danaë!" said a laughing, familiar male voice from somewhere beyond the short hallway. "Stop torturing the poor man and let him in!"

She smiled as she jerked a thumb over her shoulder. "He's waiting for you in the living room."

She moved to the side to let him pass.

One of Trejador's prostitutes, no doubt. Nasser had heard rumors of his preference for "professional" women, but this was the first time he'd encountered one. She was wearing a long, tan raincoat, so he had no idea of her figure. He turned for a better look at her face but she'd already stepped through the door and was closing it behind her.

Nasser stepped into the living room and found Roman Trejador sitting in a bathrobe and sipping a drink. From the shape of the glass and the olive sitting in the clear fluid, Nasser assumed it was a martini.

"Right on time, as usual." Trejador held up the glass. "Make yourself a drink."

"I believe I will. But not like yours."

Nasser had grown up in Qatar. Unlike other countries on the Arabian peninsula, alcohol was legal there, but still frowned upon, so he'd never developed a taste for it. Even after his years at Oxford and his MBA studies at Stanford, nothing alcoholic appealed to him. He went to the kitchenette, found the refrigerator, and removed a bottle of club soda.

"I was afraid I'd arrived early," he said as he poured a glassful.

Trejador laughed. "Oh, you mean Danaë. She's one of my favorites. Quite the character. And quite skilled. We took longer than usual."

Nasser resisted a shake of his head. Most men would hide their proclivity for prostitutes to avoid the natural and inevitable questions: *You have to pay for it? Can't you get any on your own?* Yet Trejador flaunted it.

Perhaps because, with his dark good looks and smooth urbanity, he very clearly did not need to pay for it. Though nearing fifty—or already there, perhaps—he'd become the favored actuator of the High Council of the Ancient Septimus Fraternal Order. He'd grown up in Spain—survived a rough childhood, Nasser had heard—but his English was flawless.

Nasser glanced around as he returned to the suite's sitting room. Another of Trejador's quirks: no permanent address. He lived in an endless series of hotels, staying in a given suite for a month or two, then moving to another. The only constants in his life were the Order and his mobile phone. He might not be living in the last place you saw him, but that phone kept Roman Trejador available at a moment's notice.

He seated himself opposite Trejador and watched him across the low, glass-topped table between them.

"You said you had good news."

Trejador smiled. "Much to my surprise, the High Council approved the funding we requested."

Nasser barked a laugh of relief. "That's wonderful! But why are you surprised? Didn't you present it to them with your recommendation?"

"Of course. But still, I'm only an actuator, and three million dollars is a huge amount. I thought they'd balk."

"But we're only making a loan, not a grant."

"I think that was what swayed them."

"More than a loan. We'll be returning a profit as well."

Trejador shook his head. "I didn't bring that up. Profit isn't the goal. You know that."

Nasser did know that. Chaos was the goal. "But profit must appear to be *my* goal if we are to sell this."

"I understand that. And you *will* make a profit." He raised his glass and stared at Nasser over the rim. "A fact that might prove burdensome to the High Council."

Nasser stiffened. Was he hinting that they keep the profit? An interesting concept. The High Council was expecting only the return of its loan. Nasser had no need of extra money, but Trejador's lifestyle . . . he imagined it could be costly.

The success of this venture would elevate Nasser's rank in the Order, but its success at this crucial stage depended in large part upon Trejador's contacts and tactical support. Best be cautious here.

"True," he said, choosing his words carefully. "The High Council has much on its plate since the return of the One."

"Indeed it does. The major concern they voiced to me was the possibility that one of the Arab players would abscond with the funds."

Nasser shrugged. "I cannot guarantee that it's beyond the realm of possibility, but these are zealots. I have dealt with their kind before. Their cause is everything. I don't think cash will sway them from their holy course."

"My thoughts exactly, but never ignore the possibility of that amount transforming a zealot into a rogue. *Con el dinero baila el perro*."

Nasser nodded. "I come from a land that knows the seductive power of wealth."

"Then you'll understand the need for some sort of safeguard."

"I'll watch them like the proverbial hawk."

"See that you do. I've logged too many hours setting up these contacts and working both ends of this arrangement to have an attack of greed ruin it."

"No one wants this to succeed more than I." Nasser lifted his glass. "To chaos."

Roman Trejador raised his martini. "To chaos."

FRIDAY

1

It took a moment for Jack to recognize the buzzing noise: his intercom. The only visitor he'd had since moving in was the landlord on rent day, and he knocked—hammered was more like it—on Jack's door. Someone downstairs looking for him was a new experience. He found the plate on the wall and pressed the Speak button. He hoped that was the thing to do.

"Hello?"

Silence.

He tried again, with the same result.

He lifted the window over the entrance and shouted down. "Hey! Someone looking for two-A?"

A heavy guy wearing a camouflage boonie cap backed out of the doorway and looked up. He hefted the large box in his hands.

"Yeah. Delivery for two-A."

Figuring it would be a waste of time to try to buzz him in, he hurried down the two flights to the front entrance.

"You Jack Moore?" the guy said as Jack opened the front door. He looked flushed and sweaty despite the cool breeze and overcast sky.

"The one and only."

Jack saw his name scrawled on the top of the box but no address. A clipboard lay next to his name.

"Got ID?"

Uh-oh. What now?

"It's upstairs."

"Wanna go get it?"

He put a hand over his chest. "Got a heart condition."

The guy put down the box and lifted the clipboard, glancing up at Jack after he'd read something there.

"Okay. You look like him." He produced a pen. "Sign here."

Jack complied and the guy turned to go.

"No return address?"

The guy glanced over his shoulder. "Real comedian."

That's me, he thought. A laugh a minute.

He guessed he was expected to know who sent it. He watched the guy get into a battered, grime-covered white station wagon. Its rear compartment held a number of similar boxes.

As it roared off, Jack turned his attention to the box. Only one thing it could be. Pretty quick service. He'd handed the money to Abe last night and here was the delivery. Not even noon yet. But why such a big box?

He grabbed it—much lighter than he expected, judging from the size—and carried it upstairs. He locked his door, unfolded his jackknife, and cut it open. Among the foam peanuts he found a pink plush Care Bear.

"What the—?"

He pulled it out and fished among the peanuts but found nothing. Dumped them out, still nothing.

Okay, what about the bear? He hefted it. Heavy for a plush toy. Which could only mean . . .

He checked the stitching. Definitely a poor job along one of the back seams. He slit the thread, shook the bear, and a pistol dropped out, sealed in a Ziploc bag. A box of ammo, likewise bagged, followed. Abe had come through, and whoever he'd contacted had wasted no time filling the order. Well, black markets were usually free markets. Price and performance still counted.

He pulled the pistol from the bag. *Ruger GP100®* was engraved along the blued steel of the barrel. And beneath that: *.357 MAGNUM.*

Jack turned it over in his hands. So heavy . . . so solid . . . so totally *cool.* He realized he was grinning, most likely like an idiot.

I think I'm in love.

He noticed a slip of paper on the Ziploc. He pulled it out and unfolded it to reveal a note scrawled in a crabbed hand: *Call for instruction*—NOW! A number followed.

Okay, okay. Will do.

He grabbed some change and headed for the phone in the hallway. Now was fine with him. He wanted to fire this thing.

2

He said his name was Dane Bertel. Jack doubted that was true but didn't much care. He might have been the guy who'd sold him the gun. Jack hadn't given his real name either. The only for-sure real thing between them was the hundred-dollar bill Jack had handed him.

He'd obviously taught pistol safety before. Maybe he did it for the NRA for folks with legal, registered weapons, and then freelanced on the side for people like Jack.

Jack had driven his Harley to the Calverton shooting range at damn near the end of the Long Island Expressway, almost to Riverhead at the fork. Along the way he followed the speed limits like a Sunday-only driver. If he got stopped he'd be an unlicensed driver on an unregistered vehicle transporting an illegal handgun. Talk about a bad day.

Dane Bertel met him in the parking area. He looked about sixty, with a shock of short gray hair that stood out in all directions. He wasn't dressed in fatigues or the like, but he had soldier written all over him. Make that *ex*-soldier.

After escorting Jack to the office where they paid their fees, he led him to what was basically a huge sandpit. They set up at the short, ten-yard pistol range. He grinned and shook his head when he saw the Ruger.

"Abe and his revolvers." His voice sounded as if he'd just spent a day screaming at boot-camp grunts.

"What do you mean?"

"A long-running argument: I like semiautos and he prefers revolvers."

Had Bertel given Abe shooting lessons too?

"A pistol's a pistol, right? What's wrong with revolvers?"

Bertel shrugged. "Sometimes six shots aren't enough."

"Isn't there something called 'reloading'?"

"Yes, but there's also something called 'no time.' And don't be smart, kid."

Why did people say "don't be smart"? He always wanted to stick his tongue out the side of his mouth and say, "Duh, okay."

But what Bertel said made perfect sense. Jack just hoped he was never in a spot where he needed more than six shots. Ever. Because if he found himself facing three machete-wielding *matóns* from the DR, he knew he'd want more.

He *was* definitely getting tired of being called "kid."

"And let's get something straight," Bertel added, hefting the Ruger. "This isn't a pistol. I'm something of a nerd about nomenclature, and by definition a pistol's chamber is part of the barrel."

Nerd would have been the last word Jack would have used to describe Bertel, but he was sure as hell making a nerdy distinction, and not a completely clear one. Jack couldn't resist a little fun.

"Wait a sec. That would make a shotgun a pistol."

Bertel eyed him. "What? Are you stupid or just being a wiseass?"

"I prefer it to being a dumb ass. But a shotgun's chamber is part of the barrel, so—"

"Don't sass me, boy."

"Hey, you're the self-proclaimed nomenclature nerd. You said—"

Bertel took a breath. "Allow me to rephrase: By definition a pistol is a *handgun* wherein the chamber is part of the barrel. Clear?"

"As glass."

"Therefore your typical semiautomatic *handgun* is a pistol. A revolver's chamber is in the cylinder, which is separate from the barrel. So therefore we will refer to your Ruger here as either a handgun or a revolver or a weapon, but not a pistol, got it?"

"Got it. Can we shoot things now?"

Bertel went on as if he hadn't spoken. "Your Ruger is double-action—which means you don't have to cock the hammer to fire, because the trigger cocks and releases the hammer with a single pull."

Jack fought to keep his eyes from glazing over. This was shaping up to be a long afternoon.

Although fearing another recitation, he had to ask, "What's Abe got against a semiauto then?"

"They can jam. With a well-cared-for, quality model, that concern's more theoretical than real, but yeah, the cycling is much more complex than a revolver and so a jam always remains a possibility." He laughed. "But Abe's a dinosaur. Still believes in 'down on empty.'"

"What's that mean?" Although he really didn't want to know.

"You're going to learn that real soon."

Be still my heart.

But learn he did. And as much as Jack was itching to start blasting away at something, the training wasn't so bad. Before firing a shot, Bertel taught him how to break down his pistol—make that *weapon*—clean it, and reassemble it. Then to the firing line. Finally.

"Why do you have this?" Bertel said as they set up.

"The gun?"

"Well, I'm not asking about your dick. Target or protection?"

Jack hesitated, then figured he could tell him. "I pissed off some people who might come looking for me."

Bertel didn't blink as he loaded the Ruger from a box that read *.38 Special.*

"But I've got a .357," Jack said.

"Right. A .357 will take a .38 Special but not vice versa. The .38 is a cheaper round and has less kick. Get used to these before you fire a Magnum. You'll thank me."

Bertel suggested ear guards. Jack rejected them, figuring he didn't need them. After firing one round he changed his mind.

"Kee-rist, that's loud."

"Wait till you fire some Magnums."

Bertel spent a lot of time with him on the targets, directing him to aim for the body.

"Make a point of going for center of mass. A head shot always puts them down, even if it's not a kill shot, but it's a lower percentage target. Heads can duck and bob and weave. Unless you're shooting at Michael Jackson, the torso has a lot more inertia. No matter where you hit someone with one of those .357 Magnum hollowpoints you brought along, he's pretty well finished. May not be dead, but he's out of the fight."

He started talking about hydrostatic shock and other things that happened to a human body after a penetrating wound. None of which much interested Jack. He wanted to shoot his gun, and keep shooting it until he could reliably hit a target. Because whatever happened to someone after he was hit didn't matter a whole hell of a lot if you couldn't hit him in the first place.

"And *please* use only hollowpoints for self-defense," Bertel said.

"Why?"

"Because hollowpoints tend to stay inside the target. A full-metal-jacket Magnum round can go through the target and kill someone else in the next room, or half a block away if you're outside."

Jack vowed to remember that.

Shooting wasn't as easy as it looked. At first Jack resisted the two-handed Weaver grip Bertel favored, but came to adopt it as the practice went on—that Ruger became heavy after a while.

After shooting two boxes of .38s and a few Magnum rounds, Jack broke down, cleaned, and reassembled the Ruger under Bertel's watchful eye.

"Good job," he said as Jack spun the cylinder. "Think you're ready to take on those bad guys?"

Jack looked at him. "No."

He grinned. "Right. You're not. And the fact you admit it shows you've got smarts." He clapped Jack on the shoulder. "You old enough to drink?"

"Yeah."

"Coulda fooled me. There's a bar down the road. I'll buy you a beer."

"Love one, but—"

A burst of machine-gun fire from the rifle range brought them both to a halt. Jack saw a group of Arab types with some sort of automatic weapon.

"Wow!" Jack said. "What's that?"

"Assault rifle," Bertel said, staring at the group. "Kalashnikov."

"An AK-47?" Jack had heard the term but didn't know one assault rifle from another.

One of the Arabs was staring back. They made for a motley crew with their scraggly beards and varying ages and heights. They all wore similar T-shirts, but Jack couldn't read the writing. Maybe they were an Arab gun club of some sort. One lanky guy—with red hair and an NRA cap, of all things—towered over the rest. He held the AK and began firing a series of bursts.

"Three-round bursts," Bertel said.

"What's that mean?"

"Reduces overheating."

"You know them?" Jack said.

Still staring. "Yeah." Bertel started walking again. "I know they're trouble in the making. People better wake up to that, and soon." He glanced at Jack. "You were saying you'd love a beer *but*. What's the but?"

"No proof."

"No driver's license?"

Jack shook his head.

"But you drove that motorcycle here." He used the Arlo Guthrie pronunciation.

Jack shrugged.

"Who's it registered to?"

"Nobody."

"But it's got a license plate."

"Came with the bike. Never took it off."

"You must have *some* sort of ID."

"Never got around to it."

"No shit?"

"No shit."

Bertel stared at him for what seemed like a long, long time, then said, "You looking for work?"

"Better believe it."

"Follow me. I may have something for you."

3

Kadir Allawi watched the two Americans walk away. The older one's face was familiar.

He, Tachus, Sayyid, and Mahmoud were taking turns with the AK-47 Mahmoud had brought along. When the magazine ran dry and he could hear himself think, Kadir tapped Sayyid on the shoulder and pointed to the pair.

"I've seen one of them before," he said in Arabic. They spoke English only when necessary.

Sayyid's round face darkened and his eyes narrowed as he stared. He looked almost Asian when he got like this. "You think they're FBI? You think they're watching us?"

Sayyid's passion for jihad was the glue that held them together. Kadir admired him for that passion, but he was always suspicious, always angry. Sayyid saw enemies everywhere.

Then it came to him. Kadir grabbed Tachus's arm. "That man, the older one—I've seen him with your uncle Riaz."

Tachus squinted as his gaze followed the pair toward the parking lot. "What is he doing out here?"

"Taking pictures of us, I'll bet," Sayyid said.

"No," Kadir said. "They were shooting. But now I'm sure about him—he makes deliveries to your uncle."

"Spying on him to get to us," Sayyid said. "They followed us here."

Kadir watched the younger one get on a motorcycle. "No, they were here first. I remember that motorcycle when we arrived." He'd wished he had one like it.

Tachus spat. "Whoever he is, he must bring in a lot of profit, because that's all Uncle Riaz cares about."

Sayyid snorted and turned away. "My turn!" he said, pointing the assault rifle. "But first . . ."

He pulled a piece of paper from his back pocket, unfolding it as he strode onto the range.

"What's he doing?" Tachus said.

Mahmoud grinned. "I think I know."

Mahmoud had served among the mujahideen in Afghanistan after training for combat in Peshawar. He drove a taxi now and had had special T-shirts made up, reading *Help Each Other in Goodness and Piety . . . A Muslim to a Muslim is a Brick Wall.* A map of Afghanistan was superimposed in the middle.

Sayyid attached the paper to one of the bull's-eyes and hurried back. Kadir saw now that it was a blown-up black-and-white newspaper photo of a face—the bearded face of a man wearing a yarmulke. A rabbi.

Mahmoud was still smiling as he handed the reloaded rifle to Sayyid. "Let's see how you kill the Jew."

Kadir stepped back to watch. He'd met these three Egyptians this past summer at the Al-Farouq Mosque. He'd traveled from Jersey City to Brooklyn to hear the famous holy man, Sheikh Omar Abdel-Rahman. The blind cleric had arrived in August and quickly gathered a devoted following. Kadir, a Palestinian, had been welcomed by the Egyptians who told him his struggle was their struggle.

While he did not share their loathing of President Mubarak—at least he was an Egyptian ruling Egypt—they all shared an intense hatred of Israel.

Kadir was born the seventh of nine children in Israeli-occupied Palestine shortly after the Six-Day War. He grew up under the heel of the Zionists. His father finally moved the family to Jordan where he found work in a clothing store. But Kadir could find no work in that hard place, so he came to America. It might be the ally of hated Israel, but his mother's brother had opened a bakery in Jersey City and promised Kadir a job. He saw no choice but to go. The bakery didn't pay much and so he found extra work through Tachus in his uncle's business.

Sayyid began firing wildly at the target. Most of his bullets kicked up the sand of the dunes behind. But finally he homed in and stitched a line across the rabbi's face.

Kadir joined in the cheering as Sayyid raised the rifle over his head in triumph. Although he admired Sayyid's devotion to the cause of jihad, his intensity could be intimidating at times.

He turned and watched the two Americans drive away, one in a truck, the other on his motorcycle, and wondered again why a man who dealt with Tachus's uncle would be out practicing shooting. Then again, perhaps it made sense. After all, his uncle Riaz's operation was illegal.

4

They stopped at a deli for a six-pack. Jack offered to pay for something like Heineken or Beck's or Guinness, but Bertel wouldn't hear of it.

"I may shoot foreign weapons now and again, but I load them with American ammo and I drink American beer."

"Rolling Rock then. It's made in Latrobe, Pee-Ay."

"You mean those little pussy bottles? You've got to drink them with your pinky in the air. Wouldn't be caught dead hoisting one of them."

"It comes in twelve-ouncers too."

"Yeah, but the bottles are green. More likely to turn skunky like foreign beer. Real beer—real *American* beer—comes in brown bottles, Jack." He held up a six-pack of Budweiser and rocked it before Jack's eyes. "Bud, boy. Bud."

Jack wanted to hit him but bottled it. He found that easier than usual to do. He felt oddly at peace with the world since firing that pistol—no, handgun. More at peace than he'd felt in almost a year.

He got back on his Harley and followed Bertel to a park on Long Island Sound. Fifty yards or so from the sandy beach they found a picnic area with benches and tables and grills for cooking. The only other people in sight were a man and a woman drinking wine at one of the tables. Bertel chose a spot about a hundred feet away.

"We're downwind," he said, unscrewing the cap off a bottle and handing it to Jack. "They won't hear us."

Jack wondered what he had to say that was so secret.

They tapped bottles and sipped. Jack fought a grimace. Sometimes no beer was preferable to blah beer. But other times any beer was better than no beer. This was one of those times.

He caught Bertel staring at him again. "Really . . . no ID?"

"Nope."

"What about taxes?"

This was making Jack a little uneasy, but although Bertel was a stickler for nomenclature, he didn't seem a stickler for legalities.

"I've so far avoided that particular civic duty."

Jeez, I'm starting to sound like him.

"Fingerprints on file anywhere?"

"Not that I know of."

"So you're not on anyone's radar?"

"Well, I had to register when I went to school."

"Oh?" He sipped, all idle curiosity and nonchalance. "And where might that be?"

Jack gave him a look. "Hard Knocks U."

Bertel smiled. "Good. Don't tell me. Don't tell anyone."

"Why's this so important?"

"You said you needed work. I have an interstate moving business."

Jack knew he was being "smart" but couldn't resist. "Oh, like Allied Van Lines?"

Bertel's mouth twisted. "Perhaps I should have said 'shipping.' Interested in doing some driving?"

"No license, remember? So I tend to stay off the road unless that's the only way I can get someplace."

"What if . . . ?" Bertel paused.

Jack heard laughter and glanced at the couple. They looked Hispanic and seemed to be enjoying themselves.

Bertel went on. "This is just spitballing, you understand."

"Of course."

Yeah, right.

"But what if, just for the sake of conjecture, someone gave you a license? Not in your name, and from someplace like, oh, say, Jersey, and good enough to withstand a routine check. Would you be willing to do some interstate driving a few times a week?"

"Are we conjecturing a big van?"

Jack didn't see himself backing up a semi.

"No. You'd need a CDL for that. I'm talking about keeping it simple, like a rental—Ryder, U-Haul, that sort of thing."

Uh-oh.

"Hauling what?"

Bertel hesitated again and Jack tensed, expecting to hear "weed" or "H" or something equally illegal. He noticed the couple's voices raised. They seemed to be arguing now. He wondered what had messed up their good mood.

Finally Bertel said, "I'm going to be frank with you, Jack. Abe sent you, and that gives you an excellent pedigree, plus you drove out here without a license while carrying an unregistered handgun. That takes either a lack of smarts or big cojones, and I think you're pretty smart."

Despite your telling me not to be, Jack thought.

"Either way," Bertel went on, "it means you're not afraid to break rules. So I'll tell you: You'd be hauling cigarettes for me."

After the buildup, Jack had to laugh. "Really? Cigarettes?"

"Might sound funny, but the money's not."

"Where from?"

"North Carolina to Jersey City."

"Where's the money in that?"

"NC doesn't stamp their cigarettes and, because tobacco's a big state crop, barely taxes them. They're dirt cheap down there. New York, on the other hand—that's New York the state and New York the city—taxes the *hell* out of cigarettes. They're inching toward four bucks a pack now."

Jack shrugged. He didn't smoke so he had no idea. But he saw where this was going.

"So you make money on the margin."

"I make a piece of the margin. I don't do retail. I wholesale. I supply a guy in Jersey City who has a bogus New York tax machine. He stamps the packs, marks them up, and sells them throughout the five boroughs."

The couple was getting really loud. Jack tried to ignore them.

"There's enough money in black market ciggies to make it worthwhile?"

"You wouldn't believe. I ship to Boston and Detroit too. But this Arab keeps wanting more. I need another driver and you're perfect."

"Perfect . . . first time anyone's ever called me that."

"Put you in the cab of a U-Haul and you'll look like a college kid moving his stuff to school. You won't fit the profile."

"Profile?"

"Sure. The state cops and the ATF have certain types—"

"Wait-wait-wait. You said ATF."

"Well, Tobacco *is* their middle name."

"So we could be talking federal trouble here?"

"Well, yeah. They don't take too kindly to that sort of thing."

Jack didn't take too kindly to the idea of messing with an agency of the federal government. So far he'd managed to stay off its radar. This did not seem a good way to maintain anonymity.

"And let's be fair," Bertel added, "I won't be paying you a thousand bucks a trip for nothing."

Did he just say a *thousand* per trip? Yes, he did.

"Really?"

Almost as much as Giovanni had been paying him per month working sixty, seventy hours per week. By quick estimation he'd be jumping from four bucks an hour to about fifty.

Jack heard a slap and a cry. He turned and saw the woman bent over, clutching the side of her face. He tensed.

"Domestic dispute," Bertel said. "Leave them be."

Jack had never seen a man hit a woman—well, on the screen, yeah, but never in real life.

"Guy shouldn't hit a woman."

"Real men don't. *Guys* do it all the time. Leave them to their business and let's get back to ours. I'll expect you to do three runs a week until we catch up."

That snapped Jack's head around. Three thousand a week? Just for hauling cigarettes?

Bertel smiled. "I see you doing the math. The paper had an article the other day on the median weekly pay in this country last year. Any idea what it was?"

Jack shook his head. "Not exactly the kind of statistic that catches my eye." Especially since he'd been so far below it.

"Well, check this out: The median American worker earned five hundred fifty-seven dollars a week in 1989. Which comes to about twenty-nine grand a year. This here is my busy time of year. If we start you next week, and run you three times a week, you'll make pretty much that amount by New Year's Eve. Sound good?"

The amount was almost inconceivable to Jack. Yeah, it sounded good—but the risks . . .

"Hell, it sounds fantastic. I just . . ."

Another slap, another yelp of pain. The woman was sobbing now as she clutched her face. Jack rose from the bench and stepped toward them but Bertel grabbed his arm and pulled him back.

"What do you think you're doing?"

Jack had to admit he hadn't a clue. But he couldn't just sit here and watch that happen.

"I—"

"You're going to what—brace that guy? Look at those arms."

Jack had already noticed. His chest and shoulders and biceps bulged under the yellow T-shirt, stretching the fabric. Tats snaked down to his elbows.

"So what? Those guys are always slow."

"He'll tear your head off, Jack."

"Gotta catch me first."

"And he will. You know how? She'll help him. You do *not* meddle in domestic disputes."

Domestic dispute . . . the second time he'd used the term. Had he been a cop?

"But—"

"Trust me, nobody wins. And the guy who tries to help usually turns out to be the biggest loser."

Fucking old chickenshit coward! rose to Jack's lips but Bertel tightened his grip.

"Hey. Eyes on me: I need you to make up your mind."

"Right now?"

"No. I can give you a day. But I've got the Mummy hollering for more butts and—"

"The Mummy?"

"My Arab. He's an Egyptian. He's square, but he's a tough customer. If I can't get the cartons to him, he'll find someone who can. I need another driver pronto."

Jack nodded. "Tomorrow then. I have your number. I'll let you know by the afternoon."

"Good."

"By the way, I need some ammo." He'd pretty much run through the box that had arrived with the Ruger. "Can you get me some?"

"You don't need me."

"No ID, remember?"

"You're kidding me, right? You've got Abe."

What was he talking about?

"Abe? Abe sells—"

A choking sound. Now the guy had his wife, girlfriend, whatever bent back over the picnic table. He'd forced her mouth open and was pouring wine down her throat. He was giggling as she gagged and struggled.

Bertel's expression darkened. "But first . . ." He started forward. "Wait here."

Jack started to follow but Bertel snapped around and jabbed a finger at him. "Wait and watch and see how it's done."

He stalked toward the couple. Along the way he picked up a fallen tree branch, a couple of inches thick. As he reached the table he took a two-handed grip and raised it like a baseball bat.

"Hey!"

Bertel was already halfway into a go-for-the-bleachers swing when the guy raised his head and looked. The branch caught him square across the middle of his face. His feet left the ground as he flew back. He landed in a spread-eagle sprawl on the sand and did not move.

Jack pumped a fist. Way to go.

Bertel said nothing, simply turned and walked back the way he'd come. Behind him the woman straightened and coughed up the wine she'd inhaled. She wiped her eyes and gave a cry when she saw her guy stretched out on the ground. Wailing, she dropped to his side and cradled his head in her lap.

Jack shook his head in wonder—at both Bertel and the woman. A moment ago he'd been water-torturing her with wine.

He gave Bertel a thumbs-up. "I see you've watched *The Sons of Katie Elder*."

He frowned. "Who?"

"It's a movie with—never mind."

The woman looked around and spotted Bertel, who still carried the branch. Shrieking something in Spanish—he picked up "*chancho negro*" in the machine-gun burst—she picked up a rock and hurled it at his back. It landed to his left and rolled past him. She continued shrieking but he didn't look back.

"What did I say about nobody winning?" He looked more annoyed than angry. "Do *not* get involved in a domestic dispute."

"But you just did."

He dropped the branch and brushed his hands. "There are certain things I will not abide in my sight. Let's go."

As they walked side by side back to the truck, Jack decided he liked this old fart.

5

Vinny and Aldo and Tommy stood before Tony "the Cannon" Campisi's desk. It dominated a cramped little office at the rear of his discount appliance store on Liberty Avenue in Ozone Park. Like the sign in the front window said, his store really did sell appliances at low-low prices. He could afford the deep discounts because they were all stolen. When the opportunity presented itself, Vinny and Aldo would be sent out to divert a shipment of refrigerators or dishwashers or TVs to the loading dock at the rear of the store.

Tony sat and chain-smoked, saying nothing, while the three of them fidgeted. Aldo had his hat off, clutched in the hands folded in front of him. Vinny had skipped his usual bakery stop because Tommy had said Tony was royally pissed and to get over here ASAP.

Tony Campisi got the name "the Cannon" back in the seventies. Rumor had it that after seeing *Dirty Harry* he'd gone out and bought a Colt .44 Magnum. He'd carried it everywhere. But those days were gone because he didn't get out much now. Despite his barrel chest, he couldn't walk too far without starting to wheeze. These days the .44 Mag's home was the top drawer of Tony's desk.

Tony coughed out his last drag, hacked, and spit into the wastebasket in the kneehole of his desk. He stubbed out the butt in an overflowing ashtray and looked up at them.

"How many times I told you, Tommy, dead guys don't pay no vig."

Tommy spread his hands. "I know, I know. But he just keeled over dead. Must've been his heart. Can't blame us a guy's got a bad heart."

Us? Vinny thought. Wasn't our idea to work him over.

"Wasn't his heart," Tony said. "I got a guy down the coroner's office. Says he died of a . . . a . . ." He shuffled through the papers on his desk, found what he was looking for, and read: "A 'ruptured aorta,' which, I am told, is the big pipe that comes out of your heart. His was pretty much rusted through."

"There y'go. Not our fault."

Vinny's jaw tightened at the *our*.

"Yeah, it is. You busted it. The good news is, they got him down as dead from natural causes."

Vinny and Aldo had tossed Harry's body in front of a bus rolling up Eighth Avenue. The impact would account for his lifeless state and whatever bruises Aldo had inflicted.

"The bad news is, he's dead and dead guys don't pay no vig. What's he into us for?"

Tommy pulled out his black book. "Got it right here. He was up to date until three weeks ago."

"What's the principal?"

"Three."

"And the rate?"

"Ten."

"Ten? What happened to twelve?"

"You said give him ten because—"

Tony waved a hand. "Yeah-yeah. I remember. See what happens when you give someone a break? The guy goes and dies on you."

"He's been only paying vig."

"Which is okay," Tony said. "How long?"

Tommy consulted his book. "July twenty-second."

Tony did a quick finger count, then smiled. "See? That's why vig-only is good. He's already more than paid back the principal without reducing it a cent. What's the latest total?"

"Thirty-nine ninety-three."

"So his next vig payment would have been—"

"Three hundred ninety-nine dollars and thirty cents."

"You won't mind if we round that off to four hundred?"

"Not at all," Tommy said.

"Good." Tony tapped his desktop. "Right here. Four hundred. Now."

Tommy looked like he'd been slapped, then he laughed. "You had me goin' there for a minute."

Tony frowned. "What? Did I slip into some foreign language, like Swahili or something?" He tapped the desk again. "Four C-notes. Right here. Right now."

"You serious?"

"Do I look like I'm joking? Did I forget to take off my clown makeup? Four hundred here and now or you can find another line of work."

Dripping reluctance, Tommy reached into a pocket, pulled out his roll, and peeled off four Franklins. He slapped them on the desk.

"This ain't fair, Tony."

"I made an investment. You were supposed to watch over that investment. Now that investment's gone. Somebody's gotta pay Harry's vig, and that someone turns out to be you."

"But—"

"And you'll deliver another four hundred every week unless or until you pay off Harry's loan. Or find someone to take over his payments. Now get outta here."

They filed out, walked through the store, and gathered on the sidewalk in the shadow of the El where they waited as Tommy went through a "fuck"-laced, foot-stomping, fist-swinging bitch about the unfairness of it all. What he really needed, Vinny knew, was a snort because he hadn't dared face the Cannon with a snootful.

"All right," he said when he'd calmed and caught his breath, "we are not, repeat *not* paying Harry's vig, let alone his principal."

"We kinda gathered that," Vinny said. He was hungry and would rather be having this conversation over a roast beef sandwich. Then the "we" broke through his hunger. "Whattaya mean, 'we'?"

"We're all in this together. We were all there when Harry died, so we're all on the hook."

Conversation was delayed as a train roared by overhead. Just as well.

Vinny knew better than to argue. Wouldn't do any good. The four hundred a week would make a big dent in Tommy's coke money. He was going to spread the pain.

Vinny would have his own crew, his own operation someday. Until then he'd be a good soldier. Stick with Tommy, help keep Tony the Cannon happy, and he'd move up. Everybody in the organization answered to somebody. Tommy answered to Tony. Tony answered to Sammy the Bull, who in turn answered to Gotti.

At this point, Vinny answered to Tommy. But it wouldn't always be that way. He was branching out on his own. He'd started up a scrap metal business, and it was coming along. He was careful not to step on anyone else's toes. Like he wouldn't think of doing a loan on the side. That would be poaching on Tony, a sure way to resurrect the Colt .44 Mag from its drawer. But scrap metal was a safe sideline, and totally legit. He'd borrowed a lot—and not from Tony—but it was starting to pay off. When he heard of someone with an inconvenient corpse, he offered to handle the disposal—for a price, of course. So far, those jobs had gone, well, swimmingly. Soon as he got a little busier with the scrap, he could start laundering other guys' cash. That was where the money was. Never a shortage of dirty cash around.

Not like sandwiches, of which there was a definite shortage at the moment.

Aldo didn't look hungry as he adjusted his porkpie, but apparently he also knew arguing was a dead end. "What do we do?"

Tommy scratched his jaw. "Well, let's see. What do we know about Harry?"

Vinny said, "He sucked at the ponies."

Aldo guffawed.

"Yeah, we know," Tommy said. "We wouldn't be having this conversation if he had any luck. Where'd he get his day-to-day money, though? How'd he pay his bills?"

Vinny spun through what he knew about Harry. Couldn't come up with a damn thing. He found it hard to think when he was hungry.

"No idea."

"Yeah, that's the problem. So let's find out."

"How we do that?" Aldo said.

"Research. Find out everything there is to know about this guy. Family, job, whatever. Gotta be something we can tap into. Find all the pockets connected to him, and we tap into the deepest."

"Got it," Vinny said. "On it."

As soon as he had some food.

6

"Can Dane Bertel be trusted?" Abe said, stuffing a piece of cake into his mouth and sprinkling crumbs all down his front. "That's what you're asking?"

"I guess so," Jack said.

He wasn't sure what he was asking. Bertel's offer was a big step—bigger even than leaving home—and he needed someone to talk to. He didn't know anyone else in town but Abe, so he'd brought him a cake as a sort of thank-you for arranging the gun, and as an excuse for his presence.

Abe swallowed and pointed to the blue-and-white cake box. "Did I ever mention Entenmann's was my favorite or was it just a lucky guess?"

Jack glanced at the three empty Entenmann's boxes stacked on the floor behind the counter. He'd also noticed a number of Entenmann's boxes on his previous visits. Entenmann's had seemed like a safe choice.

"I'm psychic."

"Such a talent you have. And choosing the cheese-filled crumb coffee cake marks you as a maven of baked goods."

Jack guessed a maven was a good thing.

"About Bertel . . ."

Abe took another bite and spoke around it. "Trusted how?"

Jack hadn't told Abe any details yet.

"He wants me to work for him."

"So you want to know will he pay you what he says he will? The answer to that is yes."

"What if there's trouble on the job?" Jack didn't know how much he could say about Bertel's business.

Abe looked at him. "Say it already: He wants you should smuggle cigarettes from the South and you're worried about getting caught."

Well, all right. Abe did know.

"Yeah, that's it in a nutshell."

"All I can say about Dane is that he'll do what he says he'll do. If he says he'll help you if you get caught, then that's the way it will be. If he says you're on your own, then you're on your own. What has he said?"

"Neither. I haven't taken the job yet."

"Well, if you take it, you should count on being on your own. The mob he's not. He's a small businessman. No lawyers on retainer."

Jack shook his head. "The ATF . . ."

"ATF, schmATF. It's state cops you'll see mostly."

Jack broke off a piece of the cake, then noticed Abe's wounded look.

"May I?"

"Of course," he said, but didn't sound all that sincere.

He popped it into his mouth. Pretty damn good.

"Well?" Jack said after swallowing—moist enough to go down easily without milk. "What do you think?"

"You want I should decide for you? I can't. You're a grown-up now. By your wits you want to live? Then sometimes you have to take chances." He raised his hands, palms up, and moved them like a juggler. "Does the gelt outweigh the risk? Is the risk worth the gelt? Is any risk too much? If so, maybe a school janitor you should be."

Jack realized he'd come to Abe looking for more than chitchat. He'd wanted some fatherly advice. His own father was back in Jersey and would go ballistic at the thought of one of his sons doing anything even questionably illegal. Abe, on the other hand, was treating him like an adult, like a peer, telling him to evaluate the pros and cons of Bertel's offer and make up his own mind. Jack could get used to that.

"Who is Bertel, anyway?"

"A mensch."

Mensch . . . Jack knew what that one meant.

"I get the feeling he's an ex-cop."

"Probably ex a number of things. He's been around awhile. Minds his business. Not a kibbitzer by any means. Hires young men exclusively."

"Sort of a Fagin, then?"

Abe shook his head. "No, I believe he likes women."

Jack laughed. "*Fagin*—as in Dickens."

"Oh. Sorry. I thought you said fageleh. Speaking of women, he told me once he'd love to hire females—less chance of being stopped, he thinks—but couldn't justify putting a young woman on the road alone at night."

Something about that helped Jack make up his mind.

"I think I'll give it a shot." His stomach knotted as the words passed his lips.

Abe concentrated on the cake. "You're sure?"

"Not in the least. But I'll give it a trial run. If I'm a basket case after it's over, I'll know it's not for me and I'll quit. He will let me quit, won't he?"

Abe nodded. "Of course. He may deduct certain startup expenses from your pay, but I don't believe a blood oath is involved."

"That's a relief. Do me one favor, though?"

"If possible."

"Talk me out of it?"

Abe's eyebrows shot up. "Me? Talk yourself out."

"No, I'm serious. Hit me with the downside."

Abe drummed his fingers on the counter for a second, then said, "Well, as I see it, a unique and wondrous situation you've got: The official world has no idea you exist. This can be a useful thing if you wish to maintain it. Transporting black market goods puts your unique and wondrous situation at risk. You get caught and booked and you're like the rest of us."

Jack nodded silently. A pretty good case for turning Bertel down.

Abe stuffed another piece of cake in his mouth. "What's he offering, by the by?"

"A thousand a trip."

Abe almost choked. "What? Don't be a shmoiger! Take it!"

MONDAY

1

Three days later Jack sat at a motel room's front window and stared at the parking lot. He hadn't slept much. Better to sit and watch the sky lighten than lie in bed and stare at the ceiling. A thick stand of long-needle pines bordered the cracked and rutted asphalt. He imagined that somewhere beyond them, rosy fingers of dawn were inching above the horizon.

Crappy image. He tried to remember the supposed owner of those supposed fingers. Eos? Not that he gave a damn, but he found it easier to think about things like that than what was to come.

The weekend had *flown.*

Things had begun moving immediately after he'd called to accept the job. Bertel had sent him straight downtown to a tiny camera shop on West Houston with instructions to ask for a guy named Levinson—maybe his real name, maybe not. Levinson turned out to be a skinny guy in his late thirties with spiky black hair and a sniffle. He photographed Jack, took his phone number, and said he'd call when "it" was ready. Jack figured he didn't mean a portrait.

Yesterday morning the call had come and Jack returned. Levinson waited till the store was empty—not a long wait—then handed Jack an envelope.

"Check it out," he said.

Jack pulled out a laminated card and frowned. His own face stared back at him, but . . .

"Doesn't look like a driver's license."

"It's not," Levinson said. "Your boss has the license. This here's an NC State student ID. The license is in the system, the library card isn't."

"Then what good is it?"

"It's a photo ID. Never hurts. When the name agrees with the license—which, as you will learn, has no photo—it reassures the cop or whoever stops you that you're you."

"But when they check with the school they'll—"

Levinson smirked. "Trust me, when it comes to a choice between verifying a college library ID and a state-issued license, they go with the license every time."

Jack checked the name. "Lonnie Buechner? Jeez."

"Yeah, sorry about that."

"Couldn't you come up with something simpler?"

"You want simple or safe? This guy's safe because he's real—or at least he was. Died a few years ago."

"What of?"

Jack didn't want to hear that he used to drive for Bertel.

"The big C. North Carolina DMV's got no dead file so, as long as your boss keeps renewing Lonnie's license, he's still alive . . . in a way."

Swell, I'll be a driving dead man. George Romero images followed him out of the store.

When he called Bertel to let him know he was now licensed, he was instructed to wait at the corner of Sixth Avenue and King Street, a few blocks away. Bertel showed up in a U-Haul truck. He slid over to the passenger seat and handed Jack a laminated card—the second in less than an hour.

"There's your driver's license."

"You mean Lonnie Buechner's."

"Yeah. Some name, huh?"

Jack shook his head. "Tell me about it."

"Really, who names their boy Lonnie?"

"Mrs. Mack did."

"Who?"

"Never mind."

Bertel said, "Well, when I hear 'Lonnie' I think of big blond hair and big boobs—you know, the gal on that *WKRP* show."

"Loni Anderson."

"Right. And Anderson's a lot easier to spell than Buechner. Make sure you know how to spell it like your own." He pointed ahead. "Drive."

"Where?"

"Anywhere. I know you can handle a motorcycle, but I want to see how you handle four wheels."

Jack hadn't driven a truck before, but this rig, with its automatic shift, wasn't much different from a car. Its extra width, though, made handling the narrow West Village streets a little hairy at times.

"All right," Bertel said after half an hour. "You pass. Go home and take a nap. I'll pick you up at six. We drive all night."

" 'We'?"

"I'll drive down with you the first time—make sure you get where you're supposed to be when you're supposed to be there. You'll come back on your own."

"How'll you get back?"

He grinned. "Fly."

Well, the nap didn't happen.

Bertel showed up right on time, put Jack behind the wheel, and off they went. Out the Holland Tunnel and down the NJ Turnpike. After they crossed the Delaware Memorial Bridge, Bertel handed him a sheet of directions that took him down the DelMarVa peninsula to a town he'd never heard of: Elizabeth City, North Carolina.

"Gotta be a quicker way," Jack told him.

"I know. But you'll be taking this route back and I want you familiar with it." He leaned back. "Wake me when we hit the NC line."

Then he closed his eyes and went to sleep.

The instructions were simple enough: south through DelMarVa to the tip of Cape Charles, over the Chesapeake Bay Bridge Tunnel to Norfolk, then south from there to Elizabeth City in the northeast corner of NC.

Hours later, after a stop for coffee and gas, he roused Bertel, who guided him to the Lonely Pine Motel. The name gave Jack a start. He'd grown up not far from a different Lonely Pine Motel, on Route 206 in Burlington County, New Jersey. Took its name from the huge solitary pine on its property. He'd witnessed something weird there as a kid.

A dark-haired guy, who could have been forty but might have been fifty, was waiting in the parking lot. He was good-looking and might have been better looking without the beard he was trying to grow.

Bertel introduced him simply as Tony but didn't mention Jack's name. Jack immediately found out why.

"So you're the new Buechner," Tony said as they shook. He was smiling and his big Chiclet teeth reflected the light from the motel, giving him a Cheshire cat look.

"There's been more than one?"

"Of course there's been more than one," Bertel said, sounding a bit testy. "Good driver's licenses don't grow on trees."

Maybe he didn't like being awakened at two-thirty in the morning.

"What happened to the last Buechner?"

"Got domesticated. He stashed away enough for a down payment on a house. Married a teacher and joined the nine-to-five life. Is that what we can expect from you?"

"Not likely."

Bertel looked dubious. "We'll see. This is where you'll drop off and pick up the truck. You will give Tony the truck keys, and he will give you a room key. While he takes the truck off to stock it, you will catch a little sleep. He will return at six A.M., at which time you will both trade keys again. Then you will drive north to an address I will give you later."

He sounded like he was reading from a TelePrompTer.

"That's it?" Jack said.

"That's it. I believe in keeping things simple."

And cellular, Jack realized. Jack knew neither Tony's last name nor where he took the truck to stock up. Tony knew nothing about Jack except that his name was not Lonnie Buechner; probably didn't know where Jack was dropping the cargo either. He'd bet only Bertel knew the whole operation.

Smart.

Jack checked the number on his key: room A-9. He yawned.

"See you in a few hours."

As he started toward the motel he glanced over his shoulder and saw Bertel climb into the truck cab with Tony. They were gone by the time he reached his door.

Not a bad room, not a great room. Just a room with a bed. Jack had assumed he'd conk right off, but that hadn't happened. He kept thinking about the drive back, about being pulled over for some careless minor infraction and having the cop tell him to open up the back of the truck.

So now he sat by the window and waited for that truck.

2

Bertel and Tony arrived at 6:07. They brought donuts in a box labeled "Krispy Kreme." Jack jumped on the coffee first. Not so great, but he desperately needed caffeine. He tried one of the donuts. He'd never heard of Krispy Kreme—he was used to Dunkin' Donuts—so he played it safe and chose a glazed. It all but melted in his mouth.

"Holy crap, where'd you get these?"

"Down the road apiece," Tony said with a knowing grin. "They're a local chain. To die for, right?"

"They've *got* to come to New York. They could clean up."

He grabbed one of the heavier cake donuts and found it even better than the first.

"Okay," Bertel said. "Now that you've been introduced to the local delicacies, down to business. You've got forty master cases of Marlboros on board."

"What's a master case?" Jack said as he scarfed down the second Krispy Kreme and reached for a third. He could binge on these all morning. He felt like a young Abe in training.

"Forty cartons of five hundred packs."

Jack blinked as he multiplied. "That's . . ."

"Right—twenty thousand packs."

"Can I see?"

He tried to sound innocently curious, but he wanted to make sure he'd be hauling what they said he'd be hauling.

"Yeah," Bertel said. "I wanted to show you how it's laid out."

He led Jack around the back where he keyed open a padlock.

"We could have fit a few more cases," he said as he pulled open the doors. "But we need a certain amount of camouflage."

Jack caught a short surfboard as it fell through one of the swinging doors.

"Whoa!"

"Good catch," Tony said. "That's one of the props."

Jack saw a disassembled bike, hanging clothes, a couple of floor lamps, and other odds and ends packed just inside the doors. Behind them, boxy shapes were piled to the roof and draped with moving pads.

Jack lifted the flap of one of the pads and saw a shrink-wrapped cardboard box labeled "Marlboro."

"Checking up on us?" Bertel said. He looked more amused than annoyed.

Jack gave only a shrug as a reply. Seeing a cigarette brand name on the boxes didn't guarantee they weren't filled with ganja, which would put him on a whole other level of legal trouble if he got caught. But Abe had said Bertel was a straight shooter. He'd have to go with that.

Bertel added, "I'd think less of you if you hadn't."

Tony repositioned the surfboard, then Bertel reclosed the doors and locked up.

"I'll keep this," he said, holding up the key.

Jack wasn't so sure he liked that. "What if I'm stopped for some reason and the cop wants to see inside?"

"First off, he needs probable cause. And he's not going to have that, is he?"

"Not if I can help it."

"You didn't do anything stupid like sneak your Ruger along, did you?"

"Would have liked to, but . . ." He shook his head.

As much as it would have made him feel safe, getting caught smuggling unstamped cigarettes would be bad enough, but adding an unregistered weapon to the charges—uh-uh.

"Smart." He handed Jack a sheet from a yellow legal pad. "Here's your route north."

"Same as down, right?"

"Right. Be faster on the freeways, but this way is safer. We always check the truck six ways from Sunday before we let it go. All the lights and signals work. All the rental papers are in the glove compartment. But if you *are* stopped, just turn off the engine and keep your hands on the steering wheel. Be ready to show that new license and the rental papers."

"What if he asks—?"

"You don't have the key."

"Won't that make him suspicious?"

"Explain that you're helping your girlfriend move. Her father rented the truck—his name's Robert McAllister, right there on the rental agreement—and locked it up after you helped pack it. You'd be glad to let him look, but—" He gave a helpless shrug. "What this does is deflect the cop's annoyance from you to the father. Now he's got to have *real* probable cause. He's got to see contraband in the truck cab or he's got to have a drug-sniffing dog raise a ruckus before he can do anything."

"But we've got no drugs, right?"

"Just nicotine, and they aren't trained to sniff for that. If he really wants a look, he's going to have to impound the truck to get a warrant to open it. Does he want to go through all that for what's most likely nothing, and leave himself looking like a dummy?"

Jack had to smile. "Sounds like you've really thought this thing through."

"Yeah, well, I've been doing it awhile."

"But if it's locked and can't be opened, why the bike and the surfboard and stuff?"

Bertel glanced at Tony. "Told you he was sharp." Back to Jack: "Because on one of the rare times one of our guys was stopped—this was on a Detroit run—the cop used a crowbar to pry open a corner of one of the doors and flashed his light inside. Luckily all he saw was one of the moving pads that had slipped down against the door, but it got me to thinking. If that happened again and he saw typical dorm-room stuff, he'd be satisfied."

Jack was starting to feel better about the trip.

Bertel motioned him toward the front of the truck. "Two more things." He opened the passenger door and grabbed something from inside. "Wear this."

A gray sweatshirt. Jack held it up. The front showed a cartoony wolf wearing an NCSU cap. Beneath him: *NC State Wolfpack*.

"My new alma mater," Jack said.

"And check this."

Bertel handed him what looked like a cream-colored brick with buttons along one face and a black antenna sticking out the top.

"Hey, a car phone. Cool."

"Yeah. Cool. Keep it plugged into the cigarette lighter. If you need to call me, the number's on the directions sheet—under 'Mr. McAllister.' I don't want to hear from you unless it's absolutely necessary—like you're being searched or you've had a breakdown or you're running an hour or more behind schedule. Got it?"

"Got it."

"Good." He tapped the yellow sheet. "If you keep to the speed limits—and you will keep to the limits—it will take you about eight hours, depending on traffic. I'll expect you at that address around midafternoon. Now get going."

"But when I reach Jersey City—"

"I'll be there." He held up the key. "Somebody's got to unlock those doors."

3

All that worry for nothing. The trip turned out to be a piece of cake. No one paid him the least bit of attention. Along the way, Jack did some calculations.

He had twenty thousand packs of cigarettes on board. If Bertel took a markup of just fifty cents a pack, the profit on this load was ten grand. That made paying Jack a thou small potatoes. And Bertel was talking three runs a week just for Jack. That didn't count the runs to Boston and Detroit he'd mentioned. What about runs he hadn't mentioned?

Dane Bertel was raking it in.

He had overhead, of course. Needed other employees besides Tony and Jack. Had to rent space somewhere to store all the ciggies. But still . . . all those runs a week, fifty-two weeks a year. Jack wondered how he laundered the money.

The route through Jersey City was slow, winding through a maze of rutted streets, some with exposed streetcar tracks, flanked by empty, dilapidated buildings. When he reached the address—a graffiti-coated garage looking as empty and dilapidated as everything else—he stayed in the truck.

After a good five-minute wait, a bearded guy wearing a long brown robe and some kind of embroidered pillbox hat—inanely Jack wondered what it would look like in leopard skin—stepped through a paneled door and approached. He tapped on the passenger window and held up a pack of Marlboros.

Jack fought an urge to say, No, thanks, don't smoke. Instead he nodded.

The guy signaled to another robed beard in the doorway and the garage door began to rise. As the first beard motioned him to back into the garage, Jack looked around for Bertel. He said he'd be here with the key. Where the hell was he?

Well, he'd talked about delivering the load to an Egyptian named "the Mummy," and these guys certainly fit the Egyptian mold, so Jack began the laborious process of backing the truck through the barely wide-enough opening. With helpful hand signals from the beards, he succeeded without losing a side mirror. As the door rolled back down its tracks, Jack turned off the engine.

The first guy tapped on the window again and made a turning motion with his hand, indicating the need for a key.

Jack rolled the window down a couple of inches. "The boss has it."

The guy looked baffled. Didn't he speak English?

Jack held up the key chain, showing only the ignition key. "No key for the lock."

Again that baffled look. He hurried through a doorway into what looked like a tiny office and yammered something. He emerged with a taller, heavier man following—thicker body, thicker beard, but wearing a white skullcap. If this was the Mummy, he didn't look like one.

"I have never seen you before," he said in a heavily accented bass voice.

"Well, that makes two of us."

"We need the key to open the back."

"My boss has it. He said he'd be here."

"He usually is but he is not. Usually the driver has the key."

Was that so? Interesting. But it made sense in a way.

"This is my first run."

The guy hesitated, then nodded. He didn't seem perturbed. "I see. Then we shall have to wait."

It didn't take long. Bertel showed up about ten minutes later and motioned Jack out of the truck as he handed the padlock key to one of the beards.

"You made good time. No troubles, I take it."

"None."

He clapped Jack on the upper arm. "Easiest money you ever made, right?"

Jack hadn't seen the cash, so he didn't feel he'd made it yet. But he only smiled and nodded.

The Arabs unloaded the props, then stacked the shrink-wrapped master cases of Marlboros against a wall. Jack saw a couple of cases of Kools there when he arrived, but that was it.

"Not much stock," he said in a low voice.

"Didn't I tell you? These Mohammedans can move cigarettes like nobody's business. That's—"

"Mohammedans?"

"Yeah. What do you call them?"

Jack shrugged. "Muslims?" At least that was what they were called in the papers.

"We called these oil-mongering, hummus-slurping, camel-humping bastards Mohammedans when I was growing up, and I don't see any reason to change."

"So, I take it you're not drinking buddies."

"They don't drink! Never trust a man who won't have a beer with you, Jack."

"Is that the real reason you bought us that six-pack the other day?"

"Damn straight." He looked over at the office door. "Speaking of Mohammedans, I've got to go jaw with the Mummy. Looking for an exclusive here—become his only supplier."

Bertel disappeared inside the office, and Jack watched one of the Mummy's men reload the props while another made a show of counting the cases. Eight stacks of five, like that took counting. He heard voices rise in the office but couldn't make out what was being said.

Bertel emerged from the office carrying a white legal envelope. The Mummy followed.

"I need more Kools," he said. "You can supply me many Kools?"

"Sure can. Full load?"

"Forty cases, yes. I need soon."

Bertel jerked his thumb toward Jack. "I let this guy sleep some, he can be back here day after tomorrow." He looked at Jack. "Think you can handle that?"

Jack didn't see why not. If he didn't leave until six tomorrow night, he'd have nearly twenty-four hours to recoup.

"Piece of cake."

Bertel smiled. "Famous last words. But I like your attitude." He turned to the Mummy. "Forty of Kool, day after tomorrow. Count on it." Back to Jack. "Still got enough driving left in you to get us back to the city?"

"Sure."

The door went up, they drove through Jersey City and Hoboken and back into the Holland Tunnel. As soon as they entered the tiled gullet, Bertel pulled out the Arab's envelope and counted out hundred-dollar bills.

"Put those away," he said, handing them over.

Jack slipped them into a back pocket.

Okay, *now* this was officially the easiest thousand he had ever made. In fact, the only thousand he had ever made in a twenty-four-hour period.

4

Portly Riaz Diab swiveled back and forth in his office chair and shook his head. "No," he said in Arabic. "This is trouble."

The unspoken rule was to discuss business in Arabic—the equivalent of a secret code here in America.

Nasser al-Thani had expected the refusal. Had been counting on it, in fact. Acceptance on Riaz's part would have thrown the plan into disarray. But for appearance's sake he needed to keep pushing.

"But this means a huge profit with no financial risk on your part."

Riaz's eyes narrowed. "Yes. The financial risk is all yours. The risk of jail would be all mine. But your presence concerns me more. You travel across the river from your luxurious apartment to smelly, dirty Jersey City to offer me a fortune. What is in it for you?"

"A thirty-three percent profit over a period of two or three weeks."

"If your projections are correct, you could make one hundred percent over the same period by doing it yourself."

Nasser made a face. "We have been over this. You know where I am from, you know my name. I cannot allow scandal to touch the emirate."

Though the relationship was attenuated, he did share a name and a bloodline with the emir of Qatar.

Riaz shook his head again. "No. The money is tempting, but I do not need trouble."

Nasser knew Riaz Diab's cigarette operation was highly profitable and low risk, and for that reason had counted on him backing away from this venture.

He leaned back, feigning disappointment. "There is a window of opportunity here and it is closing. Perhaps you know someone I can trust."

Another shake of the head. "No, I . . ." Riaz drummed his fingers on his cluttered desk. "Perhaps . . ."

Nasser leaned forward. "Yes?"

Now was where he was supposed to refer Nasser to his nephew Tachus.

"My brother's eldest . . . he is always involved with one jihad group or another, always looking for contributions to topple Mubarak or free the West Bank or finance the cause of the day."

"You don't share his passions?"

Riaz shrugged. "I left all that and am glad of it. I came here with nothing, now I have a business. It is not a legal business, but it hurts no one and so no one bothers me. Not only that, but I feed a number of mouths directly and many more indirectly. Can that not be considered God's work? What you propose is also illegal, but it is dangerous and can cause great anger and I am not so sure it is God's work. And for what? So much more money than I would know what to do with? Money that might draw attention to me, causing me to lose not only what I might newly gain but everything I already have." Another head shake. "No. This is not for me. But Tachus . . ."

"Tachus?" Nasser feigned puzzlement. "This is the nephew you mentioned?"

"Yes. Tachus has many contacts in jihadist circles. They have little to lose and everything to gain from this venture."

Nasser knew that.

"Will you put me in contact with him?"

"I will call him and vouch for you—you could not approach him yourself. He is too suspicious. I'll have someone take you to him."

He rose and went to the door that opened into the garage. Through the gap Nasser could see a group of young Egyptians feeding packs of cigarettes through stamping machines.

"Kadir!" Riaz called. "Kadir, come here!"

A few seconds later one of those young Egyptians appeared at the door. Riaz pulled him inside.

"Do you know where my nephew will be tonight?"

Kadir nodded. "At Al-Kifah."

Nasser nodded. He knew the Al-Kifah Afghan Refugee Center well. Brooklyn's jihadist hotbed.

Riaz pointed to him. "This is Nasser. You will introduce him to Tachus. My nephew will be expecting him."

"I will meet you there," Nasser said.

Kadir looked surprised. "You know where it is?"

"Of course. I am a regular contributor."

A truth. The place fronted as a charity for refugees, but the money it collected went to train warriors in the eternal struggle against the infidel world. The Order, through Nasser, made regular contributions. Jihad was good. Jihad brought chaos.

Kadir's eyes lit. "Sheikh Omar speaks tonight in the mosque on the second floor. You should come and listen. We can meet afterward."

Nasser suppressed a groan. Sheikh Omar Abdel-Rahman . . . since his arrival in August, Egypt's blind radical cleric had been preaching anywhere he could find an audience. The Al-Farouq Mosque upstairs from the Al-Kifah Center had become a regular stop. Nasser could think of few things he'd less like to do than listen to that crackpot. Hot needles under his fingernails, perhaps.

But he forced a smile. "I'm sure that would be inspiring."

"He is brilliant," Kadir said, his tone glowing with reverence. "I'll meet you outside before seven and take you in."

"Excellent." Nasser turned to Riaz. "And you will be sure to call him?"

"Of course."

Phase One had been securing the funding. Phase Two was connecting with the jihadists—done and done. Phase Three was convincing said jihadists that this crazy scheme was workable. Nasser al-Thani had no doubt about his abilities in that quarter. He could sell a painting of Golda Meir to the blind cleric.

5

They sat in Vinny's black Crown Vic, parked on Liberty Avenue near the Cannon's appliance store. Vinny had picked up Aldo first, then Tommy.

"All right," Tommy said. He always liked to sit alone in the back, like he was being chauffeured. "What've we got?"

Vinny and Aldo had spent the weekend "researching" Harry Detrick. The results weren't good. He glanced at Aldo with raised eyebrows, giving him the nod.

"Not much," Aldo said.

"Not what I wanna hear, guys."

Aldo shrugged. "What can we say? We visited this two-room dump in Ocean Hill he called home and turned it upside down and inside out. No stash, no nothin'."

"*Nothin'?*"

"Found a lockbox," Vinny added. "Wasn't locked. Had a bank book, divorce papers, and a will."

"No insurance policy?"

"Nope."

"That inconsiderate fuck! You said bank book? Anything there?"

"If his math is right—and it was mostly subtractions—he's got a balance of nineteen bucks."

"Shit! Any furniture?"

Aldo nodded. "Yeah, but you'd have to pay the Salvation Army to take it."

Vinny said, "His will leaves all his worldly possessions—I kid you not, that's what it said—to his son."

"Son?" Vinny heard Tommy lean forward. "How old?"

The will had listed Darren John Detrick's birthdate and Vinny had calculated his age.

"Twenty-two."

"Okay. This is good. We go after the kid. You know, the debts of the father are bestowed upon the children and all that."

"Exactly what we thought," Vinny said, "so we asked around. Ain't gonna be easy collecting. He's a marine and he's over in Saudi Arabia."

"Yeah," Aldo said. "Part of that Desert Shield thing, or whatever it's called."

Vinny added, "But the good news is maybe he'll get sent home for his father's funeral and we can tap him then."

Silence from the back. Vinny checked the rearview mirror and saw Tommy chewing his upper lip and shaking his head.

"What?"

"Tony'll never go for that. He's got this thing about guys in uniform."

Aldo straightened in the passenger seat. "Whoa! You tellin' me Tony Cannon's, like, queer?"

"Fuck no! His nephew Patsy died in Nam and ever since it's been hands off soldiers. That's why he won't lend to no one in uniform." He shook his head. "Shit."

"Too bad," Vinny said, "because now soldier boy owns Harry's share of a bar."

Suddenly Tommy was like a hyperactive kid with a full bladder hanging on to the back of the front seat. "*Bar?* As in tavern?"

"Yeah."

"That's it! We go after the bar. Where is it? What's it called?"

Vinny couldn't remember the last time he'd seen Tommy this excited.

"Somewhere on the Upper West Side. Calls itself The Spot."

6

"Miller time," Jack said.

Only he had no intention of drinking Miller—Light or otherwise.

They'd dropped the truck off and were approaching Columbus Avenue on the Upper West Side.

"Aren't you ready for some serious rack time?" Bertel said.

"I am, but I need to unwind a bit, and I owe you some beers, so I'm buying."

"Where?"

"Here."

Jack gestured to a slightly worn looking bar with a trio of windows filled with hanging plants. Raised letters coated with flaking gold paint spelled out *The Spot* above those windows.

"We're gonna hit The Spot," Jack said.

"Jesus, it's a fern bar. I'm not drinking in some lousy yuppie fern bar."

Jack stepped closer to the first window next to the door and pointed to a neon Rolling Rock sign.

"That's why we're going in."

"But it's in green—"

"No, that sign means it's on tap."

"You've been here before?"

"Never."

"Then—?"

"My dime, my choice. Come on. I drank that Anheuser-Busch swill, you've got to suck it up and drink some *real* American beer."

"No green bottles, remember?"

"Jeez, it's on *tap*. Comes from an aluminum barrel."

Bertel stared at the sign a seeming eternity, then shook his head with resignation. "Shit. Ferns. I don't believe I'm doing this. Okay. Long as you're buying and it's brewed in America."

Beer signs and a few bulbs in sconces along the wall lit the dim interior. They grabbed two seats at the mostly empty bar that occupied the left end of the room.

"What'll it be?" said the short, muscular Hispanic bartender. A thin mustache snaked across his upper lip.

"Pair of Rocks," Jack said.

"Pints or bottles?"

"Pints—as long as the glasses aren't green."

The bartender gave him a sidelong glance as he poured. After setting the beers on the bar, he headed out to the floor.

Bertel said, "Health," as he and Jack clinked glasses.

"Back atcha."

Jack quaffed a quarter of the glass. He'd hadn't realized how much he'd been looking forward to a brew. Seemed like he'd been behind a steering wheel forever.

Bertel had taken a more cautious taste, but now he held up the glass and stared at it.

"Hey, not bad. Not bad at all."

Resisting a told-ya-so, Jack sniffed the air. "Beer's good, but what's that smell?"

Bertel wrinkled his nose. "Yeah, what *is* that?"

"It's Julio," said a phlegmy voice from the far rear end of the bar.

Its owner had a full head of greasy dark hair; what Jack could see of his face looked weathered. A cigarette sent up a wavering trail of smoke from the ashtray next to the half-finished bar draft before him. Directly to his left sat an identical draft and a smoldering cigarette in a second ashtray, but the chair was empty.

"But don't say nothin'," he added. "He's sensitive about it."

"I'm not saying he's got B-O or anything," Jack said. "It just . . ."

"Sorta sets your teeth on edge, don't it," said the smoker. "It's his cologne." He coughed a laugh. "Would you believe he pays good money for that shit?"

Jack turned and checked out the rest of The Spot. Fair number of tables, but mostly empty. The guy called Julio was wiping down one recently vacated. The few soft-spoken occupants scattered about displayed good haircuts and expensive sweaters. A woman in a gray warm-up was on a step stool watering the ferns.

Bertel followed his gaze. "Looks like a slow night."

"They're all slow nights these days," said the smoker.

"Yeah," Bertel said. "I guess with the recession and all—"

"Recession, hell. Damn ferns drove the regulars away. Harry's idea. He thought—"

"Harry? Julio's not the owner?"

"Not completely. He was a minority partner—very minority—with the late, not-so-great Harry there."

The guy pointed to a black-draped photo on a shelf at the back of the bar. Some guy in what looked like a leisure suit. Had to be an old photo.

"Recently deceased?" Bertel said.

"Yeah. Thursday. Some heart thing. Fell in front of a bus. Don't like to speak ill of the dead, especially the recently dead, but Harry's one of the reasons this place is failing. The ferns was his idea."

"Didn't Julio have a say?" Jack said.

The guy shook his head. "Not really. He's only got ten percent of the place. Harry had the rest. He hardly ever showed, except to make ay-hole decisions about the dee-cor, and to decide what kind of shar-doe-nay to stock. And to water the ferns, since Julio refuses."

Jack turned again and watched the woman with the watering can. "So who's that?"

"Nita. Harry's ex. Can't call her his widow, I guess, 'cause they've been split ten years or more. Anyway, she likes the ferns."

"Too bad for Julio."

"Yeah, I guess. Harry had this idea he could get a higher class of drinkers now that we're all gen-tree-fried up here. But the place ain't shee-shee enough for the hard-core ferners, so an empty room is the result."

"You don't strike me as a hard-core ferner," Jack said.

"I'm what you call a regular. Was here before the ferns, be here after they're gone."

"Julio's gonna get rid of them?" Jack said.

"He'd love to, but where Harry's ninety percent will go, I ain't sure. Got an idea, though. Don't think it'll go to Nita, so that leaves his boy, but he's out of the country . . ." He shook his head. "I'm loyal to The Spot and to Julio, and I'll keep coming here, but I don't know how long there'll still be a *here* to come to."

"Hurting that bad?"

"Hemorrhaging. Place'll be in the morgue with a toe tag soon. Then where will Lou and me and Julio go?"

"Down by the schoolyard?"

The guy gave him a stare, then shifted to Bertel. "The kid all right in the head?"

Bertel stared at his beer. "Yet to be determined."

Back to Jack with an offended look. "You sayin' we go out lookin' for kids?"

Jack couldn't help an eye roll. "I don't believe this. You guys telling me you've never listened to Paul Simon?"

"Paul Simon?" said a guy of about the same indeterminate age wearing a faded blue T-shirt and dusty work pants. He slipped into the empty chair next to the first smoker. "That doofus senator with the bow tie?"

"Lou, would you believe this kid just said me and Julio was pee-do-files."

Lou's face darkened. "Barney, I believe those are fighting words. If he thinks he can call my best friend—"

Jack raised his hands. "Stop-stop-stop." This was escalating like mad. He pointed to the guy called Barney. "Let me buy you one and we'll forget I said anything."

Barney didn't hesitate a nanosecond. "Sold." He waved to the bartender. "Julio. Got me a contrite and generous soul here."

Julio returned and slipped back behind the bar. "Which one of you buyin'?"

Jack lifted his hand.

Julio grinned. "How'd he play you?"

"All my own doing, I'm afraid." He looked at the guy. "Your name's Barney, right?"

"You got it. And this here's my longtime pal, Louis."

"But 'Lou' will do," the other drinker said.

"I'm . . ." He hesitated, then wondered why. His was hardly a rare name. "Jack." He didn't introduce Bertel, deciding to leave that up to him. With an amused expression, Bertel sipped his beer in silence.

"A pleasure to drink your whiskey, Jack." Barney grinned at Julio and waved at the top shelf of the mirrored bottle display against the wall. "Some of that Glenlivet, if you please, Julio."

Jack pointed to the nearly empty eight-ounce bar draft sitting before Barney. "I meant one of those."

Barney looked offended. "You offered to buy me 'one.' I assumed it would be drinker's choice."

"That's right," Lou said. "Only fair."

Julio looked at Jack. "Your call."

Well, he'd just had the biggest payday of his life.

"What the hell. Go for it. And buy Lou one too."

Barney and Lou high-fived.

After Julio poured the single malts, he pulled another pint of Rock and slid it in front of Jack.

"On the house, amigo."

"Yeah?"

The little man shrugged. "You're a good sport." He held out his hand. "Jack, right?"

Jack nodded as they shook. "And you're Julio."

"That's me. Welcome to The Spot, meng." His smile turned sad. "For as long as it lasts."

Julio's cologne and the ferns notwithstanding, Jack kind of liked this place. Might come back here. No, he'd definitely come back.

7

The four were suspicious, but Nasser al-Thani had expected that.

He'd come over the Manhattan Bridge and found the mosque and Al-Kifah refugee center on Atlantic Avenue, just off Flatbush. Kadir had been waiting outside in the dark. The young Palestinian had ushered him through the entrance, framed by storefronts, and upstairs into the mosque where Sheikh Omar Abdel-Rahman was haranguing the crowd in Arabic to pursue worldwide jihad until every man, woman, and child on Earth embraced Islam. This was Allah's wish. Infidels were hated enemies, and he backed it up with quotes from the Koran.

"'We disassociate ourselves from you and from that you worship other than Allah: We have rejected you, and there has appeared between us enmity and hatred forever until you believe in Allah alone!'"

Clearly, no quarter with nonbelievers.

Nasser counted himself among the infidel horde. Worse, he was a *mur-*

tad fitri—a man born into Islam who later rejected it. As a youth Nasser had been recruited by the Order and had substituted it for Islam. That was where his loyalties lay now. In the old days, such apostasy was punishable by death.

Nasser could not understand how anyone took this man seriously. With his red cap, white beard, dumpy body, and oversized sunglasses, he looked like a cross between Santa Claus and Ray Charles, though he was so insulated and narrow in his views, he'd probably never heard of either.

But looks were deceiving in this case. He was fanatical about establishing an Islamic theocracy in his homeland. Back in the day he'd been jailed for calling President Nasser a pharaoh, and rumor had it that he was one of the plotters and instigators behind the Sadat assassination. That Mubarak had succeeded Sadat instead of a Khomeini-type leader seemed to have driven Abdel-Rahman to madness.

Nasser suffered through the tiresome tirade, and then Kadir led him to a small room below in the refugee center where he introduced his three Egyptian associates by first names only.

"My uncle said I should listen to you," said Tachus—Nasser knew his last name was Diab, same as his uncle. "He said you could help us raise a large sum for the cause of jihad."

The round-faced one named El Sayyid slashed the air with his hand. "They keep sending our funds to Egypt and Afghanistan. Jihad should be here, in America, where there are more Jews than in Israel!"

Nasser knew American Muslims contributed more than a hundred thousand a month to the Al-Kifah fund, which funneled it to radical Islamist groups. The more radical, the better, as far as the Order was concerned.

He shrugged. "I do not care where you send the profits you make through me, as long as they go to jihad."

Sayyid was unfolding a sheet of paper he had pulled from a pocket. He held it up for Nasser.

"*This* is what we should be doing!"

Nasser saw the face of a bearded rabbi, his image peppered with bullet holes.

"Is this personal?" Nasser asked.

Sayyid shook the sheet. "He hates our people as much as we hate him."

The man looked familiar. Nasser was almost sure he'd seen that face before, but the damage made identification difficult. It would come to him.

"How much 'profit' are we talking about?" said the tall, redheaded Mahmoud.

Nasser paused for effect, then said, "Three million American. After I take my commission, there will be two million left for you."

He watched their eyes bulge, saw Kadir's jaw drop.

After their initial shock, Tachus's eyes narrowed. "Why would you do this for us? We have never heard of you. Why not keep all three million for yourself?"

"Because I can't do it by myself."

"He's CIA," Sayyid said, producing a revolver with a short, thick barrel. He pointed it at Nasser. "He's setting a trap for us."

Nasser backed up a step and looked at Tachus. "Your uncle knows me, he can vouch for me."

Tachus put a hand on Sayyid's gun and pushed it down so it pointed toward the floor.

"It's true, Sayyid. My uncle says we can trust him."

"And your uncle is never wrong?"

"Not when it comes to money."

Nasser backed farther away, edging toward the door. Time for a little gamesmanship.

"Your uncle told me his nephew and his associates were dedicated to jihad and that I could deal frankly with you, but I am beginning to think he was wrong. I will leave you now and we will never speak of this again."

"Wait," said Tachus. "Put that away, Sayyid. The least we can do is listen to him."

Sayyid grudgingly complied, but glared at Nasser, saying, "His uncle may vouch for you, but that doesn't fit with what we know of the man. He cares for profit far more than jihad. Why would he pass up millions for himself and send you to us? Something is not right here."

Nasser sensed he had turned a corner with this crew.

He shrugged again. "Because one does not make that kind of profit without risk. The risk was too great for his uncle. Perhaps it will be too great for you as well."

"No risk is too great for jihad," Sayyid said. "Tell us what this involves."

Nasser began to lay out his plan. He knew he had them. He could lead them anywhere now.

8

The drinkers, what few had shown up, were gone. Julio had the chairs upended on the tables and was mopping The Spot's floor when he heard the door open behind him. He was sure he'd locked it.

"Sorry, we're closed," he said, turning, but then saw Nita stepping through. She had a key. "Kinda late to be out."

Fortyish and frumpy, she wore the same warm-up as this afternoon. It was too tight on her expanding thighs. She looked stressed, shaken even. Maybe she'd cared for Harry more than she'd realized.

She smiled. "With Harry's funeral tomorrow and Darren home for a few days, I thought I should give the plants another watering." She pointed to his mop. "A partner shouldn't be doing that."

"He does when there's no money left over to hire anyone else."

She shook her head. "Don't worry. It will turn around. It's the economy."

Sí, he thought. The economy—and those *condenado* ferns.

But he kept it to himself. Now wasn't the time.

"What time's the service?"

"Two. At Becker's in Ridgewood."

That meant he'd have to close the place after lunch and head over to Queens.

"Darren lands at ten," she added. "I'll pick him up, then maybe bring him here. He's your new partner, you know."

Julio went back to mopping. "I figured."

She bit her lip. "Something strange is going on, Julio."

"Like?"

"I went to Harry's apartment today. It's been torn apart."

He stopped mopping again. "Human *buitres.* They read someone dies, they go steal whatever they can."

"I suppose. It's just not right. But anyway, I saw the will there and Darren gets everything."

"Nothing for you?"

She shook her head. "I didn't expect anything. We've been over for a long, long time."

"He still carried a torch for you."

A small, sad smile. "My torch sank in the East River a dozen years ago. I'm glad Darren's getting it all. I would hate to have Harry will it to one of his floozies."

She went about watering the ferns, then said good-bye and left.

Julio was thinking that maybe he could sit down with Darren and agree to get rid of these ferns. If Darren stayed overseas for a while, he might turn out to be the perfect majority partner. Julio had enough to deal with, what with the falling receipts and his sister's ex giving her a hard time.

He heard the door open again and, figuring it was Nita, didn't look up.

"Forget something?"

"We thought she'd never leave," said a male voice.

Julio spun and saw two guys, one heavy, one slim, standing in the doorway.

"We're closed."

The heavy one pulled a donut from a bag and bit into it. The thinner one closed the door and locked it.

"You are now."

"My name's Vinny," the heavy guy said around a bite of donut. "This here's Aldo. We know you're Julio. We need to talk."

"About your partner," Aldo added.

"Harry? What about him?"

Julio had a pretty good idea now who had gone through Harry's apartment.

"He owes some people money," Vinny said.

Uh-oh.

Julio leaned his mop against a table and headed for the bar.

"What people?" he said as he moved.

Vinny took another bite. "People who don't like to get stiffed, even by a stiff."

Aldo laughed like it was the first time he'd heard that. Maybe it was.

"What's that got to do with me?"

"He owns part of this business—a real big part, we've heard—so we figure the business needs to settle up."

Behind the bar now, Julio removed the sawed-off twelve-gauge from its clips under the bar, but didn't show it.

"The business didn't borrow the money. You got loan papers?"

Aldo laughed again. "I love this guy!"

Vinny said, "He borrowed three G's at ten points a week and—"

"Ten a week? *Mierda!*"

"You didn't let me finish. He's three weeks behind, which means he owes four grand now. The vig is four hundred a week."

Aldo said, "We need at least that tonight to keep you from getting further behind."

That did it. Julio raised the sawed-off and rested it on the bar, pointing toward the two men. Aldo stepped back, but Vinny only paused briefly in his chewing.

"You seen *Scarface*?" Julio said. "This is *my* 'li'l fren'."

Vinny said, "You pull that trigger, the next cocktail you serve will be a Molotov."

"Chingate!"

"Whatever," Aldo said. "Look, you ain't dealin' with just a coupla clowns off the street. There's an organization involved. You hearda Tony Cannon? Well—"

Vinny nudged Aldo. "I ain't so sure Tony wants his name thrown around."

Tony the Cannon Campisi? That meant the Gambino family. *Mierda!*

Aldo said, "Who's throwin'? Just mentioning." He turned back to Julio. "Your ex-partner is in to him for four large and Tony ain't the forgive-and-forget type, so we need to walk outa here with four C-notes minimum, or we go collect it somewheres else—like from Harry's wife."

"Or maybe from his kid," Vinny said. "We know he's comin' in tomorrow."

These two *cabrons* must have been listening at the door.

Julio was ready to let loose with both barrels but held back. His older sister Rosa was always on him about what she called his "macho thing" and how he had to control it—maybe because he was always wanting to mess up her ex-husband. What if he didn't *want* to control it? Two goons come in and demand money. Was it a "macho thing" to refuse to bend over and take it up the ass?

No fucking way.

But he had other people to consider. Nita . . . who knew what they'd do to her? Darren could probably mop the floor with these two, but not the whole Gambino family. Harry had been a jerk, but Julio couldn't let his pride get Harry's family hurt.

As if things weren't bad enough.

It damn near killed him to do it, but he leaned over to the cash register, keyed it open, and removed four hundred-dollar bills from under the tray. He placed them on the bar and stepped back, raising the shotgun toward the ceiling.

Aldo stepped forward. "You're smarter than you look," he said as he snapped them up

Julio clenched his jaw and resisted the insane urge to blow his head off and tell Vinny to take *that* back to Tony the Cannon.

As they went out the door, Vinny turned to him. "See you next week. Oh, I know you didn't ask, but get rid of the ferns. They really suck."

Julio screamed, "*Metetelo en el culo!*"

MONDAY

1

In the week or so since Nasser al-Thani had last seen him, Roman had moved again. He'd called his hotel and learned that he had checked out, leaving no forwarding address. No matter. Nasser had his mobile number. He called that and Roman answered immediately.

"I'm glad you called. The funding arrived."

Wonderful. Although the amount had been approved weeks ago, putting that much cash together without raising eyebrows or leaving a trail was a delicate matter. Despite its contacts in the world of international banking, even the Order had to tread softly in these matters.

"Is that why you moved?"

"One of the reasons. Time for a change, anyway. Call me tomorrow and I'll arrange for you to take possession. We'll finalize the details of the project then."

The project . . . that was how they referred to the plan. They practiced circumlocution at an art-form level during landline phone calls, and Nasser knew to be extra cautious when speaking over a cellular network. The calls were easily monitored, but worse: conversations occasionally leaked onto a third phone for no apparent reason.

"I will do that. I have another matter I'd like to discuss. Do you remember my mentioning the piercing passion of one of our new Brooklyn associates?"

"For a certain vocal rabbi?"

"That's the one. The rabbi in question is speaking in town tonight. I was wondering if I should inform our associate. He might want to hear what he has to say."

"He might indeed. But you seem hesitant."

"There's always the possibility that it could interfere with our larger plan."

"The larger plan has a long-term payoff. If our associate takes decisive action, it could have an immediate effect. Retaliatory reaction will serve only to speed our larger plan. Tell him. This will be interesting to watch."

"I agree. Most interesting."

2

Another meeting with the man from Qatar.

Kadir joined his three Egyptian friends in a back room of the Al-Kifah Center to see what he had to say. It turned out he didn't have much new except that he would deliver the money tomorrow night and finalize all plans then.

"That is all you have to say?" Sayyid said. "You brought us here just for that? Why do you waste our time like this?"

Kadir had to agree. He'd finished up his work labeling the cigarette packs at Tachus's uncle's place, and hurried here all the way from New Jersey just to hear this?

"My friend," said Nasser al-Thani, staring at Sayyid, "you may change your mind about wasted time when you hear what else I have to say."

"I am not your friend," Sayyid said. "You say all the right things, but still I do not trust you."

Al-Thani smiled. "So who am I if not who I say I am?"

"Oh, we know *who* you are," Sayyid said. "We checked that out. But *what* you are . . . that is another question."

"You think perhaps I'm CIA? FBI? Mossad? Would I be helping you bring riches to the cause of jihad if I were?"

"And bringing riches to yourself as well."

Al-Thani shrugged. "There is more than one way to serve Allah. You bluster like a camel in heat, but so far, what have you accomplished?"

Kadir held his breath. Sayyid's round face seemed to expand as it turned red. He looked ready to strangle al-Thani.

The man from Qatar went on. "But let me ask you another question: Who do you hate most of all in this world?" A quick smile. "Besides me at the moment."

Sayyid spoke through his teeth. "You know who. You keep asking me about him."

"Yes, I do indeed know who. And as a personal favor to you, I have tracked him down. I know where he will be tonight, and exactly what time he will be there."

Sayyid shot to his feet. "Tell me! Tell me and I promise you the Zionist pig will not see tomorrow!"

What day is it? Jack wondered as he sipped a Rock at The Spot.

He knew it was early November because last week kids had been running around in costumes, trick-or-treating. He'd noticed a few Ghostbusters but Ninja Turtles definitely predominated with the boys. And he knew it was Monday, because he'd watched the Eagles trounce the Pats yesterday. But the actual date? Not a clue.

The past couple of weeks of his life had blurred into one long road, with Tony at one end and Bertel and the Mummy at the other. He'd wanted to get back out to that Long Island range to do some more shooting, but had no time. After the first run, Bertel gave him the key to the truck's padlock, but told him to keep it hidden away so he could continue to use the story about his girlfriend's untrusting father.

Girlfriend . . . good thing he didn't have a real one. She'd be on his case about never seeing him. His social life now consisted of a few brews at The

Spot at the end of a run and an occasional visit to Abe. He'd made the mistake of bringing along some sort of edible goody twice in a row; Abe had looked so heartbroken on the third visit when Jack had shown up with nothing that he vowed never to visit empty-handed again.

Each end of the road had its own ritual. The southern ceremony began with turning the empty truck over to Tony at the Lonely Pine Motel. It might be a U-Haul or a Ryder or a Budget or Penske—Jack never knew until he showed up at the garage the evening before. Then nap time in one of the rooms. As he grew used to the routine, Jack managed to get some genuine shut-eye during the break and occasionally needed Tony's pounding on the door to wake him. Then the eucharist—Krispy Kremes and coffee—during which he and Tony would shoot the breeze. Though considerably older than Jack, but younger than Bertel, Tony was easy to like—affable, always smiling, always some awful joke to tell. The facial hair thing, though . . . that wasn't making it. No way that black scraggle along his jaw would ever thicken into a self-respecting beard. At some point in every conversation, Jack would try to pry free some info on the enigmatic Bertel, and Tony would profess ignorance. Jack didn't buy that for a second.

The northern ceremony started upon his arrival at the Jersey City garage. Having the key with him allowed the "Mohammedans"—he doubted he'd ever get used to that unwieldy term—to unload the truck without waiting for Bertel. Then Jack would sit in silence until the man showed up. The Mummy's helpers spoke Arabic among themselves and the Mummy himself barely acknowledged his existence. The envelope would be passed, an order would be taken, and Bertel would wait till they were in the tunnel to pass Jack his cut. The space behind Jack's floor molding was filling with hundred-dollar bills. It became even more crowded when he was on the road because he stashed his Ruger there.

Then parking the van in a reserved space at an Upper West Side garage. Jack suspected Bertel lived up this way. He tried to follow him once but lost him. At the end of the next run Bertel said he understood Jack's curiosity but not to try that again. So much for his man-hunting skills.

And aside from a couple of post-run beers with Julio and the dwindling regulars at The Spot, that was pretty much his life.

A thrill a minute.

Of course, it could become genuinely thrilling if he got nabbed with those smuggled cigarettes. A thrill he could do without.

Today had brought a variation to the routine when he'd skipped his usual post-run brew at Julio's. He'd been bushed and had gone straight home to crash. He'd been jolted awake by a dog barking outside his door. Loud as hell and the damn mutt wouldn't quit. Finally he'd dragged himself out of bed and gone to the door to scream bloody murder at the owner, but when he opened it he found a silent, empty hallway.

Go figure.

Anyway, the damage was done. He was wide awake. So he'd wandered up to Julio's. When he reached The Spot at five the sun was already gone. Getting dark so early these days. Barney and Lou were at the bar—surprise!—but otherwise the place was mostly empty.

He stared at the foam atop his brew and thought about how this wasn't quite how he'd envisioned his new life. Then again, he hadn't had any sort of plan other than to disappear, tell the world to fuck off, kill the old Jack, and cremate his remains until nothing but ashes remained.

He'd been using Moore as a surname. He should change that to Jack Phoenix. Yeah, a new Jack, risen from the ashes of the old.

Jack Phoenix.

He shook his head. That sucked. It didn't merely suck, but clearly and sincerely sucked.

Forget the name crap. What about the smuggling? How long to keep it up?

He was making a delivery every other day, socking away seven grand in two weeks. Theoretically he could pull down a hundred and eighty thou in a year. The amount was almost unimaginable. And all tax free. He'd have to make a quarter mil or more in a straight job to net that amount after Uncle Sam and Governor Cuomo and Mayor Dinkins were done picking his pockets.

Yeah, great money, *unbelievable* money, but how long before he stretched his luck past the breaking point and got pulled over by a cop determined to see what was in the truck bay?

And really, was this all there was?

When he first arrived in the city, his main concerns had been keeping something in his belly and a roof over his head—hell, his *only* concerns. Money had been a constant problem. But now it had stopped being a problem, at least for the moment, so now other questions broke the surface.

Like, Where do I go from here?

He'd been raised to have a direction, a purpose in life. His internal compass kept searching for north. Well, fuck north. Fuck purpose and direction as well. That was why he'd come to the city. To get lost. To break out of that trap. To cut all strings.

Purpose and direction create strings, and strings inevitably control your movements. He would *not* become his father, good man though he was.

The plan: have no plan. Throw the rudder overboard. Sail the sea of Now. Live in the moment. Go where the wind takes you.

At this moment the wind had taken him to The Spot. And something was in that wind. Barney and Lou were strangely silent, and Julio . . . Julio looked like a caged tiger. He had a sense that they knew something he didn't, and weren't sharing.

"Something going on with our friend?" he said when Julio made the rounds of the tables.

Barney continued smoking but Lou said, "Lotsa shit goin' down. His sister's ex is making life miserable for her. And then—"

He cut off as Julio returned. Behind Jack, the door opened. Julio, Barney, and Lou looked up . . . and kept on looking. Their eyes told different stories. Barney's and Lou's looked a little cowed, Julio's looked angry and defiant.

What the hell?

Jack turned and saw a fat guy wearing a short black raincoat strolling toward the bar. He stopped next to Jack without looking at him. His gaze was fixed on Julio.

"Got something for me?"

Julio glared at him and said nothing. The guy snapped his fingers a couple of times. "Come on, come on. We've got other stops to make."

Another couple of beats, then Julio reached under the bar and came up with a slim, legal-size envelope. He slid it across the polished wood. The newcomer snapped it up, ripped it open, and peeked inside.

"Don't trust me?" Julio gritted his teeth.

"I only trust my mother," the guy said without looking up.

Jack caught a glimpse of some bills but couldn't make out the denomination.

The guy nodded and slipped it inside his raincoat. "See you next week."

He turned and sauntered out the door.

Jack watched him go, then turned back to Julio, but he was looking away. Jack hurried to the front windows, pushed aside the damn ferns, and watched him squeeze behind the wheel of a big black Crown Victoria. A guy in a porkpie hat sat in the passenger seat. The car roared away.

"What just happened here?" he said, returning to the bar.

"Nothing," Julio said, then slipped into the back room.

Jack looked at Lou and Barney. "Is he paying protection? Is that it?"

"Long story, Jack," Lou said.

"I got time."

Barney said, "Better you don't know."

"And besides," Lou added, "Julio wants to keep it to himself."

"Well, you guys know."

Barney coughed. "We been here a lot longer than you, Jack."

That brought home to Jack that, as much as he felt at home here, he was still an outsider. His immediate reaction was anger. And why not? Everything seemed to tick him off. But then he realized he had secrets from them as well. Had he told them he was running cigarettes? No. So they were even.

Still, it hurt a little.

4

After the man from Qatar left, Tachus turned to Sayyid. "You can't be serious!"

"This is not a matter for discussion. It will happen. He will die by my hand tonight. I do not need anyone's help for that. But escaping is another matter." He turned to Mahmoud. "Your taxi . . . you could help me."

Eyes bright, Mahmoud ran both his hands through his reddish hair. In Afghanistan, he had walked ahead of the mujahideen, poking a reed into the soil to find Soviet mines. He feared nothing.

"Yes! This man's death will shake the Zionist world. Tell me what you need me to do and it will be done."

Sayyid turned to Tachus, but Tachus raised his hands and backed away. "I want to know nothing of this. We have a once-in-a-lifetime opportunity to help jihad as never before, and you want to risk it like this? You are insane. Worse, you are traitors to jihad!"

He turned and left the room, slamming the door behind him.

Sayyid and Mahmoud turned to Kadir.

"And you?" Sayyid said. "Will you stand with us, or run like that jackrabbit, Tachus?"

Kadir tried to calm his whirling thoughts. If Sayyid was caught, the trail would lead directly to the Al-Kifah Center. The enemies of Islam would converge here and the man from Qatar might change his mind as to whom to trust with his scheme.

"How can you hesitate?" Mahmoud cried. "The Zionists have occupied your homeland since before you were born! The boots of Israeli soldiers trample Palestine soil every minute of every hour of every day! Here is a chance to strike back! You cannot refuse!"

They were right. He could not refuse. Kadir had to be part of this.

5

After reluctantly dropping the matter of paying protection, Jack had another beer and then left The Spot. Being shut out of the details still stung, but he'd have to live with that.

He turned downtown on Columbus Avenue, which would morph into Ninth below 59th Street. He'd gone maybe a block when he stopped in shock at the sight of a guy with a familiar face—at least he thought it looked familiar—strolling out from a side street. The bright brown eyes and the scraggly cheeks belonged to Tony from North Carolina, but he was dressed in a frock coat and sealskin hat and had those weird Hasidic curls dangling in front of his ears. Jack knew all Hasids were orthodox but not all orthodox were Hasids. Beyond that, they were men in black. Either way, this couldn't be Tony.

Jack watched the guy wave for a cab. When one stopped he flashed a big, bright, Chiclet-tooth smile that banished all doubt.

Tony . . . dressed as an orthodox Jew. Why? Halloween was over. And Tony was supposed to be in NC.

As he watched Tony slide into the rear of the cab, Jack made a snap decision. Nothing else going on, and he wasn't all that tired, so why not?

He stepped off the curb and flagged down a taxi of his own. As he slammed the door he said, "Follow that cab."

The bearded, turbaned driver gave him a look. "You are serious?" he said in accented English.

Telling a "Mohammedan" to follow a guy dressed as an orthodox Jew. Was that . . . kosher?

I don't believe I just thought that.

Then he recognized the distinct peaked wrap of the turban—the driver was a Sikh, not a Mohammedan. Jack hadn't lived in New York six months yet but his time here had schooled him in cultural diversity.

"Very serious," Jack told him.

The driver shrugged and hit the gas.

Not a long drive. Over to Central Park West, down through Columbus Circle to 57th, east to Park Avenue, then downtown some more. The leading cab pulled to the curb near the Pan Am Building.

"Pull over here," Jack told his driver and they stopped half a block behind.

Tony—or his Hasidic identical twin—hopped out and started walking back uptown, heading toward Jack's cab.

Shit. Had he spotted him?

He turned in the seat, angling his back toward the window. He saw $3.20 on the meter, so he threw a five onto the front seat.

"Keep it. I'll just wait here half a minute."

No confrontation on Tony's mind. Jack watched out of the corner of his eye as he strode past, oblivious. He did a slow count of five, thanked the cabbie, then stepped out and followed.

Tony moved like a man with a mission. He crossed Park at the first light and then continued uptown another two blocks. Looked like he was heading for the brightly lit Waldorf-Astoria, but before he reached it he turned east onto 49th. A block later he crossed Lexington and angled toward the Marriott East Side. Before Tony entered, Jack noticed him tugging the brim of his hat lower over his face and ducking his head.

Interesting.

Jack stopped by the knot of hotel guests waiting for cabs and checked out the ornate, pillared entrance. Pretty posh for a Marriott. It didn't take long for him to spot the security cameras in each corner of the wide entrance, aimed at the comers and goers. He realized another cam somewhere above was probably focused on him right now. And he didn't exactly blend in with this tony crowd.

He couldn't help feeling Tony was up to no good. Why leave his cab blocks away from his destination? So he could show up on foot with no cab to identify on the security tapes? He wondered if Bertel was behind it. He and Tony appeared tight, so it seemed a real possibility. And if Bertel was up to something funkier than smuggling ciggies, Jack figured he should know about it.

Dismaying thought: If Tony caused a stir, the security tapes would be fine-combed, and sure as hell someone would see Jack and ask, *Who's that guy just standing there and why's he staring at the security cams?*

If he were smart he'd keep walking.

He knew that. And he knew something else: No way he was moving on.

Jack kept his head down as he entered. Tony's black hat and frock coat were easy to spot amid the brighter clothes in the lobby. He hurried to get closer, but as he neared he noticed something different. This man was heavier and didn't have those curls in front of his ears. Oh, crap, his beard was thick and graying. Unless Tony had stepped through some sort of time-warp wormhole here in the Marriott's lobby, this was someone else.

He looked around and saw another orthodox type, this one with the curls but no way was he Tony. Then he saw a third non-Tony orthodox—this one with a black fedora. Were they having a convention or something?

Where the hell was—?

"Jack?" said a woman's voice from somewhere behind him.

He froze. He didn't recognize the voice and she could be a complete stranger, but she sounded young and the way she'd said his name . . . like the Jack she was calling to was the last person in the world she expected to find in the lobby of a New York hotel.

Which certainly fit him.

He risked a quick glance over his shoulder and saw a young, good-looking brunette, dressed to the nines, beaming at him. Had to be mistaken. He didn't know her.

As he turned away, he heard, "Jack from Johnson? Is that really you?"

Oh, Christ. Who was she?

He chanced another look and it came to him.

Cristin! Cristin from-high-school. Cristin best-friend-of-Karina. He was blanking on her last name. Didn't matter. He couldn't talk to her. Couldn't confirm that the guy she thought she saw was really him.

He saw the three orthodoxers filing into the same open elevator. He sprinted for it.

"Hold that, please?"

He squeezed between the doors just before they closed and made it a foursome. He moved straight to a rear corner out of Cristin's line of sight. He noticed the second-floor button was lit as he listened to the orthodox guys speak in low tones.

"You're going to see the rebbe?" one said to another.

A nod. "Morgan D, yes?"

"So I was told."

The doors parted and they stepped out. Jack followed, looking for Tony. His three elevator companions checked the directions plaque on the wall, then streamed in the same direction as others of their kind. Tony was nowhere in sight.

Jack held back a bit, then followed. Sounded as if they were going to hear some rabbi speak. Why would Tony want to be part of that? He wasn't even Jewish as far as Jack knew, and those ear curls sure as hell weren't his own hair. None of this made any sense.

The trio disappeared through doors labeled *Morgan D*. Jack approached the doorway and saw a room full of Hasidic types, all seated before an empty podium. Yeah, that had to be it: Some rabbi was going to lecture or pray or whatever they did. He searched the crowd for Tony but quickly realized the futility of trying to locate him from the doorway. Why did they all have to look so damn much alike? He'd have to go row to row, searching each face, and he wasn't about to do that. He doubted he'd be allowed.

Next best thing was to hang around until the show was over, catch Tony on the way out, and get in his face. Ask him point-blank what he was doing playing Hasidic dress-up.

Why the hell do I care? he wondered.

Good question. He didn't have a clear answer. Maybe because he'd seen something he couldn't explain. A guy he was dealing with a few times a week was playing Hasidic dress-up. Why?

The ideal place to wait would be in the lobby, but Cristin might still be there.

Her last name came to him then: Ott.

Karina Haddon's best friend. At least she had been. Most likely still was.

Karina . . . his first girlfriend, big-time high school crush . . . She left for college in California. They reconnected when she returned on her freshman Christmas break, but he never saw her again after that. She had simply and completely excised herself from his life. Leaving him with another kind of crush—the hurting kind. He'd got over it. But now her good buddy shows up in the same hotel, a hundred miles from home.

Wait . . . he remembered something Karina had said about Cristin going to school in the city. FIT? Or was it NYU? Not that it mattered. She'd be almost halfway through her senior year now, looking to graduate come June. But she hadn't been dressed like a college student. She'd looked kind of hot. And he'd never thought of Cristin as hot. She'd simply been Karina's friend.

So maybe she'd gone to FIT after all. Maybe the Fashion Institute of Technology had taught her how to put herself together for maximum effect.

Whatever. He just hoped she wrote off the sighting as a case of mistaken identity and didn't go back to Burlington County blabbing that she'd seen Karina's old boyfriend. Not that it would ever reach Jack's family. She lived in Tabernacle and he knew of no common contacts. But still, he didn't want anyone anywhere talking about him at any time. He wanted to be *gone*.

He found a stairway and eased down toward the lobby. He stopped where he had a view and saw Cristin standing off to the side. She seemed to be waiting for someone. A well-dressed middle-aged couple approached, spoke to her. She nodded, handed them a card, and they all shook hands. With smiles all around, they disappeared into an elevator.

Great. All he had to do was buy a paper, find a chair, and pretend to read while he watched these stairs and the elevator bank. It would also offer something to hide behind if Cristin reappeared.

6

Kadir crouched in the front passenger seat as Mahmoud angled his cab to the curb near the entrance of the Marriott.

Sayyid leaned forward in the rear seat and whispered, "*Allāhu Akbar.*"

"*Allāhu Akbar,*" Mahmoud and Kadir repeated.

Mahmoud pointed to a spot a couple of car lengths head. "We'll be waiting right there."

Sayyid jumped out and turned to face them for a moment. With his beard, black suit, and black yarmulke, he made a disturbingly authentic orthodox Jew. He nodded, then hurried into the hotel.

Watching him go, Mahmoud said, "After tonight, the name of El Sayyid Nosair shall be written on the walls of heaven."

"I pray for his success," Kadir said.

Mahmoud pulled past the entrance and parked with the engine running. The plan was to wait here for Sayyid who, after slaying the rabbi, would run out through the entrance and jump into the cab. Mahmoud would drive him to a safe place. If questioned later by the police he would say he dropped the fare off at a synagogue near Gramercy Park.

He laughed. "Imagine the confusion! They'll keep asking themselves, why would a Jew kill a Jew?"

Kadir grinned and nodded, but inside he was terrified. It had all seemed so easy and simple back in the refugee center. But here in Manhattan, the plan seemed full of risks and holes.

He jumped and almost cried out as someone banged on one of the cab's windows. A liveried doorman from the hotel was motioning them to move on. Mahmoud got out and spoke to him over the roof.

"I am waiting for a fare."

"Can't wait here."

"But—"

"Move it!"

"But my fare!"

"Want me to call a cop? Move your ass out of here!"

As Mahmoud slipped back behind the wheel, Kadir said, "What do we do?"

Mahmoud thought for a second, then turned to him. "I'll pull around the corner and wait. You get out here and watch for Sayyid. When he appears, bring him to me and we'll be on our way."

Kadir didn't want to leave the relative safety of the cab but had no choice. Mahmoud had the taxi license. He got out and moved toward the busy hotel entrance as Mahmoud pulled away. He felt terribly exposed and obvious out here. Everyone entering and leaving seemed so much better dressed than he. He shivered, but not with the cold. Why, oh why, had he agreed to be part of this?

He straightened his spine and focused on the entrance.

Stop worrying about yourself. Sayyid is inside doing a hero's work. He might end up a martyr tonight. Be alert. He will be out soon.

7

Jack checked the clock over the registration desk: pushing toward nine o'clock. He'd covered the *Daily News* from front page to back. He now knew far, far more about the current doings of Cuomo and Dinkins and the Jets' trouncing of the Cowboys yesterday and the Giants' anticipated victory in Indianapolis tonight than he wanted or cared to.

But no black-frocked horde had emerged from the elevators.

Bad.

No sign of Cristin either.

Good.

He yawned. Besides this afternoon's abbreviated nap, he hadn't had much sleep in the last thirty-six or so hours. Was this really worth it?

All right, he'd take another look, see what they were up to. He didn't know what was going on up there, so he had no idea what to expect. Maybe some religious thing that went on half the night. Then again, maybe he'd get lucky and spot Tony. Because he was only assuming Tony was there. He hadn't seen him enter the room. This could be a total waste of time.

He took the stairs and was approaching the Morgan D room when he heard a *boom!* from within. The sound froze him. It sounded just like one of the Magnum rounds he'd fired from his .357. A couple of seconds of dead silence followed the report, and then a cacophony of shocked and horrified shouts.

He spotted a swarthy guy in the doorway, bearded like the rest but wearing a yarmulke instead of a hat. One of the hatted orthodox, an old guy, was tackling him, trying to bring him down. Then Jack noticed the silvery revolver in the first guy's hand. Unable to shake off the tackler, the first guy shot him in the leg, then burst from the room and darted past Jack for the stairs. Shocked and confused, Jack stepped back as a number of orthodox gave chase.

What the hell?

He took a few tentative steps toward the door and peeked inside.

Chaos.

The old guy was down, howling as he clutched his bleeding leg. A couple of his buddies were already tending to him. At the far end of the room a clump of people were jammed around someone on the floor near the podium. Jack caught a glimpse of a bloody face and then black-clad legs blocked his view.

This was crazy! Orthodox Jews shooting each other? Whoever heard of that?

Had to get out of here. But wait. Could Tony have had something to do with this? Another quick scan of the crowd for him but no use. A milling pond of black hats. Time to go. He didn't want to be tagged as a witness. Plenty of those in Morgan D.

Jack looked around. The guy with the gun was gone, vanished down the stairs. So it made perfect sense for Jack to head in the opposite direction. He took the elevator up to the tenth floor, got out, walked down the hall. He'd kill a few minutes, then take it back down.

8

Kadir recognized Sayyid as he exploded from the Marriott entrance.

He shouted, "Sayyid!" but his voice was lost in the blare of a horn blast from a passing truck.

Sayyid bounded across the sidewalk and into an idling cab.

"No!" Kadir cried, rushing forward, "That's not—!"

A Jew in a wide-brimmed black hat ran out, spotted Sayyid in the cab, and stepped in front of it, waving his arms. Just then the driver burst from the cab and ran. Sayyid emerged next, waving his pistol. People screamed and ducked as he ran down the sidewalk—in the wrong direction! Mahmoud was waiting around the opposite corner.

Kadir ran after him, calling his name, but Sayyid didn't seem to hear. He came upon a man in some kind of uniform that Kadir didn't recognize. He must have seen Sayyid's pistol because he pulled out his own. Kadir skidded to a halt when he saw it.

"Stop right there!" the man cried.

Sayyid turned and fired, hitting him in the shoulder. But instead of falling, the uniformed man dropped to one knee and shot three times. He missed. But then another shot cracked from somewhere as Sayyid turned to run, striking him in the neck. He went down, firing wildly, as some of the Jews from the hotel rushed up and disarmed him.

Kadir backed away and crossed the street, forcing his legs to walk instead of run while he tried to make sense of what he'd just witnessed.

What had happened back at the Marriott? Had Sayyid succeeded? Something must have happened, else why would he have been chased from the hotel?

And what a string of bad luck! Mahmoud having to move the taxi, Sayyid getting into the wrong one, and then running into some sort of policeman as he fled.

But the big question remained: Who was the third shooter? Who had fired the shot that took Sayyid down?

Quickly he circled around to where Mahmoud should have been waiting but his cab was nowhere in sight. Mahmoud had deserted him.

He felt as if Allah had deserted him as well. Wasn't anything going to go right tonight?

9

After wasting a little time strolling up and down the tenth-floor hallway, Jack returned to the elevator bank and headed back to the lobby.

When he stepped out he found cops and EMTs and even firemen. He was literally pulled from the elevator cab to make room for a stretcher going up. Adopting an appropriately shocked and bewildered expression, he allowed a cop to hustle him out the door.

Once outside he crossed the street and stood with the crowd of passersby who'd stopped to watch all the commotion. People who'd seen him come out of the hotel asked what was going on. Jack played dumb: *I got off the elevator and everything was crazy. They scooted me out without telling me a thing.*

Someone arrived and said there'd just been a shoot-out farther down Lexington Avenue, and that cops and EMTs were already on the scene tending to the wounded. Part of the crowd took off in that direction but Jack stayed put.

Eventually word filtered down that there'd been a shooting in the hotel, followed by another down the street, but nobody knew who had taken a bullet in either incident. And while the crowd around him speculated wildly on the who and the why, Jack watched for Tony.

No luck on that score. Maybe he'd slipped away while Jack was upstairs, maybe he was still inside.

Eventually the black-and-white cop cars and ambulances left. Orthodox Jews drifted out in twos and threes, none of them Tony. The crowd dissolved, heading for bars or home to watch the end of the Giants-Colts game. Jack stayed. More of the black hats came out, but still no Tony.

No Cristin either, although she too might have left while Jack had been upstairs.

He figured some of the sedans parked in front of the hotel were unmarked detective cars. And for sure a forensics team was combing through the Morgan D room at that very moment.

Not much point in hanging around any longer. He grabbed a cab back to his place—taking a cab anywhere had been next to unthinkable when he'd been working for Giovanni. Now he was taking his second in one night.

Living large. Oh yeah.

He still had no TV, so he turned on his clock radio and scanned the stations. Didn't take long to learn that Meir Kahane had been shot and killed at a midtown hotel after addressing a chapter of the Jewish Defense League.

Jack had heard the name before, associated with some protest or another here or there around the city, but had never been able to drum up enough interest in him to learn more. After all, it seemed that at any time on any day, someone was protesting something in one of the five boroughs.

The newscaster repeatedly used the word "controversial" in describing the victim. Jack was too tired to listen to more. The guy sure as hell wasn't going to tell him what interest Tony No-last-name had in the Jewish Defense League.

But as Jack lay in bed, waiting for sleep, instead of his thoughts centering on Tony and all the questions he'd raised tonight, they swirled around Cristin Ott. He hadn't known her that well in high school, but under normal circumstances it would have been kind of nice to say hello, maybe have dinner together, hang out and catch up on what they'd been doing since they'd last seen each other.

But Jack's circumstances weren't normal, and smuggling cigarettes wasn't exactly a topic for casual conversation.

Why was he thinking about Cristin when a guy who he'd been working with could be linked to a shooting, maybe two?

And then it came to him: His life in the city had been a scramble for food and shelter since day one. Not exactly a happy existence, but one of his own choosing, where he profited or lost by his own decisions. He'd learned that autonomy could be exhausting. Still he wouldn't trade it for anything.

But now that he was no longer under the money gun, he could relax a little and look around. And what he saw was . . . not much.

He'd been so busy scrambling that he hadn't realized until now how alone he was.

10

Roman Trejador's message had left his new address—a suite at the St. Regis—and told Nasser to stop by between eleven and midnight. So at 11:09 he was knocking on the door.

This time Trejador answered the door himself. Again he was in a bathrobe, but his hair was wet, as if he'd just taken a shower.

"Nasser, come in," he said smiling. "I wasn't sure you'd get my message."

"I always check my answering machine."

"I won't bother offering you a drink," he said as Nasser followed him into the suite's front room. He pointed to a black nylon duffel bag on the floor next to the sofa. "Your investment funds."

Nasser nodded but made no move to pick it up. "Everything is arranged on the other end?"

"So I'm told." He nodded toward the TV that was playing without sound, and Nasser noticed a banner reading *Rabbi Kahane Assassinated.* "It looks like your friend was successful—almost *too* successful."

"What do you mean?"

"I mean, despite a comedy of errors, he almost got away with it. If he'd escaped, they would have been looking for an orthodox Jew as the perpetrator. And that wouldn't do—one orthodox Jew killing another isn't going to start any fires."

"Luckily that cop he ran into shot him."

Trejador laughed. "First off, that wasn't a cop, but a postal inspector who happened to be armed. And he missed completely. *I* had to shoot the Egyptian."

Nasser felt his mouth working without speaking. Finally he found his voice. "What? You?"

"I went over to the Marriott for insurance. Good thing I did."

Roman Trejador was known as the most hands-on actuator in the Order. Most other actuators delegated tasks to lower-echelon members. Not Trejador. He was not averse to going into the field and getting his hands dirty—or, in this case, bloody.

"Wasn't that risky?"

"Of course. But no gain without risk. Now the world will know that a radical Jew was murdered by a radical Muslim. We'll see what develops. Kahane's followers have acted violently in the past, we should expect no less now."

Nasser nodded. That was why he'd prodded El Sayyid Nosair. "If we're lucky, this will start an escalating cycle of vengeance and retaliation leading to . . ."

"Chaos," they said in unison.

Nasser glanced at the TV. "Any rumbles from Israel yet?"

"Too early. There's seven hours' difference. Not even sunrise yet. But don't expect too much. Kahane has become isolated lately, his influence waning." Trejador pointed to the duffel. "There lies the long-term jihad-feeding investment that will pay off in global chaos."

"Yes," said Nasser al-Thani. "I'll be delivering it tomorrow."

TUESDAY

1

"You were *there*?" Abe said, almost choking on one of the cream-cheese bagels Jack had brought along. "When it happened?"

"Right outside the door. I heard the shot."

On his way over, Jack had passed a fair number of newsstands where every front page of every daily had screamed the news about the Kahane killing. And a copy of just about every one of those papers, maybe even more, was spread out on Abe's counter. He'd never been here in the morning. Were all these papers part of a daily ritual? Surely he didn't read them all.

"And for why were you in such a place?"

Jack didn't hesitate. He'd expected the question. He trusted Abe but didn't know how tight he was with Bertel. Would what he said here get back to his boss? He doubted it, but couldn't be sure. So he'd come up with an answer that was neither the whole truth nor a lie—a skill he'd honed during his adolescence.

"I thought I saw someone I knew go inside so I followed." Follow the vague statement with a concrete change of subject: "So who was this Kahane?"

Good thing he'd heard the name a few times or he'd be pronouncing it *Kah-HAYN*.

"A pushy super Jew."

Jack blinked. He hadn't expected that from Abe.

"A what?"

"Super Jew. A super Zionist. He started out as a rabbi of a synagogue in Howard Beach and they kicked him out for being too pushy with the orthodoxy. He went over to Israel and somehow got himself elected to the Knesset. And you know what? *They* kicked him out."

"For being too Jewish?"

"For being too anti-Arab."

"In Israel?"

Abe nodded. "In Israel. He wanted every Arab deported, a ban on Jewish-gentile marriage, and other equally meshuggeneh ideas. He and his party of like-thinkers were banned from running for office."

"No offense," Jack said, "but I take it you don't practice."

"Practice what?"

Jack didn't know if he was stepping off a cliff on Mount Faux Pas or not, but he pushed ahead, "Uh, Jewry?"

Abe almost choked again, this time from laughter.

"'Jewry'? I've read that word, but until today I don't believe I've ever heard anyone say it."

Jack felt himself redden. "Well, then, it's a first for both of us."

"First off, you don't 'practice' being a Jew. You're *born* a Jew. You can convert, but on the whole, if your mother was Jewish, so, by law, are you. The word is 'observe,' and no, I'm not an observant Jew. You've never witnessed, but a cheeseburger I'll eat once a week, maybe more."

"What's wrong with that?"

"It's traif."

"Can we speak English here?"

"It's forbidden."

Jack couldn't help frowning. "But it's beef. I thought it was pork you folks couldn't—"

"It's meat and dairy together." He shook a scolding finger. "Traif-traif-traif!"

Jack couldn't take anymore. Big Macs forbidden? What planet was Abe from?

"Can we get back to this Kahane guy? Why would another Jew kill him?"

"Another Jew? Are you farblunget in the head? It was an Arab—an Egyptian. Didn't you listen to the news this morning?"

"No. But the guy I saw with the gun was wearing a yarmul—" The painfully obvious answer hit him then. "Never mind."

"Right. A beard he had already. Put on a yarmulke and a black suit jacket, and—" He snapped his fingers. "Instant orthodox."

"What about those curls on the side?" he said, thinking about Tony's getup.

"The side curls? They're called payot. And I don't believe an Egyptian was wearing them."

"They caught him?"

"Yes, and from what I've been reading and hearing, for an Arab this guy had a schlimazel's luck."

"Whoa. What's a schlimazel?"

"An unlucky schlemiel."

Jack balled his fists. Okay, he'd heard the words before, but . . .

"And what's a schlemiel?"

Abe stared at him. "You're kidding, right?"

"I'm a hick from rural New Jersey. I've heard the words in the opening of *Laverne and Shirley*, but—"

"*Laverne and Shirley*? I should know them?"

"From TV. You know: 'Schlemiel, schlimazel, hasenpfeffer incorporated.'"

Abe looked lost. "What's this you're telling me? 'Hasenpfeffer incorporated'? It doesn't make a pupik's worth of sense."

A real cultural gap here.

"This is a news show?" Abe added.

"No. It was a comedy series from the seventies, but they're replayed all the time."

Abe waved his hands. "No comedies for me. They think they're funny? They're not. Only news I watch, and believe none of it."

"Then why watch?"

"How else should I know what not to believe?"

"These digressions are killing me already," Jack said, and froze. Had he really said that? He shook it off. "Whatever, I always thought schlemiel and schlimazel were nonsense words."

"No nonsense. A schlemiel is a habitual klutz. I should explain klutz too?"

"No. Klutz I get."

"Well, that's something. So here it is: Give a schlemiel a bowl of soup and he'll spill it. A schlimazel is the guy he spills it on."

Jack smiled. "I've known a few of those. Okay. Why's this Arab a schlimazel?"

"Apparently he jumped into a cab outside the hotel thinking it would be driven by a coconspirator, but it wasn't. So he pulled his gun and tried to hijack the cab, but the driver jumped out and ran. So the Arab had to do the same. So far you notice that, thanks to New York's strict no-carry laws, this Arab has not encountered a single person who can shoot back. Until he runs into a postal inspector who happens to be armed."

"You and I can't carry weapons but they allow a postal worker? What's wrong with this picture?"

"Everything. So the Egyptian shoots at someone who can shoot back. Both are wounded—the postal worker not so bad, the Arab pretty bad. But Bellevue saves him."

"Okay. An Arab gunning down a rabbi. That makes more sense. Well, I mean, as much sense as gunning down someone you don't agree with can make."

"If it makes sense," Abe said, "why do you look so puzzled?"

Because he was sure Tony was part of this picture but had no idea where he fit in.

2

"No-no," Tachus Diab said, waving his hands. "This changes nothing."

He had left a message for Nasser that it might not be a good idea to meet at the Al-Kifah Center—not after what had happened last night. So they now sat in the rear of an Afghan kabob shop that hadn't opened yet for the day. The help were in the back prepping for lunch.

"I'm not so sure of that," Nasser said.

In truth he was sure, but thought it best to play dubious.

Tachus tugged his beard as he leaned forward. "Everything is set. All the buyers will be gathering Saturday night. We will return your investment and your profit on Sunday morning."

"But Sayyid is in the hospital, Mahmoud has been arrested—"

"I warned them against this. I knew it would come to no good. But they were not part of the planning."

Nasser had known that. He'd had private conversations with Tachus and found him competent and committed. But he maintained a dubious look.

"I should hope not."

Tachus tapped his chest, "That is my doing—all mine. I have arranged for everything at this end. Those reckless fools know none of the details. All we need is a safe delivery and all will be well."

Delivery was out of Nasser's hands. Roman Trejador had arranged all that.

They both had been disappointed by the news out of Israel this morning. A minor uproar over Kahane's slaying, a few Palestinians beaten by the rabbi's followers over there, but that was about it. No mass murders, no bombings, no riots. No chaos.

Ah, well. El Sayyid Nosair had been a gamble, with little downside. Trejador was right: Take the long view. Seed money into the jihadists to fund training and recruitment. A Saudi named bin Laden was feeding funds to the radicals, but nothing like the windfall that Nasser was about to provide. Best of all, none of it was traceable.

Let them recruit and train, let them become emboldened by the West's inaction. More suicide bombings in Tel Aviv, more US embassies blown up, Mubarak assassinated and replaced with a Khomeini clone, it was all to the good. As long as chaos raged and spread.

Nasser pointed to the duffel bag of cash that lay between their feet beneath the table. A *heavy* bag—a banded stack of one hundred hundred-dollar bills did not weigh much, but three hundred of them added up to considerable weight.

"Time and place of delivery are written down for you in there. If all goes according to schedule, you will have the transaction completed in time to be in mosque for Friday morning prayers."

Tachus bowed his head. "May Allah make it so."

Nasser suppressed a smile. Allah? Hardly. The Order would make it so.

3

The November sun floated high in a clear sky. He didn't have to be on the road again until around six tonight. With time to kill, he wandered down Broadway from Abe's toward the Deuce to see what Grindhouse Row had to offer and maybe catch a flick.

But at Columbus Circle he found himself veering left onto 59th Street. He felt strangely drawn to the Marriott. As if seeing it in the daytime might shed some light on why Tony had been there last night. So he turned onto Lexington and continued downtown toward the hotel.

Though dressed casually, his Windbreaker and jeans were a cut above what he'd been wearing last night. No one gave him a second look as he strolled through the entrance. Once in the lobby, he hesitated. Stairs or elevator? He chose the latter. Taking the stairs might make him look too familiar with the layout. If anyone was watching—and he had little doubt that someone was—he wanted to look like a first timer here.

He stepped off onto the second floor and deliberately turned the wrong way. After a little wandering he reversed direction and ambled back toward the Morgan D room. A yellow X of crime-scene tape crossed the closed doors. As Jack approached, a man in a wrinkled suit opened one of the doors and ducked under the tape. Looked like the detective in *Plan 9 from Outer Space*. All he needed was to be scratching his jaw with the muzzle of his revolver to complete the picture.

"You got business here, kid?" he said, giving Jack a quick up-and-down.

"Well, um, is this where that guy got shot?"

"You didn't answer my question: You got business here?"

"Well, um, no, I just—"

"You know the victim? Any connection? Know anything?"

"No, just, um, curious."

His face twisted. "One of the ghouls, huh? What's the matter with you creeps?"

"Nothing, I—"

"Move it along. This is an active crime scene." He made a shooing motion. "Go on. Git."

Jack wasn't about to argue. He got.

Ghouls? he thought. The cop must have thought he was a crime-scene groupie.

He was crossing the lobby when a voice said, "I knew it was you!"

He turned and saw Cristin Ott hurrying toward him. She wore designer jeans and a short leather jacket, and had her arms open wide.

"Jack! What a surprise!"

She enveloped him in a hug and he returned the squeeze. She smelled good. He was glad he'd showered this morning.

"Cristin!" he said as they broke, and found he didn't have to force the smile. "Of all people!"

"I'm so glad to see you. I just knew I saw you here last night. I called to you but I guess you didn't hear me."

How to play this?

"I thought I heard my name but didn't see how anybody here could know me."

"Are you staying here?"

"No."

"Really? I assumed you were. That's why I came back—to see if you had a room. I was just heading for the front desk when you popped out of the elevator." She frowned. "So if you're not registered . . . ?"

"I was on my way to meet someone here last night but then that shooting happened."

Her eyes widened. "Ohmygod! Do you believe it? I didn't know a thing about it until it was all over. From what I've heard it was like the Wild West around here last night. Hey, what are you doing right now?"

The truth popped out. "Nothing."

She beamed. "That makes two of us. Had lunch yet?"

"No."

"Great. Let's do lunch, as they say. I know this cool little . . ."

4

"Hope you don't mind," Cristin said as they settled into a rear booth of a tiny place called Salad Sentral. "I've got a thing for rabbit food."

Jack much preferred his rabbit food garnishing a burger, but said, "I eat anything."

Which was mostly true. He'd even tried tripe once, but he'd have to be pretty damn hungry to eat it again.

Now that she was seated and settled, Jack took a look at her. Cristin looked good. Like most Jersey girls in the eighties, she'd gone through the big-hair phase in high school. Now her dark brown hair lay close to her head, framing her face. Lots less makeup than he remembered, but what she wore seemed just right. Bright blue eyes and an infectious smile completed the picture. Not a beauty by the usual standards but she seemed to have learned to make the most of her assets.

She folded her hands on the table and leaned forward. "Figured out what you want to be when you grow up?"

He laughed. "Not a clue. How about you?"

"I've decided that growing up is overrated. How's school?"

"I sort of dropped out."

She brightened. "Me too! Last semester I only took three credits and I'm doing the same this year."

"FIT, wasn't it?"

"Yes! How did you know?"

"I pay attention."

She seemed delighted that he'd remembered.

"All that fashion stuff becomes a bit much after a while. I want that degree but I'm in no hurry. How about you?"

"I'm out. Quit."

"Then you didn't 'sort of' drop out. You went all the way."

"Yeah, I guess I did."

Her smile faded. "You're the last person I'd expect to drop out. What's up, Jack?"

"What do you mean?"

"You always struck me as a finish-what-you-start kind of guy. What happened?"

He didn't want to get into all that.

"No one thing in particular. Just got tired of everything and decided to reboot."

The waitress came by but neither of them had looked at the menu so they ordered drinks—a Heinie for Jack, diet cola for Cristin—and asked for a few more minutes.

"Sorry about your mother," she said, looking at him over her menu. "I heard about it from my folks. What a horrible, horrible accident."

Jack wanted to talk about something else but he couldn't let that slide.

"Not an accident—murder."

She stared at him. "What?"

"A guy stood on an overpass and dropped a cinder block, timing it to strike an oncoming car. I'm not saying she was targeted, but I *am* saying she was murdered. The lawyer types may fine-shade it differently, but that's what it was."

"Don't tell me you were in the car."

He could only nod.

The minutes after the block came through the windshield, branded onto his memory, began to replay in his head. He shut them off.

Cristin leaned back, eyes wide. "You look very scary right now, Jack."

He forced a tenuous calm. "Let's talk about you. A three-credit semester leaves you plenty of free time. What do you do with it?"

She stared at him a moment longer, then relaxed. "Would you believe I'm a party planner?"

"A what?"

She grinned. "A party planner. I just fell into it and I love it."

"You get paid to throw parties for people."

"Yes! Paid very well, I'll have you know. Isn't it crazy? Of course, if it's a corporate client, then I become an *event* planner, but it's all the same. I didn't even know the job existed until last year."

"So your clients are rich folks too lazy to do it themselves."

"Sometimes. Others are corporations who want an event to announce a new product or welcome a new officer, or Washington or state politicos who want a banquet to honor someone, or whatever. Others are well-heeled people from out of town who need to throw a party—engagement parties and destination weddings are the most common reason. They don't know a thing about the city so they call my boss and she puts me or someone else on the case. I find them a space, set up the caterer, the flowers, the entertainment, all the bells and whistles while they go about their business."

"Was that why you were at the Marriott last night?"

She nodded. "This out-of-town couple from Michigan needs to host a rehearsal dinner before their son's wedding. They don't know where to begin. I know *exactly* where to begin. So I met with them and we planned most of it. I'll be escorting them around to a couple of venues later."

Jack oscillated his eyebrows. "'Venues.' Woo-woo."

"Tons of interesting party spaces for rent around the city. You've just got to know where to look. And I've got lists of them all."

"Is this a career?"

"No way. But I'm making great money, meeting interesting people—"

"For example?"

"Oh, politicians, CEOs. You know—movers and shakers. They might come in handy later on. In this world, it's *who* you know, not what you know."

The waitress returned with their drinks and they ordered—a Waldorf salad for Cristin, and . . .

"Do you have a meat salad?" Jack asked.

The waitress paused a second, then laughed. "I've been at this a long time and that's the first time I've ever been asked for a 'meat salad.' But yeah, we've got ham salad and chef salad."

"No roast beef salad?"

"Afraid not."

"Let me try the chef's salad then."

Cristin was grinning at him. "'Roast beef salad'?"

"Well, you never know till you ask."

He wanted to avoid the subject of how he was making ends meet, so he asked the question that was eventually going to rear its head.

"Ever hear from Karina?"

She hesitated, as if gathering her thoughts, then, "Rarely. Berkeley has done something to her head. She's sort of gone off the deep end. Remember how she was always a vegetarian?"

"Sure."

In high school, everyone at their caf table used to tease her about not eating meat—she used to say, *If it had a face or a mother, I don't want it on my plate.* And she stuck to her guns. That was one of the things Jack had found attractive about her. She walked her own road.

"Well, now she's a total vegan—won't eat anything that's even been in contact with anything that moves on its own. I mean, she won't even eat cheese, Jack. And she's like totally into this whole radical feminism thing."

"Well, she always leaned that way. That's why she chose Berkeley in the first place."

"Would you believe she sent me a card for Emma Goldman's birthday?"

Jack had to laugh. "Oh, no."

"At least you know who she is. I had to look her up. She was some kind of anarchist! I could see the signs of something going on when she came home after freshman year, but—"

Jack held up his hands. "Whoa! After freshman year? But she stayed out west."

Cristin lowered her head. "Crap."

"What?"

"You weren't ever supposed to know."

"You mean she came home but didn't tell me? But those times when I called her house and her parents told me . . ."

Cristin shook her head sadly. "They said what Karina told them to say. Truth was, she was involved with someone else at the time. She didn't want you to know and didn't want to face you."

Jack leaned back. This was a couple of years gone—the summer of '88. Seemed like a lifetime ago. Yet it still hurt.

Karina Haddon had been his first love. They'd both lost their virginity to each other over the summer between sophomore and junior year and spent the rest of high school joined at the hip. A tearful good-bye in August of '87, with Jack unable to understand why she had to go to a college all the way out in California, and Karina unable to imagine going anywhere else but Berkeley. A flurry of letters and phone calls during the first semester, a passionate reunion at Christmas break, followed by a slowing of communications during the spring, but a promise of catching up during the summer. Then the first bombshell: She wouldn't be coming home for the summer. She'd offered a plausible explanation: a once-in-a-lifetime opportunity for an extended field trip through the southwest with a famous professor to study Indian cultures and volunteer at the reservations.

"So the whole field-trip story was a lie."

Cristin nodded. She looked embarrassed. "That was to keep you from flying out to Berkeley to see her."

"It worked. Because that's exactly what I would have done." He shook his head. "Sheesh. I believed every word."

"Come on, Jack," she said, her expression dubious. "You must have had some inkling."

"Well, it made her priorities clear, but I never thought she'd found somebody else."

"You mean you didn't hook up with anyone at Rutgers during that first year? You had to miss it."

"Miss what?"

"Sex."

Cristin apparently didn't believe in mincing words.

"Well, yeah, of course. And I had opportunities, but . . ."

She reached across the table and put a hand over his. "Faithful Jack. I knew it."

Her touch felt good. And then he realized something.

"Hey, wait a minute. If she was involved with someone else out there, why was she back here?"

"Jack, it was years ago. The details blur . . . it was just for a week or so. I *can* tell you she said over and over how she was going to drive down to Johnson, show up at your door, and tell you face-to-face. But she kept putting it off and before we knew it, she was flying back west."

"The 'Dear Jack' letter arrived in September."

The second bombshell, a bigger blow than the field trip. And yet not a terrible surprise. After no word from her all summer, he'd suspected something was wrong. But seeing it in black and white . . . she hit all the it's-me-not-you clichés, though they seemed sincere. He'd filled up when she'd told him he was her first love and might very well end up being the best love of her life.

"Do you see her at all?"

She gave her head a quick shake. "She was back in Tabernacle last Christmas. She called but we never got together. We swap letters once in a while, and she'll send a card now and then. Sent me a copy of something called *The Female Eunuch* for my birthday."

"Wow. Happy birthday to you. Did you read it?"

"No way. The title turned me off." She shook her head. "She's a different person from the Karina we grew up with."

"That was the gist of her 'Dear Jack.' She said she'd become a different person over the year and we both had to move on." He shrugged. "And it looks like we have."

She seemed to be studying him. "And you're all right with that?"

He hadn't been. Took him a long time to adjust.

"I wasn't given much choice in the matter. She was an important person in my life. It hurt like hell—would have hurt even more if I'd known she'd been hooked up with someone else—but I wasn't about to start stalking her."

Their salads arrived. Cristin attacked hers. Jack poked at his strips of ham, Swiss, and turkey, wishing it were a bacon cheeseburger. He started on the sliced boiled egg. After a few bites, Cristin looked up.

"So, you're over her?"

He nodded. "It's been two years. Time helps. How about you? Anybody serious?"

She shook her head. "I'm not looking for a relationship. I'm not ready for one. Maybe when I grow up, but not now." She frowned. "I might not ever grow up."

"I'm not sure how to respond to that."

She laughed. "I've kind of got my own thing going here and I don't want some guy horning in."

He remembered Cristin had been pretty popular in high school. A reputation for being easy might have contributed to that.

Hot-to-trot Ott.

"In other words, no strings."

She beamed. "Exactly."

"Interesting."

"Why?"

"Because I'm sort of in that position myself."

Her eyebrows lifted. "Oh? Don't want a woman in your life?"

"It's not gender specific."

Now a puzzled look. "I don't get it."

He knew it was going to sound weird, but he had to bring this up.

"I cut a bunch of strings earlier this year. I don't want them reattached."

"Still not following you."

"I don't want to get into the details, but I'd appreciate it if you'd keep it to yourself that you saw me."

She leaned forward, eyes bright. "You're on the lam?"

He smiled. "Did you really just say 'on the lam'?"

"Yes! You committed some terrible crime and you're hiding out, right?"

"No, I—"

"You're running from the mob, then. You're in witness protection and—"

He laughed. "Cristin, I'm not on the run from anyone. I swear."

Except maybe the old me.

"Then why don't you want me to mention I saw you?"

"It's complicated. I'm not even sure I know myself . . . not entirely. But please . . . it's a privacy thing."

"Privacy . . ." She nodded. "I can buy into that—one hundred percent. And easy to do. I mean, who would I mention it to anyway? I don't know your family, and don't think my folks ever met you. Though I most likely would have mentioned it to Karina next time I wrote her."

"Please don't do that."

"I won't. Promise. But why? I mean, is it Karina? You're not like getting into some kind of monk thing, swearing off sex and all that."

"No. Told you: I'm way over her."

"It's what happened to your mother then." Her hand flew to her mouth. "Ohmygod. I'm sorry. I should just shut up and eat."

"Hey, don't worry about it. Unlike the Karina thing, I have *not* gotten over that—it's way early yet—but I'm not huddling in some room in a ball of grief. Like I said, it's complicated. Can we just leave it at that?"

"Sure." Another smile. "For now."

"What's that mean?"

"It means I'm going to find out."

"It's no big secret, Cristin. I simply want people from my past to stay in the past."

She looked down and concentrated on her salad. "Oh."

"What?"

"I guess that means me."

He then realized what he'd said. "Aw, jeez. I didn't mean—"

"Of course you did. Sorry for intruding."

"No, listen." He reached across and grabbed her hand.

She pulled it free. "No, it's okay."

"It's not okay. Let me back up a bit. Confession time: I did see you last night and I ducked into the elevator to avoid you."

"Thanks a lot." She kept her head down.

"Don't take it personally. It wasn't because of who you are, it was because of where you're from. I didn't want anyone from home going back and saying they saw me. But you know what? I'm glad I came back and ran into you. I'm glad we're sitting here together. Because you're safe."

Finally she looked up. "Safe?"

"We don't have a history, you and I. We have a mutual friend and that's about it."

"So?"

He wanted to tell her, *So you met the old Jack but didn't really know him. So you can't make comparisons to the new Jack . . . the new Jack taking shape here . . . whoever he might be.*

But he said, "So whatever we know about each other is only secondhand."

"True, I guess." A small smile. "But I bet I've got lots more secondhand dirt than you."

"Yeah?"

She shrugged. "Girls talk."

Of course they do. True as that was, it hadn't occurred to him. He wondered how detailed Karina had been about him . . . them.

"But whatever you know or think you know is old news. In a way we're starting fresh. We can go on from here as if we just met."

She smiled. "You mean make it like a game?"

Not for me.

"You're into games?"

The smile broadened as she nodded. "Love them." She extended her right hand across the table. "Pleased to meet you, Jack. I don't believe I caught your last name."

He shook her hand. "Moore. Jack Moore."

She frowned. "Hey, that's not—"

"It is now."

"Should I change my name too?"

"No. I *am* known as Jack Moore now. Really."

She cocked her head. "You sure you're not on the run?"

"Scout's honor."

"Then what—?"

"It's really not that interesting, I swear."

She narrowed her eyes. "A man of mystery. I like that. But not for long. Told you, I'll find out."

"You're going to be disappointed."

"We'll see about that."

She flagged down the waitress and borrowed a pen. She scribbled on a paper napkin and slid it across.

"My number. What's yours, Mister Moore?"

Jack hesitated. This was kind of embarrassing. "I don't have a phone at the moment."

"What? Oh, I see. You don't want to give it to me."

"No-no-no. I really don't have a phone."

"As the saying goes, my birth certificate has a date, but it's not yesterday. Everybody has a phone."

"Jack Moore has no credit history, no bank account, no Social Security number. If you know of a phone company that'll take him on, let me know."

"So there's no way to get in touch with you?"

He told her about the phone in the hall outside his room and gave her that number.

She shook her head. "I don't think I'd want to live like that."

"Obviously it's not for everybody, but I'm okay with it."

He signaled to the waitress to bring the check. When it arrived, Cristin reached for it but Jack got there first.

"My treat," she said.

Jack cupped a hand behind an ear. "I missed that. What did you say?"

"Lunch was my idea, so—"

"Your lips are moving but I can't seem to hear a word you're saying."

He pulled a C-note from the roll in his pocket and laid it on the table with the check.

"I thought you might not have a phone because you couldn't afford it," she said, eyeing the bill, "but I guess not." Her gaze lifted. "You never did say how you were making ends meet."

The dreaded question he'd hoped to avoid.

"Making deliveries."

The waitress picked up the money.

"Must pay well."

"The tips are good."

She leaned closer and lowered her voice. "We're not talking drugs, are we?"

"Not unless you consider nicotine a drug."

"I do, but at least it's legal." Nodding toward a guy puffing away and creating a cloud around a nearby table, she grimaced and waved a hand in front of her face. "Though I wish it weren't."

Jack had never got smoking either. He'd tried it but hadn't liked the feeling.

He said, "It's not a job I want to do forever, but it pays the bills for now. I'm living below my means and socking the rest away for when *I* grow up."

She laughed. "I hear you. I don't want to be planning parties the rest of my life, but I make a good living doing something that most of the time doesn't seem like work."

The waitress brought back the change and Jack left her a tip in the twenty-five-percent range.

"Generous," Cristin said. "I like a good tipper."

Well, he was feeling flush at the moment and took advantage of the opportunity to share a little.

He shrugged. "When the bill is that small, the difference between a decent tip and a great tip can be as little as a buck. I like to round up to great."

Who knew? Tipping might turn out to be the only thing he'd be great at.

"Well, thanks for lunch," she said as they rose from their seats.

"This was fun."

No lie. Cristin had a light, easy way about her and he enjoyed being with her.

"Where do you want to eat dinner?"

"Dinner?"

"Well, yeah." She stretched "yeah" to two syllables. "New acquaintances that we are, how else are we going to get to know each other if we don't spend some time together?"

Spend some time together . . . was that wise? She seemed good company, but she was from home, from the past. She'd said she didn't want a relationship, and neither did he, especially not with someone from the other side of the line he'd drawn across his life.

Wait, what was he thinking? He had to hit the road around six.

"No can do. I'm working tonight."

She didn't hesitate. "Tomorrow night then."

Just dinner. And at a real restaurant. Be nice to have a real sit-down meal with someone. He'd eaten once at The Spot—something Julio had microwaved to death—and would not make that mistake again. Nibbling snacks and such hunched over the rear counter in Abe's store wasn't a meal either.

"Tomorrow night I can do. But we'll have to eat on the late side. I'm working all Wednesday and I'm never sure when I'll get off."

She shook her head. "Tomorrow night's no good for me. Got to see a client."

"But you just said—"

She started walking toward the door. "I know. But I wanted to see how many times you'd back out."

"I really am working tonight."

"And I'm really working tomorrow night."

When they reached the bright sunshine and cold November air of the sidewalk, she turned to face him.

"I know what's going on in your head, Jack . . . Moore. You think if we hang out too much I'm going to fall in love with you and get all clingy and possessive and start to horn in on your life."

He'd never organized the feeling into a coherent thought, but now that she'd laid it on the table . . . yeah, that pretty much nailed it. Of course, he couldn't admit it.

"Come on, Cristin—"

"Can I just tell you something, Jack? No offense, but you're no Pierce Brosnan. You're on the skinny side and not at all my type. I want a relationship less than you do. What I do want is to get to know you, learn all your secrets—"

"What secrets?"

Her mouth twisted, "Like how Karina was in bed—"

"Oh, jeez."

"—and what kind of deliveries you make and why you're hiding out here in the city under a phony name. Stuff like that. And when I've sucked you dry of everything interesting, I'm going to dump you like a week-old newspaper and move on to someone else." She put her hands on her hips and gave him a fierce look. "There. Feel better now?"

Well, truth be told . . . yeah. Lots.

He put on a hurt look. "You really think I'm skinny?"

The tight line of her lips wavered, and then she cracked up—throwing her head back and laughing. Jack laughed too. A hug seemed in order at that moment so they clinched briefly.

As Cristin stepped back, Jack said, "Who *is* your type?"

"I'll never tell."

"How about Friday night?"

She shook her head. "Friday and Saturday are N-G. But Thursday—"

"Another work night. You seem to work a lot of nights too."

She shrugged. "It's not a nine-to-five job. That's one of the things I like about it. I can go a couple of days without a call, and then I might run my cute little butt off for a week straight."

She did indeed have a cute little butt.

"But weekends too?"

"The holidays are coming, in case you've forgotten. I see corporate clients Monday to Friday during work hours. The private clients often are free only at night. As for the out-of-towners, a lot of them can only get into the city on weekends. But they're almost always gone by Sunday night, so that tends to be a reliably free night for me."

"And this one's open for me too. Let's do it. I'll leave the *venue* to you, since you're the planner."

"You did say you eat anything."

"My genus and species is *Eatibus anythingus*."

Except for the food at The Spot.

She smiled. "I'll find us an interesting place. But we need to establish an important ground rule: We go Dutch or we don't go."

She definitely seemed serious about no relationship.

"Fair enough. I'll be on the road most of Sunday, so—"

A sly smile. "On the road where?"

"I'll ignore that and call you Saturday afternoon."

"You'd better."

She waved as she turned and began walking east. Jack waved back and headed west, wondering how all this would turn out. Because he was already looking forward to Sunday.

WEDNESDAY

1

Tony was late.

Jack had pulled into the Lonely Pine's parking lot as usual and waited off to the side, idling. This was the first time he'd arrived without Tony waiting.

Okay, no problem.

But after half an hour and still no Tony, he pulled the truck into a parking space and shut off the engine. He eyed the mobile phone on the seat next to him. Time to call Bertel? He didn't want to get Tony in hot water with the boss, but maybe something had happened in New York. Jack didn't know how Tony had been involved in the Kahane shooting—maybe on the shooter's side, maybe on Kahane's side as protection, or maybe something else—but he had little doubt he'd been involved. And maybe he'd got himself caught. Maybe he was sitting in a cell in the Tombs as an accomplice.

The only thing Jack knew for sure at the moment was that Tony wasn't here.

He decided to call and was pulling Bertel's number from his wallet when someone tapped on the passenger-side window. Jack jumped and tensed, then he recognized the face. He'd shaved his beard, but no question who it was.

Tony.

"Don't sneak up on me like that," he said, leaning across and unlatching the door.

The courtesy light didn't come on when the door swung open. Jack had taped down the button in the door frame.

"The shit has hit the fan," Tony said without preamble as he slid into the passenger seat. His voice sounded shaky. "Big-time."

Swell. Just what Jack needed to hear.

"What's that mean?"

"We were raided."

" 'We'?"

"Our little warehouse. NC state cops and ATF goons showed up and sealed the place."

Jack fought a sinking feeling.

"How'd you get away?"

Tony lit a cigarette. His lighter's flame wavered.

"By not being there. I was just about to make my turn into the driveway when I saw the flashers. I kept on driving, parked down the road, and came back on foot for a look-see."

"They didn't get Bertel, did they?"

Tony exhaled a cloud. "Naw. He hardly ever comes down from New York. Twice a month, maybe, and this wasn't one of those times."

"He lose a lot?"

Tony nodded. "We unloaded a shipment of Winstons just this afternoon, but that's not going to burn him up as much as somebody ratting him out."

Jack rolled down his window—as much to let out the smoke as to allow a better look at the Lonely Pine's parking lot. All quiet.

"Who'd do that?"

"Good question. It's a small operation and Bertel keeps it broken into compartments."

"Are we in trouble?"

"You and me? I don't think so. But Billy is."

"Who's he?"

"One of the warehouse guys who helps me load the trucks. I saw him sitting in the back of one of the cop cars."

Jack gave the lot another quick scan. "Shouldn't we be on the move?"

Tony shook his head. "Billy knows me but doesn't know you or the other drivers. And he doesn't know where I meet up with you guys. All he knows is I show up out of the night with a truck that we load up, and then I disappear back into the night. He can't even tell them what kind of truck I'll arrive in because Bertel rents different kinds in random order. He doesn't know my last name, I don't know his. He doesn't know Bertel's name at all—just knows him as 'the boss'—and doesn't know where he's from. And you . . . you don't know Billy and don't have a clue where the warehouse is."

"All compartmentalized," Jack said, nodding with appreciation. He'd suspected as much, and expected nothing less from Bertel. "Smart."

"But none of that protects against one jerk with a big mouth." He shook his head. "Billy, I bet."

"But he got caught."

"Billy likes his beer. Five'll get you twenty he had a few—more than a few—and mouthed off in front of the wrong person, who then went and dropped a dime."

"Really?" Jack found that hard to believe. "You hear a guy in a bar blabbing about running cigarettes and you say to yourself, 'I think I'll go give ATF a call.' People really do that? I can see if he's bagging heroin for kids, but cigarettes?"

"Never know where you're going to run into a busybody. But more likely someone traded Billy for a future favor. Whatever, Billy got himself tailed and blew a sweet operation." He shook his head. "Shit."

"What now?"

"You go back empty. But don't count on getting paid for the trip."

"Hey, it's not my fault."

"If Bertel doesn't get his dough, you don't get yours."

Jack banged his fist on the steering wheel—once. Ah, well, he should have known it was too sweet a gig to last.

"Bertel know?"

Tony nodded. "Course. Called him, and is he *pissed.* This could screw his whole deal with the Mummy. If he can't guarantee a steady supply of butts, the greasy bastard will get 'em from someone else. So the boss has got some scrambling to do. Take him a while to get a new operation set up and running, though."

Jack sighed and leaned back. He should head north now. Since the truck was empty, he didn't have to worry about getting stopped. He could take the interstate all the way and make good time. But he'd been on the road all night. A short nap would hit the spot.

"Do we have the usual room?"

Tony shook his head. "Never got around to renting it. You don't want to stay here anyway."

"I thought you said this Billy guy doesn't know about it."

"He doesn't. But Elizabeth City isn't exactly Raleigh. The ATFers are probably at the warehouse waiting for me to show up with the truck. When I don't, they'll go looking. So I'm not staying here and neither are you."

Jack bristled at that. "I'll decide—"

Tony jabbed a finger at him. "You know what I look like. They nab you, they'll sweat you, and before I know it, there's a drawing of my puss circulating all over the mid-Atlantic states."

"I wouldn't—"

"Maybe you wouldn't, maybe you would. I don't know you, Jack. I get to see you for maybe twenty minutes every few days. You seem like a standup guy, but I can't risk it. Neither can the boss. And I've gotta look out for him too. So we put some distance between this town and this truck and we bunk you somewhere else."

Much as he resented taking orders from Tony, the logic was unassailable: Staying here was plain stupid.

He reached for the ignition. "Where do you suggest?"

"Well, we can get lost in Newport Beach. I'll think on it while you drive me to my car."

"Your car?"

"Yeah. It's a few blocks away. You didn't think I was just going to tool in here and park, did you?"

Duh, Jack thought, and drove him three blocks to a black BMW 530i.

"Nice ride."

"Nothing else to spend it on," he said as he hopped out.

He opened the Bimmer's door and Jack heard a ringing within. A bag phone sat on the passenger seat. Tony lifted the receiver and slammed the door as he took the call. After what looked like an animated phone call, he hung up and rolled down the driver window.

"Bertel again. Like it's my fault this happened." He shook his head. "I'll deal with it in the morning. Meanwhile, you need to crash somewhere." He drummed his fingers on the steering wheel. "Hey, I know a place on the Outer Banks that's—"

"Outer Banks?" Jack knew where it was on the map, knew the Wright Brothers had lifted off on their first flight there, but mostly he knew it from news footage of its population evacuating during hurricane threats. "How far is that?"

"A quick jump. We're in the off season now, so it's empty. No one'll bother us. You can sleep as long as you want, then take off."

2

Tony's quick jump took more than an hour. But he was right about the lack of people. Granted, the hour was early, but once they hit the barrier island—or was it a peninsula?—the roads were empty.

Jack followed Tony's speeding Bimmer north through some town with the unlikely name of Duck and farther along to where the houses thinned out to the point where each sat alone on the high dune that ran along his right. On his left a nameless bay reflected a half moon in the predawn sky. When the land had narrowed to the point where little more than a thousand feet of sandy soil separated the bay from the Atlantic, Tony made a sudden right into a driveway. A huge house loomed on the dune ahead. Jack saw a car and a truck like his in the driveway. A light glowed in an upper window. He'd expected an empty house.

Tony pulled to a stop near a detached garage and walked back to the truck.

"Looks like we've got company."

"Should we move on?"

"I'll see. I recognize the truck. These guys have a game like ours."

"Game?"

"You know . . . moving merch. They may be staging here. If our being here is gonna queer their action, we'll move on and find some other place. If they're cool, we'll stay. You'll get some shut-eye and we'll grab breakfast and be gone our separate ways before noon."

That sounded good to Jack. As Tony headed inside, Jack shoved the keys under the driver seat and slid out of the cab. He walked around the truck to stretch his cramped legs. The sky behind the house was doing that rosy-fingered thing. He could smell the ocean on the breeze flowing over the dune. Chilly out. Weren't the Carolinas supposed to be warm?

He heard a door slam and saw Tony moving his way, motioning him forward.

"It's all good. We can stay. Their shipment's not due in yet, so they'll be hanging out till after dark when the boat arrives."

Jack felt his neck muscles tighten. "Shipment of what?"

He smiled. "My first question too. I don't want to get caught with bales of MJ either. But these guys move hooch."

"Booze?"

"Moonshine. But it's colored and flavored and sold in Jack Daniel's bottles." He winked. "Most folks can't tell the difference, especially those that mix it with Coke." He made a face. "Can you imagine—pouring real Jack into Diet Coke? Makes a grown man want to cry. Anyway, the markup is *huge*. Lots more than Bertel's cigs."

"But you can't sell hooch to Arabs."

"Not *to* them, but I'll bet you could get them to act as middlemen. I'm sure they'd grab a fee for handling just about anything."

Jack followed Tony around the side and up an outside stairway to a porch that wrapped around the beach side of the place. He stopped and stared a moment at the bright orange crescent just breaking the surface of the Atlantic.

"Be nice to have a house like this and watch that happen every morning."

Tony snorted. "People around here don't buy these houses to live in. They buy them to rent out. And the true locals never go near the beach."

He led Jack inside through a huge kitchen. He stopped at the fridge and pulled out two Coronas, used the magnetized church key stuck to the door to pop the tops, and handed one to Jack.

Jack looked at it and said, "What? No lime?"

Tony laughed and clinked his bottle against Jack's. "Up yours."

A beer at dawn. Why not? Not as if it was too early in the day—it was way late.

They moved on and came upon two men lounging in the family room. Both had Coronas in hand; a porn movie was running on the wide-screen, rear-projection TV.

Jack put on a gawky expression. "Man, I was like totally into you guys when I was a kid."

Tony pointed to a skinny guy with long mullet hair. "Reggie."

Reggie lifted his beer.

Jack wondered why anyone would name a kid Reginald—unless it happened to be the name of a rich uncle or something.

"And that's Moose."

Moose didn't look up. His build fit the name. His sleeveless denim jacket revealed pale, muscular, tattoo-bedizened arms; his scalp was bare to the middle; long blond hair flowed straight back from there.

"No kidding? Moose and Reggie? Where are Betty and Veronica?"

Reggie pointed to the screen. "You missed them. They were just getting it on together."

"This is Lonnie," Tony said.

Jack raised his beer. "But you can call me Archie."

Reggie laughed, Moose still made like he wasn't there.

"Which bedrooms are free?" Tony said.

"Either of the streetside ones upstairs."

"How about downstairs?" Jack said, figuring he could make a quicker exit from there if need be.

"Stay the fuck away from downstairs," Moose said, eyes still fixed on the screen.

It speaks, Jack thought.

"You got it," Tony said. "Any particular reason?"

"Reserved for product."

"Gotcha."

Jack found a room upstairs. The bed was stripped but the mattress looked relatively new. He pulled the drapes closed and emptied his pockets onto the night table. After polishing off the beer he lay back on the bed and closed his eyes.

He thought about Tony. Should he mention sighting him in New York or let it slide? How to bring it up? How far to push it? Mention that he followed him to the Kahane shooting? That could open multiple cans of worms.

As sleep claimed him he had a feeling his life was going to take another turn.

THURSDAY

1

"Lonnie! Hey, Lonnie! Get your lazy ass out of bed!"

The voice finally broke through and Jack realized he was "Lonnie" for the time being. He lifted his head and blinked at Tony standing in the doorway.

"What?"

"Let's go get some lunch."

Jack's mouth tasted like stale beer. And then his brain grasped the words—

"Lunch? What time is it?"

"After two."

"Aw, hell." He rolled to a sitting position and rubbed his face.

Tony shrugged. "'Aw, hell' what? You got someplace to be? Not as if you're gonna miss a delivery."

He had a point. And Jack was starving.

Tony turned away from the door. "Come on. I'll drive. I know a sandwich place up the road that's open all year."

"Long as they have coffee."

They took Tony's Bimmer. It had a nice smooth ride. Jack didn't say much as they cruised south on the only road, passing through Kitty Hawk to a town with the unlikely but cool name of Kill Devil Hills. He knew he wasn't exactly a loquacious sort, but he found morning small talk, before coffee, physically painful. Plus he was thinking about Tony dressed as a Hasid and when to raise the subject.

They found a diner—appropriately named the Kill Devil Grill—where Jack washed down a foot-long ham-and-provolone sub with a carafe of coffee. Tony poked at a clump of tuna salad on lettuce.

"Not hungry?"

"I used to have a metabolism like you. Could down a whole pizza and a six-pack without gaining an ounce. But once you hit that half-century mark you need to start watching the carbs."

Fifty? Tony didn't look it.

"You seem to keep yourself pretty trim."

"Yeah, but it used to come naturally. Now I have to work at it."

Jack liked Tony. He seemed centered. And best of all, he didn't call him "kid." He figured the drive back would be the best time to broach the sighting.

So, as they cruised back north toward the house . . .

"This'll tickle you," he said when they'd reached the halfway point. He fixed his gaze not on Tony's face but on his hands where they gripped the wheel. "I swear I saw you in New York the other day."

The hands tightened their grip.

"I wish. Nothing to do in these parts."

"Wait. It gets better."

"What?"

Jack forced a laugh. "You were dressed like a Hasidic Jew!"

The knuckles whitened slightly as Tony looked at him and grinned. "You gotta be kidding me!"

"No, I swear. Black hat, black coat, beard, the works. Even had . . ." What had Abe called them? ". . . payots."

"What's that?"

"The long hair by the ears."

His laugh sounded as forced as Jack's. "With all that, how the hell could you possibly think it was me?"

"Well, he had the same coloring, the same eyes, and, well, I never forget a face. Can't always come up with a name to go with it, but faces stick with me. And that face was yours."

Silence in the car as Tony sat rigid behind the wheel. Jack let it run.

Finally Tony said, "That wasn't me."

"That's what I kept telling myself. But I gotta tell you, if it wasn't you, it should've been."

"What's that supposed to mean?"

"Because he looked so much like you. You got an identical twin?"

"No."

Another silence. When Tony spoke again, his voice was low, almost menacing. "What was my Jewish doppelganger doing?"

Doppelganger . . . Jack had suspected him of being better educated than he let on, now he was sure.

"Getting into a cab." Jack had a feeling it might be wise to ease back some now. "I hollered at him but he just drove off."

Tony seemed to relax a smidgen. "And this was last night?"

"No, Monday. I'd got off the last run earlier and was coming from a couple of beers when I spotted you."

"*Not* me. Couldn't have been me. I was here. And if I was in NYC, believe me, I wouldn't be dressed like that."

"Yeah, I guess you wouldn't. And it was too late for a Halloween party, so it must have been someone else."

They both laughed and the tension eased some.

After a brief silence, Tony said, "Where are you going?"

Jack wondered at the question and decided to take it at face value.

"Back to New York—ay-sap."

"I meant in a more existential sense. You seem like a bright guy. You want to do this sort of thing the rest of your life?"

Existential sense? Yeah, this guy had more going for him than it seemed at first glance. But Jack didn't want to get into that, so he turned it back on him.

"How long have you been at it? And as for brains, you seem like you should be *running* an operation instead of working for one."

He shrugged. "I've done my share of running things. The details drag you down after a while. I've found I prefer to do my job, collect my check, and be able to walk away whenever I want. No strings."

No strings . . . there it was again. Cristin . . . now Tony. He kept running into people who didn't want strings.

"But I've got a lot more mileage on me," Tony added. "Experience informs my decisions. I've been there, done that, and know what I don't want to do again. You can't say the same. You ought to think about going back to college and—"

Jack stiffened in his seat. "Back to college? How do you know I ever started."

Had Tony been checking into him?

Tony laughed. "Easy, easy. I haven't been backgrounding you. It's obvious you've had some higher ed. Unless you're an autodidact. All I'm saying is that this is the time in your life when you ought to be getting drunk and laid and sleeping in class."

"Like you said: Been there, done that, don't want to do it again."

"What I'm telling you is there's a big picture out there."

"And I want no part of it."

"You're sure of that? Even if you could be part of it without strings?"

Jack looked at him. "What are you getting at?"

"Just roll with me here. If you could be a mover and a shaker with no strings, would you?"

Jack didn't have to waste even a nanosecond of thought on that. "Nope. Not interested."

He found Tony staring at him . . . for too long.

"Um . . ." Jack pointed through the windshield. "The road?"

Tony focused ahead again, saying, "If that's really true, you're a rare bird. That Tears for Fears song doesn't apply to you then?"

The reference surprised him. "You listen to rock?"

His mouth twisted. "John Lennon and I are contemporaries—or would be if some asshole hadn't wanted to impress Jodie Foster. My generation *invented* rock. And let me tell you, Tears for Fears isn't rock."

"Yeah, well, no argument there."

"But you didn't answer the question."

"Do I want to rule the world? Not even a little bit. In fact, I can't think of anything I want less. How about you?"

He laughed. "Oh, I definitely want to rule the world. And as soon as I figure out a way, I'll jump on it. You, on the other hand, are headed for trouble."

His tone was light but Jack sensed a serious train chugging beneath it.

"In what way?"

"It won't take Bertel long to get another operation up and running—rent a new warehouse, get a couple of guys to man it, contact his suppliers, and he's in business. I mean, he's already got his drivers and his routes. The money's good, so you'll keep driving for him. After a while you'll get bored and start taking shortcuts and cutting corners, and that'll lead to you getting caught. Then you're in the system and your options start shrinking. Then guys like Bertel will be the only ones you *can* work for, because they're the only ones who'll have you."

A grim scenario . . . but Jack considered Bertel a stepping-stone, not a career—a way to build a nest egg that would free him up for the next step. Trouble was, he had no idea what that next step might be.

"Speaking from experience?" Jack said. "Was that your life story you just told me?"

Tony shook his head. "I've never been caught. I choose my work carefully. With Bertel my only exposure's been when I help load the truck and drive it back to the Lonely Pine. Work a couple of hours every night, collect my generous check, and go home. The rest of the time I play an unemployed construction worker looking for work and having no luck in this bad economy."

"Bertel is further on in years. If he quits, would you take over?"

Tony shook his head. "Uh-uh. That would mean strings—guys like you depending on me. I don't want to depend on anyone, and I don't want anyone depending on me."

Jack understood perfectly, but didn't believe a word.

Because he *had* seen Tony dressed as a Hasid. And that meant he had strings attached.

Who was pulling them?

2

When they pulled up to the house they found Moose waiting outside by Jack's truck. He wore the same denim cutoff and torn black jeans. This was the first time Jack had seen his face straight on: his small eyes and lipless mouth seemed to have gravitated toward his large nose. A chrome chain swung between a belt loop and a back pocket. His skin looked fish-belly white in the sunlight.

"Tony, we need to talk," he said as they exited the Bimmer.

"Sure. What's up?"

"Not here."

"Okay. Let's go inside."

As they started to walk toward the first-floor door—the level reserved for "product"—Jack followed. Moose turned and pointed to him.

"Not you."

Tony gave him a placating smile. "It's okay. Be back in a minute."

Jack faced the sun, closed his eyes, and leaned back against the Bimmer to bask. Probably wouldn't have a chance again until spring.

After a few minutes he heard the screen door slam. Tony was walking his way, hands in pockets.

"They've got a problem."

"What's that?"

"They need two trucks for their haul and their other driver cracked up number two early this morning on his way home from a bar. They need a replacement."

Jack saw where this was going. "Mine?"

"Yours. And you. The cops ran a check on their driver after the crash and found a warrant on him, so he's in some local clink inland. The route's pretty much the same as yours except their drop is in Staten Island instead of Jersey City."

"Why didn't they ask me?"

Tony smiled. "Because for some reason they got the idea I'm your supervisor or something."

Yeah, Jack could see that: an older guy driving a Bimmer, a "kid" following in a truck. No brainer who's the boss.

"They're offering double whatever Bertel pays you."

"Two grand?"

Tony's smile broadened as he leaned closer. "No, three. I told them you get fifteen a run. I figure two for you and one for me. Fair?"

A few minutes ago Jack had said he couldn't think of anything he wanted to do less than rule the world. Now it had just been offered to him.

"More than fair. But I think I'll pass."

"Why? You're making the trip anyway."

"I don't want to work for Moose."

"Why not? He was our host. It would be the courteous thing to do."

"I'll leave him a nice tip."

"No, tell me: What've you got against him?"

Jack shrugged, not sure how to put the feelings into words. "Something in his eyes. Or maybe, something not in his eyes."

Tony stared at him. "You mean, like a soul?"

So . . . Tony felt it too.

"You could put it that way."

Tony continued to stare, then said, “You know, in the unlikely event I ever start up my own operation, you’re the first one I’m going to bring in.”

Jack took that as a compliment, but wasn’t so sure he’d accept. Tony seemed to be playing an open hand, but Jack sensed he was hiding cards—a lot of them.

“Yeah, well, right now all I want is Moose and Reggie watching the taillights of my empty truck heading down the driveway.”

Tony grinned. “I’ll tell them.”

As he returned to the house, Jack opened the truck and reached under the driver’s seat for the keys. The space felt empty. He pushed the seat all the way back and leaned inside for a look.

Not there.

His neck muscles tightened. Not good . . . not good at all.

He moved around to the passenger side and did the same. No keys there either. And Bertel’s car phone was missing too.

“Shit.”

He was almost to the house when Reggie appeared in the doorway.

“Hey, Archie.” He might have been smiling but his face was blurred in the shadows beyond the screen. “We need to talk.”

Jack wasn’t in the mood for talk, just wanted the answer to one question. “Where the hell are my keys and phone?”

“In here. Shouldn’t leave them outside. Might get stolen.”

Reggie backed up as Jack pulled the door open. As he stepped in he saw a blur of motion to his right and a fist rammed into his belly. As his gut exploded in agony, someone kicked him behind one of his knees, dropping him to the floor. Jack’s ham-and-cheese sub threatened to hurl but he kept it down.

As his vision cleared and he straightened, he saw Tony seated against the opposite wall, duct-taped to a chair, tape over his mouth. His eyes were angry and a trickle of blood leaked from a nostril down over the tape.

“You’re gonna drive,” Moose’s voice said from close behind Jack. “Give us any shit and we start using your old pal here for target practice.”

Jack didn’t know what to say. “He’s not my ‘pal,’ ” he blurted. “I barely know him.”

Tony rolled his eyes.

Okay. Poor word choice. Bad thing to say. Even though he’d said it only once, he felt like Judas.

“Yeah? Reggie, get your bow.”

Bow?

Jack twisted and looked at Moose. He held a black semiautomatic casually pointed in Jack's direction. Its slide had a dull finish and a composite look. A Glock?

"No, wait. That's not necessary."

Moose's lipless mouth widened into a shark grin. "Oh, but it is."

Jack watched Reggie exit through a door to the right and heard him pound up a set of stairs. He looked around for a way out. A pair of narrow windows, too small to crawl through, were set high in the outer wall; a door to his left—where it went he couldn't guess; then the door to the parking area. He noticed a double-key Yale dead bolt, an odd choice for a door with no glass within reach.

Reggie returned a few minutes later with a quiver of arrows and a massive fiberglass hunting bow that looked like it had been designed by Rube Goldberg, what with the cams and pulleys and sights and other attachments. Whatever happened to the simple English longbow?

"Reggie hunts with this baby," Moose said. "Killed a buck at eighty yards last week. Gave me a hind quarter. I *love* venison."

"Me too," Reggie said as he pulled out an arrow and notched it on the string. He maintained his happy-go-lucky demeanor as he spoke, which made his words all the more chilling. "But you know what I love more? Shooting this thing. It can release at over three hundred feet per second. At this range I should be able to put this right through Pops here."

"Not necessary," Jack said. "I'll drive."

Reggie pulled the arrow back to his ear and aimed at Tony. Jack's bladder clenched.

"I'll DRIVE!"

The bow gave a soft *thwang!* and the arrow buried itself in the wall an inch from Tony's left ear.

"Fuckin'-A right, you'll drive," Moose said. "Just so you get it straight in your head that we're not fucking around, I'm gonna lay it all out for you plain and simple. This is an important shipment for us. We ain't playing games, and we ain't taking no chances. It's a bigger load of product than we've ever handled and it's gotta arrive on time. And it's all gotta go at once. Can't leave none behind. To move it all we need two trucks, but shitty luck left us with only one. We can't wait till tomorrow for a replacement truck because the product has to go out tonight as soon as it comes in. So your truck is now *our* truck, and you are now driver number two. You got that clear in your head?"

Figuring it was best to play along, Jack nodded. "Got it."

"Good. Now get this: You will drive half our product to its drop-off point. You will lead the way. I will follow in our truck. You will not stop along the way. You gotta piss, you bring a bottle. If you stop, I call Reggie here and he starts target practice on the old guy. Got it?"

Jack was pretty sure Tony was bristling at the "old guy" remark, but old was relative, and he probably looked old to dumbasses like Moose and Reggie. Anyway, what they were calling him was the least of Tony's concerns right now.

"Got it."

"Good. And along the way you will not pull anything cute like speeding or running a light or anything that'll get you stopped. If a cop pulls you over for *any* reason, even if it's not your fault, I make that call. I'll be checking in with Reggie every half hour."

Reggie smiled. "And if I don't hear the right code word, I start playing make-believe. Like I'm Robin Hood and he's the sheriff of . . ." He looked at Moose. "Who was that sheriff anyway?"

"Who gives a fuck?" Moose looked at Jack. "We clear on all this?"

They had him pretty well boxed.

"Crystal."

"When the delivery is made and the product is off-loaded, I call Reggie and he lets Pops go."

Jack pushed himself to his feet. His gut still ached.

"What guarantee do I have?"

That shark grin again. "None. You'll just have to trust us."

Like hell, Jack thought.

If these two were half as cold-blooded as they seemed, they wouldn't be leaving a couple of guys with grudges in their wake.

How had he let himself get boxed into this? Oh, yeah. The lure of easy money. What about the next question: How to get himself out? And Tony too.

No easy answer for that one. He'd have to play it by ear and hope that an opportunity presented itself.

"What time does this 'product' arrive?"

"After dark," Moose said.

"What do we do till then?"

"'We' don't do nothin'." Reggie opened a door behind him. "You stay in here until we need you."

Moose shoved him from behind and Jack entered a cramped, windowless furnace room. The door slammed closed behind him, shutting off all light. He felt along the wall until he found a switch. A single bulb flared to life overhead.

Swell.

3

Shortly after nine-thirty, the door reopened. Jack had spent much of the six hours in the tiny room seated on the floor with his back against the cold furnace. Good thing the heat wasn't on or the little room would have been a toaster oven. He might have dozed once—he'd kept an eye on his watch and he seemed to experience a gap along the way.

He'd spent the first hour or so looking for a way out. With no windows, that left the door. He'd scrounged around and found a few slim scraps of metal that he tried to fashion into lock picks, but no go. He'd learned to pick locks as a kid but hadn't tried in years. But even at the peak of his skills, these bits of steel wouldn't get the job done.

Reggie stood outside the open door, holding what Jack was pretty sure was a Glock. Now that he was a gun owner, he'd taken an interest in them, picking up copies of *Gun Digest* and the tabloid *Shotgun News* and the like. Among the nice things about living in New York were the huge newspaper and magazine stands that sold damn near everything printed in the U.S. along with lots of foreign publications as well. And Reggie's pistol looked like a Glock. Jack wasn't well versed enough yet to identify the model but the muzzle looked about right for a 9mm.

"Product's arriving," Reggie said as he stepped back and waved Jack forward. "You gotta move upstairs."

Jack stepped out and found Tony still taped to the chair. Had he been there all this time? Their eyes met. Tony's held a mixture of angry accusation and humiliation. What was that all about?

Then Jack noticed a wet stain darkening his crotch. Poor guy had peed himself. Jeez. Couldn't very well ask for a bathroom break with his mouth taped shut.

"What are you doing with Tony?"

"We'll move him after we get you settled. You're only gonna be here a coupla hours. He's gonna be here all night."

Reggie pointed the Glock toward a stairwell and Jack led the way up to the second floor. He was prodded into a big, unlit bedroom with an ocean view.

"You bringing Tony up now?"

Reggie grinned. "Put the two of you together? You must take us for real dumbasses."

"Worth a try," Jack said.

Reggie sighed. "No, it ain't. Look. All y'gotta do is drive, just like you was gonna do anyway. Why you making such a fucking big deal out of it?"

Because it's not my choice, Jack thought.

But Reggie wouldn't get that.

"Why are you threatening to make a pincushion out of Tony?"

"Not my idea, but that's *your* fault. You'da taken the money and made that run, everything woulda been cool."

Was that behind Tony's accusing look? This was all Jack's fault?

Uh-uh. No one was going to lay Moose and Reggie's thuggery on Jack's doorstep. He'd never been a part of their operation. The failure of their second truck to show up put no obligation on Jack.

"Hey," Reggie added, his voice edging toward a whine. "You think I want to shoot him up? I don't. But I will. Because I gotta. Count on it. That's how important this shipment is." He gestured to the windows. "We don't have a good place up here to lock you up. You can get out real easy. But don't. Your buddy will pay the price. Guaranteed. Understood?"

Crap.

"Yeah, understood."

"Good. All y'gotta do is cool your heels a couple more hours without doing anything stupid, then we hit the road. By tomorrow morning you'll get your cash and this will all be a memory."

"You're still going to pay me?"

"Sure. Three grand, just like we said. We're stand-up guys."

Yeah, right. The money was the carrot, Tony was the stick. They figured they had Jack boxed. And maybe they did.

For now.

Reggie indicated the doorknob. "As you can see, this locks from the inside. I can't lock you in, so you're on the honor system. Be smart."

He closed the door, leaving Jack alone.

Honor system . . . right. Well, maybe the smart thing to do was play this their way—for Tony's sake. No guarantee that that would work out in his favor, but it was the only play he had right now.

He stepped to the windows and looked out at the moonlit sea. The dark blotch of a boat, either anchored or idling, floated beyond the surf. From the booms jutting this way and that, it looked like a good-size trawler. A smaller boat was motoring toward the beach through the small, low-tide rollers.

The precious "product" had arrived.

Both Moose and Reggie had stressed the importance of this shipment to their operation. Fake Jack Daniel's. Big deal. How important could that be? No more than cigarettes. Maybe it was the amount. Enough that they needed two trucks to move it. But enough to take up the whole first floor? Enough that they had to move him upstairs? They must be talking a *lot* of booze.

Someone hopped out of the skiff or whatever it was as it nosed into shallow water and pulled it the last couple of dozen feet toward the shore. As it nosed against the beach, Jack got a look at its cargo. His gorge rose as he realized what the "product" was.

"Aw, no! They've gotta be kidding! *No!*"

4

Jack watched with mounting dismay as the skiff beached for the third time and unloaded its cargo.

Girls . . . little girls.

Some chunky, most skinny, all young-young-young. He got a good look at them as they trudged over the dune and around the side of the house. The oldest he saw could be no more than fourteen, and some looked as young as ten or eleven. Most were somewhere between. All had black hair and were dressed in T-shirts and shorts, all had their hands clasped in front of them. That could mean only one thing: plastic wrist ties.

The sex trade. He'd heard of it. Now he was going to be a part of it.

They all looked Hispanic. Where were they from? Mexico? Central America? Probably not as far as South America.

Christ, who cared where? Didn't matter. They were *children*—snatched from streets and villages and towns, maybe some even sold by their parents—and herded aboard a ship and brought to this deserted stretch of coast.

And Jack was expected to drive them north and deliver them to some piece of human slime who'd either pimp them out or sell them as sex slaves.

No way. No fucking way. I'm outta here right now.

He unlatched a window and pulled it up, unhooked the screen, pushed it out, and was readying to duck out onto the porch when he remembered Tony.

What about Tony? If they found Jack gone, Tony would take an arrow. Or maybe they'd just put a bullet in his head.

He pulled his leg back inside, and as he did he spotted a phone on the nightstand next to the bed. Really? They'd left him in a room with a phone? If he'd turned the damn lights on he might have noticed it sooner. Didn't help that it was the same beige as the top of the nightstand.

He snatched up the receiver. A quick anonymous call to 911 about a boat unloading suspicious cargo off Duck should bring a quick response. Moose and Reggie and the rest would take off—ideally to the trawler—leaving Jack, Tony, and the girls behind.

He listened for a dial tone . . . and listened. Nothing.

Dead.

Crap.

He resisted the impulse to smash it against the wall and gently replaced it on the cradle. He checked the wire just in case . . .

Nope. Plugged into the wall. Right. A working phone was too much to hope for. Made sense for the owners to cancel service during the off-season. They—

Noise outside the door. He flopped onto the bed and tried to look like he'd been there a while. The door opened and Reggie stuck his head through.

"Just checking."

"Where am I gonna go?"

"Never know when someone's gonna try something stupid."

"If you didn't have Tony, I'd be smoke."

Reggie grinned. "But we do. And don't you forget it."

"When do we leave?"

"Soon, my man. Real soon."

As soon as the door closed, Jack rose and returned to the window. Maybe he could slip out, run down the dune, and find a house with a working phone. After he called 911 he'd race back here before anyone knew he was gone. No houses close by, but—

Something moved outside. The moon had risen high enough to light up the sand. Two dark blotches were moving away from the house toward the dune . . . one big, leading the way, the smaller one behind, stumbling, being dragged.

His gut twisted as he recognized the bigger one.

Oh, Christ. Moose heading over the dune with one of the girls. No need to wonder what was about to go down.

Before he knew it, Jack had kicked off his sneakers and socks and was through the window. He pushed the screen back into place and moved along the porch in a crouch. Yeah, if Reggie found the room empty, there'd be hell to pay for Tony, and maybe for Jack too. But Bertel's words kept echoing in his brain.

There are certain things I will not abide in my sight.

Jack had never understood that more clearly than at this instant. Because he'd just seen one of those things.

He had no illusions about taking Moose mano a mano, at least not without raising a ruckus. Whatever he did had to be quick, silent, and final. The scene with Bertel in the picnic area replayed in his head.

Yeah.

The moon cast stark shadows all around him, but they couldn't compare with the darkness encroaching on the edges of his sanity. He pushed it back. Had to stay cool, had to keep quiet. This was neither the time nor place for a screaming rage.

When he reached the stairway at the end of the porch he took the steps as quickly and silently as possible. His bare feet made little sound on the gravel as he hurried toward the truck. He always made a point of knowing the location of the spare tire in whatever truck Bertel arranged for him, and making sure it was inflated. Never knew when you'd have to change a flat. The spare on this model was stored in a compartment under the cargo bay. He knelt by the rear bumper and yanked on the drop-down hatch behind it. He reached in along the side of the tire and found the jack; farther along his fingers closed around the tire iron.

Yes.

He pulled it out and immediately headed back toward the dune, inspecting it along the way. Solid iron, good weight, flat pry edge on the straight end, lug wrench on the curved end.

Yeah. This would do. This would do just fine.

He ran up the dune, his footfalls silent in the sand as he pelted through the sea grass. Time to lay a little John Elder action on Moose.

He found him and the girl just over the dune. Looked like he couldn't wait to take her any farther from the house. His back was to Jack and the girl's shorts lay in a wadded clump to the side. Moose was unzipping his fly as he knelt between her kicking legs. Jack wondered why she wasn't screaming, but only for a second . . .

. . . because the darkness was engulfing him. Not with a snap, like with Rico. More gradual this time, because it had been lapping at him since he'd seen Moose and the girl heading over the dune. More like an irresistible flood now, seeping into all his nooks and crannies. It would have its way . . . oh, yes, it would have its way.

Without slowing, he tightened his grip and lowered the iron as he stretched it behind him.

"Pssst!"

Jack twisted his body and swung with all he had as Moose turned his head. The curved end of the iron, powered by Jack's arm, the added body weight lent by the torso twist, plus the momentum of his headlong rush, caught the slimeball square in the teeth and flipped him onto his back.

Jack slewed to a halt and stared in shock as Moose made a gurgling noise and rolled over onto his belly. He raised his head.

How could he still be conscious, let alone move after that shot?

A few feet away on the sand, the little girl was crabbing away from them on her back.

Moose spat teeth and began to push himself up from the sand.

Uh-uh. Not gonna happen.

Darkness ruled. Jack stepped up beside him and smashed the tire iron against the back of his head, flattening him. Then a third shot, because . . . well, just because.

He turned and saw the girl's bare pubes as she continued the crawl away on her back. God, how old was she? Ten? Eleven? He saw the glint of duct tape across her mouth and knew why she was so silent. Moose loved his duct tape.

He stepped toward her and she whimpered behind that tape. Moonlight glistened off the tears on her cheeks. To show her he was on her side, he dropped the tire iron, then picked up her shorts and tossed them to her. She reached for them but couldn't hold them. Jack noticed then that her hands were taped as well, locking down her fingers. Probably so she couldn't pull the tape off her mouth.

Moose had thought of everything. That kind of thoroughness didn't come without experience. He'd done this before. How many times? Jack didn't want to know. Didn't matter. Once was too many.

The darkness remained on the periphery as he dropped to his knees beside the girl. She whimpered and tried to roll away, but when he grabbed her hands and began to strip off the tape, she quieted. Beneath the tape her wrists were bound with a plastic restraint, impossible to break or loosen. These suckers had to be cut off.

"*Silencio?*" he whispered as he gripped the corner of the tape across her mouth.

She nodded.

"*Silencio,*" he repeated, pulling it off as gently as he could.

He handed her the shorts and turned away, wadding up all the used duct tape as she stood and pulled them on. When she was dressed again, he turned and stared at her. So little. Just a child. The darkness bloomed as he glanced over at Moose's still form.

You filthy piece of—

He pushed it down. Had to think. He'd acted without a plan but he had a good excuse for that: no time for a plan. Had to get this girl, this child out of harm's way.

Okay, he'd done that. At least temporarily. Now what?

Good question. What to do with Moose?

Harder question: What to do with the girl?

First, Moose. The perv creep was going to be out for a while. Leave him here and let it look like he got into a fight. With whom? Not Jack's problem, because Moose's not talking at the moment. And even after he comes to, he probably won't remember what happened, let alone who did it.

But the girl . . . the girl, the girl, the girl . . . only one way to handle her. He took her bound little hands in his and looked into her dark eyes.

In his best Spanish, he asked her name.

"Bonita," she whispered.

That meant "pretty." She lived up to her name. And his heart broke at what he had to say next.

"Bonita . . . you must go back to the others."

Even in the moonlight he could see her eyes widen. *"No-no-no!"* She released a single sob, but at least she did it softly. The kid was tough. What had her life been like till now?

He carefully assembled his response before speaking. "You must go back but only for a little while. I will save you."

Still she shook her head.

"If you run, they will know. They will find you and hurt you and hurt me." He nodded toward Moose. "I saved you once. I will save you again. I will save you all."

Her head stopped.

I will save you all . . . a tall order.

He tugged on her hands. She resisted a second, then rose to her feet.

"No moverse," he said, then hurried over to Moose.

He found the chain that ran to his front pocket and tugged on it. Keys jangled as they pulled free. He found the clasp and undid it, then he led the little girl to the top of the dune. He peeked over. Nothing moving outside the house.

He led her down the dune and around the house to the parking area and straight to the ground-floor door. She whimpered a little as they neared it and began to dig in her heels. He squatted beside her and turned her to face him. Tears glistened in her lower lids, readying to fall. Fine if they did. It added realism to the situation.

He told her that he needed her to go back inside. But tell no one about him. No one must know. Say nothing and he could save her. *"Comprende?"*

She sniffed and nodded.

"Buena." He reminded her: Tell no one. Not even her friends.

He pulled on the door. Locked. No surprise there. Now he understood the double-key dead bolt.

He held Moose's key ring up in the moonlight, looking for a Yale. At least he wasn't one of those guys who carried ninety keys wherever he went. Only half a dozen here; two looked like good candidates for the Yale. The first one fit but wouldn't turn. The second did it.

Jack turned the key slowly, teasing the bolt back. When it clicked, he eased the door in until he could see inside. The room was packed with prepubescent Hispanic girls, some sitting, some standing, some stretched out on the hard floor, all looking dejected. But not a single adult in sight.

Quickly he pushed the door open, guided the reluctant Bonita through, then closed it behind her. But as he was relocking it, an idea so obvious, so beautiful in its simplicity, struck him like a . . . well, like a tire iron.

Why not simply open the door and shoo them out into the night, scatter them north and south. Reggie and the others would be able to corral some of them, but the majority would be gone. Locals were few, but by morning one of them had to stumble across some of the girls and then the story would be out, blowing Moose and Reggie's sick operation for good.

He was just about to reverse direction on the key twist when he heard voices to his right. He recognized one as Reggie's.

Shit.

He ducked away from the door and put a car between himself and the voices. He realized he was hugging Tony's Bimmer.

"—ain't keen on this mystery driver you got," said the voice he didn't know.

"No sweat," Reggie replied. "Kid's not a mystery and not as young as he looks. He's experienced—runs ciggies, and he's made the run through DelMarVa and Jersey plenty of times."

"That may be, but I don't like all the arm-twisting involved. I prefer a guy who *wants* to be on board."

"Hey, you think *we* need that shit? Rather have Ace drive any day, but he fucked up. Shoulda run over the dog."

"What're you talking about?"

"He called from the cop station last night, or should I say, early this morning. Said he was driving along—okay, it was late and he'd had a few—"

"Driving the truck—*our* truck?"

"Nobody said he was a rocket scientist. Anyway, he's driving along and suddenly there's this mutt sitting in the middle of the road. So the dog-loving asshole swerves and hits this car coming the other way. Bad enough, but he's got beer on his breath, and worse, there's a warrant out on him for child support. And on top of that, his license is expired."

"This is your *driver*?"

"Hey, it wasn't expired when he started driving for us. I guess he never got it renewed. The long and the short of it is, Ace and his truck are outta circulation. So if we're gonna make the schedule, we need the kid."

Why was he always "the kid"?

"I still don't like it."

"Hey, you know that thing about a gift horse? This guy dropped right in our laps. Almost like fate. And he won't give us no trouble. We got him boxed."

"Yeah? But what about after the run? He'll be a loose end—an *unhappy* loose end."

"Not so unhappy once we pay him double his usual rate. Bet we can bring him in—take Ace's place."

"And if he doesn't want to?"

"Moose'll be there. He'll handle him. One way or another, the kid won't be a problem."

"Better not be."

The kid is already a problem, Jack thought. Ask Moose.

But the implication was chilling.

He heard the door rattle as one of them tested it to double-check it was locked.

"Speaking of Moose," the new guy said, "where is that fucker?"

"Oh, uh, tying up some last-minute business."

"How soon before you put this show on the road?"

"I'm guessing half an hour or less."

"Shit. You *guess*? Listen, we've traveled over two thousand miles with those little bitches and—"

"You started with thirty, right?"

"Yeah. And delivered twenty-eight."

"Just two lost? Not bad."

Just two lost? Not bad? Jack's blood began to boil.

"Yeah, well, always some spoilage with any cargo. One got hurt bad in a fall trying to sneak out of the hold, and the other came down with a bad case of some kinda dysentery. Had to toss them."

Toss them . . . Jesus. Those poor kids.

"Anyway, what I'm getting at, Reggie my man, is me and my crew ferried the product over two thousand miles and we want our cut."

"You get paid when we get paid," Reggie said. "Same as always."

"Yeah, but the longer you dick around here, the longer till payday."

"Shit, Tim. Half an hour ain't gonna make no difference."

"Just load 'em up and roll 'em out, okay? The sooner me and the boys are back beyond the twelve-mile limit, the better."

They walked off, back toward the side of the house, bickering as they went. Jack waited till they made the turn, then followed. He peeked around the corner as they reached the porch and went inside. Good thing he'd closed his window behind him. Now, all he had to do was slip back inside, put on his sneakers, and play dumb. Reggie would never—

Shit! The tire iron. He'd left it by Moose.

Instead of sneaking up the stairs to the porch, he raced over the dune to where Moose lay. The tire iron jutted from the sand next to him. Jack grabbed it and was swinging around for a run back to the parking lot when he noticed that Moose seemed to be lying awfully still. Like not-breathing still. He bent and gingerly touched him.

Cold.

Aw, no.

Not that he felt bad for Moose. He felt nothing for him, especially not remorse. Nothing too bad could happen to a guy who'd rape a little girl. But this complicated things up the wazoo. No big thing for this crew to have to deal with a banged-up member, but a dead one . . . a corpse was a major liability. They'd have to figure out how to dispose of it.

Only one way out: Hide Moose.

He grabbed an arm and dragged him into the shadow of the steep slope of one of the bigger dunes. Using his feet, he collapsed the dune onto the body. He used his hands to finish the cover-up, then stepped back for a look.

Not bad. A good flashlight might pick out the disturbed sand, and no way that lump would look natural in daylight, but all things considered . . . as good as he was going to get.

Now for the tire iron. Jack didn't want to risk another trip to the parking area. He grabbed it from the sand, ran down to the water's edge, and reared back to toss it as far as he could. In the unlikely event anyone ever found it—no worry about it floating ashore—surf and saltwater would take care of the blood and fingerprints.

But he stopped. If they found Moose, they might guess he'd been done in by a tire iron. Unlikely for Reggie to glom onto that, but Tim might. And it wouldn't do for Jack's truck to be missing a tire iron.

He wiped the iron in the wet sand to remove any bloodstains or bits of hair, then raced back around to his truck. He restored it to its place with the tire and jack, then climbed onto the porch and eased back through the window into the room. As he was pulling on his socks he realized he was covered with sand—not just his feet but his clothes as well. Burying Moose had been messier than he'd realized.

He didn't know how much time he had, so he stepped to the center of the throw rug and gave himself a frantic brush down. When he'd got himself as clean as he could, he slid the rug with its telltale pile of sand under the bed.

With his socks and sneakers back on his feet, he rose and took a breath. Now what? Voices rose beyond his door. He stepped closer and listened at the crack.

Tim's voice was the louder of the two.

"—told me he was 'tying up some business.' Well, where is he and what's this business he's tying up?"

"Hey, it's okay—"

"No, it's not fucking okay. We've never had this much product. If one of them, just *one* of them gets away, we're screwed." His voice rose to a shout. "*WHERE THE FUCK IS HE?*"

A pause, then, "He's out on the beach with one of the girls."

"*WHAT?*"

"Hey, he does it with every shipment. Calls it 'sampling the product.' He—"

"Are you shitting me? You fucking asshole! They're supposed to be virgins! That's why we get primo dinero for them!"

"Hey, don't get on me. Not my idea."

"Listen to me, you dumbass. I don't know what he's doing on the beach, but he ain't with one of our girls."

"What do you mean?"

"I just did a head count and there's twenty-eight downstairs."

"Naw. You're sure?"

"Course I'm sure."

"But then . . . ?"

"Yeah. Where's Moose? Where the fuck is Moose?"

Jack had known this moment would come. Still, it tied a knot in his gut. The next step was to go looking for him. He heard footsteps pounding his way so he jumped back on the bed. The door swung open.

"You seen Moose?" Reggie said.

"Yeah, he's under the bed."

"Don't be a wiseass."

Reggie flipped the wall switch and the ceiling light came on. He stepped over to the closet and pulled open the doors. Empty. Jack saw him glance at the foot of the bed—no room for Reggie under there, let alone Moose.

"You're not serious," Jack said.

He hoped to hell not. If Reggie looked he might get curious as to why the rug was there.

"Deadly." He pulled a pistol and pointed it at Jack, his eyes cold. "I'm asking you again: You seen Moose?"

"En-oh."

Reggie slammed the door on his way out, and Jack leaped back to the crack.

"Maybe he's asleep in one of the rooms," Reggie said.

Tim made a noise like a growl. "Goddamn better be. You search the house. I'm checking out the beach."

Jack moved to the window and felt his palms grow sweaty as he watched Tim head for the dunes.

5

"I don't fucking believe this!" Tim raged. "We're fucked-fucked-fucked!"

Jack stood in the house's great room with Reggie and a couple of guys from the trawler who had been ferried in to help find Moose. No luck in the house and none out there on the dunes—much to Jack's relief. He'd been pulled from his room and now he and the others stood in a semicircle and watched Tim rant. This was his first good look at him: barrel-chested with a bushy beard. And red-faced with anger.

"Hey no, we ain't," Reggie said. "We got two trucks and two drivers." He jerked a thumb at Jack. "Archie here can take the first, I'll take the second. We can deliver on time if we leave now."

Tim shook his head. "That means I've got to stay here with what's his name."

Reggie nodded. "Yeah. Lucky you. That's the easy job. No one's gonna bother you here. You just gotta cool your jets till I get back with your cut."

"This ain't how it's supposed to be."

"But it's how it is. And hey, if Moose shows up, you bust his face for me, okay?"

"With pleasure."

Tim started barking orders, and within fifteen minutes Jack was behind the wheel of his truck, heading for the mainland. They'd kept him upstairs while they were loading the girls. He didn't know how many he had on board. Half? That meant fourteen.

I will save you.

His promise to Bonita. How was he going to keep it?

He could save the ones in his truck simply by driving to a police station. But that would mean a death sentence for Tony. Plus, he had no way of knowing if Bonita was even on board. She could be in Reggie's truck. And who knew how crazy-desperate Reggie would become if Jack pulled a stunt like that?

I will save you all.

Had he really said that? What had he been thinking? Where had his head been to let him think he could pull *that* off?

He didn't see any options except to stick to their plan for now. That meant Jack in the lead, Reggie behind, watching Jack's every move, calling in every twenty minutes or so with the code word that would keep Tony alive.

But would anything keep Tony alive? Or Jack? The conversation he'd heard between Reggie and Tim in the parking area made it pretty clear that Jack and Tony were expendable. Jack was a "loose end," and if he didn't join up after this run, the plan had been to have Moose "handle" him.

One way or another, the kid won't be a problem.

Well, Jack was pretty well set on being a problem, and with no Moose around to "handle" him, maybe he could find a way to become a big problem.

Maybe when they reached Staten Island and the girls were being transferred to their new owner . . . maybe then he could make a move.

Maybe.

This was all new to him. He needed a plan, but he had no idea where the transfer would take place, so he'd have to play the whole damn thing by ear.

The only thing he knew for sure was that he'd have to do *something*, because Bertel's words kept echoing back to him.

There are certain things I will not abide in my sight.

FRIDAY

1

Ghost time.

Neil Zalesky's intestines were complaining as he crouched in the dark on Rosa's roof and tied the rope around the chimney. Seemed his gut wanted to know what he was up to. Well, it would find out soon enough.

He'd called the bitch's floor at Downstate where she worked as a ward clerk. He'd recognized her voice when she answered, so he'd asked in a singsong voice if Dr. So-and-so was there. He wasn't, of course, so he'd thanked her and hung up.

She worked the eleven-to-seven shift on the orthopedic floor, so she'd be there all night. Her job was half her life. The other half was school. Gonna be a nurse. That was what broke them up. All about her—always all about her. What about him? Where did he fit in? He brought home enough for both of them, set them up in a nice apartment, and in a much better neighborhood than this crap hole. Longwood? Really? She couldn't do better than that?

Some bitches never knew how good they had it. Especially this one. Little Miss Overachiever had to have her own thing. And then when he got all blabby once and told her all he had to go through to bring home the good ol' bacon, did she thank him? Hell, no. She got on her high horse and things went steadily downhill from there.

He'd gotten a little frustrated, lost his temper a few times—all her doing—and she walked out. He still couldn't believe it. The bitch walked out. Got a fucking restraining order on him. He still couldn't believe it.

Well, no restraining order could stop the Ghost.

He double-tied the knots on the half-inch cord, then tested them: solid.

He carried the rest to the edge of the roof and dropped it over. He had this down to a science by now—the rope all measured out with knots at twelve-inch intervals with an extra big one at the end. He pulled on a pair of gloves and lowered himself over the edge.

An easy drop down the brick wall to her third-floor window over the alley. He lifted the sash, and eased himself in. Her brother had nailed down the windows that opened onto the fire escape—all sorts of code violations there, but Neil wasn't about to say anything. He wasn't supposed to know about it. He was never here, so how could he? But her devoted brother had never bothered with the alley window. After all, it was three stories up, with no way to move a ladder in and out without making a huge racket and attracting all sorts of attention. Too bad the greasy little spic never considered the possibility of the Ghost climbing *down* to the window.

But Neil had. Neil knew all the angles. That was why he brought home those stacks of cash and never paid a dime in taxes.

Once inside, he pulled out a flashlight. He didn't need it to get around—the place was small and he had the floor plan down cold by now—but he had to be on the lookout for booby traps. Could be something as elaborate as a trip wire to trigger an alarm, or as crude—and effective—as a bear trap sitting in the middle of the hallway.

He took his time and found nothing. No surprises.

Well, she'd added a bar to her apartment door—a steel rod, hooked under the knob and wedged against the floor. He checked the lock on the door and smiled. Yeah, she'd had a new one installed—again. Stupid cow thought he was getting in through the door. Since he wanted her to go on thinking that, he threw the bar on the floor and unlocked the door.

His unhappy gut growled, telling him it was time.

No need to argue. He pulled a folded sheet of paper from his pocket as he trekked to her bedroom. He opened it and flattened it on the nightstand. Too dark to see what was written, but he didn't have to see.

a gift from the Ghost

Then he pulled down her covers and stood on the mattress. He dropped trou, then squatted over her pillow and let loose a major loaf.

When he was done, he used her sheet to wipe, then fled the stench. He'd been holding that all day and it was wicked. He closed her bedroom door behind him to lock in the stink. He grinned, imagining her face as she opened the door and the smell slammed her nose.

He returned to the window, slipped through, and took hold of the rope. He swung out, got his feet on the sill, and pushed the sash down. When it was fully closed, he began the climb back up to the roof.

The Ghost had struck again.

2

Kadir hid a yawn as the limo swayed along a rutted road. He hadn't been sleeping well since all the excitement Monday night; here it was almost dawn and he hadn't slept at all since yesterday morning. He might have been more awake if he were behind the wheel, but he had no license and Tachus wanted someone more experienced, someone familiar with Staten Island. Kadir fitted neither description. The man to his left in the driver seat, who he knew only as Osman, fit both.

All in all, six men on the mission—four here in the rented limo, and two more in the truck, also rented. Both Faraq in the backseat with Tachus, and Saleem in the truck, worked with Kadir in Tachus's uncle's place. They had all gathered at a kabob shop and left from there. Kadir knew no one but Tachus, and would have preferred to stay safe at home, but Tachus had insisted he come along. Of the original group of four approached by the man from Qatar, only Kadir and Tachus remained free. Sayyid was in custody in a hospital recovering from his wound, and Mahmoud was being held as a material witness.

"I ask you," Tachus said from the rear seat, "what did you three accomplish? What? If you're going to strike a blow for jihad, choose a worthy target. This rabbi had few followers and little influence. Even the Israelis didn't want him. Only two days now and you cannot find mention of him in the papers."

Kadir said nothing. He was glad Kahane was dead, but not glad that Sayyid had suffered a bullet in the neck.

Tachus lapsed back into silence as he studied the directions given him by the man from Qatar.

"It should be at the end of this road," he told the driver.

They cruised into a low, flat, marshy area. Kadir didn't see any way out besides the path they'd come in on.

"This is the place," Tachus said. "Drive to the far side and turn around. That way we will be facing them when they arrive."

The limo driver did as he was told and the truck followed.

When they were situated, Tachus said, "Leave the engines running."

"What is going to happen?" Kadir said as sweat pooled in his armpits.

Monday night he had been just a lookout. Tonight he was a full participant. He admitted—only to himself—that he was frightened.

"They are bringing two trucks, but small, and both their cargoes should fit nicely into our big truck."

Cargo . . . no one wanted to say "little girls."

Tachus had told him over and over how the Quran allowed slaves, but Kadir wasn't so sure about selling children, even if they were infidels. He was glad his mother and father were far, far away. They would be ashamed of him, even if the ultimate purpose was for the glory of Allah and jihad. They would say, *Find another way, because . . . little girls . . .*

"We do not know these men, do we," Kadir said.

"No. Nasser brokered the deal."

"Then they know we have money . . . lots of money." He saw danger.

"*Nasser's* money. He arranged this. He would not put such a fortune in jeopardy."

Kadir didn't care about money in jeopardy. How about him?

"That is why we brought these," Tachus said, handing a revolver to Kadir. "We are all armed. Now you are too. I've seen you shoot. That is why I brought you along."

Kadir's fatigue vanished as he hefted the weapon. It reminded him of Sayyid's .357 Magnum. Suddenly he felt as if a weight had been lifted from his shoulders. He glanced through the windshield and saw headlights.

"Look!"

"Quickly!" Tachus said, poking his shoulder. "Get out and stay out of sight by the side of the car. Keep your gun ready. I don't expect any problems, but we are dealing with infidels. Allah rewards honesty in trade, but these do not follow Allah. I do not want any surprises unless they come from us. We must be prepared."

Kadir slipped out the door and crouched near the rear fender as two trucks approached the boggy clearing.

3

Jack had been to every NYC borough except Staten Island; he knew nothing about it. All he did was follow the written directions Reggie had given him. He took his usual route until he reached the two-thirds point into Jersey, then turned east over the Outerbridge Crossing onto Staten Island. He recognized the man-made mountain of the landfill—everyone knew about that—but the rest was terra incognita.

Follow this highway, turn on that boulevard, go down this road . . .

Finally he pulled to a stop at the edge of a marsh in a deserted lowland. He thought he could see houses in the distance through the trees that rimmed the area, but they seemed far off.

Those rosy fingers were stroking the sky again. Fifty yards away, a large truck—big enough to hold all the girls—idled next to a black Lincoln Town Car. He jotted down the license plates of both on the sheet of directions, but didn't know why. Maybe they'd come in handy later.

Later . . . what about now? He pounded his fists on the steering wheel. He'd driven all night, ferrying a truckload of young girls—children—toward a future of horrendous abuse, and still he had no plan.

Reggie pulled his truck to a stop to the right of Jack's. He hopped out and opened Jack's passenger door. He'd added a gray hoodie to his ensemble.

"I gotta go talk to them."

"Want me to come along?"

"Hey, no. Moose usually handles this so I'll be playing it by ear. We got money and shit to discuss. Plus, these are new customers, so it might take me a little longer. You stay here with the product."

Product . . . Christ, how he'd come to hate that word.

Jack's offer to go along had been bogus. He'd been counting on Reggie turning him down. He wanted to stay with the truck. He kept it idling while he examined his options.

He could take off now and save his half of the girls. That would mean the end of Tony, but . . .

Yeah . . . *but*. Risk Tony's life to save fourteen girls from being sold as sex slaves. One life for fourteen, or fourteen lives for one.

He shook his head. Who was he to make that decision? Good question. The answer: his decision, by default. He was the only one behind the wheel, the only one with the option. A judgment call.

But if he took off with his girls, what happened to Reggie's group? Would they be switched to the other truck and carted off? Jack had the license plate number, but was it even real? Could he get to a phone in time to tell the cops to stop it?

Too many questions, too many ways for things to go wrong.

As Reggie approached the other vehicles, two men stepped out of the limo and another pair from the cab of the truck. Two had towels wrapped around their heads, the others wore pillboxes, all four wore ankle-length thobes—he knew what they were called now because he'd looked it up.

"Holy—"

Mohammedans. Two looked familiar. He was pretty sure they'd helped unload the cigarettes at the Mummy's place, but in the dim light he couldn't be sure. He had the impression that someone remained in the Town Car. The Mummy himself?

He saw Reggie lean into the rear compartment.

4

"The deal was for thirty," Kadir heard Tachus say.

He remained in a crouch, revolver ready, looking up at the lighted interior of the car. He could see neither Tachus nor the driver, but he could hear them.

"We had a little spoilage," the driver replied. "It's a long trip. Y'gotta expect that."

"We will adjust the payment accordingly."

"Fair enough. But since we've never dealt with you before, I gotta see the money before this goes any further."

"Of course. Osman!" Tachus raised his voice and spoke in Arabic. "Open the trunk and let him see." He lowered it again and returned to English. "And you—do not be foolish. We are honest businessmen, but we will protect what is ours."

Kadir smiled as he envisioned Tachus showing the driver a pistol.

"Hey, no need for that. We're businessmen too. We just want to get paid what was agreed on and be on our way."

"Good. Then there will be no problem."

Kadir heard the trunk open, heard a zipper slide, followed by rummaging sounds. He peeked and saw a thin, scruffy man with hair cut short in the front and long at the back of his neck. After a while . . .

"Okay," the driver said as the trunk slammed and he returned to Tachus. "Looks good. Let's make the transfer."

"We will need to inspect the cargo."

"What's that mean?"

"You understand, of course, that we must make sure the count is correct and that there are no damaged goods."

"They're all fine."

"So you say. But as you also said, we have never dealt with you before. Your idea of 'fine' may not agree with ours."

"All right, all right. But we gotta make this fast. Gonna be light soon."

"Back one of your trucks up to ours and we will transfer one at a time."

"That's gonna take time."

"If all is as it should be, this will not take long. But I will not pay for damaged goods."

"Shit, okay. Let's just get this show rolling."

The driver moved away, but Kadir maintained his position, unsure of what Tachus wanted him to do. As his legs started to cramp he began to rise, but froze as he heard a new voice say, "Hello, fucker!"

A stream of bullets shattered the rear passenger widow. Blood and brains and bits of glass sprayed into the night over Kadir's head, spraying him.

Someone—the driver?—was attacking with a machine gun!

5

Jack watched Reggie talk, gesture to the trucks, then one of the robed guys opened the Lincoln's trunk and showed him something. Jack couldn't see what it was, but the way the glow from the courtesy lights within lit up Reggie's face reminded Jack of the suitcase in *Kiss Me Deadly*. Money, he supposed.

Whatever. Reggie seemed satisfied. The trunk was closed and Reggie headed back toward Jack's truck. He opened the passenger door again.

"They want to check out the product."

That word again.

Jack unclenched his teeth. "What's that mean? They bring a gynecologist along?"

"A what?"

"Never mind. What do we do?"

"Back your truck up to the back of theirs. We transfer the girls one at a time and—"

A rapid series of pops followed by cries of pain and terror cut him off. Two ski-masked figures had emerged from the brush and were shooting everyone in sight. One was firing into the rear compartment of the Town Car.

"Oh, shit!" Reggie cried as he jumped in. "Go!"

Jack sat frozen in shock, unable to respond as he watched the Mohammedans drop. The two attackers each carried some sort of submachine gun with a long silencer on the barrel. They moved quickly and operated with deadly efficiency. One of the Mohammedans pulled out a pistol but never got a chance to fire it. In seconds all four were down.

"What—?"

"Go-go-go!" He rammed a fist against Jack's shoulder. "Get the fuck outta here!"

The punch did it. Jack shook off the paralysis, slammed the truck into drive, and stomped the gas. As he yanked the wheel hard to the right, a spray of bullets stitched the hood and smashed the passenger window. Reggie screamed like a girl and ducked, slipping to the floor. Jack kept driving.

As the truck angled away, the shooters lost their line of sight on the cab. Jack prayed they wouldn't keep shooting—they'd hit the girls. But a glance in the passenger-side mirror showed that they'd shifted their interest from the truck to the Town Car, then they were lost from view.

"Who are they?" Jack shouted. His heart felt like it was going to pound its way out of his chest.

Reggie straightened from the floor. "Dunno!" He was panting like he'd just finished running a marathon.

Jack felt a little short of breath too. An ambush was the last thing he'd expected.

"What do they want?"

"The money, what else? There's three mil in the trunk of that car."

"Three—!"

"Hey, a hundred grand apiece for the product."

"You say 'product' once more and I'm going to punch out your lights."

"What? Who the fuck you think—?"

Jack gave him a shove that bounced him off the door. "You heard me."

He stared at Jack in shock for a second, then reached for his waistband.

Oh, no. Going for his pistol—

But he came up empty-handed.

"Shit! The gun and the phone are back in my truck!"

"You were going to *shoot* me?"

"I don't—" He shook his head. "Just don't you ever lay a hand on me again."

"Fine. And you just remember what I said."

Jack reached the pavement and picked up speed. Reggie had mentioned the phone. Christ! Tony!

"When did you last call in with the code word or whatever it was?"

"Just before I got out of the truck. Told Tim we were at the spot."

"We've got to find a phone before twenty minutes are up."

"Keep driving! And don't worry. We were just kidding about killing him. Moose's idea to make you cooperate. We ain't killers."

Jack wasn't buying that. But even if he was telling the truth, what would they do if they found Moose?

Reggie was peering in his rearview. "Don't see nobody. Had to be the money—that was all they wanted." He slammed the dashboard. "Shit! How'd they know?"

"Who cares? What if they come after us? We had one gun between us and now we don't have any."

"Hey, I couldn't walk up to the buyers carrying. And no one's coming after us. I mean, what for? They was wearing masks. We can't identify them."

Good point. Reggie was obviously more attuned to this sort of situation than Jack. But Jack was more concerned about the girls. These were safe, but what about the others?

"What do you think they'll do with your truck?"

Reggie shrugged. "Who cares? It's rented with a credit card that don't belong to nobody. Ain't worried about the truck. The prod—" He cut off. "The girls are what worry me."

"Why?"

"They've seen us."

"Haven't seen me."

Well, Bonita had, but none of the others. And he didn't think Bonita was going to accuse him of anything.

"Hey, they seen *me*, okay? I loaded them into the house and I loaded them into the trucks. They can identify me."

"Well, you'll be back in North Carolina and they'll be shipped back to wherever they came from. Where *did* they come from?"

Reggie shrugged. "Who knows, who cares?" He chewed a fingernail. "We gotta do something with the ones sitting behind us. We get caught with them, we're fucked."

"Why don't we—"

"Turn here!" Reggie said, pointing to the right. "I got an idea. I know a place on the north shore we can go. No one'll see us."

"No one'll see us what?"

"Hey, just drive and lemme think, okay?"

Jack glanced at him. Reggie and thinking . . . not exactly a match made in heaven.

6

Kadir didn't have to look to know Tachus was beyond help. He glanced down at the revolver in his hand—what chance did this little thing with its six rounds have against a machine gun?

He dropped flat and slithered under the limo. He heard shots, shouts, screams, saw Osman hit the ground on the far side of the car. In the light from the open car door he watched his torn throat pump dark blood. The man stared at Kadir, blinked twice, twitched, then lay still. The blood stopped pumping.

"That all of them?" said a voice.

"Yeah," replied another. "But we've got to go after that truck."

"No kidding," said the first. "But first—"

Kadir jumped as a short, sharp burst sounded at the rear of the car. He heard the trunk pop open. Cold liquid began to splash his legs.

"Damn! I hit the money."

"You also hit the gas tank."

Gas! Kadir could smell it now, but didn't dare move his feet.

"Jesus, bro," said the first voice. "Will you look at that? Beautiful or what?"

"Yeah, beautiful. Meanwhile the other truck is getting away."

"Yeah. But a couple of details first."

As Kadir watched, booted feet kicked Osman's body onto its back. It jerked as more bullets were fired into it.

What were they doing? Clearly he was dead.

More bursts of gunfire from farther away in the clearing. Kadir used the sounds to cover him as he squirmed from under the car and rolled into the rank grass at the nearby edge of the clearing.

He held his breath as one of the attackers returned to the car. He could see only two figures moving about the clearing, both wearing ski masks. They reminded him of the Palestinian heroes from the Munich Olympics.

"Last one," the approaching attacker said.

He fired a few more rounds into the rear compartment—why shoot Tachus again?—and then stopped by the trunk. There he used a cigarette lighter to set fire to a piece of paper the size of a dollar bill—it might even have been money—and then dropped it at the rear of the limo. Kadir could not contain a gasp of shock as the gasoline on the ground burst into flame. His sound apparently was covered by the *woomp!* of ignition, because the attacker hurried away without a second look.

Kadir stayed low until he heard the remaining cargo truck start up and drive off. Then he rose and reentered the clearing, giving the burning car a wide berth. He glanced into the open rear section where Tachus sprawled, the top of his head missing. His crotch had been blasted to a bloody ruin.

Kadir backed away and saw that Osman's genitals had been blasted away as well. As he staggered about the clearing he noticed that the same had been done to Faraq and Saleem. Why? What did this mean?

He jumped as the limo's gas tank exploded, sending a ball of flame into the air.

He hurried to the truck they'd brought but the keys were not in the ignition and he couldn't bring himself to search the ruined body of the driver. So Kadir did the only thing he could think of.

He ran. He didn't know where he was going. He simply ran.

7

Jack followed Reggie's directions to the northern limit of the Staten Island waterfront. He didn't know the island's geography, but figured those dockyards across the channel had to be in Bayonne. Reggie hadn't been kidding about it being deserted—at least at the moment. Who knew what it would be like once more people were out and about. Clouds had scudded in and it looked and felt like rain.

"There's a boat ramp around here somewhere," Reggie was saying, craning his neck as he peered through the windshield.

"Boat ramp? You've got a boat around here?"

He looked at Jack as if he'd grown a third eye. "What? No. Did rent one here once, though."

"Fishing?"

Another look. "Hey, no. Had to get rid of something."

Jack hesitated, then decided he had to ask what. But before he could speak, Reggie straightened and pointed to the left.

"There! Get us over there."

As Jack approached he saw a ramp sloping down from the pavement to the water, lined on either side with wooden bulkheading.

"What do we need this for?"

"You're going to back the truck into the water."

"What for?"

"We're gonna sink it."

"What? But the girls—"

"Yeah." Reggie nodded, a small smile playing about his lips. "You catch on fast, Archie."

Jack stared at him. He wasn't kidding.

"No way!"

"Yes, way. Yes, fuckin-A way! This way they don't talk and they don't give out no descriptions."

He was really serious. Jack couldn't wrap his mind around the casual cold-bloodedness.

"Uh-uh. Not happening."

Reggie made a disgusted face. "Or what? You gonna pussy out on me? All right, get out. Get out! I'll do it myself! Move!"

The only move Jack made was to slide his right hand to the noon position on the steering wheel.

Reggie slid closer. "Come on, Archie! Get the fuck out and let—"

Jack straightened his elbow, slamming the knife edge of his hand against Reggie's throat. The short chop didn't carry the force to crush his larynx, but enough to spasm it. As Reggie clutched his throat and made choking noises, Jack felt the dark break loose again. He grabbed his head and smashed it back against the passenger door. The glass had been blown out by a bullet, but his skull landed with a thud against the bottom of the window frame. Jack slammed it a second and third time until Reggie's eyes rolled up in his head and he went limp.

He released him and let him slump in the seat. Jack leaned back, panting. He watched Reggie breathe. Okay. Still alive. Now what?

He had a truck rented by someone who probably didn't exist, with fourteen illegal young girls in the back and an unconscious man in the front.

He was in deep shit.

The girls. The girls came first. Had to figure out what to do with the girls. Had to put some distance between himself and them. And quickly. He could walk away from the truck, but that left him conspicuous and vulnerable to being picked up.

He could dump Reggie here, let the girls out, drive away, and report them at the first pay phone he found. Some sort of social services agency would pick them up, feed them, keep them warm, and find a way to get them back to their families.

Yeah. That seemed like the best for all concerned.

He checked Reggie's hoodie pouch and found a set of keys. As he slipped out of the cab and hurried around the back, he prayed one of them fit the lock on the rear doors or his plan was shot. The air temperature was probably in the forties but the wind off the water made it feel sub-freezing. His second try was a hit—the padlock shackle popped up. He pulled one of the doors open and saw a crowd of frightened faces.

"Usted es libre! Correr!"

They stared at him.

He motioned toward the ground. *"Salte! Usted es libre! Correr! Correr!"*

Something hard and round jammed against the back of his neck as a voice said, "What the fuck are you up to?"

That didn't sound like Reggie.

The girls screamed as a hand grabbed the back of his neck and slammed his face up against the unopened rear door. Hurt like hell but he refused to groan.

Who the hell was this? One of those dead Mohammedans' friends? Probably thought he and Reggie had double-crossed them.

"You listening?" the voice said. "What do you think you're doing?"

Might as well tell him.

"Letting them go."

"Go where?"

"Anywhere but here."

Another voice came from around the passenger side of the truck.

"We got one already down here, bro."

Someone must have found Reggie.

"What?"

"Looks like a little falling out between slimeballs."

Slimeballs? Did he think—well, what else would he think?

"Quedense!" the first guy said and closed the truck's back door. The girls inside wailed.

"They've been cooped up in there all night," Jack said.

"Like you care."

The guy tightened his grip on Jack's neck and dragged him toward the passenger side. Jack got a glance at him and his bladder clenched when he saw the ski mask.

A second masked guy, shorter, heavier, was standing by the door.

"How come he's still breathing?" the second one said.

"Found him letting the girls go."

"Yeah?" The second stepped closer. He had blue eyes and the skin around them was pale. Not a Mohammedan. "A little disagreement over who gets first choice of the girls?"

Jack shook his head as best he could. "No. Over what to do with them."

"And you won. What was your bright idea?"

"Let them go."

"Really." His eyes narrowed as he jerked a thumb toward the cab. "And what was his?"

Well, why not tell him? If they got pissed at Reggie, so what? He had something coming for what he'd been about to do. A lot coming.

"Back the truck into the water and sink it."

The second's eyes widened. "With the girls inside?"

Jack nodded.

A long silence followed as the second guy peered through the shattered window at Reggie. Then he looked at Jack.

"How do we know that wasn't your idea?"

"Because like I told you," said the first, still behind him, "he was letting the girls go when I nabbed him. Telling them to run."

Another long silence, then the first tightened his grip and said, "Still doesn't let you off for driving them up here."

"Not like I had a choice."

"What's that supposed to mean?"

Jack considered what to say next. These were two cold-blooded killers who hadn't hesitated a second to shoot up the Mohammedans, but he was still standing. Maybe they weren't after him.

"What do you care? You've got your money. I can't identify you. Let's just call it a day."

"You think this is about money?"

"Tell you the truth: I don't know what the hell to think."

"Mouthy, aren't you?"

"So I've been told." And then he realized something. "Aw, no."

"What?" said the first.

"You want the girls too."

"So what if we do?"

"They're just kids. Let them go."

"You're the one who delivered them to the brokers. Now you're all concerned about them?"

"Like I said, I didn't have much choice."

"We heard you," said the second. "Convince us."

Might as well lay it all out: He gave them a quick rundown of the situation, leaving out what happened to Moose.

"Nice story," said the first. "Make a good movie. Was this guy Tony a good friend of yours?"

Something in his tone . . .

"Why? What do you care? You know something?"

"We found a phone in the other truck," said the second. "We redialed the last number." His gaze flicked to the first. "Told them the delivery had been made. He asked for a password. When we couldn't give it, he asked if this was Archie. Then he said 'Kiss your friend's ass good-bye.'"

"Shit." Poor Tony.

"You're Archie?"

Jack nodded, silent.

"Think your buddy's gone?" said the second.

Jack thought about Tony as he'd last seen him—taped up with blood leaking from his nose. Would Tim shoot him? No question Moose would have. Probably Reggie too. He'd said, *We ain't killers*, but he'd been more than ready to drown the girls. Why expect any mercy for Tony? He was a liability, a loose end. He could point a finger . . .

The sons of bitches.

"Yeah. I do."

"Then you'll want a little payback. You can tell us how to locate their depot house."

Jack definitely wanted payback.

"It's on the Outer Banks. Easy to find. But listen. Can you call the cops down on the place? Just in case he's still alive."

"Why would we want to do that?"

"Because he's a good guy and has nothing to do with this."

The second looked over Jack's shoulder at the first. "Believe him, bro?"

"Spins a good tale, but . . ." He tightened his grip. "Got any references?"

It took Jack a few seconds to process that. "You're kidding, right?"

"Your life could depend on it."

His mind raced. His father? Who'd buy that? Giovanni? Maybe. Then he knew—

"There's this guy who runs a sporting goods shop on the Upper West Side who—"

"Abe?" said the first. "You know Abe?"

A ray of hope: They'd heard of Abe.

Wait. Why did these two killers know Abe? And how, out of all the sporting goods shops in the city, had they picked out Abe's first thing?

"Yeah. Isher Sports Shop. I worked for his uncle when I was a kid and—"

"Spare us the details," said the first as he handed a cell phone past Jack. "Call him."

The second took it and started walking away, dialing as he went.

He didn't even have to look up the number . . .

"Tell him I'm the guy who worked for Uncle Jake!"

Jack watched him have a short conversation out of earshot, then he returned.

"Abe says he's okay." He looked at Jack. "Jesus, man. Talk about shitty luck. You landed yourself a truckload."

Jack had been thinking the same thing, then something occurred to him.

"One way to look at it. But on the flip side, if I hadn't been along, this truck would be underwater right now."

The first released him. "That's the way the world works: The early bird gets breakfast, but it's one shitty morning for the worm."

Jack shivered. He hadn't realized till now that he was cold—freezing in this wind. He'd left his sweater in the cab. He rubbed his arms.

"Cold?" said the first. He was taller and had brown eyes instead of blue.

"You could say."

"And you were going to put those girls on the street with just T-shirts and shorts. They come from a much warmer place."

"I was going to call them in."

The second nodded. "Yeah, that'd work—to a point. The system isn't very good at getting illegal minors back home, and those departments have their share of creeps."

"I didn't know what else to do."

"We do," said the second. He jerked a thumb toward the cab of the truck. "But first, help me with your buddy here."

"Help what?"

"Carry him. My brother's got a bad back."

Brothers? Jack guessed the "bro" wasn't just street talk.

"Where we taking him?"

"We're dumping him in the channel. Where else?"

"But he's out cold. He'll—" Now he got it. He felt like a dumbass.

"Yeah," said the first brother. "You catch on slow."

Jack backed up a step. Their eyes showed no emotion. They were disposing of trash.

"Wait. No. I mean, I don't think I can do that."

"Why not? You didn't mind denting his skull. And it's what he was gonna do with the girls. Turnaround's fair play."

"Yeah, I know that. But it's so . . ."

The skin around the second brother's eyes crinkled, as if he was smiling behind the mask. "Cold-blooded?"

"Yeah. I guess that's the word."

"Not as cold as his blood's gonna be."

Maybe Reggie was trash—okay, definitely trash. Murderous trash. Jack hadn't felt bad about killing Moose. And if he'd hit Reggie too hard—like fatally hard—well, that would be acceptable. The heat of battle and all that. But to take a helpless man, even a scumbag like Reggie, even with Tony dead, and dump him facedown in a river . . . Jack didn't think he was up to that.

"Can't we just dump him in the bushes?"

"Right. And when he wakes up and gets over his headache, he'll be back next week with another truckload of slaves." He shook his head. "Uh-uh. No way."

Jack looked for options. Why, he couldn't say. The world would be a better place without Reggie, no question, but . . .

Killing a guy to protect someone else was one thing. This would be something else. This would be flat-out murder.

Thinking about killing brought to mind Moose and what had happened down on the beach. And that gave him an idea.

"What if I can fix him so he won't be driving for a real long time?"

The brothers looked at each other, then gave simultaneous shrugs.

"Whattaya got in mind?" the second said.

8

"Let's hope you don't regret this," the second brother said as he and Jack carried Reggie's dead weight into the reeds.

It turned out the brothers—he assumed they were using the term literally instead of figuratively—had followed Jack and Reggie out here in Reggie's truck. After letting Jack talk them out of drowning Reggie, the second brother shoved the unconscious Reggie to the floor of Jack's cab and put Jack in the passenger seat while he drove. The first took Reggie's truck and promised to use Reggie's phone to call in a raid on the Duck house. Jack didn't think it would accomplish much, but he had to try.

He'd slipped back into his sweater; that, along with the heat blowing from the dashboard, had eased the chill in his bones.

The second brother seemed to know where he was going. After about a mile they'd arrived at a swampy area, then turned onto a dirt road. When they'd stopped, the first brother had stayed in Reggie's truck while Jack and the second hauled Reggie out and lugged him away. For a skinny guy, Reggie was heavy as hell.

"What do you mean?" Jack said as they dropped him in a stand of cattails.

Cattails . . . he remembered picking them as a kid and drying the corn dog–like tops, then lighting them. They'd smolder and the smoke was supposed to keep mosquitoes away. Never did, though.

"These subhumans are like boomerangs. They somehow find their way back to you."

Jack didn't like the sound of that. He'd stuck the truck's tire iron into his belt before hauling Reggie, and he pulled it out now. He was getting a lot of use out of this thing.

The brother added, "You'd be better off using that on his head."

"Then I might as well have helped you dump him in the water. Same thing."

He shrugged. "I'm not saying this for my benefit. He doesn't know me. He's seen a ski mask from fifty yards. But you . . . he knows stuff about you. Save your goody-goody worries for all the kids this guy has hurt."

Maybe he was right. Jack looked at Reggie. A couple of good swings to the head . . .

He sighed. "Nope. Can't do it." He glanced at the brother. "Is that how you handle everybody who gets in your way? Take them out?"

"Just the subhumans. Once they're gone, you don't have to give them another thought. And believe me, they're not worth a thought after they're gone."

"And you decide who's 'subhuman'?"

The brother looked him in the eye. "Don't have to. They tell you straight out. Actions speak louder than words. And I'm telling you: He's one of them."

"I think I'll settle for keeping him in a wheelchair for a while."

He stared at Reggie's knees. In theory it had sounded easy, almost humane, considering the alternative offered. But the actual doing was something altogether different.

Without giving himself a chance to reconsider, Jack raised the tire iron and smashed it down on Reggie's right kneecap. He felt it give under the iron. Reggie might have been edging back toward consciousness, but this yanked him the rest of the way. He screamed and clutched at his knee. Fighting a rising gorge, Jack swung a second time and shattered the left.

Then he turned and walked away, leaving Reggie moaning and wailing as he clutched his useless legs. A damn long time before he'd be working gas and brake pedals again.

"You just turned your back on a cold-blooded killer," the brother said, following close behind.

"You don't know that."

"I've got your word that he would have backed that truck into the water with the girls in it if you hadn't stopped him. You telling me that's not true?"

"It's true."

"So? That isn't killing? That isn't cold-blooded?"

"Yeah." His stomach didn't feel so good. "Yeah, it is."

"Okay. Now, I don't want to sound like a broken record, but you just turned your back and walked away from a stone killer who knows who you are—"

"He only knows me as Archie."

"Doesn't matter. He knows what you look like. He knows someone you know. He can track you down and hurt you and people who matter to you."

"So what should I do?"

"Remove the threat. Don't crush his knees, crush his head. Or you will live to regret it."

As they reached the dirt road Jack stopped and dry-heaved. Once. The second brother stopped by his side and patted him on the back.

"You're all right, kid. I think you made a mistake back there, but it's yours to make."

"I'm not a kid."

"No, I guess you're not."

9

"Where are we going?"

They were rolling again—the second brother insisted on driving—and Jack's stomach had settled.

"You can't know that. Even though Abe gave you a thumbs-up, you already know too much about our operation."

"What *is* your operation?"

He pulled off his ski mask, revealing mussed-up blond hair and a pale face. He looked younger than Jack expected. Late twenties at most.

"Can't drive around wearing this." He handed it to Jack. "But you can."

"What?"

"Put it on—backwards."

"You're kidding."

"Do I look like I'm kidding? Put it on backwards and sit down there on the floor. You can't know where we're going."

Okay. That seemed reasonable. They didn't know Jack and wanted to keep him literally and figuratively in the dark. He turned the mask backward, slipped it on, then slid down onto the passenger-side floor. He couldn't see a thing, but he could feel every rut on the pavement.

He needed to know: Who were these guys? What was their game? Cold-blooded killers—he'd witnessed that firsthand—but they seemed genuinely concerned about the girls.

"How did you know where we were meeting?" Jack said.

"We belong to certain, shall we say, discussion groups."

"What's that mean?"

"You've heard of the Internet?"

"Sure."

They'd had computers at Rutgers connected to the network.

"Ever hear of Usenet?"

"No."

"It's part of the Internet where people transfer information. The pervs have gotten into Usenet big-time."

"They use computers?"

"Damn right. Because it's anonymous as all hell and they can trade pictures. Takes forever to upload and download them, but it's lots safer than the U.S. mail."

"Jeez."

"Yeah. They've got bulletin boards and discussion groups they keep secret. They try to disguise them, but if you know their lingo, you can suss out what they're about. They've got online forums that restrict access. It took time and patience and more vomit buckets than Mister Creosote used—especially on sites where they post pictures—but we've worked our way into the restricted levels of quite a few."

"You track them through computers?"

"That's where they've all gone. Coupla weeks ago we learned through one of their forums about a huge auction set for tomorrow night brokered by some Arabs. It dovetailed with whispers we'd been getting about a big shipment coming from the South. We learned where the auction was being held—an off-season rental of a big place in the Hamptons—and poked around the agency that handled the rental. Got a name—fake, but tracked it to an Arab named Tachus Diab."

"Diab?"

"You know the guy?"

Somewhere along the way Jack had learned that the Mummy's last name was Diab. But not Tachus. Riaz or something like that . . .

Jack shook his head. "No. Heard the name Diab somewhere, though."

"Not exactly rare in the Arab world. We figured he wouldn't take possession of the girls until as close to the auction as possible, so the closer we got to Saturday, the closer we watched him. When we saw Diab and his buddies take off in a limo followed by a rental truck, we figured the time had come. When they pulled into that swamp and started checking their weapons, we had all the confirmation we needed."

"What are you going to do with the girls?"

"Send them back home."

"How do you work that?"

"We have an affiliate. She works it out."

"What's in it for her?"

"Does there have to be something?"

"There usually is."

A laugh. "My-my. So young, so cynical."

"You're not exactly Methuselah."

"No . . . I just feel like him. You wouldn't believe the shit you see . . ."

Jack could almost feel the loathing flowing from him.

"So, you turn the girls over to this gal to be returned home. That takes money."

"Not exactly what you'd call a 'gal.' She's got a lot of miles on her. But she's got the necessary bucks."

"How do you know she really—?"

"Sends them home? You're a real trusting bastard, aren't you."

"If you knew what my last twenty-four hours were like, you wouldn't wonder."

"Maybe not. Anyway, she does send them back. I don't know her story, but I suspect she was abducted as a kid and went through hell, and now she wants to do right by other kids in the same fix."

"How'd you come to work for her?"

"Whoa-whoa-whoa. My brother and me don't work for anybody."

"I don't—"

"Understand? You don't have to. We do our thing, she does hers. She gave us a little logistical support in the beginning, but we're independent operations. She's not equipped to do what we do, we're not equipped for her end, so we cooperate."

"Synergy," Jack said.

"Yeah. Good word."

"But what *do* you do?"

"I think you've got an idea."

"I saw you shoot some people and—"

"No, you didn't. At most, you saw two guys in ski masks do some shooting, but not at people. Those weren't people. They were insects. Vermin. You exterminate vermin."

This guy and his brother sure as hell had done that.

Jack sensed real heat behind the words. He might call whatever he and his brother were into an "operation," but Jack sensed it was more of a *mission.*

"Well, whatever they were, I thought I recognized a couple of the Mohammedan types around the car."

He laughed. "*Mohammedans?* Hell, I haven't heard that word since Sister Margaret's history class in grammar school. What are you, a hundred years old?"

Jack felt his face redden behind the mask. "An acquaintance calls them that, and I sort of picked it up."

"Well, drop it and call them *Muslims.* A lot fewer syllables. But where'd you see these guys before?"

Instantly Jack wished he'd kept his mouth shut. He didn't want to get Bertel involved. He remembered helping Giovanni with a couple of jobs in Astoria and seeing that squiggly Arabic writing on a lot of the shop windows and awnings along Steinway Street.

"Astoria. Used to date a Lebanese girl there. Her uncle owned a bakery. I think I saw a couple of those guys in there a lot."

"Well, looks like her uncle is minus a few customers. Astoria's rotten with Arabs."

"You got something against them?"

"Just the slavers. It's part of Arab tradition."

"Didn't know that."

He knew Arabs had developed a thing for suicide bombings and blowing up innocent civilians in planes and street markets, but slaves?

"Their religion—and that's *Islam*, not Mohammedism—is okay with it.

A big part of the slave trade in North and West Africa was either run or brokered by Arabs for centuries. The Barbary pirates raided ships and towns and carried off people to be sold as slaves. Big business. Still a business. But though the misery isn't as widespread, it's more concentrated in each of these kids who gets sold."

"Sold . . . jeez, I don't mean to sound naïve, and I can see people getting away with it in Third World countries, but how does this go on in this day and age in the U.S.?"

"Welcome to the wonderful world of human trafficking. A ten-billion-dollar business."

Ten *billion*? Jack shook his head within the mask.

The truck slowed and Jack got the impression the brother was paying a toll. Bridge? Tunnel? He couldn't say. That huge dollar amount was dominating his thoughts.

"You said ten billion dollars. What does one of these little girls go for?"

"Depends where they are on the supply chain. The limo's trunk contained a duffel bag holding three million cash. A hundred grand apiece. That's the wholesale price. The Arabs were going to hold an auction. Some of the prettier girls could easily go for a quarter mil, three hundred, even more. None go for less than two."

"But who can afford that?"

"Lotta rich pervs out there. Or you get a pedophile ring where they each chip in and pass her around. Then there's those that'll put her straight to work earning back her price by servicing pervs. When they get a little too old for the creeps who like them prepubescent, they're sold again, to those that like teens. And when they get too old for that, the survivors—who are all junkies and crackheads by now—they're put to work out on the street."

"How . . . ?" Jack felt numb. "How do you do that to a little girl?"

"They do it to little boys too. They're not people to the pervs, they're *things*. They're property. They're—"

"Product," Jack said.

"Yeah. 'Product.' "

"Sounds like the two who didn't make it would have been the lucky ones."

"Didn't make it?"

"I overheard the boat captain say one got sick and another hurt trying to escape."

"What happened to them?"

"Tossed overboard."

A lengthy silence followed, during which Jack thought about Tony. He'd been half hoping they might not be up to killing him, but now he remembered how casual Tim had been about the two dead kids.

Poor Tony . . . didn't have a chance . . .

Finally the brother said, "So only twenty-eight made it?"

"That's what I heard."

He banged the heel of his hand against the steering wheel. "Fuckers."

"They told me I'd be shipping 'hooch.' Moonshine. I didn't want to do that, but I'd have preferred it like all hell to little girls."

"I hear ya. This is the largest one-time shipment of kids I've ever seen. Half a dozen at once has been the top so far. Usually it's one or two at a time."

"But—"

"We're here. Stay down."

10

When Jack was finally allowed to remove his mask—after big rolling overhead doors had closed behind the trucks—he found himself in a wide-open space that could have been a small warehouse or a big garage. He had no idea whether he was still on Staten Island or in one of the other boroughs, or even back in Jersey. But whoever the benefactress was, she'd seen to everything.

Four Porta-Pottys lined the left wall; portable showers waited behind a curtained-off area at the rear. Tables piled high with pizza boxes and bottled water and soft drinks stood to the right.

Three uniformed nurses helped the girls from the backs of the trucks. The kids were dirty and weak and scared but the nurses all spoke Spanish and began to check them over immediately. Some of the girls headed straight for the potties—more than a few looked like they hadn't been able to wait—and some for the food.

Jack looked around for Bonita but couldn't pick her out among the milling crowd. He'd seen her in the moonlight and didn't have a good sense of what she looked like beyond her large brown eyes. But they all had brown eyes.

The first brother had taken off his mask. His hair was as brown as his eyes.

Jack realized he was starving so he wolfed down a slice of sausage pizza and opened a Pepsi. He was reaching for a second when a body slammed against his right side and a pair of arms wrapped around his waist.

He looked down at the little girl who had a death grip on him. Tears streamed from her eyes as she looked up at him and sobbed.

"Bonita?"

She nodded and rattled off something he couldn't understand through the sobs. But he did catch "*asustada*"—scared.

"Hey-hey, Archie," said the second brother, approaching. "You know this girl?"

"We met last night."

His eyes narrowed. "Met how? What's going on here?"

The brother knelt beside Bonita and asked in Spanish how she knew him. Bonita told him he'd saved her from a "*bestia*" by hitting him on the head.

The brother was smiling when he rose and faced Jack. "That wouldn't have been a curved tire iron, would it?"

"It would."

The grin broadened. "Weapon of choice. Now you're going to have two of them to watch out for."

Jack shook his head. "No. Only one."

It didn't take the brother long to catch the meaning. He looked puzzled. "Then why all the agonizing with the other driver?"

"Different circumstances. Her *bestia* was in the process of unzipping his fly at the time. I just wanted to stop him."

"I guess you did, Archie." He slapped Jack on the shoulder. "Stopped him for good."

He signaled to one of the nurses to come over. She spoke to Bonita in soothing tones and started to lead her away. Bonita looked at him with pleading eyes.

"*Vaya con ella*," he told her. "*Ella le ayudará.*"

Bonita left with the nurse as the first brother wandered over. He had a good-size backpack slung over a shoulder.

Jack looked from one to the other. He was tired of thinking of them as first and second brother.

"What do I call you guys?"

"Don't," said the first.

"Ever," said the second.

"Seriously."

"Okay," said the first. "Call me Deacon Blue."

The second laughed. "If that's the way we're playing it, call me the Reverend Mister Black."

"Black and Blue," Jack said. "Got it."

"Grab another slice and find a place to sack out for a while. We've got cots for the girls. Get one for yourself."

"What are you two going to do?"

"Pretty much the same," Black said. "We work the night shift and we've got ten, twelve hours to kill."

"Oh, and this is for you," Blue said, slipping the backpack off his shoulder and handing it to Jack.

Jack hefted it. "What is it?"

"Your cut."

"Cut of what?"

"The three mil we confiscated."

"You guys keep the money?"

"Well, we sure as shit ain't handing it back to the pervs. You saved half these girls from going into the drink. You deserve at least a ten percent finder's fee."

Three hundred thousand?

"I can't."

Black looked baffled. "Why the hell not?"

Good question. Why indeed not? That kind of nut meant a nicer place, and no more driving for Bertel. It would set him up pretty for a long, long time. With his low-rent lifestyle, damn near indefinitely.

But no . . .

He shoved the backpack at Black. "Give it to the girls."

Black reached inside and pulled out a neat, half-inch stack of hundred-dollar bills, labeled *$10,000*. It had a hole through it.

"Look, we even gave you some of the shot-up bills. They're still good but we thought you'd like a little memento."

Jack shook his head. "Give it to the—"

Black shoved it back. "Don't worry. They'll each be going home with cash."

"Well, then, send them home with more." He tossed it to Blue this time. "They need it more than I do."

They both stared at him.

Finally Blue said, "What planet are you from, man?"

Probably the planet Stupid, Jack thought, but he couldn't help it: The money didn't feel like his.

11

Al-Thani's call had been cryptic at best:

"We have big trouble."

The Arab hadn't wanted to say anything more over the phone, so Roman had given him his present address and waited.

Mid-morning now. The deal should have been completed. He had a bad feeling something had gone wrong between the Outer Banks and Staten Island. The big question: *How* wrong?

One look at al-Thani's face as he stepped through the door told Roman things had gone *very* wrong.

"Are you alone?" the Arab said as the door closed behind him. He sounded breathless.

Roman almost smiled. It had been too busy a night for the company of one of his ladies, but even if he'd had the time, no one stayed over. Ever. Not even the wonderful Danaë.

"Yes. Quite."

"The jihadists are dead and the money's gone!"

Roman liked to use al-Thani because he was smart and resourceful and unusually direct for an Arab, but this was almost too direct. The words were like a slap.

"What? How?"

"I don't know!" He pressed his hands against the sides of his head as he paced the suite's front room. "They were ambushed at the exchange point. An inside job! Had to be!"

"But only you and I and one of the jihadists knew the location on this end."

Al-Thani lowered his hands. "Tachus was a true believer. He would not betray jihad."

"Don't be so sure. Three million is a lot—"

"He is among the dead."

Well, that eliminated that possibility.

"What of the auction and its participants? This Tachus . . . he arranged it?"

"Yes. He let it be known to a certain circle of interested parties. They use computers now, so word spread like lightning. In no time he had more than enough bidders, so he set it up. But the prospective bidders knew only of the location of tomorrow night's auction, no details of the delivery."

"You're so sure?"

"Tachus himself didn't know until the last minute—I made sure of that. It has to be someone on the shipping end."

Roman couldn't argue against that. But who . . . ?

"The delivery drivers were killed too?"

Al-Thani shook his head. "Both gone, along with their trucks. It has to be them. You arranged that end."

It wasn't an accusation, not yet, but Roman could see it escalating to that once the High Council heard.

He chose his words carefully. "There were last-minute complications down there. They had to use a new driver."

"It must be him."

"No . . . not him." He felt a burst of fury as he realized who it had to be. "I learned that one of the Outer Banks men named Moose, who has been with the operation for many shipments, disappeared shortly before the trucks departed. It has to be him."

Al-Thani stopped pacing. "You think the money was too much to pass up?"

"What else can I think?"

"But wouldn't the drivers have to be involved as well?"

"Perhaps, perhaps not."

Roman could not imagine why, if involved, they wouldn't abandon the trucks and the girls and simply run with the money. But one of the drivers had been pressed into service; and the other, Reggie, had not been scheduled to drive.

"We found no trace of them."

"What if they were marked for the same fate as the Arabs and managed to escape?"

Al-Thani stopped pacing. "Then we must find them! They may know something."

"They certainly would have seen something." He jabbed a finger toward the Arab. "You get out to Staten Island and start asking around. I'll provide you with the makes and models of the trucks. Meanwhile, I'll start looking for Moose."

"You're going down to the Outer Banks?"

He shook his head. That had been his first instinct, but he'd discarded it immediately. He'd imagined himself as Moose—not his real name, of course, but that hadn't mattered until now—and tried to think like a piece of human slime. He'd deserted the Outer Banks house for . . . where? Where else? He'd raced to where the money would be.

"No. If he's anyplace, he's up here."

"Do you have any idea where?"

"No, but I intend to start looking for him . . . as soon as I inform the High Council."

Al-Thani straightened. "I handed the money to the jihadists. I will take full responsibility."

A noble gesture on the surface, but Roman dismissed it for what it was: empty. The betrayal hadn't originated with the jihadists, it had come from the Americans Roman had dealt with. He was the actuator and he'd made a miscalculation, therefore he would have to face the music.

But the heat he would feel for losing—even temporarily—three million dollars from the Order's coffers would be nothing compared to the suffering that would befall Moose when Roman found him.

12

Kadir opened his eyes and cried out in shock at sight of the man from Qatar standing over him.

He had a moment of disorientation until he realized he was back in his Jersey City apartment. He remembered his trek through Staten Island to the ferry, the ride to lower Manhattan with all the commuters casting side-long glances at his blood-sprinkled, gasoline-reeking clothes. Then taking the Path to the Jersey side of the Hudson. He'd collapsed with mental and physical exhaustion when he'd reached his apartment.

But how had the man from Qatar found him?

"You were supposed to go with Tachus," he said in Arabic. "Did you?"

Kadir saw no use in denying it, so he nodded. "Yes."

"Yet you live and he is dead."

Kadir made the only reply he was capable of at the moment. "Yes."

The man's expression never changed. He looked neither angry nor sad, simply . . . concerned.

"You will explain this."

Not a request, a statement. And in truth, Kadir was desperate to tell someone about the worst experience of his life.

"It all happened so fast, I—"

The man wagged his finger. "Not here. Downstairs. You will come with me and then you will talk."

Kadir led the man down four flights to the twilit street where an idling car waited with a stranger behind the wheel. Kadir settled into the rear with the man from Qatar and the car took off.

"Talk," said the man, watching him intently.

As the car found Kennedy Boulevard and drove west, Kadir told every-thing he could remember.

"Two men in masks . . ." the man from Qatar said softly after Kadir had finished. "You are sure there were no more?"

"Perhaps, but I saw only two. They spoke English to each other."

"What of the drivers of the delivery trucks—were they involved?"

"I don't think so. The killers shot at them as they fled, and talked of chasing them. The killers took the truck the drivers left behind."

The man rubbed his jaw. "Interesting."

Kadir wasn't sure why that was interesting, unless the man was wondering what the killers intended to do with the girls.

The man said, "And you say they shot Tachus and his men in the genitals after they were dead?"

Kadir winced at the memory of the mutilation. "Shot them *off*."

After a pause, the man from Qatar said, "Castration by machine gun. This makes me think this was more than simple murder-robbery. Is someone sending a message? Are we dealing with more than mere greed here? Is this someone motivated by anger?"

"But they did take the money."

"Well, why shouldn't they? It will finance their anger."

"Is this bad?"

"No. I rather think it is good. Angry people are easier to find."

In the silence that followed, Kadir noticed that the sun was gone; they had left Jersey City and were cruising through Bayonne.

"Where are we going?"

"To Staten Island. That is where this all happened, that is where we will begin. And you will help."

Again, not a request, a statement.

13

Jack jerked awake to the sensation of something moving on his shoulder. The first thing he saw was a dark-skinned young girl, standing close to his cot, reaching across him.

What—?

And then he recognized her: Bonita. She was adjusting the blanket over him.

He rubbed his eyes and sat up, mumbling, "*Buenos días, Bonita*."

She grinned. "*Es de noche*."

She'd had a shower and been given clean clothes. Her slightly frizzy hair was pulled back into a short ponytail. She looked like a different person.

He looked around. How could she tell? No windows here. How long had he been out? He'd had the damnedest time falling asleep on the cot, but when he'd finally dropped off, he must have crashed like a stone.

She stepped back and ran her hands over her brand-new pink sweatsuit. "*Le gusta?*"

Did he like it? Most of the girls her age in the city would probably think the look was a total disaster, but to her this sweatsuit was obviously a fashion coup, and just might be the newest thing she had ever worn. Plus it was warm and practical.

"Yes. I mean, *Sí. Me gusta mucho*." He smiled. "*Muy bonita, Bonita*."

She averted her gaze, and he wondered if anyone had ever told her she was pretty. She was. She had a dark beauty that would have fetched top dollar at the auction the Arabs had been planning.

His stomach turned at the thought of what would have followed.

Black strolled up.

"Sleeping beauty awakens at last. Time to roll, Archie. Our work here is done. The girls are out of our hands now."

Jack looked at Bonita and fought a powerful protective urge. But he had to go. He told her he had to leave. He pointed to the bustling nurses who seemed tireless and told her they'd take good care of her.

"*No!*" she wailed, tears springing into her eyes. "*Yo necesito que me proteje!*"

He assured her that she didn't need his protection, that the people here would keep her safe and see her home.

With a sob she turned and ran off.

"Let's go, Archie," Black said. "She'll be fine."

Jack felt a little uneasy about leaving her. What if this was all a sham and the girls would be shunted to an auction as soon as he left?

He shook it off. He had to get over that. Black and Blue had proven they had no compunction about pulling their triggers. No reason to spare Jack unless they were on the up and up.

Jack followed him toward the truck. "Hope so."

"Having a little trouble letting go?"

He shrugged. "That's usually not a problem for me."

He'd let go of everything else in his life. Why the reluctance to let go of her?

Black climbed in behind the wheel. "Maybe because you saved her life by preventing her from being drowned like a rat. Some say that makes you responsible for her."

"So I've heard."

He wasn't too comfortable with that. Being responsible for himself was turning into pretty much a full-time job.

"And when you think about it, you didn't just *save* her life, down on that beach in NC, you *killed* somebody to protect her. Yeah, no question about it: You two are bonded for eternity."

Swell, he thought as he dropped into the passenger seat and slammed the door.

"Well, it's going to be a really tenuous bond with me here in New York and her back in—where's she from, anyway?"

Black shrugged. "Don't know. Could be Puerto Rico, could be the DR, could be as far away as Guatemala. Someplace where they speak Spanish. Our job is cutting them loose from whoever's holding them, no matter where they come from. Getting them back there is her job."

"Does 'her' have a name?"

"Yeah, but you don't really expect me to tell you, do you?"

No. Not really.

"She here tonight?"

Black didn't bother answering, so Jack glanced through the windshield and saw Bonita staring at him. He waved, but she turned away.

"The female of the species," Black said. "Can't make sense of them."

Jack shook his head. "I think she was counting on me safeguarding her all the way back home."

"You just might be the first hero she's ever had."

Jack heard the garage doors rising behind them.

"And I walked out on her."

"But you didn't. You left her safe and in good hands."

"That's not how she sees it."

As the truck started to back up, Jack tried to put Bonita out of his mind. She was better off right where she was, and staying there now was the best thing for her.

"What's the plan?"

Black said, "My brother's wiped down the other truck. He's going to park it by a midtown fire hydrant and walk away. I'm going to drive you around for a bit, then get out and let you do whatever it is you do with your truck when you return from a run."

"And what'll you do then?"

"Train home."

"To the wife and kids and a blazing fireplace."

A prolonged silence followed, then, in a soft voice, "That'd be nice." Black shook it off and tossed him the mask. "Time for hide-and-seek."

"Again?"

"You seem okay, but the less you know, the better for all concerned, including you."

"What if I refuse?"

"I shoot you in the eyes."

Not a blink, not a hint of hesitation or smile. Jack had posed the question for the hell of it, but he couldn't tell if Black was kidding or not.

"Then I guess I'll put on the mask."

14

Reggie was sure he was dying.

His head hurt, maybe the worst headache of his life, but that paled against the agony blazing from his knees. He'd never felt anything like that. At first he thought he'd been kneecapped, but when his vision had finally cleared and he'd looked, he'd seen no blood. He'd felt them through his jeans, gingerly touching where they were swollen up like watermelons. Just broken . . .

Just broken? Nothing *just* about it. He'd never hurt so much in his life. How? He had no memory of breaking them. And he'd probably never get a chance to remember because he wasn't going to survive the night.

He'd barely survived the day. He was cold, wet, exhausted, hungry and thirsty as all hell, and now the sun was down. That meant he was going to get colder and wetter, and with no food or water, weaker and weaker.

When his vision had cleared, he'd spotted the roof of some sort of warehouse above the grass and reeds. After screaming his voice raw, he'd tried to stand, but that wasn't possible by any stretch. Getting on his hands and knees was even more out of the question. So he'd tried to crawl on his belly but his broken knees howled as they were dragged over the rough ground. Finally he'd rolled over onto his back and managed to crawl that way through the grass.

Took him fucking forever, but he made it to what he'd thought would be a road, but turned out to be little more than a rutted path. He tried again to scream for help, but could manage little more than a croak. His voice was shot.

Reggie lowered his head and sobbed. If anyone used this road, it was once in a blue moon. Had to face it: He was a goner.

He lay quiet, trying to remember how he'd come to this. Asshole Moose, disappearing, Reggie forced to take his place behind the wheel, arriving in Staten Island, meeting the—

Holy shit! The shooters! And that guy . . . Archie . . . he'd slammed Reggie's head against the door. Had he busted his knees? Reggie seemed to have a vague memory of—

Yeah! Shit, *yeah!*

Archie . . . standing over him . . . swinging a tire iron.

Archie broke his knees.

Reggie remembered someone else there, talking to him, but he never saw his face, and the words were a blur. But no mistake about Archie, that son of a bitch. He—

Lights! Headlights coming down the road.

Reggie dragged himself half onto the road and waved an arm. The car slowed, then stopped. A door opened and he heard voices babbling in a foreign tongue. He was lifted under the arms and dragged into the backseat of a car. His knees screamed at being bent and he would have screamed too if he had a voice.

And then he saw who was dragging him and almost wished he'd stayed hidden in the grass.

Arabs.

15

They'd been riding in silence for a while, with Jack safe inside his mask, wondering at the story behind these brothers. Where'd they get such a vendetta against pedophiles? Jack agreed the world would be a better place without them, but he wasn't about to make a career out of hunting them down and administering street justice. Had they been abused as kids? That was the only reason he could imagine two brothers winding up on the same path.

Then again, *were* they brothers? They sure as hell didn't look alike. Then again—

"Hey, Archie," said Black. "You can take off the mask and sit up now."

"You're not going to shoot me in the eyes if I catch a glimpse of the street?"

He laughed. "Nah. In fact, I want you to see something."

Jack straightened from the floor and pulled the backward mask off his head. He looked around at five-story tenements with fire escapes clinging like spiders to their brick faces. At street level, a parade of XXX and PEEP SHOW and MASSAGE signs. The doorways sported shills and hustlers; the sidewalks were full of girls in hot pants

He spotted a passing street sign: 46th Street and Eighth Avenue.

"Welcome to Hell's Kitchen," Black said. "Specifically, the Minnesota strip."

Jack had strolled here many times. Lots of offers of coke, weed, speed, rock, whatever, and come-ons from teen girls in hot pants—teen boys in hot pants too—though none as young as the kids in the trucks.

"Never knew why it's called that."

"Because back in the mid-seventies, Minnesota passed hard-assed antiprostitution laws that drove all their hookers here. They do tons of business when conventions are in town." He slowed and nodded toward Jack's side window. "Check out the kid at two o'clock."

Jack peered at the bustling sidewalk and saw a young boy in tight leggings, a skintight shirt, androgynous blond hair, and heavy eye makeup, shivering on the curb.

"Got him."

"Can't be over fourteen, you think?"

Jack gave him a closer look. The eyes looked old, but the rest of him . . . "Not a day."

"A chicken, waiting for a hawk."

Jack had heard the term—chicken hawks were older gays who went for young stuff. But this kid was definitely underage. He gave them a hopeful look. Jack shook his head.

Black said, "He look like he wants to be out there?"

"Looks like he's freezing his butt off."

"Right. That means somebody's running him. Wonder who?" He scanned the sidewalk as they moved on. "He won't be far away."

Jack sighed. "Man, this is sad."

"Yeah. Ten blocks of the dregs of society. They're on their way down, but haven't quite hit bottom yet."

He stayed on Eighth up to 53rd, cut over to Ninth, then headed back downtown. Different here. Still some peep and massage places, but mostly dingy storefronts, the darker doorways offering temporary shelter to shapeless homeless folks with their plastic bags and shopping carts, their gender uncertain beneath myriad layers of grime and old clothes.

A red light halted their downtown cruise at 44th. Up ahead Jack could see the bus overpass arching above the street into the Port Authority's upper levels. Suddenly his view was blocked by a splash of soapy water.

"That window's dirty as all get-out!" a voice shouted. "Needs a good cleanin'!"

One of the dreaded squeegee men. A lot of them worked by intimidation. They'd clean your windshield without asking, then demand payment. Some of them got real nasty if you refused. This one was bearded and could have been forty or seventy. Jack pulled a single out of his wallet and rolled down the window.

"Thanks," he said, holding out the bill. "It really needed that."

"Pleased to be of service," the guy said with a toothless grin.

"You gotta be kidding," Black said as the light changed and they rolled on. "These guys are a fucking plague. You don't encourage them!"

"The last thing I wanted was to draw attention to the truck. Well worth a buck to make him go away."

"Well, in that case, okay." Black pointed ahead and to the right as they crossed the Deuce. "There's rock bottom."

Skinny women, mostly various shades of brown, with a few whites sprinkled among them, stood along the curb under the overpass and hailed the passing cars headed for the Lincoln Tunnel or farther downtown. Their eyes were glazed and they looked unsteady on their feet.

"Under the overpass—a favorite site for the crack whores. Doesn't matter if it's raining or snowing, they stay dry."

As Black slowed to give Jack a better look, one of them waved and pulled up her top to reveal saggy breasts. The one next to her did the same.

"Know why they're doing that?"

Jack shook his head. "Well, if they think it's enticing, they need to think again."

"It's to show they're female." He barked a laugh. "Because some of those gals on the curb there ain't gals at all."

"What's to keep the ones who aren't from getting implants?"

"Can't afford it. In their world, all your income either goes into your arm or up your nose."

They speeded up, continuing downtown.

"That's where your little girls—the ones who somehow survived years of sex slavery and enforced drug addiction—would eventually wind up. We prevented that. And that's a good day's work, as far as I'm concerned."

Jack thought of little Bonita out there. It made him ill. Yeah, it had been a good day's work.

Black turned east on 34th, then headed back uptown on Eighth Avenue. He pulled into a loading zone near the Port Authority bus terminal.

"We split here. You're on your own." He thrust out his hand. "You're good people, Archie. You've got a lot to learn, but you're gutsy and your head's in the right place. Keep that compass pointing north."

They shook.

Jack still hadn't got a grip on Black and his brother. What was going on in their heads? Was this anti-pedophile "operation" as they called it a sideline or their life's work?

"Well," Jack said, for lack of anything better, "it's been interesting. Hardly a dull moment."

Black opened the driver door and slid out.

"You hear or see anything you think might interest us, tell Abe to give us a holler. He knows how to reach us."

Abe seemed to know everybody, and everybody seemed to know—and trust—Abe.

"And listen," Black added, "my brother and I were talking. We like the way you handle yourself. Sometimes we need an extra hand along. You up for that?"

What to say? These guys seemed on the up-and-up, but they had a lot of cowboy in them.

Jack shrugged. "Depends on what's involved. I'm not much of a shooter."

He smiled. "You can leave that to us. That's our favorite part."

"I'm low on ammo anyway."

He laughed. "Abe vouches for you and you're low on ammo? That's rich."

Whatever that meant. Figuring turnaround was fair play, he said, "Call Abe if you need me." He glanced over at the Port Authority. "Taking a bus somewhere?"

Hard to believe he lived in Jersey.

"Nah. Gonna walk up the Strip, see if that chicken's still there."

"And if he is?"

"I'll see if I can scope out who's running him."

"And if you do?"

"Watch him, find out where he hangs, where he lives, who he associates with, how many kids he's running, who else is in with him."

"And then what?"

He shrugged. "People go missing all the time in this city."

The casualness of the remark sent a chill through Jack.

"You two ever take a day off?"

"My brother and me, we're like rust."

Jack caught the reference. "A Neil Young fan?"

Black winked. "We never sleep."

He slammed the door and walked around the front of the truck as Jack slid into the driver seat. He put it in gear and headed uptown, tooting as he passed. Black waved. In the side-view mirror, Jack watched him start walking up Eighth Avenue with his hands thrust into his jeans pockets, looking like just another New Yorker ambling along the West Side.

No hint that he was a predator hunting other predators.

16

On the upside, the car was warm inside and the head Arab spoke English pretty well. When he heard Reggie's voice, he had his driver run into a 7-Eleven and get some water. It wasn't kindness. It enabled Reggie to talk.

On the downside, he wanted answers and he wanted them now.

"Our young friend here says he's seen you before," said the trim, well-dressed bearded guy who was obviously in charge. "I think you know where."

They'd positioned him on the backseat with his legs straight out on the cushions. His knees wouldn't bend so they didn't have much choice. A beefy guy was hunched behind the wheel, and a young, skinny, and scared-looking Arab sat at the end of the rear seat by Reggie's feet. The leader guy was twisted around in the front passenger seat to face him.

No use in playing games.

"I don't remember him, but I know whereof you speak."

"Good. Then you know that our money is missing. We want it back."

"Who's 'we'?"

"I will ask the questions. The money?"

Reggie sipped the Poland Spring. "Wish I knew. A couple of guys mowed down your people and—"

"*Not* my people, I assure you. Describe these . . . guys."

The scene was etched on Reggie's brain. "Two guys in ski masks with submachine guns came out of nowhere and started shooting. I was in Archie's truck at the moment—"

"Archie?"

"The new guy—that's what we called him. They started shooting at us so we took off."

The boss man looked at the young Arab by Reggie's feet. "Your stories agree. That is fortunate for you. And it gives us a start." He turned back to Reggie. "How did you wind up at the side of the road with broken knees?"

"Ain't rightly sure of that. Me and Archie had a fallin' out. Motherfucker left me for dead."

"Do you have a last name for this Archie?"

Reggie thought about that. Tony had introduced—shit, Tony. He wondered if Tim had offed him as threatened. Probably. Tim didn't like loose ends. Too bad. Reggie had met Tony only a couple of times and he wasn't a bad guy. But hey, he'd walked into the middle of a big omelet and got his shell broke.

Shit happened.

Did it ever. Look what had happened so far on this run, and Reggie had a feeling he'd only seen the tip of this stinking turd.

But what had Tony called the new guy when he'd brought him in? Larry? No, Lonnie. That was it.

"Archie's not his real name. We just called him that. Real name's Lonnie. But that's all I got. No last name."

"What was the nature of this falling out?"

What had it been? What had set him off? Oh, yeah. Archie—Lonnie—had kinda lost it when Reggie suggested sinking the truck with the girls on board. Pussy.

"We disagreed on what to do with the product."

"Where do you think he took the truck and its cargo?"

"Don't rightly know. But I'd like to catch up with that boy. We've got some settling up to do."

"That is your affair. We are interested in him only so far as he can lead us to these masked men. Do you think he was part of the plot?"

Plot . . . listen to this dune monkey.

Reggie was about to give him a hard *no*, but bit it back. This deserved a little thought.

Lonnie's reaction when the two masked guys started shooting had been pure shock. He hadn't been prepared for anything like that. But if Reggie said that to these Arab boys, they'd have no use for him. Might dump him in the harbor just to see how long he could stay afloat with two bum legs.

Probably a good idea to keep them interested in Lonnie.

Especially because Reggie was interested in Lonnie too. He craved a little face time with that boy—more like removing his face, or pounding it to a pulp. Yeah, they had a score to settle. Reggie was due some major payback.

He had an idea where he might find Lonnie, but he had to play this real careful. If he said Lonnie was part of the heist, and getting a share of the three mil, they wouldn't look for him where Reggie figured he'd be.

"No," he said finally. "Lonnie was just as scared as I was when those guys were chasin' us, but shortly before we had our falling out, I think he got a look at them."

The boss was instantly interested. "You are sure?"

"Well, yeah. Pretty sure. They took off their ski masks when they started chasing us. I guess they didn't intend to leave us alive to talk. I was on the wrong side of the cab, otherwise I woulda seen them."

"Do you think he could identify them?"

"Don't see why not. And I can identify Lonnie. I'm kinda anxious to find that boy myself."

"We seem to have a convergence of purposes."

Reggie had been counting on him seeing it that way.

"If I help you find him, you'll allow me a little alone time with him when you're done with him?"

"That depends on how cooperative he is."

Reggie allowed himself a smile. Poor ol' Lonnie wasn't going to be cooperative at all. Couldn't be. He hadn't seen any more than Reggie had.

Reggie wanted to be there when all this went down.

"I'll tell you how I think we can find him . . ."

17

Jack parked in the space Bertel rented for the trucks. He'd backed out of this same spot a little over three days ago. The damnedest seventy-two hours of his life.

He'd have preferred that the trip had gone down as just another cigarette run, but he couldn't deny that it had been—to quote Black from just a little while ago—"a good day's work." He was glad he'd interrupted Moose's assault on Bonita, even if it had meant killing Moose. Couldn't dredge up any regret for Moose—the human gene pool was better off with him in the skimmer. He'd spared Reggie's life at the cost of his knees. The pool would have been cleaner without Reggie as well, but Jack's blood simply wasn't that cold.

No question about being glad he'd saved those girls from brutalized futures.

The only part he regretted was Tony. He was probably—okay, most likely—dead. If Jack believed prayer worked, he would have prayed for his safety, but . . .

He'd liked Tony. Another guy living on the fringe. He'd been at it a lot longer than Jack and would still be at it if only they'd picked a different place to crash on Wednesday.

What strange turns his life had taken since that fight with Rico.

With the truck secure now, his next step was to find a phone and call Bertel. He'd probably been ringing the phone in Jack's hallway off the wall.

As he did a last-minute search of the truck's cab before getting out—didn't want to leave anything of his or Reggie's behind—he found a plastic shopping bag shoved between the driver and passenger cushions. Didn't remember seeing that before. He pulled it out and looked inside.

Money. Three banded stacks of hundred-dollar bills, each showing bullet damage. And a note:

If 10% is too much, how about 1%?
Deacon Blue

The bands on the stacks were each labeled *$10,000* . . . thirty thousand dollars.

Christ!

Only a small fraction of what they'd wanted to give him but still more money than he'd ever seen in his life.

Well, he didn't need to risk his freedom driving for Bertel anymore, but he owed him an explanation.

He went in search of that phone.

18

Bertel didn't want to discuss anything on the phone so they arranged to meet at The Spot.

Jack arrived first and found the usually cheerful Julio in a frowning funk, short with the patrons, slamming things around. The place was half empty—not a good sign on a Friday night—and although Julio couldn't be happy about that, the low turnout didn't seem to be what was bothering him. Without saying what was in it, Jack asked him to stow the shopping bag with the money behind the bar for safekeeping.

Jack worked on a pint of Rock near Barney and Lou, ensconced in their usual spots with their shots, drafts, and ashtrays arrayed before them on the bar. Smoke from their cigarettes blunted whatever stinky cologne Julio had splashed on tonight. He wondered if their butts came from packs he'd smuggled out of NC.

When Julio went out on the floor to take table orders, Jack leaned toward Lou.

"What's eating Julio?"

Lou, the closer of the two, shook his head. "Lotta shit comin' down."

Barney raked his long, greasy hair back with nicotine-stained fingers. "*Lotta* shit. You don't wanna know."

I don't? Jack thought. Yeah, probably not. Then again . . .

"Maybe I do," he said. "Try me."

Barney and Lou appeared to be asexual, and they lived in different neighborhoods, but as Jack had got to know them, they struck him as an old married couple. They'd been drinking together so long they could finish each other's sentences—and often did.

Lou leaned closer and lowered his voice. "Well, he's getting pounded on multiple fronts."

Barney leaned around Lou's shoulder. "Yeah. First off—" He glanced up and over Jack's shoulder. "Later. Here's your buddy."

Jack turned and saw Bertel pushing through the door. He looked tight, tense, haggard, and years older. He pointed to a table toward the rear of the room.

Jack nodded to Lou and said, "To be continued," then grabbed his beer and joined Bertel.

"Why the fuck didn't you call before tonight?" Bertel said as they seated themselves.

Jack bit back a fuck-off retort and said, "I'm glad you're okay too. You had me worried there for a while."

Bertel stared at him a moment, then leaned back. "Sorry. Been a shitty day. And knowing you—which hasn't been very long, but long enough—you probably had a good reason for staying incommunicado."

Jack nodded. "Twenty-eight of them."

Julio swung by then, dropped off a pint of Rock for Bertel, and sailed away without a word.

"Maybe I don't want a beer," Bertel said to his retreating back.

Without looking around, Julio raised a single-digit salute over his shoulder.

"You don't want it," Jack said, "I'll see it doesn't go to waste."

"Nah, that's okay. Just felt like something stronger is all."

"He'll be back. Where do you want me to start?"

"When you reached the Lonely Pine is as good a place as any."

"All right. I got there and no Tony, so I—"

" 'No Tony,' " Bertel said, closing his eyes. He took a shuddering breath. "Ain't that the truth."

Jack went cold. He'd suspected, but he'd kept hoping . . .

"Aw, no. What?"

"They killed him."

"How do you know?"

"It's involved. He called me Wednesday morning to tell me about the raid. Said he was going to pick you up and get you away from the motel in case it had been compromised. Called later and said he had you stashed at a place on the Outer Banks and was sending you home empty in the morning. Last I ever heard from him. I knew the place he meant—smugglers use it a lot—"

"Smuggling what?"

"Everything from drugs and guns to handbags and hooch. You name it. Why?"

Did Bertel know about the girls? If he did, so help him—

He forced calm. He'd get to that. "What about Tony?"

"Early this morning I headed down there. Found it crawling with cops."

"Cops?" So, Deacon Blue had made the call as promised.

"Yeah. So I drove on and contacted a guy I've got on the tab in the NC State Police."

"You own a state cop?"

"I don't *own* him—I just contribute to his retirement fund to keep him looking the other way."

"And he didn't warn you about the raid?"

"The tip went to ATF. He was off duty when the feds informed the staties that they were raiding. But here's what he told me: They found a body inside they identified as Tony Zahler."

"Zahler?"

"That's our Tony. That was his real name. He'd given me a phony last name when he joined up but I traced him. He'd been double-tapped in the head. Brains all over the wall."

Jack felt his jaw muscles bunch. Tim . . . that bastard.

"Shit."

"Found another guy half buried in a dune nearby, skull stove in. Know anything about that?"

Jack shook his head. None of Bertel's business.

Bertel leaned forward, face tight, expression tense. "But what I want to know is why Tony's dead down there and you're alive and well up here?"

Jack gave him a quick rundown, involving only minor details about Blue and Black—he implied that they never took off their masks—and leaving out the thirty thousand they'd left him. Bertel might get the idea he deserved a piece of that. He didn't.

Bertel gave his head a baffled shake. "No idea who these two crazies were?"

"Never saw them before, hope never to see them again."

"Well, I'm glad for the little girls. I just hope those crazies were dealing straight with you."

"I don't think I'd be sitting here if they weren't."

"Yeah, good point. What gets me is none of this would have happened if some lousy snitch hadn't dropped a dime on my operation. You been talking to anyone you shouldn't?"

Jack gave him a look. "Think about what you just said. How can I talk when I don't know what *town* your warehouse was in, let alone the street address?"

Bertel was reaching into the pocket of his jacket. "Yeah, well, be that as it may, I want you to listen to the bitch who called in the tip."

"Where'd you get—? Oh, right. Your guy inside."

"He managed to get a copy from ATF."

He pulled out a battered Walkman cassette player and hit a button. A woman's voice with a heavy Southern drawl talked about a warehouse she knew of that was being used for all sorts of smuggling—drugs and guns, for sure—and how they'd better get on it and shut it down or she was going straight to the *News and Observer.* She was hard to hear at times over the dog barking in the background. She hung up without giving her name.

Jack almost laughed. "Trust me, I don't know anyone who sounds even remotely like that. Tony mentioned someone named Billy as a possible leak."

Bertel nodded. "Yeah. Billy's a good possibility." He pounded the table once with his fist. "Damn! Tony'd still be alive if he'd just kept his mouth shut."

Well, that was true. Tony also would still be alive if he hadn't gotten fancy and simply let Jack drive back north with an empty truck. And he'd be alive if they'd gotten up Thursday morning, eaten lunch, and just kept on driving.

Jack hesitated, then decided what the hell. "How well did you know Tony?"

"How well do you know anyone in this business?"

"He gave you a phony name."

Bertel shrugged. "So what? Just a layer of protection. You should talk, Jack *Moore*."

Uh-oh. Had he found Jack's real name?

"But I don't care about your real name. You came with a good recommendation."

"Me?"

"Abe said you could be trusted. Good enough for me."

Abe's word seemed to carry a lot of weight with people. The brothers, and now Bertel.

"You trust Abe?"

Bertel stared at him. "Abe is not a frivolous man. Anyone who has dealt with him knows that. His word is gold."

Dealt with him how? He sold sporting goods. Or was he something more? Was he a banker to shady enterprises?

"Did Abe vouch for Tony?"

"Naw. Never heard of Tony, I'm sure. No, Tony bought his way in, so—"

"Wait-wait. *Bought?*"

"He came to me about six months ago and connected me to a guy in Detroit. He wanted a piece of that business in return. He wasn't asking anything unreasonable, so I brought him in. He worked the Detroit shipments, made sure they went out on time. Did a good job so I put him on running the Mummy's flow as well." He shook his head. "Good man. Why all these questions about Tony?"

Jack told him the Hasid story.

Bertel's expression could have been carved from stone, but his eyes carried a strange mixture of disbelief tinged with alarm. Yet when Jack finished he brayed a laugh and pointed to Jack's empty pint glass.

"How many of those did you have Monday night?"

"Not that many."

Bertel hadn't touched his so Jack hoisted it and sipped.

"How many Orthodox guys would have the same scraggly beard—"

"Plenty."

"—which, by the next time I saw him, he'd shaved off, as if he didn't need it anymore. Add to that his big bright smile and you've got Tony playing dress-up."

Bertel shook his head. "It just doesn't make sense, Jack."

"Well, not to me. And he denied it when I asked him—"

"Well, there you go."

"But he wasn't completely convincing. I was hoping you could shed some light."

"Well, I can't. If it's true, it's disturbing—more than a little. But I can't see him getting involved in Arab-Israeli politics, especially an assassination. He wasn't the type."

Jack had to agree. Tony seemed to be a career criminal, but not violent. But you never knew. Whatever the facts, Tony was dead and gone, so Jack would most likely never know. He didn't like not knowing, but Bertel's remark triggered another question.

"Speaking of Arabs, is your Mummy still alive?"

Bertel made a face. "Is he ever. Spent too long on the phone with him today listening to him complain about missed shipments. Why?"

"When we met up with the slavers, they were all Arabs. I'm sure I saw a couple of them in the Mummy's warehouse."

The Mummy's Warehouse . . . sounded like a movie he didn't want to see: Kharis as a tanna leaf wholesaler.

Bertel shrugged. "I'm not surprised. Some of them are raising cash any way they can and they're not squeamish about how."

"What for? Using sex slave money to build mosques?"

"I think some money is going back home to less savory groups."

"The kind who like to blow up civilian shoppers in Tel Aviv?"

"Very likely."

Well, Jack knew of three million of their cash that was going to be put to a different, better use.

"And you don't mind being a part of that?"

Bertel bristled. "Who says I'm a part of anything? You saw—*think* you saw—some of my Arab's minions. That doesn't mean they were working for him then. Could all have been extracurricular."

He had a point.

"Could be."

Bertel looked away. "Listen, I provide a service—at least I did until someone put the FUBAR on it. I supplied a *number* of people and I will supply them again. But I can't help what one of them *might* do with his earnings. If you take the money I pay you and go buy crack, am I responsible for increasing drug cartel profits?"

"Not quite the same as blowing up innocent people."

"Don't be so sure. And why are you asking me about the Mummy anyway?"

The sudden switch to another subject wasn't lost on Jack, but he let it go. Bertel was on the defensive and pushing him would get nowhere.

"Because there was somebody in the limo before the brothers arrived and started shooting up the place. Whoever he was, that was his last ride."

"Well, it wasn't my guy. The Mummy's alive and complaining. I should be up and running again next week—on a reduced scale, of course—so be ready for a call."

Jack shook his head. "I don't know . . ."

"What? You're not going to leave me high and dry, are you? Kick me when I'm down?"

Sheesh. "Nobody's kicking you. I've just . . . lost my taste for it."

Bertel leaned forward. "You're putting me in a real bind, Jack. Tony's gone, and now you're quitting—without giving notice? Without time for me to find a replacement? You think that's fair?"

No, it probably wasn't. And Abe had vouched for him, so he owed him to play square with Bertel. He didn't really know what this Mummy guy was doing with the money. Could be building mosques.

"All right," Jack said. "Consider this my notice: I'll give you three more runs and then I'm out."

Bertel nodded. "Fair enough, I guess. But if I can't find a replacement by then—"

"Three and out."

Jack hoped his tone carried the finality he felt. He wanted to put a period on this very brief chapter of his life. He wasn't going to do this anymore.

19

After Bertel left, Jack wandered back to the bar with the remnant of the second beer. Lou and Barney were exactly where he'd left them.

"You didn't make your friend happy while he was here," Barney said.

"Maybe because I took his beer."

Lou exhaled a cloud of smoke. "He looked as unhappy going out as he did coming in."

"Yeah, but for different reasons." Julio was back out on the floor, so Jack said, "You were saying about our friend? Like, what's eating him?"

"Well, first off," Lou said, "he got word that Harry's kid is putting his share of The Spot up for sale."

Barney nodded. "Between the recession and his late, great, fern-brained ay-hole father screwing around with dee-cor and serving shar-doe-nay, the place is runnin' in the red."

"But he's gone. Julio can change the place and—"

Lou was shaking his head. "The kid's in Saudi Arabia and he put his mother in charge, and she's worse than Harry."

Saudi Arabia . . . Arabs seemed to keep popping up one way or another.

Barney added, "He don't want the business. He says if he don't find a buyer by the end of the year, he's closin' the place down."

"Can he do that?"

"Owning ninety percent, yeah, he can."

"Well, that's a great opportunity for Julio to buy that ninety percent."

"Julio ain't got no, whatyacallit, discretionary income."

Jack wasn't surprised and tossed his suspicions up for grabs. "Because of the protection he's paying?"

Barney and Lou stared at him for a long moment.

"Where'd you get that idea?" Barney said.

"I saw him pass an envelope to that mob type—I mean he was right out of central casting."

They did their married couple thing. Lou started.

"That's Vinny Donuts—"

"—works for Tony Cannon—"

"—with the Gambinos—"

"—and it ain't protection—"

"—it's for a loan Harry had before he died—"

"—and if Julio don't pay—"

"—the Cannon's gonna sic Vinny on Harry's wife—"

"—so Julio's fronting the vigorish."

Julio soared a bunch of notches in Jack's estimation.

"So Julio's got nothing to buy with," Barney said. "And if sonny boy do find a buyer, there's gonna be lotsa changes made. And it's a damn good bet—"

"—I'd say it's a *sure* bet, wouldn't you?" Lou added.

"I won't disagree, my friend. It's a *sure* bet the new owner's gonna do a clean sweep."

"Which means, anyhow you look at it, Julio's out of a job by New Year's Day."

"Maybe sooner."

"But he's part owner," Jack said.

Barney shrugged. "Yeah. Which means he gets ten percent of the profits—ten percent of zilch."

"But that's just the background noise," Lou said.

"The Muzak, you might say."

"What's really chewin' on his ass—"

A phone began to ring behind the bar. Barney waved to Julio but he'd heard it and was already on his way. He ducked under the service counter and snatched a receiver from somewhere out of sight.

"The Spot."

As he listened, his face darkened and his lips drew back from his teeth into a fierce snarl. He began shouting in Spanish so rapid Jack could barely make out a word. Then he slammed the receiver down, yanked the phone from the wall, and threw it across the room.

"Awright!" he shouted. "Everybody drink up and get out! We closing!"

Lou and Barney looked at each other in alarm, then at Julio.

"Hey, it's Friday night, Julio. You never—"

"Closing time!" the little man shouted.

He grabbed a Louisville Slugger from under the counter, then ducked back out onto the floor.

"Closing time!"

He kept repeating the phrase as he moved around the room. Not many tables were occupied, but he went from one to the next, slamming his bat on each tabletop, sending drinks flying and customers scurrying for the door.

SLAM! "Closing time!"

Jack watched in awe. "No wonder the place is dying."

"Never seen him like this," Barney said.

Lou said, "Gotta be Rosa again."

"Rosa?" Jack turned to them. "Who's Rosa?"

"His older sister. Married a gringo a few years back. Neil . . . ?" He looked at Barney.

"Zalesky."

SLAM! "Closing time!"

"Right. Neil Zalesky. He kept wailing on her, so she cut him loose. They're divorced now but he keeps coming back."

Jack said, "Why doesn't she get a restraining order?" He wasn't sure exactly what that was, but knew it was supposed to keep stalkers and abusive spouses away.

"She's got one," Barney said.

"Yep. Got two or three."

"But they don't matter to this ay-hole."

SLAM! "Closing time!"

"Nope. He sneaks in whenever he pleases and scares the shit outta her."

Jack shook his head. "That's why they've got police. All she's got to do is report him and . . ." Lou was shaking his head. "What?"

"She does."

"Every time."

"But his buddies always say he was with them."

"Got half a dozen alibis."

"Every time."

SLAM! "Closing time!"

"He just laughs and calls himself 'the Ghost.'"

"Should call himself 'the Ay-hole.'"

"Used to do it just once in a while."

"But now that Rosa's got a new boyfriend—"

"—he's doin' it more and more."

"Musta just scared the shit outta her again."

"She keeps calling Julio—"

"—seein' as he's the man of the family."

"—askin' him to do something."

Julio returned to the bar then. He'd emptied the room. Only Jack, Lou, and Barney remained.

"Sorry, guys. Gotta close."

"The *hijo de puta* again?" Barney said.

"What he do this time?" Lou said.

Julio's lips peeled back from his clenched teeth. "Took a dump on her pillow."

"Aw shit!"

"That ain't funny, Lou," Barney said.

Lou looked confused a second, then shook his head. "Oh, no. Didn't mean it like that, Julio."

Jack winced at the thought. That was low. Really low.

"S'okay. But you guys go. Got somethin' I gotta do."

"Like what?" Lou said.

Barney squinted through the smoke from his cigarette. "You ain't gonna do anything stupid now, are you, friend?"

Julio tapped the business end of the baseball bat against his palm. "Gonna find out if ghosts bleed."

Sounded as if Julio had been pushed over the line and was going to "do something" about Rosa's problem.

Barney and Lou started yammering at once.

"You don't want to do this."

"He'll know you did it."

"The cops'll tag you."

"You'll be locked up."

"And he'll be laughing all the way back to Rosa's place."

Julio glowered as his dark eyes fixed on a point in space, as if imagining how good it would feel to swing that bat and hear bones snap. "Not if he's in hell."

Lou threw up his hands. "Oh, yeah! Get sent up for life!"

"That'll show him!"

Julio still had that thousand-mile stare. "At least he won't be botherin' Rosa no more."

Part of Jack wanted to walk away, but another part had to speak.

"There's a better way."

Julio looked at him. "Hey, Jack. You a nice guy an' all, but you don't know—"

"We told him about Zalesky," Barney said.

"Yeah." Lou's voice dripped scorn. "The *Ghost*."

"Right now the law is on your side," Jack said.

"The law ain't doin' shit, meng."

"Yeah, but you go off half-cocked, it'll be on *his* side, and he'll use it against you."

"So what do I do?"

"Two can play his game," Jack said.

Julio looked interested. "How you mean?"

"Well, he's got guys lying for him when he's out messing with your sister. When something bad happens to him, you can have a whole roomful of people vouch for you."

"Who?"

Jack gestured to the room. "Everybody drinking here—I mean, when you haven't chased them all away."

Lou and Barney guffawed.

Julio frowned. "But if I'm here, who's bashin' his skull?"

"Somebody else. Like me, for instance."

"Why would you bash him? You don't even know Rosa."

Jack shrugged. "I know you. And head bashing is a last resort. Maybe his life can become so miserable he'll forget about Rosa."

"Yeah? How?"

"Don't know yet. How's he make his living?"

"Any way he can," Barney said.

Lou waved a hand. "Told Rosa he was in sales but he's mainly in cons."

"As in scams?" Jack said.

All three of them nodded.

"He lie to my Rosa," Julio said. "Said he was in real estate."

"Commercial real estate," Lou added. "But he ain't. Just another one of his scams."

A con man . . . interesting.

"Who does he target?"

"Little old ladies with money," Barney said. "He stays away from people who can come back at him."

"Sounds like a swell guy. Why don't you let me check him out?"

"Check him out how?"

"Find out his weaknesses. Everybody's got weaknesses."

"And then you bash his head in?" Julio said.

Jack thought of Moose. He didn't want to make a habit of that.

"If it comes down to that . . . if there's no other way . . . let's just say we leave that on the table. But if his head's gonna get bashed, it would be nice to work it so somebody unconnected to all of us does the bashing."

He got three puzzled looks.

"A guy like that's got to have enemies, right? And if he doesn't have the right kind, maybe I can make him some."

"You do this for me?" Julio said.

"Haven't done anything yet. Just going to check him out and see if there's a way to hurt him and keep you out of jail." He pointed to the bat. "Meanwhile, you put that away, I'll buy us all a drink, and you can tell me all about this Neil Zalesky."

Julio stowed the bat back under the counter. "Okay. For now. We try it your way. But I'm buying."

Jack had no idea where this would lead. His money worries were gone for the moment, so why not see where this took him? He'd fixed problems and situations for people at home and at school—sometimes they knew it, sometimes not—so why not try his hand here in the city?

Might be fun.

SATURDAY

1

Jack placed the black plastic platter on the counter and, with a flourish, whipped off the clear cover.

"Oy!" Abe cried as he took in the array of bagels, lox, cream cheese, sliced Vidalia onion, and capers. "For me?"

First thing this morning, Jack searched out a kosher deli and had them put together a breakfast platter for four. This was what they gave him. From what he'd learned of Abe over the months, he couldn't think of a better way to express his appreciation than through food.

"The least I can do. You saved my life—literally."

"How? When?"

"Yesterday—when you got that call about me."

Abe had produced a Special Forces knife from somewhere and was already slicing a bagel.

"You're here only a few months and already you're running afoul of the Mikulski brothers. You managed this how?"

Mikulski brothers . . . so that was their name.

"Wasn't easy."

Abe began smearing cream cheese on the bagel halves.

"You're very lucky I was here. They were thinking bad thoughts about you, and it's *nisht gut* to have those two thinking bad thoughts about you." He slid the knife across the counter to Jack. "Have a shmear."

Jack took the knife and began sawing at a poppyseed bagel. It sliced through so quickly he almost cut his hand.

"Sharp!"

Abe was positioning a slice of onion on the cream cheese. "I should bother to keep a knife that isn't?"

"These Mikulski brothers . . . what's their deal?"

Abe shrugged. "I should know? No one knows. Some say Mikulski might not even be their real name. That it's maybe the name of an abused child who died. What I do know: Like ghosts they move. It's a name you fear if you involve children with sex. You don't want those shtarkers to find out, because that's when you disappear."

Jack mimicked what Abe was doing with the onions and slices of smoked salmon.

"Well, I think you saved me from disappearing."

Jack placed the bagel top over the goodies in the middle, making a sandwich. He took a bite and the combination of flavors exploded in his mouth—the saltiness of the lox, the sweetness of the cream cheese, the tang of the onion.

"Holy crap! This is great!"

Abe stared at him in wonder. "You've never had bagel and lox?"

"Never."

"Such a deprived childhood you had."

"Hey, you know where I grew up. We were lucky we got mail delivery. I never tasted Chinese takeout till I got to college—"

Abe's expression was horrorstruck. "No Chinese—?"

"—and no one was serving lox and bagels in Johnson, New Jersey, I promise you."

"Well, then, welcome to Hymietown."

Jack pointed at him. "Jesse Jackson . . . 1984, right?"

"Such a memory."

He remembered discussing that remark in Mr. Kressy's civics class back in his freshman year of high school.

Abe said, "With that memory, you must recall how you crossed the Mikulskis." He waggled his fingers in a come-to-me motion. "Tell."

Jack gave him a somewhat different version from what he'd told Bertel—more emphasis on the brothers, less on Tony.

Abe had finished his first bagel-and-lox sandwich during the story and was assembling a second by the time he finished.

"Such a string of good luck for those girls," he said.

"What do you mean?"

"First, the raid on Bertel's place. That leaves you with no job and at loose ends. So your friend just happens to take you to a place where the girls will be delivered."

"But not till the following night. We were going to take off the next morning."

"Yes, but the driver of the second truck has an accident and is arrested. You are drafted into driving in his place. The Mikulskis are tipped and are waiting. You escape with this mamzer Reggie who would have drowned the girls if you hadn't been there."

Jack had to agree—an impressive string of good luck for them.

"Had a bit of luck myself at the end," he said as he placed a shopping bag on the counter.

Julio had kept the grocery bag behind the bar and knew from the get-go it contained cash. On returning it he'd given Jack the paper shopping bag because he thought it was safer.

Abe took a big bite of his second bagel. "Nu?"

"The brothers, shall we say, *confiscated* some cash from the dead Arabs and—"

"A cut they gave you? Such charity. And you're giving it to me?"

That hadn't been Jack's intention at all, but he did owe Abe his life.

"Well, not all of it, but I'll be glad to split—"

Abe waved him off. "A vits! I don't want your gelt. How much they give you?"

"Um, thirty grand."

His eyes widened. "Thirty—" He looked in the bag. "A hefty percentage."

"Just one."

"One? That means . . . oy. But it stands to reason, considering the buyers were ready to purchase thirty little girls." He shook his head. "Those words—like smutz they taste." He tapped the basket. "Nu. Why you bring this here? You like basketball? A whole court I can sell you."

"I need someplace to put it."

"You mean invest?"

"No. Store it. I never realized how bulky cash can be. I'm running out of space. And if there's ever a fire—"

"A storage locker?"

Jack shook his head. "Don't trust it."

Abe rubbed his chin, smearing cream cheese along it. "You need the money right now?"

"No. I've been making good bucks and the long hours leave me no time to spend it. So it's piling up. I can't get a bank account or safe-deposit box, so—"

"Ever consider gold?"

A weird suggestion. "Like a gold bar?"

"Bullion coins. Like Krugerrands. Gold closed yesterday at three eighty-five an ounce. You could convert all three hundred bills in that bag into seventy-five or so Krugers. Easy to hide and they don't burn."

Jack shook his head. "Like I said, I'm not looking to invest it."

"Invest, schmest. If you keep the bills, you're investing also."

"In what?"

"In the fiscal responsibility of the politicians who run your government."

"I don't think I like the sound of that."

Abe picked up the knife. Was that a third bagel sandwich he was making? Yes, it was.

"You shouldn't. Any investment is a bet. Hold on to cash and you're betting the government will rein in inflation and control deficit spending."

"I might be better off in a casino down in AC."

"Bullion coins are portable, anonymous, and liquid. If you can hold on to gold, expect fluctuating value in the short run, but, as inflation continues, expect a steady rise over the long run. Hold on to paper and inflation will steadily sink its value."

"I'll have to think about this."

"Thinking is good. What? You're done eating?"

2

Jack left the Isher Sports Shop with the intention of heading straight home and stashing his cash. He was supposed to meet Julio in an hour or so and didn't want to be lugging all this money around.

He was just turning away when a sixtyish guy in a yellow Windbreaker and plaid pants hurried up and pulled open the door to Abe's shop. The bell attached tinkled as he rushed in.

Jack wondered what the hurry was, then realized this was the first customer he'd ever seen in the Isher Sports Shop. He followed him back inside to see what was all the hurry.

"Got any golf balls?" the man said as he approached the counter.

Abe didn't look up. "Some," he said around a mouthful of bagel.

"Where would I find them?"

Still not looking up, Abe waved toward his left. "Over there."

"Where over there?"

"Somewhere."

"Could you be a little more precise?"

Finally he looked up. "I should know where every little thing is?"

"Isn't this your store?"

"Who else's would it be?"

"Well, then . . . ?" After a raised-eyebrow/and-your-point-is? look from Abe, the guy threw his hands in the air and trudged off in the indicated direction. "Fine! I'll find them myself."

He disappeared behind one of the high, disordered shelves. Grumbling and rattling soon emanated from the far side.

"You really don't know where they are?" Jack said in a low voice.

"You're back?"

"Yeah, I'm back."

Abe shrugged. "I'm not even sure I have any."

"Want me to help him?"

"Why? You know where they are?"

"Well, no, but—"

"Then stay put already."

A few minutes later the guy returned, red-faced as he blew dust off a twelve-pack of Titleists.

"What the hell are golf balls doing under a badminton net? And what are these—antiques?"

"Yes, antiques," Abe said as he held out his hand. "Fifty dollars, please."

"What?" The guy got even redder. "You've got to be kidding!"

"Like you said—antiques."

Now the guy was speaking through his teeth. "If I wasn't going to be late for a foursome, I'd—"

"Plus tax," Abe added.

The guy looked ready to explode as he reached for his wallet. "There's got to be a law against this." He pulled out a credit card.

"Cash only."

He violently shoved the card back into its slot and pulled out three twenties.

As Abe hit some keys on an old-fashioned steel cash register and made change, he said, "Why for you should want to chase a little ball around? Don't you have better things to do?"

"It relaxes me."

"You don't look relaxed."

His red complexion deepened. "That's because I—" He shook himself. "Never mind."

"Read a book already," Abe said, handing him his change. "You'll relax and maybe learn something."

The guy said nothing as he grabbed his change and pointed to his dusty purchase. "Got a bag for that?"

Abe shrugged. "Bag, schmag. Who needs a bag? Not me. I should carry something I don't need?"

The guy snatched up his golf balls and stormed away, shouting, "This is the worst goddamn service I've ever—" He made a choking sound. "In the *world!* Hell will freeze over before I ever come back. I'm telling everyone I know to avoid this place like the plague!"

The door slammed behind him, cutting off further clichés.

"Have a nice day," Abe said and took another bite of his bagel.

Jack stared at him, dumbfounded. He'd just witnessed customer relations from hell. What was Abe trying do, drive customers away? He—

And then wheels turned and gears started meshing in his head. Bits and pieces of seemingly unrelated data—occurrences, comments, and knowing looks—collided and clung, allowing a realization to take form.

Jack stepped back to the counter and slapped his hand on the scarred surface. "I need some ammo."

Abe concentrated on his bagel. "So? I need a watch battery. This is conversation?"

"To load the Ruger you sold me."

Now Abe looked up, his expression neutral, his voice flat. "Go lock the door."

Jack hesitated—this was not the expected denial—then did as Abe said. When he returned to the counter, Abe was already on his way to a rear corner. Jack followed. Abe unlocked what looked like a storage closet but turned out to be an empty space. He pushed on the rear wall, which swung away on hinges, then flipped a light switch and started down a narrow stone staircase. Words flickered to neon life on the staircase ceiling.

FINE WEAPONS
THE RIGHT TO BUY WEAPONS
IS THE RIGHT TO BE FREE

Something familiar about that.

They passed it, reached bottom . . .

. . . and stepped into an armory.

Jack froze on the threshold, gaping. Light from the overhead incandescents glinted off racks of pistols and rifles and other instruments of destruction like switchblades, clubs, swords, brass knuckles, and miscellaneous firearms from derringers to bazookas.

It all made sense now.

The scene upstairs had demonstrated the impossibility of Abe selling enough sporting equipment to pay even the rent, let alone put food on the table. Add to that the quick arrival of the Ruger, the offhanded comments from Bertel and the Mikulskis, and it all made sense.

He closed his gaping mouth and found his voice. "Your real business."

"You're surprised?" Abe said as he stepped over to a wall cabinet and opened the doors.

"Well, *yeah*."

"You're offended?"

A man he knew and trusted had just revealed that he was a gunrunner. The term had such an evil sound. But no way Abe was evil. Was he offended? He searched his feelings and couldn't come up with any disgust or revulsion. Offended? Not at all . . .

"More like fascinated. Did Mister Rosen know about this?"

"My dear uncle? Of course."

Jack closed his eyes . . . the neon words in the stairwell were a quote . . . and the store was called the Isher Sports Shop.

"A. E. van Vogt!" he blurted.

Abe glanced at him. "You've read him?"

"Used to belong to the Science Fiction Book Club. *The Weapon Shops of Isher* is a classic."

"I'm glad you get it. Hardly anyone else does." He held up three boxes of ammo. "One three-fifty-seven Mag and two thirty-eight Specials for target practice—good enough?"

That should hold him for a while. "Sure."

"I'm adding a nylon SOB holster as well."

"Son of a bitch?"

"Small of the back."

"Cool. Can I look around?"

"I should stop you? Look already."

Jack wandered the aisles.

"Who do you sell to?"

"Individuals. No bulk sales. Some want one gun for protection. Some want one of everything—it's like porn for them. And like a porn shop, I stock some novelty items."

"Like?"

"M-fifteen, AK-forty-seven, grenade launcher—fun stuff."

Jack had to ask: "Um, you ever worry that one of the guns you sell will kill an innocent person?"

Abe shook his head. "If I sold cars I should worry whether my customer is a drunk and will run down a lady pushing a baby across a street?"

"But a car—and I'm just playing devil's advocate here—a car isn't designed to make holes in things."

Abe gave him a hard look. "You read the papers or listen to the TV or the mayor, you're told over and over there are too many guns on the street. They like to parade around the latest shooting victim of the crack wars and say we—some nerve they've got saying 'we'—must pass more laws to control this deadly plague."

"Well, you can see their point: You can't shoot somebody if you haven't got a gun."

"But you can stab them. Should we have knife control laws too? And we can crush their skulls with a Louisville Slugger. Should we have baseball bat control laws as well?"

Jack held up his hands. "Okay, I get it."

"Do you?" Abe said, approaching. "Do you really? How many guns in the U.S.?"

"I have no idea."

"Most people don't. Well, it averages out to one per person. One in four own a gun, and gun owners average four apiece. The new census is expected to show the population now at around a quarter billion. That means there's two hundred fifty million guns in the U.S. You want to talk gun violence? Okay, let's talk about how many of those quarter-billion guns were *not* involved in violence yesterday. Or the day before. Or the day before that. There's no gun problem. There's a media problem and a politician problem, but there's no gun problem."

His intensity was a little intimidating. Jack noticed a sudden lack of Yiddishisms but decided not to mention it.

Obviously he'd touched a nerve. Might be a good idea to change the subject. He glanced to his left and saw an array of semiautomatic pistols.

"Ooh, pretty." No lie. He was starting to understand the guns-as-porn concept. "I-want-I-want-I-want!"

Abe paused, shifting gears. "Which?"

"All."

"More lessons you should take before you go semi. The care and feeding is more complicated. More moving parts."

"I don't know if Bertel is up for that. I think I've been crossed off his list of favorite people."

"I can show you breakdown and cleaning. But get comfortable with your Ruger first." He placed the ammo on a counter—smoother and cleaner than the one upstairs. "You pay for these down here."

As Jack counted out the money, Abe slipped the boxes into a plastic Gristedes bag.

"Should I feel special?"

Abe gave him a quizzical look. "Nu?"

"I mean, I'm getting a bag."

"No bags upstairs, always bags down here. I should let you walk out my front door carrying live ammo for all to see?"

3

After leaving Abe's, Jack returned to his place and stowed the money and ammo behind another section of molding. Gold coins would probably weigh more, but they'd take up less space . . . and they wouldn't burn. At least he wasn't living over a restaurant or anything like that, but he didn't know how many of his neighbors smoked in bed. A fire . . . that would put him back to square one financially. No, behind square one, because he'd lose all the savings he brought with him.

He gave in to an urge to call Cristin. They'd had no contact since Tuesday and he wondered if they were still on for tomorrow night. He stepped out into the hall and dialed her number on the pay phone. She wasn't home so he left a kind of pointless message on her answering machine saying he'd call her back to firm up Sunday. Well, if nothing else, it would act as a reminder.

He'd thought he could live without a phone, but an answering machine might make life easier.

Okay . . . he had the rest of the day ahead of him to check out Julio's sister's nemesis. Julio had offered to take him by Neil Zalesky's place in the Bronx.

They met outside The Spot where Julio stood sipping his coffee from one of those blue-and-white paper cups that all real New York delis seemed to use—with the Greek urn on the side and "We Are Happy to Serve You" in red. Last night he'd been all gung-ho about accompanying Jack this morning; now he didn't seem so sure.

He wore snug jeans and a tight black T-shirt that showed off his bulging pecs. Obviously he worked out. He'd topped it off with an unzipped bright red jacket of some satiny fabric. Jack would have loved to see *Sharks* stitched across the back, but no . . .

Jack sniffed the air. "No cologne?"

Julio made a face. "You ain't gonna start, are you, meng. I get enough of that from Lou and Barney."

"Just making an observation."

"Too early for a scent. Ain't gonna see no chicks, anyway. And no matter what you guys say, chicks love scents."

Some guys were born with peacock in them. Jack supposed it was natural. The male cardinal was bright red, the female dull gray. The male peacock had all the feathers. That gene had missed Jack. Maybe it had never been in the cards anyway. The only time he'd ever seen his father stand in front of a mirror was to shave, comb his hair, or tie a tie. At least Dad wore suits. Jack tended to wear the first thing his hand touched when he reached into the closet.

Julio had peacock in his blood. The thin, carefully trimmed mustache, the work he put in on his body, the way he dressed. Maybe his height had something to do with it, but here was a guy who strutted his stuff for the ladies. Jack didn't know how successful he was, but if he failed, it wouldn't be for lack of trying. For his cologne, maybe, but not for lack of effort.

Jack said, "We need a car."

"Ain't got a car."

"Neither do I, but I figured we could borrow one."

Julio frowned. "Borrow? No one's got a car here, meng."

Jack gestured to the long row of cars parked along the curb in front of The Spot, a solid line broken only by spaces left for fire hydrants. "What do you call these?"

"They're decorations. We locals got subways, we got buses, we got feet."

"Yeah, but if Zalesky's got a car, we need to follow him."

He still had his Harley garaged downtown. It could carry them, but that was too exposed.

"Shoulda told me last night. I coulda asked around."

Jack shook his head. "Not what I want. Our ride's got to have no connection to you or me."

"We gonna rent one?"

"No. Renting would make a connection. I meant steal one."

Julio made another face, more dubious than the first. "Steal? How?"

"Figured we could hot-wire one."

Dubious morphed to incredulous. "You know how to hot-wire a car?"

He used to. He'd done it back in high school when he felt like a joyride. But he'd only wired old cars where he could hide his handiwork afterward and return the car to the spot he'd found it. No one had ever caught on.

Cars were tougher now, and he was out of practice.

"I was depending on you for that."

Julio choked on his coffee. "Me? Hey, meng, why you asking me? Because I'm Puerto Rican?"

Jack hadn't expected this. "Well, no, I just—"

"Yeah, I know what you *just*. You just *assume* the PR knows how to steal a car, is that how it is?"

"Hey, listen—"

"No, you answer me, meng. Is that how it is?"

"So you're telling me you do *not* know how to hot-wire a car."

"Course I do. But you shouldn't just assume, know what I'm sayin'?"

"All right, all right. I—"

Julio grinned and backhanded Jack across his upper arm. "Gotcha!"

Jack shook his head and smiled. "Bastard. So, we gonna do it?"

"Sure."

"What's the first step?"

"We get a flat-head screwdriver and a hammer and find the oldest car we can that ain't locked."

"Why old? I might want something flashy."

"You want flash, I'll flash you my ass. We want old because they got less safety shit on them. If you're lucky, you just hammer the screwdriver into the keyhole, give it a twist, and she start up."

Jack shook his head. "Not looking to screw up anybody's car."

"What, you got like ethics 'bout boostin' a car? You kiddin' me?"

"Just want to borrow it, is all."

"Then we need some tools."

Julio knew a mom-and-pop hardware store around the corner. He bought rubber cleaning gloves—pink, because that was the only color available in the cheap brand—a wire cutter/stripper, and a Phillips screwdriver. Then they walked down the block, Jack on the street side, Julio on the sidewalk, testing door handles. They found a 1984 Plymouth Reliant coupe with an unlocked passenger door. This had been a new car when Jack had been hot-wiring. It might have come off the assembly line some sort of blue but that had faded to a dull gray trimmed with rust.

Julio slid over behind the wheel and motioned to Jack. "Get in. I'll show you how it's done."

He knew how it was done, but he'd never done it in daylight. He looked around, suddenly feeling exposed.

"Right out here in public?"

"It's still early on a Saturday. People are asleep, like I should be. Get your ass in here. The whole thing is looking like you belong here. Do that and nobody give you a second look."

As Jack slid in and slammed the door, the smell hit him. By all appearances, the owner was a cigar smoker and a sloppy eater. Spilled drinks stained the seats, petrified French fries dotted the floor. It smelled like he'd been smoking rotten food. No wonder he'd left the door unlocked. Who'd want this rolling landfill? On the other hand, maybe he was hoping it would be stolen.

Where was Julio's cologne when you needed it? Even his worst was better than this.

Julio pushed the seat back and checked under the steering column. He found what he wanted and put the Phillips to work. In less than a minute he'd popped the plastic cowl. He tossed that in the backseat and tugged some wires loose.

"See the two reds? One's always hot, the other's not until the key turns and connects them. Since we don't have a key, we connect them by hand."

Jack played naïve as Julio put on the pink rubber gloves.

"That color is so you," Jack said.

"Hot pink to help a hot guy do a hot wire."

Snip-snip, strip-strip, twist-twist, and the wires were joined. Jack jumped as Richard Neer's voice came through the radio.

Julio grinned. "Easy, man. It's only the FAN."

Jack turned it off. He'd noticed a change in Julio's diction since he'd entered the car.

"What happened to 'meng'?"

Julio looked flustered for a second. "Oh, yeah, well, that's just my Rican thing. Gotta project a certain amount of street, y'know?"

"You a native?"

"Full blood Nuyorican—born in Harlem Hospital, grew up on East 102nd."

"You sound like you grew up speaking English."

"Yeah. My mother insisted. My grandmother never learned so we had to speak Spanish to her, but the rest of the time it was English all the way. I could sound pure gringo if I wanted to, but I don't. 'Cause I ain't pure gringo. I'm no kinda gringo."

"I hear you, *meng*."

Julio dropped his head and groaned, then looked at Jack. "I say this as a friend: You don't *ever* wanna do that."

For kicks, Jack pushed it. "Really? I don't sound 'street'?"

"No, you sound beat—as in *lame*, not -nik."

"I get the feeling you're saying I'm too white bread to be street."

"In a nicer way, but yeah, that's what I was getting at. You saying 'meng' is wrong in so many ways, too many to count. It's wrong like . . . like turkey-flavored ice cream is wrong."

Jack's gorge rose at the thought. "*That* wrong?"

"Yeah, that wrong. Anyway, the red wire's now hot—"

"Thus the term 'hot wire.' "

Julio gave him a sour look.

Jack shrugged. "Can't help it. When I was a kid I ruled at Master of the Obvious."

"We don't play that in Harlem, but I believe it. Okay. Here's your ignition wire."

He snipped that and stripped a half inch of insulation from the tip.

"Now watch," he said.

As he put his foot on the gas, he touched the ignition wire to the exposed area of the hot wire. The engine roared to life.

"You da meng!" Jack said.

Julio's face showed real pain. "Jack . . . please?"

"Okay, okay."

Julio put it into gear and pulled out onto the street.

"We head for the Bronx."

Jack couldn't resist: "No thonx."

4

Julio drove him to a mixed commercial-residential area along Crosby Street in the Pelham Bay section. It reminded Jack a little of his own current neighborhood.

Julio pointed to some apartments over an Italian bakery. "The *hijo de puta* lives on the third floor there."

"Think he's home?"

Julio shrugged. "Who knows?"

"You know his number?"

"By heart. I call him alla time, tellin' him to stay away from Rosa."

Jack pointed to a phone booth a block up. "Pull in up there and tell me the number."

Jack hopped out, dropped a coin, and punched in the number. He hung up when a man answered.

Yep. Home.

They parked the car and wandered into a used-book store across the street. The delicious smell of old paper engulfed him as he stepped inside the door. Two small tables, each flanked by a pair of ladderback chairs, sat in the sunlight streaming through the window. He found a bin full of paperback books with their covers missing. Fifty cents apiece. Such a deal, as Abe might say. Keeping an eye on Zalesky's door through the front window, he poked through them until he found an author he'd heard of. Robert Ludlum: *The Icarus Agenda*. Hadn't read that one. For half a buck, how could he say no? He found a Stephen King novel for Julio.

A carafe of coffee sat beside the cash register. Jack paid for the books and two paper cups. They each poured themselves a cup and settled at one of the sun-soaked tables.

Julio looked askance at the coverless book. "This is all messed up, meng."

"The whole box was like that."

"We gonna sit here and *read*?"

"No, we're gonna pretend to read while we keep an eye on the *hijo de puta*'s doorway."

"Hey, you say that pretty good."

Well, why not? He'd heard Julio say it enough times.

Jack flipped the title page and the first thing that caught his eye was a warning:

> *If you purchased this book without a cover you should be aware that this book is stolen property. It was reported as "unsold and destroyed" to the publisher and neither the author nor the publisher has received any payment for this "stripped book."*

Swell.

So far this week he'd smuggled illegal alien minors across numerous state lines, killed one man, broke another's knees, and now this.

A life of crime, that's what I'm living.

He started reading. He was participating in robbing an author of a royalty. Not quite on a par with the rest of the week, but still it bothered him. However, he'd already bought it and needed it for a prop. Could be a long while before a *hijo de puta* sighting.

Not so long, it turned out. Less than two hours later, a trim, darkly handsome guy in his early thirties stepped out of the door next to the bakery.

"That him?"

Julio looked up. His lips twisted into a snarl as his fists crushed the book. He opened his mouth to speak—

"Never mind," Jack said, rising. "I'm going to follow him." Julio began to push back his chair but Jack waved him down. "Stay put."

"But—"

"He knows you. Never seen me."

Jack stepped out into the cold fall air. He'd been getting a little drowsy inside and found it bracing.

Zalesky was wearing a dark suit with a white shirt and conservative striped tie. A long way from the Saturday morning dress code of his neighbors. As he walked south he adjusted a dark fedora over his slicked-back hair. Looked like he was on his way to a Mormon prayer meeting. Or a con.

Jack followed him around the corner onto Roberts Avenue to a plain black Dodge Dynasty sedan parked on the street. As Zalesky got in and started the engine, Jack realized he was pointed away from Crosby. If he headed up that way, they'd lose him. He looked around for a taxi. He could follow and call Julio later. His pulse picked up a little as he realized the street showed not a trace of yellow. To Jack's relief, Zalesky pulled out of his space, did a three-point turn, then cruised back Jack's way.

Jack turned and beat him back to Crosby. Zalesky passed him on the corner and turned south. Jack ran to the bookstore and signaled Julio through the window.

"Come on! Gotta move!"

He and Julio raced for their car and got it rolling. Fortunately, lots of other cars were traveling south on Crosby as well and Zalesky hadn't gone far.

Even better when Zalesky turned into a car wash. Julio pulled over and they waited.

"Car don't even look dirty," Julio said.

"I'll bet he's got a good reason for wanting it spotless."

"Meeting a mark?"

"Why else?"

They waited. About five minutes later the Dodge, all shiny and glittering with a few remaining drops of water, emerged from the car wash and turned their way.

Julio trailed Zalesky to the Bruckner, and then all the way south to the Brooklyn-Queens Expressway. They exited the BQE into Brooklyn Heights. Jack admired the panoramic view of the lower half of Manhattan Island. Beautiful, even if marred by the gray jutting towers of the World Trade Center. Jack called them the Twix Towers. They weren't simply too damn big, they were obnoxiously unimaginative, unbalancing the skyline. He might have forgiven them all that, but then they'd gone and provided a location for that awful remake of *King Kong*. Unforgivable.

"Looks like we're in *Moonstruck* territory," he said aloud.

"What's *Moonstruck*?" Julio said.

"A movie. With Cher."

Julio grinned. "You a Cher fan?"

"She's okay. Got dragged to it. It was set right around here."

Karina had wanted to see it when she was home that first Christmas break after starting college. Nicolas Cage must have turned her on because the sex was hotter than usual that night.

These local streets were slow and narrow, and Jack started to worry that Julio was staying too close behind Zalesky.

"Let a car or two get between us."

"I might lose him."

"Better than him realizing he's being tailed. Worse yet, recognizing you through the windshield."

"Got it."

True to his word, at the next opportunity he let a car pull out of a parking space and get between him and Zalesky.

Jack figured losing Zalesky would be bad luck, but it left the option of following him another day. If they were made, however, Zalesky would be on guard from then on and another chance would be unlikely.

They followed the Dodge on a winding path until it double-parked before a three-story row house. Jack turned his head as Julio glided past.

"What now?"

Jack thought about that. He'd been playing this by ear. He still wasn't sure he was going to see anything happen today, although the suit, the tie, and getting the car washed were pretty good indications.

"Drive around the block and park where we can watch."

Julio did just that and idled in a no-parking zone by a fire hydrant with a view of the row house and the Dodge. A few minutes later Zalesky emerged with a dowdy woman who appeared to be in her seventies. He held the door for her as she lowered herself into the rear of the Dodge, then he walked around to the driver side.

"That looks like one of the marks he used to brag about to Rosa."

"Always old ladies?"

"Sometimes old guys, but mostly the ladies. Mostly because he's a charmer. You know, good-looking, big smile, talks the talk. People like him. Even I liked him. Didn't like him sniffing after Rosa but she was *loco* for him and I was her younger brother, so what did I know about love?"

"Why old? No jealous boyfriends to get in the way?"

"You'd think, but he told her he needed his marks from a certain generation because he had to be able to 'appeal to their sense of civic duty.'"

"He said that? Their 'civic duty'? What the hell did that mean?"

"Yeah. I asked Rosa but she didn't know. He wouldn't say. Wouldn't say a lot about his scams. Said it was 'proprietary information.'" Julio shook his head. "Told her not to marry a gringo."

"Hey, we're not all bad."

"Ain't sayin' that. But if she stayed in the community, well, we got ways of handling certain situations."

Jack understood. "But Zalesky's out of reach. Nobody can take him aside and straighten him out."

"Some guys don't straighten out so easy. Some *never* do. That *hijo de puta* is one of those. But he ain't outta reach. He may think so, but he ain't."

Jack wanted to keep him out of reach of Julio's bat—for Julio's sake.

"How does this work again?" Jack said.

Julio shrugged. "Don't 'xactly know. Like the man say, 'proprietary information' and all that. He told her he convinces the marks to take money out of their bank accounts and give it to him. How he do that, I dunno."

"Tell me what you *do* know."

"Okay. First thing the *hijo de puta* do is he find himself a lonely old person. Some guy who lose his wife, some lady who lose her husband. Like I said, he prefer the ladies 'cause he so fucking charming. That how my Rosa fall for him. But he swing both ways as long as they got enough money."

Jack couldn't help making a face. "This doesn't involve sex, does it?"

Julio laughed. "Doubt it, meng, but nothin' too low for that—"

"—*hijo de puta*, right. But where's this 'civic duty' come in?"

"Don't know. He showed Rosa some kinda badge once, said he pretends to fight fraud. Ain't that somethin'? The *hijo de puta* con man pretends he's fighting fraud."

"Well, if I wanted to rob somebody who had a burglar alarm, I'd pretend to be a burglar-alarm repairman."

When Julio didn't respond, he looked over and found him staring.

"What?"

"You been planning to rob a place with a burglar alarm? Or that just pop off the top of your head? 'Cause either way it's kinda scary."

Jack didn't think so. Just seemed logical.

"So somehow he gets them to help him fight fraud by giving him money? Doesn't make sense. He makes a living out of this?"

Julio nodded. "Six figures."

"Yow. Doesn't anyone report him?"

"Who knows? All I know is he don't get caught. At least not yet. He did tell Rosa he make a point of not cleaning them out. He sting them and move on. They poorer and he's richer."

Jack thought about someone doing that to his grandmother when she was alive. Or old Mrs. Clevenger from town. He frowned. Why had he thought of her? She hadn't seemed like the type to fall for a scam. He shrugged it off. Didn't matter.

Either way, it would have pissed him off.

The next leg of the trip was short. They followed the Dodge a few blocks to the local Chemical Bank branch. Again Zalesky did the chauffeur thing by opening the rear door for the mark. She stepped out carrying a small black briefcase and went inside.

"What's this?" Jack said.

"Only thing I can see happening in there is she's gonna fill that thing with cash."

Jack shook his head. "Does not compute. If I'm a bank teller and I see a little old lady coming in to withdraw a large amount of cash, I'm suspicious. I'm wondering if maybe this lady is being coerced—you know, someone's holding a gun to the head of her grandson or her cat until she comes up with the money."

"I dunno, meng."

Less than ten minutes later she emerged and reentered the car.

"That was quick," Jack said. "Gotta be something else going down."

They followed the Dodge a short distance until it parked. Julio found a space for their car where they could sit and watch it idle.

"What the hell?" Jack said.

This was weird. If Jack hadn't been told this was a con, he might have expected Zalesky—sorry, the *hijo de puta*—to clock her, kick her out of the car, and run off with the money. But that would change it from a con to a mugging. He would have paid a princely sum to know what was being said in that car.

Suddenly the driver door opened and Zalesky stepped out with what looked like the same briefcase. Only this one had two pieces of bright yellow tape stretched across the top, one over each lock. He placed it in the trunk and returned to the driver seat.

Jack was baffled. He glanced at Julio. "Does any of this make *any* sense to you? Ring any bells from what Rosa told you?"

Julio shook his head. "No. Nothing."

After a twenty-minute wait, Zalesky retrieved a taped briefcase from the trunk and returned to the car.

"Okay," Jack said. "He had two identical briefcases in the trunk. He puts in the one with the cash and takes out the duplicate filled with—what? Newspapers? But no mark is *that* stupid. Anyone with half a brain is going to open that briefcase to make sure the money's still there."

The Dodge started moving again, straight back to the row house where Zalesky opened the rear door for the lady who emerged with the briefcase—sans tape. He walked her to her door and, after a brief hug, hurried back to the car and sped off.

"A hug?" Jack said, totally bewildered. "He gets a hug? What's going down here?"

"Told you the *culo* was smooth."

Yeah, but this was beyond smooth. This was supernatural.

As Jack watched him drive off, he wondered if there was anything here he could turn against Zalesky. He didn't see it. He didn't know enough. At least not now.

But letting him drive away with that old lady's money didn't sit well either.

"Keep on him," Jack said.

5

Zalesky drove straight back to Pelham Bay, found a parking spot on the same street as before, and reentered his front door carrying the briefcase.

"Gotta go," Julio said. "Gotta open up. Gotta keep the place open as many hours as possible."

"Keeping that baseball bat behind the bar wouldn't hurt either."

Julio smiled. "I hear you, meng."

"Go ahead," Jack said. "Take the car. I'll train home." During their cruising around he'd noticed elevated tracks a couple of blocks away. The subway wasn't sub this far up in the Bronx.

Jack let Julio roar off and returned to the bookstore where he pretended to browse but kept his eye on Zalesky's door.

He didn't have to browse long. Zalesky popped back out a few minutes later—in casual clothes and with no briefcase—and headed in the opposite direction with the stride of a man who knew where he was going.

Jack followed, but not before passing close enough to Zalesky's door to see what kind of lock it had. A Schlage. Good. He knew Schlages inside and out.

Jack closed in on Zalesky and checked him out. He'd changed into jeans and a sweatshirt. Did he have the old lady's cash on him? Probably not. Didn't make sense to carry heavy cash. Which meant he'd left it in his apartment. Did he stash all his dough there as Jack did, or did he have a safe deposit box somewhere? He was a real citizen with a real-person identity, and a box would make better sense than a cash cache or a bank account. An account would track deposits and withdrawals; if he ever was investigated for anything, the IRS might want to know the source of those deposits and why taxes hadn't been paid on them.

So Jack figured it was a relatively safe bet that Zalesky's latest haul was sitting somewhere in his apartment, at least for the remainder of the weekend.

He followed the man to a bar-restaurant called The Main Event. Jack passed the place, walking on for about half a block, then doubled back. He strolled in and took a seat at the bar. In the mirror he saw Zalesky standing by a table where three other guys of varying ages were seated. All were grinning. Then he turned and headed Jack's way.

"Yo, Neil," the bartender said.

Jack tensed as Zalesky leaned on the bar not a foot away. But Jack might as well have been invisible.

"Hey, Joe."

"'Sup?"

"Lemme have a Bud Light and a round for the guys. Put it on my tab."

"You got it."

He returned to the table and seemed in a great mood.

Well, he should be, Jack thought. He'd just ripped off somebody's grandma. Buy *two* rounds, Neil-baby. You're one helluva guy.

"So you're really Joe the bartender," Jack said, chatting him up. "*The* Joe the Bartender?"

Joe smiled. "The original. When Sinatra sings 'Set 'em up, Joe,' he's talking about me."

"Can you set me up with a Bud Light draft, Joe?"

He ordered a Bud because that was what Neil and company were drinking and Jack wanted to fit in.

"Need to see some proof."

Jack showed him the Lonnie Buechner license Bertel had supplied.

"North Carolina, huh?" Joe handed it back. "You're a long way from home."

"Just checking in on my grandmother," he said, thinking of the old lady Zalesky had scammed.

The bartender filled a glass and Jack sipped it slowly. It tasted like cold piss cut with seltzer, which fit his mood just fine.

"Bad day?" Joe said.

Jack looked up. The bartender was staring at him.

"Me?"

"You look ready to punch someone."

Jack blinked. *Exactly* how he felt. Did it show so clearly? He needed to work on an everything's-cool face.

"Outta work," he said.

Joe nodded. "I hear ya. A lot of that going around. Wish I could help but things are tight all over."

"Thanks anyway."

The bartender wandered away, leaving Jack to watch the *hijo de puta* in the mirror and ponder his next move.

6

Roman Trejador glanced at the bowl of curried shrimp that room service had just delivered, then looked up at Nasser. His eyes seemed wary.

"So, the only witnesses we have are a frightened Palestinian who was hiding most of the time, and a driver whose prospects are best served by telling us what we want to hear."

That's quite a negative spin, Nasser thought, but pretty much on target.

"We also have the name of the other driver, who got a look at the thieves."

"Whom we are *told* got a good look. Do you believe we can trust this—what was his name?"

"The driver we have is named Reggie—"

"So he says."

Nasser knew a good actuator survived by being suspicious of everything and everyone.

"He also says the other driver's name is Lonnie."

"Just . . . Lonnie? That's almost as bad as having no name."

"Reggie says he knows how to find him."

"I think you should strangle this Reggie for being a liar. Or shoot him in the knees to see if he's telling the truth."

"His knees are already broken."

Trejador smiled briefly. "Touché."

"And he thinks Lonnie broke them, so we can assume he's motivated to find him."

The actuator poked at his shrimp. He didn't seem to have an appetite.

Nasser was about to ask a very important question when a door opened and a woman wearing only a black teddy stepped through. He recognized her as the young prostitute from last month. In midafternoon?

She looked surprised when she saw Nasser.

"Oops, sorry, I didn't—oh, it's you again." She smiled at Trejador. "You didn't tell me this would be a threesome."

"It's not, Danaë."

She pouted. "But I *like* threesomes."

"I'm sure you do. Why don't you go take a bubble bath in that ridiculously huge tub while I talk to my associate here."

"You'll scrub my back?"

"Of course. Now shoo."

As she turned and closed the door behind her, her teddy lifted to reveal a delightful pair of bare buttocks. Nasser felt a stirring in his pelvis that almost made him forget his question. But not quite.

"How did the High Council take the news?"

Another poke at the shrimp. "About as expected."

"They needn't worry. We will get the money back."

"It's not the money; you know that."

Nasser did. The Order was richer than the Vatican, and far older. Even so, three million U.S. was hardly a negligible sum. But the amount didn't matter. The principle mattered. Someone had stolen something that belonged to the Order. No members of the Order had been hurt or killed in the process—the only bright spot in this cesspool—but the fact remained that someone had stolen from the Order, and that could not stand.

Which brought up the most important question. "Did . . . did they say anything about me?"

Trejador nodded. "Very disappointed."

Nasser swallowed. "What does that mean?"

"They said 'adjustments will be made.'"

Nasser didn't like the sound of that. "'Adjustments'? What does that mean?"

"I'm not sure they knew at the time. We'll find out when they decide."

For an instant Nasser wished he were back home in Qatar, but then, the Order had a presence in Qatar. The Order was everywhere.

He looked at Trejador. "Do you want to speak to him? The driver?"

"Why would I want to do that?"

"Maybe you can get more information out of him."

"I sincerely doubt that. I have more pressing matters."

Like what? Nasser thought. A soak with your whore?

But he said, "Anything I can help with?"

Trejador paused, then said, "Yes, I believe you can." He reached behind him and produced a floppy computer disk. He held it out to Nasser. "Before giving you the money I had the serial numbers recorded."

Nasser took the five-inch disk and stared at it. "You suspected?"

"No, but I prepare for the worst. Distribute copies to our brothers in the banking industry. Many of the bills have consecutive runs. Have them alert their people to be on the lookout for those numbers."

"This is brilliant!"

"No, it's a long shot. No bank can afford to check every bill that comes through, but they can keep their eye on large cash deposits or large cash transactions." He shrugged. "Who knows? We may get lucky."

Nasser's spirits lifted at this ray of hope. "What about the driver—Reggie?"

He sighed. "Get his knees repaired and put him to work."

Nasser hurried off with the disk, leaving the actuator with his cold shrimp and the very hot Danaë.

7

He watched Zalesky's door.

Earlier in the day, Jack had left The Main Event to make a quick trip by train to his apartment where he retrieved his lock-pick kit.

He'd worked in Abe's uncle's store as a teen. Every so often Mr. Rosen would buy an old piece of furniture—an armoire, a china cabinet, a bureau—that would arrive locked with the key long lost. The old guy had a lock-picking kit and had taught Jack how to open the doors and drawers without a key. Later, Jack had bought a kit of his own and had kept it through college. The skill had come in handy many a time when drunken dorm mates would find themselves locked out of their rooms.

He'd returned to Zalesky's neighborhood in time to see him wander home from The Main Event. With nothing better to do, Jack hung around, hoping to see him leave. And sometime after dark, he did just that, carrying a small duffel. But he was dressed all in black—black jeans, black sweatshirt, black sneakers and socks, even a black watch cap. Not nearly as dashing as Cary Grant in *To Catch a Thief*, but he did look like he might have a little B & E action on his mind.

Jack's plan had been to break into his apartment while he was out and relieve him of a certain black briefcase. But Zalesky's commando-like get-up piqued Jack's curiosity. What the hell was he up to?

Only one way to find out.

Going after the briefcase could wait until later.

He followed Zalesky to the nearby train station where he hopped the 6, just as Jack had earlier. Jack boarded one car back. He stood by the door at the front end of his car so he could watch Zalesky. When he got off at Longwood Avenue, Jack had a pretty damn good idea where he was going.

Rosa's.

Julio had given him her address, and the *hijo de puta* was headed in that direction. He gave Zalesky a half block lead on Longwood and watched him turn onto Rosa's block on Hewitt Place. But when Jack reached the corner, he was gone.

Not good. Was he in the building already? If so, Jack had to warn Rosa. He found a phone booth on the opposite corner and called The Spot.

"Is Rosa home?" he said when Julio answered.

"No. She working. Why?"

"I think 'the Ghost' is about to pay another visit."

Some garbled Spanish, then, *"I be right there."*

"No-no-no. You stay put. Be your usual less-than-charming self. Make sure everybody knows you're there."

"What're you gonna do?"

"Zap him with my neutrona wand."

"What?"

"Never mind. Just stay there and be noticed."

Jack found a shadowed doorway and watched the three-story building. Julio had said Rosa's apartment was on the top floor but Jack didn't know which windows were hers. So he kept watching the third floor, waiting for lights to go on. And while he was watching, he spotted movement on the roof—just a hint. As if someone dressed in black was lurking up there.

Had to be Zalesky. Either he knew how to pick a lock or he'd gotten hold of a key. Jack had no key, but he had something almost as good.

He removed a tension bar and a couple of picks from his kit, then crossed the street toward Rosa's front door. The outer door opened into a small vestibule; the inner door was locked. The doorknob was a Kwikset. Cool. He loved Kwiksets.

With his left hand, Jack inserted the tension bar into the knob's keyhole and applied gentle clockwise pressure. He worked the pick in and began raking the pins in the cylinder. He didn't have to crouch to watch what he was doing because it was all done by feel. Eventually the pins fell into place and the cylinder turned. He gave the tension bar a final twist, the latch retracted, and the door swung open.

He slipped inside and immediately started up the steps. He hurried to the roof door and found it wasn't alarmed. He eased it open and peeked out. No movement, no sign of anyone up here. Had Zalesky slipped back down while Jack had been fiddling with the lock? If—

He spotted a length of rope running from the chimney to the edge of the roof. He padded over and peeked. The knotted end of the rope dangled next to a third-floor window. This cheater of old ladies had more guts than Jack would have thought.

Keeping to a crouch, he moved to the chimney and found the duffel—empty. Must have held the rope. He inspected the knots fastening it to the chimney. He couldn't identify them but they looked sturdy.

Okay . . . how to play this?

He could pull the rope up and make Zalesky improvise, but all he'd have to do was leave by the apartment door and walk downstairs.

Jack had a three-inch folding knife in his back pocket. He could wait till Zalesky was climbing back up and cut it. But the cut end would leave no doubt he'd been sabotaged.

Hmmm.

8

Ghost time again.

Neil was feeling pretty good as he stood in Rosa's hallway. He'd had a few beers at the Event but he'd paced himself and had some food too. Their pepperoni pizza was tops.

Like last night, he'd called the bitch's floor at the hospital and did his hang-up bit. So, he knew where Rosa was. And he knew where her brother was. Julio wasn't very big but he was a tough little spic and would probably take a box cutter to Neil's face if he caught him here. But Neil had had one of the guys from the Event call Julio's bar and he'd answered. His friend had asked how late he'd be open, got his answer, then hung up.

He did a flashlight scan again and found nothing. No surprise. Even if she was planning a trap, the Ghost had never visited two nights in a row, so this was going to blow the bitch's fucking mind.

When he reached her bed he pulled down her covers, unzipped his fly, and let his bladder go. He sighed with relief as the stream started. A lot of it was beer and he'd been holding it for a good hour. Man, he soaked that thing through and through. No just changing the pillow this time around. She was going to have to get a whole new mattress.

He finished, shook a few times, then tucked in and zipped up.

This was just too easy. He was tempted to do something else, but stifled the urge. Save it. He was going to be back again and again. But he couldn't resist opening the refrigerator. He saw the carton of skim milk on the top shelf. He'd have to do some thinking and come up with something interesting to drop into that.

Something whitish that might mix unnoticed in the milk.

He smiled. Next time.

He returned to the window, leaned through, and grabbed the rope. He swung outside, lowered the sash, and started to climb. He'd gone only two steps when suddenly the rope went slack and he was falling.

"Oh, Christ!"

His left hand shot out and his fingers caught the ledge of the bitch's windowsill. He had a grip for a second but lost it before he could cross his right hand over. He saw the rope falling past him as be began to drop again. He grabbed at the ledge on the second-floor window below but his momentum was too great.

He hit the floor of the alley with a gut-wrenching, bone-crunching thud that sent pain shooting through his shoulder and chest, and down his left thigh. It took every ounce of will to keep from screaming like a girl.

Cutting through the pain was the razor-sharp realization that someone must have cut the rope. But then he saw the blue-taped upper end lying on the dirt a couple of feet away. He'd put that tape there himself. The knots must have slipped and come undone. But how?

He looked up at the edge of the roof.

How?

Never mind. Had to get out of this alley. Couldn't get caught here. With that restraining order and all, he'd be in deep shit. He tried to rise but a burst of agony forced a yelp of pain past his clenched teeth.

He was going to have to crawl.

9

Jack had untied Zalesky's knots and just begun retying the rope with his own when it went taut and started to vibrate. Someone was climbing it. Jack yanked on the free end of his knot and it came undone. He heard a cry of *"Oh, Christ!"* from below as the rope whipped away and disappeared over the edge.

Oops.

He couldn't help wincing at the *thud!* that immediately followed. Not a pretty sound.

He held off a full minute—timed it with his watch—before peeking over the roof edge. He spent the time listening to the soft moans and groans filtering up from the alley floor. When he finally looked, he saw Zalesky crawling on his belly, dragging himself with one arm and one leg, toward the sidewalk. Took him a while to reach it, and when he finally did, he began calling out in a strained voice.

"Help! Call an ambulance! Help!"

Had the knots slipped or had someone untied them? The Ghost would never know for sure.

Jack waited until the EMTs came by and carted him off to the emergency room, then he descended the stairs and left by the front door.

10

The Schlage knob on Zalesky's door took longer to pick than Rosa's, mainly because Jack found his hands a little unsteady, what with all the people passing on the sidewalk and going in and out of the bakery next door. He'd worn a Mets cap and had it pulled low over his face; he'd turned up the collar of his peacoat. Probably all for naught. No one seemed to notice and the lock quickly yielded.

Upstairs, Zalesky's apartment door was double-locked—the doorknob plus a dead bolt—and those took a while, but at least his only worry was one of the neighbors stepping into the hall and spotting him.

Once inside, he turned on the lights. The city's ERs were famous for their overcrowding and long waits, worsened by the recession. No matter where Zalesky was taken, he wouldn't be home anytime soon. And if he had a major fracture, not at all tonight.

Jack found the briefcase in the bedroom closet. It had a three-dial combination lock, immune to picking. He found a screwdriver in a toolbox and used that to pop the case open.

"Hello, hello," he murmured as he lifted the lid and saw the banded stacks of twenties—three of them, each labeled *Chemical Bank* and *$2,000.*

He chose one and fanned through the crisp new bills—

"Whoa!"

Only the top and bottom notes were twenties. All the bills in the middle were singles. What was labeled $2000 contained only $138. Obviously the switch money. Take in six grand in exchange for a little over four hundred—not a bad day's work.

But Zalesky hadn't taken the six grand. He'd kept the doctored stacks.

The old lady still had her money.

What the hell?

What was he missing here?

Maybe a look around would clear up the mystery. And maybe produce a little more cash. According to Julio via his sister, Zalesky took down six figures-plus a year. A guy like that had to have a stash. He began to search.

The place was furnished for utility, not comfort, which indicated Zalesky didn't spend much time at home. Not much beyond underwear and socks in his dresser drawers. He did have three business suits in his closet along with an array of a half dozen ties and white shirts. Jack recognized the suit he'd worn today and checked the pockets. He found a badge and ID that identified him as a member of the New York State Banking Department, fraud investigation unit—whatever that was.

Okay, where did he hide the cash?

Jack found a stash behind the bathroom molding. The discovery was a cause for celebration as well as concern—he kept his own stash in the same place.

He pulled out a pair of banded stacks labeled *Chase* and *$2,000* each. But these weren't dummied up—all twenties here. Another day's haul? After those came a stack of hundreds held by a red rubber band. He fanned through that—easily a hundred bills. The total came to fifteen, sixteen grand. Jack stuffed it all in his pockets, then grinned as he fitted the molding back into place. Might be *days* before Zalesky discovered he'd been robbed. And he couldn't even report it.

He considered adding insult to injury by emptying the briefcase of its four hundred or so bucks. Yeah, why not?

He left the apartment on a high. If mainlining heroin felt anything like this, he could see why it was addictive. He was totally buzzed.

11

"Is he hurt bad?" Julio said. "He break anything?"

Jack and Julio were locked in The Spot's tiny kitchen. Jack hadn't wanted Lou and Barney to hear this.

"All I know is he's hurt. He won't be sneaking in windows for some time."

"I wish the *cabron* break his back!" Julio said through his teeth. "I wish he's so crippled he can never bother her again!"

The thought gave Jack a queasy feeling. He didn't wish paralysis on anyone. Truly a fate worse than death. To change the subject, he pulled out the cash he'd taken from Zalesky's place and put it on the counter.

Julio's eyes bulged. *"Por Dios!"*

"Does Rosa get alimony?"

"No. She didn't want it from that *mierda*."

"Well, she's got it now."

Julio shook his head. "She never take it. She want nothing to do with the *culo*."

"Well, she doesn't have to know. In fact, she *can't* know. That was part of our deal. Just say it's a gift from you."

"Rosa won't take it from me neither. She too proud. Sooner or later she hear he been robbed. And her crazy brother who got no money suddenly giving her thousands? What she gonna think? She ain't stupid."

Yeah, Julio had a point. Her ex robbed, Julio suddenly flush, the truth would be too obvious.

"Well, what do I do with it all?"

"Keep it."

"Naw."

"You earned it, meng. It's yours."

He looked at the pile of stolen money . . . he didn't like to think of himself as a thief, but then again, this money had been stolen from other people. Which made it twice stolen.

Stealing from a thief . . . he guessed he could live with that. The thirty grand from the Mikulskis had been stolen too—stolen from dead sex slavers. Jack could definitely live with that.

But what was he going to do with it? Abe's idea about the gold coins was sounding better and better.

And then a thought.

"Hey, pay off the Gambinos with it."

Julio gave him an angry look. "How you know about that? Who's been—never mind." He jerked a thumb toward the door that led to the bar where Lou and Barney were ensconced in their usual spots. "The guys?"

"Right." Jack jumped in as Julio opened his mouth for a sure refusal. "Think about it: One jerk gets you into a hole and another gets you out. It's perfect. Cosmic symmetry."

Julio gave a slow nod. "Real cosmic." The nod turned to a shake. "But I can't take your money."

"It's *not* my money, dammit. It's Zalesky's. The *hijo de puta* is going to simplify your life."

Julio thought about this, then sighed and shrugged. "Okay. We make him pay."

Jack clapped him on the shoulder. "Excellent! But . . ."

"But what?"

He had a sudden urge to go slow.

"Let's make a few more payments—with Zalesky's dough, of course—before settling the loan."

"Why?"

Yeah. Why? Curiosity? He wasn't sure. Julio was being squeezed by some genuine Mafiosi, the bigger-than-life kind who got their pictures splashed in the *Daily News* and *New York Post* above headlines with bad puns. Jack had seen the bagman—chubby with a thick gut and a piggy face. A far cry from the Teflon Don Gotti with his blow-dried hair and felt-collared overcoat.

Couldn't hurt to get a little firsthand knowledge about someone like that.

And knowledge was power.

Or so they said.

12

Roman opened his suite door expecting al-Thani. Instead he found a Caucasian wearing a white three-piece suit and carrying a slim cane wrapped in black hide. Equally black hair, slick and glossy, swept straight back from a widow's peak. He knew the man. And had never liked him.

He forced a smile. "Drexler."

"Good evening, Mister Trejador." He spoke with a vaguely German accent. "I know it's late, but the Council is anxious to settle this affair."

So this is what the High Council had meant by "adjustments." But Roman put on a puzzled expression.

"Affair? What affair?"

"The incident. May I come in, or shall we discuss the situation in the hall?"

Drexler seemed to be feeling cockier than usual. Roman stepped back.

"Of course."

He turned and walked into the suite, leaving Drexler to close the door behind him.

"I hope I'm not . . . interrupting anything," Drexler said.

Roman caught the inference. The Council would have preferred all its actuators be functional eunuchs living lives of quiet desperation in cold-water flats between assignments. Like Ernst Drexler.

They'd made veiled references to Roman's "aberrant" lifestyle with no permanent address and hired companions. But he got results, and as long as his string of successes held up, he'd be free to conduct his personal time as he wished.

Drexler's only quirk was the white suit. He wore it year-round, an egregious fashion faux pas that could be due to either ignorance or arrogance.

Roman suspected the latter. He almost appeared to be going for a Tom Wolfe look but the severe black hair ruined it. Roman might have found a silly sort of charm in it if Drexler weren't such a prick.

And that cane. Wrapped in rhinoceros hide, they said. The figure Drexler cut with the combination was hardly subtle. But then Drexler was one of those hands-off actuators. Never got his hands dirty. Embraced the rear-echelon general model, watching from afar as his troops did his bidding. At Drexler's level of personal involvement, he could have spent his days in a pink tutu for all it mattered.

So unlike his father. The cane originally had belonged to Daddy, and had been much less of an affectation in his day. Ernst, Sr., remained a legend among actuators. His work in the Weimar years ultimately had paved the way for the One's return to the world. He'd been the epitome of the hands-on actuator. Roman had modeled his career on the example set by this twit's father.

Ernst, Jr., would turn forty next year. Roman had nearly ten years of wisdom and experience on him. Drexler had proven himself competent, but not exceptional. Why had the High Council sent him, of all people? Only one reason: The legacy of *vati* Drexler. They expected a flash of his progenitor's brilliance. Roman didn't see that happening.

"Not at all. I was expecting al-Thani with an update."

"I contacted him and came instead."

So that was how he'd learned the address.

"And your interest is . . . ?"

"I should think that is obvious: I have been assigned responsibility for retrieval of the Order's loan." He quickly added, "I've been pressed into service on the matter to allow you to continue pursuit of the creation of chaos without further distraction."

Pressed into service? Oh, Roman doubted that. Doubted that very much. Given the nod after a campaign to wheedle his way into Roman's business would be more like it. The part about reducing Roman's distractions from the pursuit of chaos was no doubt the argument this cream-coated Austrian strudel pressed when presenting his petition to the Council to be allowed to come to the aid of actuator Trejador and help "settle" the "affair."

"I see. That's very considerate of the Council. Will Nasser be assisting you?"

"Only in the most peripheral way. I have debriefed him and may call on him from time to time, but I have my own operatives to put into the field."

"Of course you do."

Roman let the statement stand.

After a rather lengthy silence, Drexler said, "Well, I stopped by as a courtesy and to inquire after any insights you might have."

"At the moment, none. A pair of wild cards has been dealt into the game—whether by themselves or by another hand remains to be seen."

"Where do you think the treachery occurred—this end or the other?"

Clearly, Drexler was pumping him. Roman decided to give him what he wanted. Be the bigger man. Appear to be above all that petty territoriality. Because none of it would help.

"At first I was sure it was the other end—that fellow Moose's disappearance right before departure pointed that way, but it turns out he didn't show up because someone broke his head out on the dunes."

"The driver called Reggie?"

"Possibly. But I believe you'll find that the Egyptian, Tachus, will prove to be the indirect source of the leak. He rented a place for the auction and issued invitations. That was the weak link. Someone connected the dots."

"What do you make of the genital mutilations?"

"*Obliterations* is more like it. Someone making a statement."

"Exactly my conclusion." Drexler smiled. "And this can work to our advantage. Anyone making a statement has an agenda that goes beyond profit. A simple thief is more likely to take the money and run, never to be seen again. But someone making a *statement*, someone with an *agenda*, will be heard from again. Because money isn't the object—the *cause* is all. Somewhere, at some time, those two will resurface, and we'll have our chance."

"You're planning on luring them out?"

"Only as a last resort. They appear to take violent umbrage at those with a sexual predilection for children." Drexler made a face. "To bait a trap will require dealing with that sort. I am in no hurry to do so."

"So you're left with . . . ?"

"The driver. I'm having one of our brothers in the orthopedic field patch up his kneecaps. Then we'll see what he can do to locate this Lonnie."

"You should get on that as soon as possible."

Yes, Roman thought. Waste your time, not mine.

The chances of finding Lonnie were remote. And if they did track him down, he'd know nothing. Tachus had made a critical error and paid the ultimate price for it. Who knew? Drexler might make a similar error, and pay a similar price.

One could only hope.

SUNDAY

1

Neil Zalesky staggered up to his apartment door. He'd never minded not having an elevator before, but today he wished to Christ his building had one. The stairs damn near killed him. God, he hurt. He'd never hurt like this in his whole life.

And what had the hospital discharged him with? Half a dozen Percocets—Percocet fives, no less. They didn't even touch the pain. The guys up at the Event would be able to fix him up with tens, maybe some OxyContins. He had a major hurt on and he needed a big gun to shoot it down.

He switched the cane the hospital had given—no, *sold* him—to his slung left hand, found his key, and unlocked the door. It was stuck; without thinking, he rammed his good shoulder against it and—

Shit!

He yelped as sharp agony speared through the left side of his chest.

The whole night had been like that. Doze off and then get jolted awake by pain from his broken shoulder, his cracked ribs, or his bruised hip. Certain positions were fine, others sucked ass, even with the morphine needle the hospital had given him. Hardly a wink of sleep.

He limped into his apartment.

The hospital . . . fuck 'em. The EMTs had wheeled him into the ER and left him there, and four hours later someone finally got around to x-raying him. Wound up he'd broken his left shoulder—"humerus," the doctor had said—fractured three left ribs, and banged up his left hip. "Sprained, strained, bruised, and contused" was how the nurse had described his hip in some ass-backward attempt to lighten him up. Had she really thought that was in any fucking way the least bit amusing? It hurt like a son of a bitch. His left side wasn't worth shit right now.

They kept him overnight and kicked him out this morning. What? No cast for a broken shoulder—excuse me, *humerus?* No, just some sort of fancy strap-down sling-brace-whatever. He'd wanted to stay for a few days, wanted them to put him on IV morphine, but they weren't buying.

Could've been worse, man. Could have broken his back and ended up a cripple. He'd got off lucky, even though he looked like someone had worked him over with a baseball bat.

That was what he'd told the EMTs. He didn't know what else to say. Couldn't tell them he fell off his ex's roof. Not with that restraining order. But the mugging story meant the EMTs had to report it, and a couple of bored-looking cops had shown up in the ER and taken a statement. Neil told them three or four guys attacked him from behind with no warning. He hadn't got a look at their faces, had no idea why they'd attacked him. A gang initiation, maybe? He'd been in Longwood, after all.

He could tell neither of the cops believed him. After all, he still had his wallet. But they didn't seem to care what really happened. Neil was alive and talking and hadn't been hurt bad enough to warrant more than an overnight stay. They'd file the report and forget it.

Fine. Neil wanted to forget it too.

What had happened up on the roof? He'd studied knots and tried them out before the first time he'd hung his ass over the bitch's back alley. They'd held every time before. Last night he'd tied that rope to the chimney with a double buntline hitch. No way that knot had come free on its own.

But who'd do that? Nobody had known he was up there. The bitch and her greasy brother had been miles away. How—?

Unless those beers at The Main Event had affected him more that he'd thought. Fuck no. He could hold more beer than that. Lots more.

Still . . . he'd seen the end of the rope. It hadn't been cut.

Shit, talk about bad-ass luck.

He coughed and that earned him another shot of agony. He groaned and cupped a hand over his broken ribs. He'd never been stabbed but this was what getting knifed in the chest must feel like.

He hobbled to the kitchen, filled a glass with water, and washed down three Percocets. He emptied his pockets on the kitchen table—mostly bills from the hospital and the ambulance service. He didn't have any medical insurance, so he was going to have to pay cash. His initial instinct when they'd handed him the bill was tell them to fuck off and shove it. But wisdom had prevailed.

The grifter game was a tightrope. He needed a clean record if he ever got caught—Mr. Neil Zalesky was an upstanding citizen with no arrest record who always paid his rent and his bills on time. Once a year he even declared some income and paid city, state, and federal taxes. He hated to throw money away on taxes, but he never paid anywhere near what he'd have to fork over if he declared it all. He could afford it—and he didn't see how he could afford not to.

But even with all that legitimacy up front, he couldn't risk bill collectors coming around and looking into his finances. First thing tomorrow morning he'd mail out checks to the hospital and the ambulance service.

Trouble was, he didn't remember how much he had in the checking account. He always kept enough to pay the rent and utilities, but these new bills hadn't been in the cards. He was due for a run to the bank anyway. The bucks had been stacking up—the Schmidt haul last week had put him well past his ten-grand limit for cash in the house—and that called for a visit to the safe deposit box. He'd throw a couple, three thousand into the checking account while he was there.

Oh, wait. Today was Sunday. He'd go tomorrow.

As he was relieving his bladder, he looked at the shower. How the hell was he going to shower with this shoulder brace? Was he allowed to take it off? The assholes at the hospital hadn't told him a goddamn thing. Or maybe they had and he wasn't listening. He'd figure it out.

One thing he couldn't figure out was how to handle old Mrs. Cohen. He'd set her up for a big sting next Saturday. He couldn't show up looking like a mugging victim. He couldn't drive or open doors or handle the briefcases with only his right arm.

Shit. He was going to have to call her and put her off until his shoulder healed, and the orthopedist had told him that would take months. *Months!*

He went to his bedroom and eased himself down to sit on the bed. The Percocets were kicking in. Maybe a little nap if he could get comfortable. He—

His closet door was open a crack. He always closed it tight. He hated open doors. Groaning with the effort, he rose and looked inside. The briefcase was where he'd left it. No, wait. He always placed it flush against the wall. This was angled out a bit.

Concerned now, he bent and grabbed it with his good hand. Light . . .

Oh, shit, it couldn't be. A closer look showed scratches and dents by the locks. Someone had popped it open. His hand was shaking as he worked the combinations. The lid popped open and inside was—nothing.

"Fuck!" he shouted.

It was only four hundred dollars, but that wasn't the point. Someone had broken in while he was in the hospital.

But what if that wasn't all they'd taken? What if—?

He hobbled as fast as he could to the bathroom and grabbed the screwdriver he kept in the medicine cabinet. His left hip screamed as he gingerly knelt on the floor. A couple of twists of the screwdriver popped the molding free. He snaked his fingers into the space where he'd left the banded stacks he'd liberated from Mrs. Schmidt last week—

—and found nothing.

No, wait. Not possible. He'd stuffed them in there himself. Had they been pushed farther back? Trouble was, he couldn't feel anything but dust and plaster rubble.

No!

He struggled to his feet and limped to the kitchen for the flashlight he kept in the cabinet near the window. Moving as fast as he could, he returned to the bathroom. Ignoring the agony from his chest and his hip and just about every-goddamn-where else, he crouched and forced his head down to the floor so he was eye level with the molding space. The flashlight beam picked up just that—space. *Empty* space.

He'd been robbed! Some cocksucking, motherfucking son of a bitch had snuck in here and ripped him off! He didn't know who'd broken in, didn't know how they knew where he hid the money or how they even knew he kept cash here, but he knew who was behind it.

2

Julio's head kept shaking back and forth, like some sort of flesh-and-blood metronome.

"No, meng. Can't do it. Can't do it."

"Why the hell not?" Jack said.

The scene was kind of a replay of last night. Jack and Julio in The Spot's tiny kitchen, a stack of cash on the counter between them, but the subject was different.

Jack had been wondering what to do with all his cash, then it hit him: Harry's interest in The Spot was going up for sale, so why not lend Julio a down payment so he could make an offer?

The head kept shaking. "No, meng. Can't do it. Can't do it."

"You sound like a broken record."

Broken record . . . Jack idly wondered how long that expression would last—or at least be comprehensible. Tapes and CDs had largely replaced vinyl, and they didn't skip.

Julio shrugged. At least he'd stopped shaking his head. "It is what it is."

"But why not? Look, I'm not offering you a handout. I'm talking about a *loan.* I lend you the money for a while, you pay me back when you can."

The head began shaking back and forth again. "We known each other since when? Last month? I can't take money from you."

"You're not *taking.* You're *borrowing.* Big difference. And I've known you long enough to know you'll pay me back."

"You want to be a partner with me, maybe we can work something out. But—".

"No-no." Jack waved his hands in the space between them. Him? A business owner? Talk about scary. That occupied a spot on his to-do list somewhere below getting syphilis. "No partnership. I like this place. I like you—"

Julio's turn to wave his hands. He added a step back. "Hey, meng. I like you too, but—"

"You didn't let me finish. I like the way you pour a beer, I like the way you run the place. You've got a real feel for it. Give you free rein and this place will be turning a profit in no time. That's when you can start paying me back."

Back to the shaking head. "No."

"Julio, for Christ's sake, I've got nothing else to do with the money!"

"Buy youself a car. Buy youself—"

"Hey, Julio!" Lou had stuck his head between the two drapes that served as a divider. He spoke in a hushed tone. "Y'got company."

"Who?"

"*El hijo de puta.* He's all banged up and royally pissed."

"I'll stay back here," Jack whispered to the two of them. "I don't want him to see me. He might remember me from his bar."

They nodded and Julio followed Lou through the curtains.

"There he is!" a new voice said, dripping belligerence. "There's the man I want to see!"

Jack turned off the light in the kitchen and moved to the curtains. He peeked through the slit between them and spotted Zalesky standing near the bar, leaning on a cane. He wore sweatpants and an oversized Islanders jacket. His left arm was in some sort of sling-brace under the jacket. He looked like he'd been hit by a truck.

"What's a matter with your leg?" Julio said, pointing to the cane. "Your dog bite you? I hope he's okay, you know. I hope he don't die of poison."

Lou and Barney cracked up at this. Zalesky reddened.

"Listen, you little—"

"Or you finally pick on someone your own size—that it?"

Zalesky looked like he wanted to take a swing at him with the cane. He had considerable advantage in height and weight, but he had only one arm to work with. Too bad he wasn't in better shape. Maybe he'd start something. Which might not be a bad thing under these circumstances: his ex-brother-in-law comes in on a quiet Sunday morning and starts a fight and Julio kicks the crap out of him—all in front of witnesses. No foul for defending yourself and your business.

But Jack figured Zalesky wouldn't start anything even on a good day. He was a con man. The way Jack saw it, con men didn't like to get physical. That was why they were con men. And even if Zalesky were in the mood for violence, he was in no shape for it—not even with Rosa. Lucky for him he'd landed in a way that saved his face. Not a mark on it. But the rest of him had to be hurting like hell. Jack had been hoping for major internal injuries that would lay him up for weeks, but no such luck. The guy was up and about the next day.

What was the expression? God looks out for drunks and shitheads. Or something like that.

"Get out," Julio said.

"Gladly. I wouldn't take a drink from you if you had the last bottle on Earth. Probably catch the AIDS from it."

Lou and Barney made mocking sounds at the lame remark.

"Ooh, that cut," Lou said.

Barney nodded. "Cut deep. Look at Julio. He's bleeding all over the floor."

Julio's expression didn't change. "Out."

"Not before I've had my say. I was robbed last night."

Lou and Barney clapped and cheered.

Zalesky ignored them. "I know you were behind it."

"He was with us all night!" Barney said.

Zalesky smiled. "You can trot out all the lushes you can find, won't matter. You didn't do it yourself, I'm sure—you wouldn't know how—but you put someone up to it. No doubt about that. And I know why. I know this place is on the skids and you've gotta be wondering about whether you're gonna have a job soon. So you think you can build a little cushion by ripping me off?"

"You crazy," Julio said.

"No!" He jabbed a finger at Julio. "*You're* crazy if you think I'm gonna take that kinda shit lying down! You been unhappy with the way things've been going down? Wait! You just wait, motherfucker! You ain't seen shit!"

He turned and started limping toward the door.

"I don't know about you, Barney," Lou said, "but I think I see shit right now. And damn if it ain't got feet."

Barney laughed.

Zalesky turned at the door and pointed at Julio. "You *will* be sorry. Sorrier than you ever thought you could be."

Then the door was swinging closed behind him.

Jack waited until he'd passed from sight, then stepped out of the kitchen.

"You catch that big dramatic move? He's probably seen it a zillion times in movies."

Julio turned to him, his expression grim. "He means it."

Jack nodded. He'd sensed that too. "Yeah. He does."

"That guy gotta go."

"Yeah. He does."

Julio stepped behind the bar and produced the Louisville Slugger. He slapped it against his palm. "Time for this?"

"Don't give up on me yet."

"What you gonna do?"

"I'll think of something."

Al least he hoped he would. The bat was looking better and better.

3

"You've gone meshugge, is that it?" Abe said, munching on one of the powdered-sugar donuts Jack had brought for an afternoon snack. "You want to invest in a bar?"

"No, I want to invest in Julio. He's a hard worker, he's a straight shooter, and he's got a feel for the business. I think he can make a go of the place."

"And he won't take your money?"

"Not a cent."

Abe's eyes narrowed. "You sure he's not conning you?"

"Julio? Sure I'm sure. Why would you say that?"

"It's an old grifter trick: Such a great investment opportunity I've got, but sorry, you can't get in." He held up his hands in a stop gesture. "No, really, it's not for you. I'm only taking in friends or people recommended by friends. You, I haven't known long enough, so, sorry. Take your money somewhere else." Abe lowered his hands and reached for another donut. "And so what's the result?"

From what Jack knew of human nature, the answer was obvious: "The mark wants in more than ever."

"Exactly. He begs, he pleads, he searches out friends of the grifter and pleads with them to put in a good word. Finally, the grifter relents, but only if the mark contributes more than he originally intended. It's such a good deal, such a sure thing, and the mark is so glad to be allowed in, that he begs, borrows, and maybe even steals to meet the investment threshold."

Jack shook his head as Abe bit down on the donut, sprinkling himself with powdered sugar. "That's not Julio."

"You're so sure? Twenty-two years old not even and already you're a Freud on character?"

"Call it gut instinct."

"He gets you to like him—like an old friend he welcomes you—and his two shills you've told me about who are always there sell you a story about the bar being sold and him out on the street, and all of a sudden it's Jack to the rescue."

Jack had to admit that, on the surface, it might look that way, but . . .

"Anyone ever tell you what a cheery guy you are?"

"Cheery is not my nature. I've seen it happen too often. Don't think that just because you're not a little old yenta living alone in Brooklyn you can't be scammed. It's happened to wiser heads than yours."

The mention of a little old yenta brought Zalesky to mind. An idea had been perking since Jack had left The Spot earlier.

"On that subject, do you know any hit men?"

Abe choked briefly on his donut, then swallowed. He grabbed his neck. "Call a doctor. Whiplash I've got from the change of subject."

"Okay, doesn't have to be a hit man, per se. Any sort of enforcer or guy who specializes in strong-arm stuff."

"You've got someone you want hurt?"

"Yeah."

"You can't do this yourself?"

"It's got to come from somewhere else. Can't have any connection to Julio, and I'm connected to Julio."

"Julio-Julio-Julio . . . your life he's taking over."

"He's like the second friend I've made in the city. I want to help him out."

Abe frowned. "Second? Who was the first?"

"Well . . . you? At least *I* consider you a friend."

Abe looked uncomfortable. "Yes, well, what makes you think I know such people?"

"Considering your other line of merchandise, I just thought—"

"No thoughts, please—at least not that thought. The mob has its own sources. The likes of me they don't need. I sell to the little guy."

"But you've been around awhile. Everybody seems to know you, and so I assume you know who's who and what's what and who's into what."

"You could maybe be more specific?"

"Like if somebody gets knee-capped, you might hear who did it. Somebody got a broken arm for being late on a payment, you might know the name of the breaker. Am I out of line here? If so, just let me know and I'll shut up."

"Out of line? No. But how much I can help you, we'll see. I hear things. I'll write down some names."

"I need more than just names. I need to know all you know about them or can find out about them."

"And you'll use this information how?"

"Not sure yet. Won't know till I see what I've got to work with. In the meantime, can I use your phone?"

Abe pointed to the black rotary squatting on the far end of the counter. "Help yourself."

Jack pulled out a slip of paper with Cristin's number and dialed it. He had no way of knowing whether or not she'd returned his call. If she had and one of his neighbors picked up, they hadn't told Jack. She answered on the second ring.

"This better be important," she said.

"Hey, Cristin, it's Jack."

"Is it now? The guy who doesn't exist?"

"What do you mean?"

"Well, I called that number you left but the guy who answered never heard of you."

Crap. "Sorry about that. Some of my neighbors aren't too bright. Or spend most of their days whacked out. Are we still on for tonight?"

"If you're up for it, so am I. I need a blast from the past."

"Um, we just met, remember?"

She laughed. *"Oh right. Okay, I want to get to know my new friend."*

"That's it. Where do you want to meet?"

"Why don't we start out at a little tapas bar I know. Rioja. It's on Second between Seventy-third and Seventy-fourth."

"When? Five? Six? Seven?"

"How about six-thirty?"

"You're on. See you there."

He hung up and turned to Abe. "What's a tapas bar?"

Abe shrugged. "I should know? A kind of beer maybe?"

"The name's Spanish. I'll call Julio later. He should know."

"Speaking of calling, one of the Mikulskis phoned in yesterday. Said they needed to talk to you."

"Really."

Black had asked if they could call on him should they need a hand with a job. Obviously something had come up.

"They leave a number?"

"They did. When are you getting a phone? An answering service I'm not."

"Sorry about that. They wanted to know how to get hold of me and since we had you in common—"

" 'In common' is what I've always wanted to be."

"—I said to call you."

"You shouldn't worry about it. But you need a phone and an answering machine."

"First thing I'll do after I get some genuine fake New York ID. I'm gonna check back with that Levinson guy and—"

"You should maybe try somewhere else. Levinson's connected to Bertel, and Bertel, good man though he is, is maybe not your biggest fan right now since you've handed in your notice. Levinson I don't know well enough to vouch for the tightness of his lips. I do know a fellow not far from here. Like a sphinx, he is. Name's Ernie and he's an ID maven. He'll get you a foolproof soshe—"

"Soshe?"

"Social Security number."

"He could do that?"

Jack had never had one of those. Be kind of weird having one, even somebody else's.

"For a price, of course."

"Of course." Jack shrugged. "He should work for free?"

Abe gave him an amused look. "You're making fun, maybe?"

Jack suddenly realized what he'd done. "Oh, jeez, I don't know where that came from."

No lie. That had not been intentional.

Abe looked dubious. "Really?"

"Really. It just came out."

"Interesting. Like a chameleon you change."

"No offense. Really."

"None taken. Anyway, Ernie will set you up as a new person. You want?"

"I want."

"I'll tell him to expect you sometime. I'll give you the address and you mention my name."

"Thanks a mil, Abe. How can I repay you?"

"On your next run, bring me back some of these donuts you've told me about."

"Krispy Kremes?"

He held up yet another sugared donut and rotated it back and forth. "As good as this is, you say these Krispy Kremes are better?"

Saliva began flowing at the memory. "I've never had anything like them, especially the glazed cake—"

"An assorted dozen will make us even."

"That's all?"

"That and getting your own phone so you won't be arranging trysts on mine. Someone you've met in your travels?"

"Someone from home, actually."

Abe's eyebrows lifted, wrinkling his extended forehead. "From your old life? You think that's wise?"

"Well, it's not a 'tryst.' Neither of us wants a relationship. It's just dinner."

"Dinner with someone from home. Not what one expects from someone who says he wants to start anew . . . someone who is going to be set up with a new identity."

"I don't see the conflict."

Abe sighed. "Never mind then."

"No, seriously. You're seeing a problem I don't. I'd appreciate knowing what I'm missing."

Abe looked at him. "You've erected a dike. The sea of your past is on the other side. This girl, this woman is a leak in that dike. If you don't plug it, the past will flood your new present."

As much as Jack respected Abe's greater age, experience, and wisdom, he wasn't buying.

"It's just dinner."

"Just dinner, he says. Until a mutual friend visits the city and calls on this girl. 'Oh, you'll never guess who's in town,' she says. 'Jack. Let's the three of us get together for lunch.' That's two leaks. And then that mutual friend mentions you to someone else who mentions you to someone else and so on until one of those someones knows your family has been wondering where you took off to, and before you know it, your father or sister or brother is on the phone asking where you are and why haven't you called?"

Jack couldn't imagine his brother giving a damn, but the rest . . . yeah, he could see Karina or someone else from high school coming to town and Cristin arranging a get-together.

Leaks in the dike . . .

Abe was right.

"But it's kind of moot now. She's seen me. We've talked. It was all by accident, but she already knows I'm here."

"She knows where you live?"

"No."

"She has your phone number?"

"The hall phone, yes."

"But I have a feeling you're going to be changing your address soon, yes?"

That took Jack by surprise.

"Are you psychic? Yeah, I was thinking of looking for a quieter neighborhood. How did you know?"

"With your financial situation improved, you should be looking for better digs. I would."

Jack grinned. "Did you just say 'digs'?"

"Just because I don't get out much, I shouldn't know the argot of the street?"

"Okay, yeah, I'm thinking of moving."

"So. You'll have a new address, a new phone number, and a new name. No reason she should know these things. You simply do your disappearing act again."

"Just drop her?"

"What? Her heart will break?"

"Hardly. We were never involved and we're not going to be involved. I'm not her type and she's not mine."

But yeah, her feelings might be hurt. Jack could see how: Someone you consider a friend breaks off contact, stops returning your calls, for no reason at all . . . that's got to hurt.

But Cristin was tough. And she didn't want strings. So how much would it hurt her? Not much, if at all.

"Okay. Dinner tonight, then no forwarding address."

Abe shook his head. "Why show up at all? Make up an excuse. Beg off."

"Can't do that. Doesn't feel right."

"Feel right for her, or you?"

Jack knew the answer but wasn't about to admit to Abe how much he was looking forward to hanging out with her tonight. Could barely admit it to himself.

To change the subject, he put on a sheepish grin and said, "Mind if I call the Mikulskis from here?"

4

Jack didn't know which brother he spoke to on the phone, but his presence was requested on the 40th Street side of Bryant Park, near the east corner. He wouldn't give any details, just be there in an hour and make sure he wasn't followed.

Followed? Who would follow him? Especially from Abe's. Then he realized the Mikulskis had no idea where he was calling from. A routine request, he guessed. But he honored it and took an intricately circuitous route back to his apartment. No one followed. He wanted to change into something warmer, just in case the brothers needed his help right away. And he wanted to add some iron to his wardrobe. Or was "heat" a better word?

Toward the first end, he added an extra sweatshirt over the one he was already wearing. Toward the second, he pulled his Ruger and a brand-new SOB holster from their hiding place among his cash stacks. He removed the wrapping from the holster and slipped the gun inside. A good snug fit. Then he clipped the assemblage inside his jeans at the small of his back. Had to loosen his belt to make it fit.

Christ. Felt like he'd stuffed a cantaloupe back there.

He headed for midtown, knowing that the two sweatshirts hid the bulge, but still feeling as if everyone on the subway was staring at it. He was glad it was only two stops. He walked to the designated corner of the walled-off park—mid-block on West 40th between Fifth and Sixth—and waited.

The sun hung low, still hours from setting but behind the buildings, allowing shadows to rule the street. A cold wind whipped along from the west. Not exactly a private spot for a meeting. The sidewalks were filled with shoppers with store bags, getting a pre-Thanksgiving drop on the Christmas season.

"Jack!"

He whirled at the voice behind him—only a wall was supposed to be there—and saw the Mikulski who'd called himself Deacon Blue standing in a makeshift doorway in the plywood wall running around the park. He wore a big fatigue jacket, a knitted watch cap pulled low, and jeans.

He motioned Jack toward him. "Step into my office."

Jack stepped through and looked around. Bryant Park had been under construction since he'd arrived in the city, so he had no idea what it looked like before, but it sure looked like crap now. Everything was dug up, retaining walls were half built, wood scraps littered the ground, and saw horses and cement mixers were scattered everywhere.

"Nice taste. Who's the decorator?"

"Dinkins and Company," Blue said as he fitted the door back into place. "A friend of a friend works here."

"Your brother coming?"

"He's here."

Jack looked around again. "Where?"

"Out on the street, making sure you didn't bring company."

Anger flashed. Didn't they trust him by now?

"Hey, I wouldn't—"

Blue raised his hands. "Not on purpose. We've been picking up word that the Arabs are looking for their money."

"Aren't they dead?"

"The ones on the scene were just part of a group culled from a number of mosques. They borrowed the money."

"Uh-oh. The mob?"

"No."

"Then who?"

"We don't know, and that bothers us."

"Maybe one of the Arabs knows."

"They don't."

"How do you know?"

"We interviewed one of them."

"Interviewed?"

"He'd been slated to help with the auction and was asking an awful lot of questions, so we decided to ask a few of our own."

Jack had seen how the brothers operated, so he didn't really have to ask, but did anyway.

"Is he still asking questions?"

"No."

"Ooookay. Was he cooperative?"

"Very, but no help."

"Why not?"

"Because he didn't know. The guy in the limo the other night was the go-between to the moneymen and he's with Allah. All our interviewee knew was that they expected a quick return on their investment, and now the principal is gone."

"No idea who they are?"

"No, but word is they have bank connections and the bills are recognizable in some way and so their inside people have got an eye out for them. You haven't done anything stupid like depositing thirty K to an account or anything, have you?"

Jack couldn't help feeling insulted. "Not likely. It's all tucked safely away for my retirement."

He was suddenly glad Julio had turned him down.

Blue looked relieved. "Good. You seemed too smart for that, but you never know."

"What about you guys?"

"We don't need it now. And if and when we do, we've got ways of laundering it offshore. But we're not off the hook. We still have a weak link."

"What?"

"Not what." His eyes locked with Jack's. "Who."

"Me?" Jack didn't like the way this was going. He began sliding his hand toward the small of his back. "You don't think I'd—"

"—be so stupid as to pull that gun in your belt? Nah. I don't think so. That would be *real* stupid, and you're not stupid."

Jack let his hand fall away. "Why am I the weak link?"

"Because of your pal, Reggie."

"He's not my pal."

"You left him breathing. That makes him your pal for life."

"Hardly."

"After you took off with my brother that night, I drove back to our neighboring borough to check up on him."

"Why do I have this feeling your idea of 'check up' is not the same as a doctor's?"

A smile played about the corners of Blue's lips. "I was concerned about his welfare."

"I take that to mean you were concerned that he might be faring well."

Blue nodded.

"And you were going to fix that."

Another nod.

Deacon Blue hadn't been able to let it go. The brothers saw Reggie as a liability, a loose end, and Blue had returned to Staten Island's north shore to tie it up.

Jack said, "I take it it didn't go . . . well?"

"Not at all. He wasn't there."

"Well, he had plenty of time to crawl off and flag down someone to take him to a hospital."

Blue shook his head. "Did some checking through some cop friends. No one with two busted knees showed up in any of the city's ERs that night."

"Could have been driven into Jersey."

"Possible. Or taken to a private doc. Either way, your guy's out there. The Arabs know him. If he can talk his way out of them killing him, he'll give you up. He'll spit you out faster than a vegan biting into a Big Mac."

"What about you guys? He saw you."

"He saw a couple of dudes in ski masks. We're zeros to him. You, on the other hand . . ."

Jack had a bad feeling about this.

"So that means what? I'm expendable?"

Blue laughed. "We don't work that way with the good guys. This is just a heads-up to watch your back."

Jack felt his tensing muscles relax. "He doesn't know anything about me. And he and his buddies killed the guy who did."

"The Tony you mentioned?"

Jack nodded. "All the ID I was carrying says North Carolina. Reggie had to guide me on the drive through Staten Island because I really and truly know nothing about it. So if he's talking about me, he's talking about somebody from down south."

"Does he know the guy who was running you?"

Jack almost blurted Bertel's name but bit it back. The less anyone knew, the better.

"Not unless Tony told him."

Blue slapped his hand against his thigh a few times as he eyed Jack. "Never know what a guy will say when he thinks he's got only a few moments to live."

Jack didn't like the sound of that. "What's that supposed to mean? Even if I told everything I know about you, I can't hurt you. The backward ski mask, remember?"

He was glad now that Black had made him wear it.

"You know that, and we know that, but *they* don't. They may think we planted you. So watch your back is all I'm saying. We're not talking a few grand here. We're talking millions. They'll be turning over every rock looking for you."

"Swell."

"And they'll be using your pal Reggie to help them. He's probably given them a detailed description. One day real soon you might see your likeness posted on a telephone pole with a reward offered." His smile was grim as he shook his head. "You went and let a subhuman live. Told you you'd regret it."

Jack guessed the brothers had been right, because right now he *was* regretting it. But he still didn't see how he could have crushed an unconscious man's skull. He'd had a hard enough time cracking his kneecaps.

5

Julio wasn't much help on the subject of tapas. He said it was a Spanish thing—Spanish as in *Spain*—and he was Puerto Rican. He said they were like *bocas*, as if that explained it. What Jack came away with was snacks—tapas were snacks.

Cristin had asked him to meet her at a Spanish snack bar. Well, okay. A lot of days he lived on what could be considered snacks—Pringles, Doritos, Cheetos, Sour Patch Kids, and the like. And if it was a bar, it must have beer. Jack didn't see how he could go wrong.

Then he remembered that ruthless people were looking for a guy named Lonnie. Looking in North Carolina, most likely, but still . . . not a comforting thought.

He found a Brooks Brothers and bought khaki slacks, a long-sleeve button-down white shirt, and a blue blazer. After a shower at home he dressed and checked himself in his only mirror. He didn't recognize the guy in the reflection.

But the blazer would hide the pistol holstered at the small of his back.

Cool.

He took a roundabout way over to Second Avenue, going so far as to double back a couple of times. No one was following him. Or if someone were, he was a ninja.

Rioja turned out to be anything but a snack bar. A real restaurant with lots of dark wood and glass, and many small tables. Jack arrived early and found the place already half full. He learned that a table had been reserved by a certain Cristin Ott. The hostess seemed to know the name. He asked for a corner table against the rear wall. He took the seat that put his back to the wall and gave him a view of the entire place.

He saw Cristin step through the door a fashionable five minutes late. She wore tight jeans and a denim jacket over a white blouse. With her short dark hair and her high heels she looked very East Side. Jack had never understood high heels with jeans, but then that could be added to the very long list of things he didn't understand about fashion. The hostess pointed him out but Cristin stared without recognition until he stood and waved to her.

"I didn't recognize you," she said, grinning as she reached the table. "I mean, look at you: all dressed up and nowhere to go."

"I guess this is nowhere."

A quick air kiss–hug combo and they sat.

"Seriously," she said, "I chose this place because you can dress down here. Look at me and look at you. I didn't think you owned clothes like that."

Jack shrugged and looked down at himself. "What? These old things? I've had them forever."

Her blue eyes sparkled as she reached across the table and plucked a tag from his sleeve. "Really? All those years and you never removed this?"

They had a laugh over that.

"Truth is, I've owned this outfit a couple of hours."

"Who picked it out, Joe Prep?"

"I told him to check out what I was wearing, and dress me exactly the opposite."

No lie there.

"You want *real* opposite?" she said, laughing. "I'd have put you in a dress."

"I think he wanted to."

A waitress arrived then.

"Hi, Cristin. The usual?"

"I think I'll be adventurous tonight. House Rioja."

Jack ordered a Spanish beer, whichever the waitress preferred. He knew nothing of Spanish beers.

"I gather you come here often."

She smiled. "It's around the corner. Great place to stop for something light when I don't feel like cooking—which is pretty often."

The waitress returned with a glass of red wine for Cristin and something called San Miguel for Jack. Cristin seemed to like her wine; Jack's San Miguel was awful. But he kept working on it. Better than no beer.

She guided him through the menu which was pretty much a list of appetizers. They ordered a bunch to share. Lots of seafood—*gambas salsa negra, bacalao, chopitos, calamares*—plus various veggies—*papas arrugadas, pimientos a padron, bandarillas*—and a couple of meats in the form of sausage and skewers.

They got through the obligatory chatter about how her party planning was going—very well, thank you—and she asked how his delivery job was going—he'd forgotten he'd told her about that, so he said he was looking into "other opportunities."

As the dishes came in successive waves, they sampled and talked about everything but politics and religion. Cristin had been to a lot of plays—so far this year she'd liked *Six Degrees of Separation* best. Jack couldn't add much on the subject, because he wasn't a theater fan. His mother had filled his youthful ears with Broadway soundtracks, but he preferred movies.

Cristin proved no slouch on that front either. And she liked the same kind of genre movies as Jack. She thought *Total Recall* cool and *Dick Tracy* crap. Jack agreed. They both liked a couple of sequels: *Robocop 2* and *Predator 2*. She declared *Pretty Woman* "totally clueless but soooo romantic." They disagreed on *Flatliners*—she liked anything with Kevin Bacon, Jack was disappointed with the ending—but both loved *Miller's Crossing.*

New music–wise they couldn't have been more different. They both still dug the music of their youth—Def Leppard and the Police and *Thriller*—and Cristin almost choked on a baby squid when Jack mentioned how he was beginning to have doubts that Dexy's Midnight Runners would ever make a comeback. Nowadays she liked Michael Bolton and Wilson Phillips. Jack found Wilson Phillips tolerable in small doses, but Michael Bolton was fingernails on a blackboard.

"I've gone retro and roots," he said, rolling a shrimp in some spicy sauce. "Reggae and blues, although as new stuff goes, I really like *Goodbye Jumbo*."

"Which is pretty retro itself."

Jack smiled. She'd nailed that one. Pretty sharp.

He found himself relaxing. Concerns about Reggie and Arabs and stolen money receded, allowing him to enjoy the moment. Beer certainly contributed. After that one San Miguel he'd switched to Heineken, but alcohol wasn't the only reason. Cristin was good company, easy to be with. They went way back and had nothing to prove to each other. They laughed a lot, and best of all, the subject of Karina didn't come up once.

The waitress appeared. "Dessert?"

Jack patted his belly. He was tapased out. "I don't think so."

"You can't leave here without tasting their flan," Cristin said.

"You can still eat?"

"Always save room for dessert." She added an impish grin. "Which was easy with you here."

"Uh-oh. Did I pig out?" Had he hogged all the food? He hadn't noticed. He'd been hungry and it had tasted so good. "I'm sorry. I didn't realize—"

She reached across the table and touched his hand. "Just busting you."

Her hand lingered there, lightly, just for a second or two, but long enough to send a warm tingle up his arm.

And then it darted away as she glanced up at the waitress. "One flan, two spoons."

Cristin rose as the waitress moved away. "Off to the facilities. Back in a flash." She put on a stern expression and pointed at him. "And leave me some flan."

Jack laughed and waved her off.

He watched the gentle sway of her hips as she strolled away. He'd always thought Cristin kind of plain, but she was looking pretty good these days. Beer goggles? Maybe, but he didn't think so. This was the third time he'd seen her in a week—a glimpse last Monday when she'd been meeting clients just before the shooting, at lunch the next day, and now tonight. She'd been more dressed up Monday, but she'd been working then; more casual at lunch and tonight, but whatever she wore, she wore with a certain flair.

But more than that, she seemed comfortable in her skin . . . like she knew who she was. Jack envied that. He was still treading water in that regard.

But the biggest revelation was Cristin herself. Lunch last Tuesday had been his first one-on-one with her, tonight the second. Back in high school she'd been overshadowed by Karina. If the three of them were hanging out, it was all Karina. Not that she was pushy or anything, she simply had all these offbeat interests she couldn't stop talking about. Cristin tended to be obscured in her shadow.

He watched her stop by the hostess's station before heading for the ladies' room. They seemed to know each other. He tried to come up with a word that best described her now that she could shine on her own.

Vivacious.

Yeah. That nailed it. She radiated a field, a glow of vitality that had magnetic qualities. It made Jack want to edge closer so he could siphon off some of that energy and make it his own.

Cristin had definitely come into her own.

The waitress brought the flan and two spoons. Even though he wasn't big on desserts—as much as he loved junk food, he'd been born without a sweet tooth—he'd had flan before and liked it.

Cristin appeared again at the far end of the room and he watched her stop for another brief exchange with the hostess. Then she strolled his way, waving to the bartender as she passed.

When she arrived he rose, and pointed to the flan. "Only through supreme effort of will did I resist slurping that down."

"Look at those manners," she said. "Rising when a lady arrives. Your mother taught you well."

"Actually, it was my father."

"He must have been old school."

"And how."

"Well, he did a good job."

"All by example."

His dad had been very old school about that—rising when a woman at the table rose and not sitting until she was seated. It became almost comical at a large, crowded table.

She sat and immediately dug into the flan, closing her eyes and moaning with her first bite.

"I so love this stuff."

Jack took a bite. A little too sweet for him. He took tiny bits, letting Cristin finish the bulk of it.

They talked awhile longer, then he said, "Where do we go from here?"

"For a nightcap. I know a good place."

Well, this was her turf.

"Sounds good to me."

He signaled the waitress and waggled a finger against his palm in the universal *check, please* sign.

She came over and said, "All settled."

Jack looked at Cristin. "Oh, no you don't—"

She raised her hands. "Don't get your macho nachos in an uproar. It's on the house."

"Do I look like a dummy? I saw you talking to the hostess."

"And she told me the owner said my money's no good here tonight."

Jack had expected a minor struggle for the check but had assumed he'd prevail. "On the house" hadn't even been on the radar.

"This was supposed to be my treat."

She shook her head. "No-no, Jacko, this was never going to be your treat. We agreed on Dutch, remember?"

"You don't expect me to believe—"

"I've arranged a few parties here where my clients have rented the whole place. They loooove me here."

"Really?"

"Really."

"What about the tip?"

"Taken care of."

Not knowing what else to do, he pulled out a twenty and dropped it on the table. "Gotta leave something."

She tilted her head toward the waitress. "Estella will love you. Let's go."

6

Outside, a chill wind blew down Second Avenue. Cristin wrapped her arms across her chest.

"Should have worn something a liiiittle warmer."

Jack resisted an impulse to throw an arm across her shoulders and snuggle her against him. Nice as that might have been, he opted instead for giving up his jacket. He had it halfway off before he remembered the revolver in the small of his back.

Crap.

He let her pull half a step ahead, then shrugged off the jacket and draped it over her shoulders.

"Here."

Before she could look around, he untucked his shirt to hide the weapon.

She smiled up at him. "And I thought chivalry was dead."

"Find a puddle and I'll lay it across it."

She held up the blazer's sleeve. "You really hate it that much?"

"Loathe it."

He couldn't imagine ever wearing it again—unless he wanted to look like someone else.

"But now *you're* cold."

"Yes, but I'm a man, and real men don't feel cold."

"Or at least don't admit it."

He had to admit—to himself—that he *was* cold. That breeze was cutting through his shirt like it was fishnet.

"Um, where are we going? Is this nightcap place far?"

"Right around the corner," she said as she led him in a westward turn onto 73rd Street. He followed her to the front of an apartment building halfway down the block.

"But—"

"My place," she said, smiling as she handed back his blazer. "Best nightcaps in town."

Jack couldn't help a tingle of anticipation. Was this really going where it seemed to be? And if so, what did he do? How did he handle it? Getting involved with someone from home was the worst possible move at this point in his new life. But the flip side . . . would backing off shut her off? Make her cut off contact? That might be for the best—Abe's warnings echoed in his head—but the last thing he wanted to do was hurt her in any way. But even beyond that, he'd enjoyed the hell out of tonight. He delighted in her company. He didn't want to lose that.

He could beg off right now—bad stomach or something equally lame—and avoid the situation altogether. Or maybe he was kidding himself, creating this whole conundrum when sex was the furthest thing from Cristin's mind. After all, hadn't she made a point of saying "no strings" last week?

He was still vacillating as they stepped into her third-floor apartment a few minutes later.

"I've been here only a couple of months so I'm still decorating," she said.

Compared to Jack's place it looked like a designer showroom. She had real curtains on the windows instead of room darkener shades, her couch looked firsthand instead of third or fourth. And she had art on the walls.

"Name your poison," she said as she opened a cabinet in the tiny kitchen.

"What've you got?"

While her back was turned, he removed the SOB holster and wrapped it in the blazer.

"Cuervo Gold."

He'd never been a tequila fan. In margaritas, sure, but the few shooters he'd done had left a burning tongue but no burning desire for more.

"What else?"

"I'm looking. Got some Cuervo Gold, and some Cuervo Gold, and let's see . . . oh, here's some Cuervo Gold."

He laughed. "I'll let you choose."

She turned and stared hard, as if studying him. "Judging from the look of you, I peg you as a Cuervo Gold type."

"Straight up?"

"The only way."

He'd never had that particular brand. Steely Dan's "Hey, Nineteen" drifted through his head. *Cuervo Gold . . . make tonight a wonderful thing . . .*

He really should go.

But he stayed and wandered to one of the framed pieces on her walls. It ran about three feet tall and two wide. From afar he'd thought it some kind of abstract, but close up he realized it was a sketch of a dress. The woman in the dress was almost a stick figure, barely recognizable as human, let alone female. The dress was the focus. He moved on to the next—different dress, same focus. Same with the third. He bent closer and realized they were originals on slightly wrinkled sketch paper.

"Did you do these?"

"Yes," she said, close behind him. "Like them?"

As he turned she pressed an elongated shooter glass filled with golden fluid into his hand. She was close. Very close.

"I do like them," he said. "I have no way to judge them as far as fashion design, but I think it's cool you've got your own work on your own walls."

"They're okay," she said, slipping past him and staring at the third. "I did them at FIT and had them lying around. I needed something for the walls so I figured, why not? Something different. Better than a Seurat print or Matisse that nine zillion other folks have. So I had a few framed and now I'm the only person in the whole world with Ott originals on her walls."

Jack felt a toast was required. He raised his glass.

"To the artist!"

She grinned. "I'll drink to that."

They clinked glasses and tossed back the Cuervo. It burned just a little going down, but left a soft and surprisingly pleasant aftertaste. Nothing like the harsh tequilas he'd had in the past.

"Not bad," he said, staring at the glass. "Not bad at all."

She lifted the bottle from a nearby table and poured them another, saying, "This isn't shooter tequila. This is almost like sipping whiskey."

He took a sip and let it roll around his tongue. He could get used to this stuff.

He looked around. "Nice place. Looks like you've got a pretty good life for a college dropout."

"Drop-*down*," she said. "I'm still taking a few credits. And as for this place, I'd love to buy it. They're asking only ninety-five thousand."

Seemed like a lot to Jack.

"'Only'?"

"I could probably get them down to ninety."

"Still pricey, if you ask me."

"City real estate is going to go through the roof, Jack."

He didn't want to ask flat out how an FIT dropout—or drop-down—knew this. So he opted for . . .

"Based on . . . ?"

"My clients. I arrange events for CEOs' families and companies and they all tell me to put any spare money I've got into real estate here in the city."

Real estate . . . that was for real people, with real identities. Not for him.

"So what's holding you back? Money?"

"You betcha. But I'm putting away all I can for the down payment. I'll get there."

Jack couldn't help but think of Julio's need for a down payment. Maybe the combination of that plus the tequila caused him to blurt out, "I can lend you the money."

She laughed. "I know you said the tips were good, but they can't be *that* good."

Oh, right. He was supposed to be a deliveryman. And then he remembered the Mikulskis' warning about keeping that money out of circulation.

"I've got savings from my previous life."

She gave her head an emphatic shake. "Thanks, but no way I can take money from you."

He hid his relief with a hurt look. "What's wrong with my money? Just a loan."

Still shaking her head—had she and Julio taken lessons together?

"No strings, remember? A loan is a string."

"But you'd be getting a mortgage from a bank. That's a loan. That's a string."

"Not the kind of string I'm talking about. A bank's an *institution.* You're a person. No strings, no strings, no strings."

"I get it."

"Good." She finished her second tequila and put the glass down. "Now let's fuck."

Jack blinked. Did she just say . . . ?

"Um, what?"

"Fuck, fuck, fuck. Like bunnies. Or, if you prefer, 'Have sex.'" She stepped close and began unbuttoning his shirt. "Notice, I didn't say 'Make love.' Because we're not in love. We may be in 'like' but we're not in love. Love would mean strings, a relationship, and neither of us want that."

Inanely, through all the sudden turmoil in his bloodstream and in his brain, he mentally corrected her: *wants* that.

He gripped her wrists as she opened a second button.

"You've had a lot to drink."

She smiled. "And you think I'll regret this in the morning. Aw, that's sweet. But I haven't and I won't." She twisted her wrists free and began working on the third button. "I know exactly what I'm doing."

"Which is?"

"Getting ready to fuck your brains out and hoping you'll reciprocate."

"Cristin . . ."

"Just pure physical need and want, Jack. Don't make any more of it than that. I like you. I find you attractive. So, unless you find me repulsive . . ." Her hand trailed down to his zipper and gave a gentle squeeze to the growing hardness there. She smiled. "Apparently you don't. So then, I'm going to pleasure you and you're going to pleasure me. Nothing more. Fair enough?"

She gave him another squeeze. That did it. It had been too long a time, too many nights alone.

His voice sounded like a croak. "Fair enough."

She took his hand and pulled him toward her bedroom.

"Follow me."

7

"So if we're not making love, are we making like? I've never made like."

"Then this will be a new experience for you. And I guarantee something."

"What?"

"You're going to *like* it. Comfy?"

"Yeah, but it's awful dark in here."

"I like it dark. Am I rushing this too much?"

"Not at all."

"Sometimes I just want to get to it, you know."

"You won't hear me complain. But there's this strange sensation of a weight on my chest."

"That's my butt. Are you telling me I'm fat?"

"No way."

"Then get used to it . . . it's gonna be there awhile. Now take your hand and—yes!"

"Mmmm, you're wet."

"I should be . . . been hoping all week we'd end up here."

"Like slick silk."

"Right there. That's the spot."

"You like that?"

"Yesssss . . . now stop talking. This is *my* time and I know you can find better things to do with your tongue. Aaaaah! You do! That's it . . . that's it . . . find the little pearl . . . there! Now the fingers, don't forget the fingers. Right there. Gimme! Gimme! Gimme! Gimmeeeeeeee!"

8

"How're you doing?" she said, her breath warm against his chest.

They'd untangled the sheets and now lay stretched out on the bed, Cristin snuggled against him, her head on his shoulder, a thigh draped across his groin.

"Wiped out."

She giggled. "Good. Then my work here is done."

No lie. He felt physically drained. But emotionally . . . strange. It had been over sooner than he would have wished. And he'd never expected the evening to turn out like this.

"I wanted to last longer but, well, it's been a long time."

"It's okay. I came four times."

She was counting? Well, why not? She knew what she wanted and she'd definitely been in charge, even to the point of slipping a condom on him. When he'd questioned her, she'd whispered, *"I play it safe . . . and it's got ridges. I loooove ridges."*

Did she ever.

He pouted. "Only once for me."

"Well, your tongue-fu is verrrry strong."

"You are an excellent teacher."

She laughed. "Seriously, though, you haven't been getting any?"

"Nope."

"Oh, man, I'd go craaaazy!"

"I'm not very good with pickup lines. Never have been."

"You don't really need them in this town. 'Wanna fuck?' is often enough."

He shook his head. "Somehow I don't see me saying that."

"You can say it to me. Anytime you want. I mean, I like sex, you know."

Jack laughed. "Really? I never would have guessed."

"Seriously. I discovered that in junior high school when I gave myself my first orgasm. I didn't have the nerve to get it on with a guy until well into high school, and that was even better. At least most of the time. So many guys, so little time."

Jack remembered how Cristin had gained quite the reputation by senior year.

"It just came back to me: Hot-to-trot Ott."

She smiled. "That was me. I did most of the football team."

"Oh, come on."

"Well, varsity first string, anyway. All except Tommy Lampman. Turned out he was gay."

"No way!"

"Way. Way gay. You know who else was gay? Sheila McKim."

"But she was dating that jock, Warner."

"And he wasn't getting any."

"How do you—oh, wait. Him too?"

"No. Her."

Jack rose onto an elbow and stared at her. "You and *Sheila*?"

She nodded. "We got assigned to a science project together—she told me later that she'd finagled me as a partner—and one night we're working on it at her house and her folks are out and she starts playing footsie with me and, well, one thing led to another and . . ." She shrugged. "She was my first girl."

"First?"

She glanced away. "There've been others."

"So you're telling me you're bi?"

"I don't look at it that way. The queers make it all so political and go around labeling everybody. I . . . like . . . *sex*. I like getting it on and I loooove getting off. The sex of the other person doesn't matter so much as long as I like them. I could use a little more Cuervo. You?"

The change of subject caught him by surprise. He laughed. "After hearing about you and Sheila McKim, yeah. A double."

She rolled out of bed and strolled away. As he fully appreciated the curves of her body, he couldn't help envisioning Cristin and Sheila going at it. The images caused a little stir down below. She returned with the bottle, completely nonchalant about her nakedness.

"Did you have that body in high school?"

She sat on the edge of the bed and poured a shot. "Pretty much."

"You hid it well."

"Just 'cause you're the school slut doesn't mean you have to look the part."

Jack didn't like to hear her talk about herself that way. "Don't call yourself that."

She shrugged. "It's just a word."

Holding the shooter glass, she reclined on the bed.

"We're sharing?"

"Uh-huh."

She poured some onto her belly, filling her navel.

"That's yours."

He looked at her. "Seriously?" He put on a disgusted face. "What if you've got lint?"

She giggled. "Don't make me laugh. You'll spill it." And sure enough, some of it tricked down over her left flank. "And after where your tongue has been tonight, you're going to worry about a little belly-button lint?"

"Point taken."

He leaned over her and slurped the tequila. She squirmed as he licked the residue from her navel.

"That tickles. Now my turn."

As she rolled him onto his back and pushed the sheet down to his hips,

Jack did a quick check of his navel. No lint. He'd showered just a few hours ago, but who knew where that stuff came from anyway?

She poured the rest of the shot and licked. It did tickle. She lifted the sheet and took a peek at him.

"Ooh, I think you'll be ready again reeeeal soon."

He had no doubt of that.

She rested her head on his abdomen and looked at him. "Your fuck drought is over. We'll be fuck buddies—as long as you want. Just don't get attached."

He thought about that. Her vivaciousness, her in-your-face approach to sex and life in general were so refreshing . . . he might get attached.

"You never get attached?"

She lifted her head. "Nah. I'm too young to get involved with anyone. Plenty of time for that. Guys are the problem. They get all territorial and possessive. A couple of bouts in the bedroom and they think they can't live without you and you can't live without them. Wroooong! They get all worked up when you tell them it's over. A guy in my first year at FIT beat me up when I broke it off. Said it wasn't over till he said it was over."

A surge of anger cooled Jack's afterglow. "Did you report him?"

"No. I didn't want the attention."

"You just let it go? How did you get free of him?"

"He had an accident. He was always late for class and used to run down this stairwell every morning. One day he tripped. Had a terrible fall. Broken bones, bad concussion. He was out cold for a day or so. He's got a permanent limp now."

Jack had to smile. "What did he trip on?"

"When he regained consciousness he said he remembered a bunch of marbles on the landing, but nobody ever found any."

Jack could only stare at her. Her matter-of-fact attitude was a little chilling. More than a little. He liked her even more.

"A guy shouldn't hit a woman, Jack," she added. "Don't you agree?"

"Absolutely."

"That was when I started working on my little speech, so that everyone knows the ground rules going in."

She refilled the shooter glass, then lay back and dribbled some onto her belly.

"More?" she said.

"How can I say no?"

Indeed. He slurped, then reclined. She filled his navel, then licked it empty. But she didn't stop there. She pushed the sheet farther down, exposing him.

"This might feel a bit cold." She poured the rest of the shooter over him and the tequila did feel cold. "But not for long."

She licked him, then took him in her mouth, and made it warm . . . made everything warm.

9

"Wake up."

Someone was shaking him. Jack opened his eyes. Cristin was standing over him, wiggling his shoulder.

"What?"

"Wake up."

He pushed himself up to one elbow and rubbed his eyes. "I think I fell asleep."

"I *know* you did." She'd put on an oversized Bon Jovi T-shirt and plaid comfy pants. "No sleeping allowed."

He flopped back. "It's your fault."

Their second bout of lovemaking—despite her insistence, he couldn't call it fucking—had lasted much longer than the first, and had left him literally and figuratively drained. He must have dozed off.

"Up-up-up!"

"I can't move."

"I'm serious, Jack. No sleepovers."

"Really?"

"It's a rule."

He forced himself to a sitting position on the edge of the bed.

"Why not?"

"I like my mornings to myself."

"No strings, no attachments, and now no sleepovers. You do like rules."

"Only if they're mine. And sleepovers lead to all sorts of domestical, attachy feelings, and that leads to strings. And as I said, I like my mornings to myself."

Jack spotted his boxers on the floor and pulled them on.

"I'm going to try to stand," he said, "but I'm not sure my knees work."

He was only half kidding.

Cristin laughed and held out a helping hand. "I'm not *that* good."

He took her hand and let her pull him to his feet. His knees held. He found his shirt and slipped into it.

"In my limited experience, you are beyond fantastic."

"Better than Karina?"

He looked at her. Was that important? He'd tell her the truth.

"No comparison. But it's apples and oranges. We were both beginners." He pulled on his slacks. "Back then I thought Karina and I had the greatest sex in the world, but I had nothing to compare it to."

"But now you do. You've got to admit she's kind of passive in bed."

He smiled. "Compared to you, I imagine . . ." His voice trailed off as a realization grew. "You and Karina?"

She looked guilty. "I thought you should know."

"When?"

"That summer after freshman year."

"But you said she was involved with someone else back in Berkeley and came home only for a week."

Cristin shook her head. "No, she was home all summer but made me swear not to tell you."

Jack's head swam as he tried to put the pieces together. He still had tequila plus Cristin-triggered endorphins roiling through his bloodstream, so it wasn't easy.

"So let me get this straight: There was no field trip to volunteer at the Indian reservations and study their cultures."

"I told you that."

"And there was no new guy in Berkeley."

"No. That was my lie—or semi-lie."

"You could have told me the truth."

Her eyes widened. "Jack, we hadn't seen each other in years, and we're sitting down for our first conversation since high school, and I'm going to tell you that Karina's 'other man' was me and we spent part of that summer munching each other's carpets?"

"Swell way to put it."

The image both hurt and excited him.

"Actually 'carpets' isn't exactly accurate because we both decided to shave our—"

He held up a hand. "Okay, okay, I can see why you might hesitate, but jeez, Cristin."

"Jack, you wouldn't believe how messed up she was. You know she'd always been a vegetarian, right? Well, she'd gone total vegan out there and was into all that gender politics and alternate lifestyle stuff and somehow got the idea that she ought to be a lesbian."

"'Ought to be'?"

"Yeah, like you decide, right? It seemed to have more to do with politics than sex. When we got high once in senior year I slipped about doing Sheila. She'd been all 'Oh, yuck' then, but now she wanted to know what it was like and, well, you know me—or at least you do now—I said there's only one way to find out."

He shook his head. "My first love became a lesbian."

"Only for a little while. It wasn't real for her and she couldn't get into it."

"Were you into it?"

She shrugged. "It was okay. She was kind of passive. At least we didn't have to worry about condoms and pregnancy and all that. When she got back to Berkeley she went hetero again."

"But not with me."

"You weren't radical enough for her, Jack. You aren't at all political. Gender politics—that was pretty much all she'd talk about. But sometimes, after we'd finish up, we'd lie in bed and she'd talk about you."

"How to avoid running into me?"

"Yeah. But not just that. She was trying hard to get over you, but hadn't succeeded yet. She'd been soooo crazy about you back in SBR. Freshman year, the first day on the bus, she spotted you getting on and right away wanted to know who you were. At first we thought you were hooked up with that weirdo Weezy Connell."

"Don't call her weird."

"Everyone did."

"Because they didn't know her. She was good people."

But definitely weird. No getting around that. Jack wondered how she was doing.

"Anyway, when Karina found out there was nothing going there, she set her sights on you."

Jack remembered how Karina and Cristin always managed to wind up at his lunch table.

"Well, she got me."

Cristin grinned. "But I bet you thought you got her."

Jack had to nod. "Yeah, I did."

She laughed. "Guys. So clueless. Say, whatever happened to that Weezy chick?"

"I don't know. We grew apart. She was a year ahead of us, so she's probably graduated by now."

He and Weezy had been so close. They'd had some bizarre adventures together, seen some strange things, and he'd gone way out on a limb for her once. But then some doctor put her on medication to ease her mood swings and she changed. Her life evened out, her moods became less volatile, and she became less . . . Weezy.

Had the meds made her life better? He couldn't say. But wherever she was, he hoped she was happy.

He grabbed his blazer—and the revolver swathed within—before Cristin could hand it to him, and glanced at the clock on her nightstand.

"It's not even midnight yet."

"It's been a long week and I need my beauty rest. So, when will I see you again?"

"Anytime." Had he said that too quickly? He added, "You could see me again in the morning if you weren't kicking me out."

She smiled. "Don't look at it as me kicking you out. Look at it as me doing you a favor. I'm not a morning person. I like my wake-up time to myself. Having someone else around makes me *very* irritable. You wouldn't like me at all. Trust me, you're better off waking up in your bed rather than mine."

Jack didn't feel like braving the cold.

"Okay," he said slowly. "Dinner again?"

"Sundays are best for me. You pick the place this time. Come up with something interesting."

"Will do."

Interesting? He ate at sub shops and delis. Who could he ask? He'd figure that out later.

She led him to the door and when he went to kiss her good night she held him off and pointed to her cheek.

"Friends kiss here. A peck and no more."

So he gave her a quick kiss on the cheek. She returned the favor.

"Night, Jack."

"Night, Cristin."

And then he was walking down the hall, cradling the blazer and its contents in his arms and thinking what a strange, quirky, intriguing woman the former plain-jane Cristin Ott had grown into.

And damn she was good in bed.

10

The man in the white suit frightened Kadir. He had opened the door to his apartment to the man from Qatar, but this man and two other Westerners had entered with him. The man in the white suit seemed to be in charge. The man from Qatar acted as an interpreter when Kadir's limited English failed him. The two others positioned themselves by the door and said nothing.

"Do you know Seif Jalil?" the man in white said.

"Yes. Not well. I work with him."

"Do you know that he was found dead?"

Kadir gasped. "No! When? How?"

"Apparently he was tortured. You know nothing about it?"

"No-no! Of course not!"

"Do you know of any reason why he would be tortured and killed?"

Kadir searched for an answer. He'd barely known Seif Jalil. They worked together labeling cigarette packs for Tachus's uncle Riaz. But Jalil had been unusually talkative lately. And Kadir had a feeling he had better give this man something useful.

"He was involved in the . . ." He looked to the man from Qatar for clearance to mention the unmentionable.

The man nodded. "Go ahead, Kadir. He knows all about it."

"Seif was involved in the auction."

"Yes, we know. He was in charge of arranging the seating and the rooms for inspection of the merchandise. Tell us something we don't know."

"He . . . he heard there was a reward for return of the money."

The man in white looked at the man from Qatar. "Reward? Who authorized a reward?"

"Our brother in the hotel."

The man in white's eyebrows lifted. "Since when do we reward people for returning what they lost?"

The man from Qatar made no reply and the other turned back to Kadir. "Why would that lead to his death?"

"He said he was asking around, looking for clues."

This seemed to amuse the man in white. "'Clues'? How quaint. Apparently he asked the wrong person." Kadir quailed as his eyes narrowed and his gaze bored into him. "And what about you? Were you hunting 'clues' as well?"

"No! They might lead me to those two killers. I don't want to find them."

"Ah, yes. The two killers. We'll get back to them. You didn't happen to mention Jalil's interest to anyone, did you?"

"No. Who would I—?"

"We are always suspicious of anyone who survives a massacre. Everyone dead but one. How does that happen?" Kadir opened his mouth to explain, but the man waved him silent. "Never mind. Tell us about these two men—*all* about them."

Kadir did the best he could with what limited knowledge he had.

When he finished, the man said, "And you are sure they were Americans?"

"They sounded like Americans."

"Would you be able to recognize their voices?"

Kadir very much doubted that, but sensed he must remain useful to this man, or risk being discarded . . . disposed of.

"I think so."

"You might get that opportunity. Stay easily available. We may call on you at a moment's notice. Do not make us search for you. Because, no matter where you go, we *will* find you. We are everywhere, and you will suffer for any inconvenience you cause us."

The man in white led the way out, followed by what appeared to be his two bodyguards. The man from Qatar turned at the door. "Do as he says, Kadir. This is very serious."

And then he too was gone, leaving Kadir alone again.

What was happening? How had he got himself into this horrific mess? All he had wanted was a job. Then he had met El Sayyid Nosair and came to share his devotion to jihad. The man from Qatar was supposed to help them support jihad with a windfall. He'd made it seem like he was using his own money, but obviously it came from somewhere else, from someone he answered to.

Who was the man in white? Who did he represent? Never once during the entire interrogation had he said "I" or "me." Always "we" or "us."

Who was the "we"? Who was the "us"?

Kadir felt that his life was no longer his own, that he was being lifted and carried along by a great force he could not resist, a force greater even than jihad.

MONDAY

1

Jack stepped out of the narrow storefront a thousand bucks poorer than when he'd gone in. He paused by the yellow A-frame sandwich board sign on the sidewalk.

ERNIE'S I-D
ALL KINDS
PASSPORT
TAXI
DRIVERS LICENSE

It should have had an extra line: LEGAL AND OTHERWISE.

He glanced back through the smudged window at the display of dinky castings of the Empire State Building and the Statue of Liberty surrounded by dusty snow globes encasing the Manhattan skyline and the Brooklyn Bridge and other landmarks.

The weaselly guy inside had been all sorts of accommodating. He took a number of pictures of Jack and pocketed a large deposit, guaranteeing "totally locked-down, foolproof, atomically secure ID." For that price, it had damn well better be. The only hitch was that Ernie didn't have a "John" or a "Jack" ID in the hopper. The only one he had that started with a "J" was "Jeff Cusic." Jack went with that one.

When Jack returned from his next trip to North Carolina, Ernie would have a New York State driver's license, a Social Security card, and a Visa card with a modest credit history ready for him. The Jeff Cusic they purported to identify was not fictitious. He'd died at age two. But his name lived on.

Jack tried to shake off the morbid feeling of assuming a dead kid's identity, but it followed him through a nearby Gristedes, where he picked up an eight-pack of Entenmann's crumb donuts, and from there as he hopped on his Harley and rode to the Isher Sports Shop.

Abe was delighted with the offering and immediately dug in.

"Nu," he said, biting the crumbs off first and littering the counter with donut debris, "your tryst with the girl from home went well?"

Jack gave a casual shrug—at least he hoped it looked casual as Cristin's voice echoed through his brain saying, *Now let's fuck.*

"Yeah, pretty well."

"And she won't be talking about you next time she visits home?"

Damn, he'd never got around to discussing that with her. He'd brought it up at their lunch but he'd wanted to reinforce it. Somehow the subject never came up. Funny thing about that . . .

Fuck, fuck, fuck. Like bunnies.

Next time . . . next time he'd bring it up.

"Not a word."

"Good. And Ernie—he treated you right?"

Jack nodded. "You weren't kidding about him being expensive."

"Quality costs. When a member of officialdom is inspecting your license and calling the DMV to see if you've got any outstanding violations, you don't want the DMV saying, 'Never heard of the schmuck.' For peace of mind, you should expect to pay extra."

"If he's that good, then it's worth every penny. By the way, how's that list coming?"

"Of the strong-arm types?" He reached under the counter. "Half a dozen I've got."

"Any background?"

"Some. You want to know about John Gotti, you look in the *Post*. You want to know about these guys, not so easy. But I put down what I could."

He passed Jack two handwritten sheets of yellow paper. Jack glanced at them, then folded them.

"I'll study these later."

"You should maybe think twice before getting involved with these golems."

"Golems?" Jack remembered seeing the Paul Wegener silent film. "Wasn't the golem made of clay or stone?"

"These are men of stone. Be very careful in your dealings with the likes of them. Like the golem, they have no souls."

Jack slipped the papers into a back pocket.

"I'm counting on that."

2

Jack Harleyed over to The Spot to meet Dane Bertel. He'd called the old guy first thing this morning and learned he wanted a meeting ASAP. So Jack suggested The Spot.

Bertel seemed grumpier than usual and Jack had a pretty good idea of the who and the why.

"You're really screwing me up, Jack. You know that, don't you?"

Yep. Jack was the reason.

"I'm sure there's no shortage of drivers," Jack said, sipping coffee as they sat in the deserted bar. Not even Lou and Barney yet. "There's a recession going on."

"I can find a driver in a minute, but not one I can be sure won't take off with the shipment and try to sell it on his own."

"Sorry."

"I hope it's not because you blame me for what happened on the Outer Banks."

Well, Tony was Bertel's guy and he led Jack to that beach house, so yeah, indirectly Bertel had to take some responsibility. But Jack had made the decision to follow Tony instead of heading straight back, so he wasn't about to point a finger.

"I don't."

"So what is it then? You want to squeeze me? Okay. Three Gs per run."

"That's not—"

"All right, damn it—four."

"It's not the money," Jack said. "My . . . situation has changed."

"How?"

No way Jack was going to tell him about his double windfall. How could he put this?

"I need to stay around town more."

"What? You've suddenly got a wife and kids who don't want you on the road?"

Jack had to laugh at that. "Hardly. But I have some opportunities that need watching."

Bertel shook his head, his mouth twisting in distaste. "'Opportunities' . . . Well, I wouldn't want you to miss out on any 'opportunities.'" He pulled a folded sheet from the pocket of his coat and slid it across the table. "New meeting spot. New guy to meet you. And a change in schedule."

"Change how?" Jack said, unfolding the sheet.

"The Mummy wants the shipment first thing tomorrow morning."

Jack hadn't been expecting that.

"That means I'll have to leave soon."

"And haul ass on the way down. The Mummy is desperate for product and pissed off at me for the hiccup in his supply stream."

"'Hiccup'? Your operation was busted and Tony's dead."

"You and I may care, but he doesn't. All he cares about is product. If he can take delivery on the butts in the morning, he can have them all stamped and distributed by nightfall. Can you get it done?"

That meant driving all day and all night. What the hell . . . the only other thing he had going was the Zalesky fix, and that wasn't on a timetable.

"Yeah. No problem."

Bertel shook his head again. "See? That's what I need. A guy who says, 'No problem.'"

"Gotta be a lot of them around."

"You'd be surprised." Bertel rose and threw a ten on the table. "Don't let me down."

"I won't."

As Bertel left, Julio approached with his coffeepot.

"You want another?"

"Sure. A quick one." He was going to need all the stimulant he could stomach.

He pulled out an envelope containing four hundred-dollar bills. "Vinny Donuts is due today. Here's Zalesky's contribution."

"Zalesky." Julio's voice sounded strangled.

Jack glanced up at him. He'd thought he'd noticed a grim cast to his expression before. A closer look now left no doubt.

"What's up?"

Julio dropped into the chair Bertel had vacated. "Nita called last night."

"Who's Nita?"

"Harry's ex. Harry owned the place and—"

"Right-right. Left it to his son—who wants to sell it."

"That's it. She said Darren got an offer on the place."

"Crap. Well, my offer still stands."

Maybe the Mikulskis could help him find a way to launder the money. But Julio was shaking his head.

"It's worse than that. She didn't call me out of the goodness of her heart. She call because the seller want her to. He also want her to tell me his name."

Jack remembered the *hijo de puta*'s parting words just twenty-four hours ago.

"Aw, no. Zalesky?"

Julio nodded. "I gotta do him, Jack."

"Don't be a dummy, Julio. It's not a done deal yet, right?"

"Darren's got leave comin' up. Nita wants to get rid of the place but Darren don't want to do nothin' till he comes home."

"When's that?"

"A few months."

"Then we've got time to put together a counteroffer."

"I gotta do him. It solve two problems at once."

"And you wind up in the joint for life? He's not worth it."

"I do it so no one knows."

"He's your ex-brother-in-law with a restraining order on him from your sister and he's made an offer to buy your workplace. Who's gonna be suspect numero uno?"

"Don't care. I do it so no one can prove it."

Jack doubted that. Julio had a big-time emotional stake in all this and Jack suspected he'd wind up with a plan as subtle as a front-end loader.

"Let me handle it, Julio."

Another shake of the head. "You not the killing type, Jack."

A guy named Ed and a guy named Moose might disagree . . .

"I'm not talking about—"

"But I am, meng. This is double personal now. Not right I let somebody else solve my problem."

Just then the door opened and a burly guy in a dark suit stepped inside.

Vinny Donuts.

Jack pushed the envelope toward Julio and whispered, "Let Zalesky pay him."

Julio hesitated and Jack could tell it was eating Julio to give this creep a single cent, no matter whose money it was. But he took it, handed it to Vinny without a word, then returned to the table as if he'd ceased to exist.

Vinny tucked the envelope inside his coat pocket and left.

Jack jumped to his feet. "Look. I've got a run to make, and I can't put it off. When I get back, we'll work this out."

Julio shook his head. "I dunno—"

"Julio, promise me. We'll work this out so you don't get caught. Promise me you'll sit tight until I get back. It's an overnight run. We'll talk tomorrow. I won't let you down."

"No, I—"

"One fucking day, Julio. Okay?"

A long pause, then, "Okay. But you ain't gonna change my mind."

Jack knew he had to, but had no idea how. Worry about that later.

Right now he had to follow Vinny Donuts.

3

Jack kept plenty of distance between himself and the big black Crown Victoria. Vinny was driving. The same guy with the porkpie hat sat in front in the passenger seat. A third sat in the back. Jack had seen Vinny hand Julio's envelope to the third guy.

He followed them deep into Queens to a store—Elite Discount Appliances—on Liberty Avenue. The two passengers got out and went inside, the Crown Vic took off.

Jack stayed with the Vic, which turned around and started heading southwest, leading him into Brooklyn. In a warehouse section of Canarsie, the Vic pulled into a car salvage place on Preston Court. Vinny got out and disappeared into a trailer that seemed to serve as an office. Rusted cars littered the large lot, side-by-side in the front, piled atop each other in the back. Jack spotted a few steel cubes that used to be cars. Must be a compactor somewhere on the lot.

Jack didn't know how long Vinny would be there, and didn't have any more time to waste. But he made a note of the sign—Preston Salvage—and filed it away.

Elite Discount Appliances and Preston Salvage . . . data to add to the bank. He didn't know what he'd do with the information, but bits and pieces might adhere and come in handy someday.

He headed back to Manhattan to collect Bertel's truck and start the long haul south.

TUESDAY

1

The Suburban's dashboard clock was closing in on one A.M. as Reggie adjusted his screaming legs on the backseat of the car.

What a clusterfuck.

At least he was still alive. Unlike Tony and Moose.

The Arab, the one they called al-Thani, had grilled him about the Duck house. Told him a guy had been killed execution style in the house—that would be Tony. At first Reggie figured Moose for it, but then learned that someone had crushed Moose's skull out on the dunes. Probably Tim. He'd been royally pissed at Moose for disappearing. And then Tim, who didn't like loose ends, had done Tony. Or maybe Tony first and then Moose, didn't matter. He'd cleaned up and headed back to his boat to wait for his money.

Son of a bitch had a long fucking wait ahead of him.

Reggie couldn't see a reason not to be straight with al-Thani about the Duck house. He seemed to know a lot already, and Reggie didn't want to get caught in a lie. So he told him what he knew.

After that they'd fixed his knees. Both legs were now locked straight in casts, but supposedly on the mend. The pain was a bitch, and they weren't giving him a goddamn thing but Tylenol for it.

They . . . that was the big question: Who the fuck were *they*?

Some sort of club or secret society like the Masons or the Illuminati, he guessed. But what did that mean? Those were just names to him, anyway. He'd heard a couple of references to "the Order," but what was that? A religious sect? Whoever these people were, their "Order" was *big*. Arabs, Eurotrash, probably chinks as well.

And connected. He'd seen a guy in a white suit that everyone kowtowed to. He'd snapped his fingers and the next thing Reggie knew, he was in some private clinic getting plugged into IVs. He spent the late half of Saturday and the early half of Sunday in a daze, then he was shoved into the back of this Suburban with one of the Arabs who'd found him and driven south.

They were looking for Lonnie and hell-bent on finding him. They'd grilled Reggie on the best place to wait for him. Like he knew. But he could guess.

Tony had said the kid knew the route, even told them how much he got paid per run. And Reggie remembered Lonnie himself mentioning that he knew how to get to Staten Island but would be lost once he reached it.

Reggie was close to absolutely sure that Lonnie'd had nothing to do with the hijacking. That meant Lonnie was going to have to keep working. Tony had said he ran cigarettes—wouldn't say who for, but that was okay. If Lonnie went back to his old job, he'd be on the road again soon.

So Reggie had directed these Order guys to this spot on Route 13 just outside Salisbury, Maryland, where they could park close to the road with a long view of the northbound traffic. If Lonnie quit or changed his route, they were all fucked. But this was the perfect route to drive contraband between NC and NYC.

Last night the Suburban and another car—a Cherokee—had spent hours and hours parked here with no hits. Now they were back, same time, same station.

Two foreign guys, Eurotrash types, occupied the Jeep idling to their left. Reggie had the backseat of the Suburban to himself. Another Eurotrasher—a kid named Kris—had the wheel, and the second Arab who'd found him, the young one whose English sucked, sat shotgun. Why they had him along, Reggie couldn't say. He'd managed to learn that his name was Kadir and he was from Palestine, but that was it. He seemed scared and useless.

At thirty-two, Reggie was the old fart in the car.

"See?" said Kris from the front. He was pointing through the windshield. "Truck."

His English wasn't so hot either. Sounded like he was Russian or from one of those other commie countries over there.

Reggie spotted the northbound U-Haul, same model as Lonnie had used before, doing the limit and no more. He lifted the binocs Kris had brought along and focused on the windshield. Nothing but shadow within shadows until it passed under a streetlight. He caught a glimpse of the driver's face as the light flashed across it, but that was all he needed.

"That's him! Let's go! Let's nail that fucker!"

Kris gave his horn a toot and rolled down his window. He pointed to the truck and yammered something. The Jeep chirped its tires as it raced off. Kris rolled up his window but the Suburban stayed put.

Reggie slapped the back of Kris's seat. "Whatta you waitin' for? Let's go!"

Kris shook his head. "No. We stay."

"Fuck that! I got payback comin'!"

"You go nowhere. We stay. Orders."

Orders from the Order. And Kris wasn't about to disobey.

Reggie leaned back. This sucked. But the idea was to take Lonnie alive. Maybe after the Order was through with him, they'd give Reggie some time to get up close and personal with the son of a bitch.

2

Jack cruised north on Route 13, glad to be halfway home. A box of a dozen assorted Krispy Kremes sat on the passenger seat. He'd spent much of the empty road time thinking pleasant thoughts about his next encounter with Cristin. The taste of her tequila, the taste of her soft skin and the soft sounds she made as she came . . . memory and anticipation helped keep him awake and alert. Had to remember to remind her not to mention him should she talk to anyone from home.

In-the-moment reality intruded somewhere north of Salisbury when he began to suspect he had a tail. A dark SUV—black or blue, he couldn't tell—had been lingering in his side-view mirror.

Up until then he'd had smooth sailing. He'd left New York at noon and, despite heavier than expected traffic, made the trip in just under eight hours. The new contact, a fat guy in bib overalls, was waiting for him as planned at a Fairfield Inn outside Elizabeth City. He called himself Vern—that might even have been his real name—and reminded Jack of Junior Samples in need of a shave. He took the truck in exchange for a room key. Jack had lain on the bed but it was too early for sleep, so he watched a painful *Head of the Class*, followed by *Roseanne.* He didn't have a TV in his apartment and had been planning on buying one. He decided to revisit that decision. It didn't seem like he was missing a damn thing.

A knock on the door saved him from *Coach*.

Vern handed him the truck keys. "All yours," he said and started to walk away.

"Whoa-whoa," Jack said. "Not so fast. Let's take a look at the cargo first."

His round, unshaven face darkened. "What? You don't trust me?"

The guy was big and evidently had a chip on his shoulder. Jack did not want to get into it with him.

"I just met you, Vern. And I had a bad experience with the cargo on my last run. So humor me, okay? We'll just walk out to the truck and I'll take a peek inside, okay?"

Vern obviously didn't like it but he went along and a peek showed the bay packed to the ceiling with Marlboro master cases. Satisfied, Jack had driven off, leaving Vern standing in the parking lot.

He checked his side-view mirror for the tenth time in the past minute. The SUV—he'd pegged it as a Jeep—was hanging back, pacing him. When Jack slowed, it slowed; when he picked up speed, it did the same. He spotted a truck stop ahead on the right and pulled in. The car followed.

Shit.

His heart picked up tempo as he pulled up to the pumps. He didn't need gas but went inside and prepaid for five bucks' worth anyway. The car—a dark green Jeep Cherokee—had pulled into a parking space. As he waited for change, he watched out of the corner of his eye. Two figures in the front seat but he couldn't make out their faces. They remained in the car.

Unless they thought he was totally stupid, they had to know they'd been made. What next?

He picked up a wrapped toothpick from a shotglass on the counter and went outside. The guys were still in the car. What were they after—the truck, or him? He needed the answer to that.

Well, he wasn't without resources. Against Bertel's rules, he'd brought the Ruger and stashed it under the front seat. The last thing he wanted was a shoot-out. His aim wasn't all that great under range conditions; he could imagine how accurate he'd be with someone shooting at him.

While the gas was pumping, he climbed into the truck's cab and stuck the Ruger into the back of his belt line. When he finished with the gas, he started the truck and left the door open as he walked back to the shop. If that didn't shout *Steal me,* nothing did.

Without going inside he asked loud and clear about a restroom. The guy jerked a thumb over his shoulder—toward the right side of the building.

Jack rounded the corner and paused. After hearing two car doors slam, he ran to the restroom, pulled the door open, and checked the inside knob. As expected, a standard lever model with a push-button lock. He pushed the button and squeezed the toothpick in beside it, jamming it in the locked position. Then he slammed the door and ran around the rear of the building.

He emerged on the other side and checked the Cherokee—empty, with neither occupant in sight. If they were after his cargo, one of them would be behind the truck's steering wheel and hauling ass out of here.

So . . . they were after him.

He would have preferred the former.

He dashed past the Jeep to his truck. He wished he'd brought a knife so he could slash their tires or cut a couple of valve stems. He could shoot the tires, of course, but that would have the attendant calling 911.

He hopped behind the wheel, slammed the door, and roared back toward the road. Along the way he saw two men outside the men's room, tugging on the doorknob. They spotted him and started to run.

All right. Now even more obvious that they were after *him,* not the cigarettes. Only one reason for that: to find the money. Which meant they'd want him alive. And that was a good thing.

Jack's heart was pounding now. He couldn't outrun them, and he sure as hell couldn't call the cops. So what the hell to do? Route 13 was a glorified country road around here. Should he stay on it or get off? He discarded the get-off option—the side roads were darker than 13 and looked like narrow, macadam traps. If he could find some other cars heading north he could hang with them, but the road was deserted. Okay, yeah, it was a Monday night—or early Tuesday morning, rather—but didn't anybody around here go out during the week?

He wished he had more experience with this sort of thing.

He kept the gas pedal floored, passing eighty, pushing toward ninety miles an hour when headlights flashed in his mirror, coming up fast. Now what?

The Cherokee swerved into the southbound lane and pulled up on his left side. The passenger was leaning out the window, his arm extended, gripping a semiautomatic. Jack instinctively ducked back, then noticed that the pistol was pointed down, not up.

He was shooting at the truck's tires.

Maybe they wanted him alive, but a blowout at this speed could leave him just as dead as a bullet through the head.

He saw muzzle flashes but the reports were reduced to pops through the closed window. He was reaching around to the small of his back, figuring two could play this game, when he realized: Hey, I'm bigger than they are.

Taking a tight, two-handed grip on the steering wheel, he wrenched it left. The truck sideswiped the Cherokee, crushing the arm of the shooter and sending the Jeep careening off the road into a ditch where it flipped rear over front. The shooter flew from the window and pinwheeled through the air while the Jeep landed on its roof, pancaking the top and blowing out all the windows as it spun a one-eighty, then rolled onto its passenger side.

Jack slammed on the brakes. After the truck swerved and skidded to a halt on the shoulder, he pulled his Ruger and ran back to see what was what. He had some questions that needed answering.

The Jeep's engine had died but its headlights remained on and aimed across the road. The shooter's semiauto lay in the middle of the blacktop. Jack kicked it to the side and approached the shooter himself. Pale-skinned with blond hair, he lay crumpled on the shoulder, eyes staring, arms, legs, and neck at impossible angles.

No answers from this guy.

He moved on to the side-resting car, approaching the crushed roof. The radiator was hissing, sending up plumes of steam. He looked down through the shattered window space and saw the roof resting on the headrests of the front seats. The driver, another white guy—Jack had expected Arabs—hung from his seat belt. Jack leaned closer and saw bloody bubbles forming and popping between his slack lips. Alive, but not a font of information at the moment.

"Looks like we wasted our time, bro."

Jack spun, Ruger raised.

"Whoa!" said one of the two figures approaching across the road.

They both stopped midway and raised their hands. A dark blue sedan idled with its lights out on the opposite shoulder. He hadn't heard it over the hissing steam.

"We're on your side."

Jack recognized that voice. Deacon Blue. The Mikulskis.

"What are you two doing here?"

"Looking out for your ass," said Blue as they resumed their approach. "But you seem to have taken care of business."

Black picked up the shooter's pistol. He turned it over in his gloved hands, popped the magazine, and examined it. He shook his head, tsking.

"Trying to shoot out a spinning truck tire with nine-millimeter hollowpoints."

"Really," said Blue as he crouched beside the dead shooter. "Somebody was watching too many movies."

He patted the shooter's body and removed his wallet. Pocketing it, he rose and moved toward the Jeep.

"I don't get it," Jack said.

"Low-percentage shot. 'Specially with hollowpoints."

Black was turning the pistol over in his hands. "I'll be damned. It's a Tokarev."

"What's that?"

"Old Russian Army pistol now made by the Chinese."

Jack looked down at the shooter. "He's not Chinese."

"They're still popular in Europe."

"Piece of crap," Black said and tossed it into the field at the side of the road.

Blue looked in on the driver. "Hey, this guy's still breathing."

He reached in with both arms. After fumbling around a bit, he came up with a second wallet. He reinserted his arms and made a sharp jerking motion.

Jack stepped forward. "What'd you just do?"

"Solved the breathing problem."

"What? I wanted to talk to him!"

"Wasn't going to happen," Blue said. "If he survived long enough to get to a hospital, he wouldn't be talking for days. And we've all got to get out of here."

"Haven't you learned your lesson?" Black said, stepping closer. "You leaving the wrong guy alive is why we're all standing here."

The accusation startled Jack. "You think Reggie—?"

"Is this the route you and him followed up to Staten Island?"

Jack nodded as a sick feeling grew in his stomach. "Yeah." Reggie must have laid out the path for whoever was after the money. "But why are you guys here?"

Black said, "We figured this might happen. I kind of blame myself for letting a green newbie make a decision that I just knew was going to come back and bite him in the ass."

"Not so green," Blue said. "Take a look around."

"Yeah, you did all right. But you were lucky. The bad news is Reggie wasn't in the Jeep. That means you're going to have to deal with him again."

Blue patted the pocket where he'd stowed the wallets. "Maybe these guys can give us an idea as to who's behind this."

"Meanwhile," Black said, looking up and down the road, "let's get out of here. We may be in the sticks, but sooner or later somebody's gonna come along."

"Thanks, guys," Jack said.

The brothers headed back toward their car.

"We didn't do shit," Black said.

"Still, I appreciate the thought."

"Yeah, well, we'll follow you back," Blue said, "but from here on we're staying home. And you should do the same. You make another one of these runs, you're on your own."

"I hear ya."

He hurried back to his truck and resumed the trek north.

Good advice from the Mikulskis. And he was going to take it.

Bertel was going to be royally pissed, but too bad. Jack was a sitting duck out here on the road. Next time he might be the one lying in a ditch.

3

Kris had dialed his car phone about a dozen times, but his buddies in the Jeep weren't answering.

Not good. Not that Reggie thought for an instant that Lonnie had bested those two Eurothugs. He might be quick with his hands when a guy wasn't suspecting anything, but this was different. The guys after him were about

Reggie's age, maybe older, and carried themselves like seasoned vets. Lonnie wasn't going to sucker-punch those two. But that didn't mean they couldn't have got themselves on the wrong side of some state or local mounties.

"Maybe we'd better cruise on down the road apiece and see what's what," Reggie said.

"Orders are to stay."

"Yeah, well, you've done your stayin', now it's time to do a little reconnoiterin'."

"We must wait for them here."

"If they were coming, they'd be here by now, or they would have called. Something's wrong, Kris. That's obvious. And your higher-ups might be asking you later why you didn't go see if you could help."

Kris chewed his upper lip for a few seconds, then gave a quick nod. He threw the car in gear and started rolling. A couple of miles past the truck stop they came across a couple of cop cars with their lights flashing. Behind them a steaming Jeep Cherokee lay on its side.

Reggie let slip a "Holy shit!" while Kris blurted something unintelligible and Kadir mentioned Allah before slapping a hand over his mouth. They slowed to watch a cop covering a sprawled body with some sort of tarp. A second cop was crouched by the Jeep, shining a light into the front compartment. The first cop looked up from the body and motioned them to keep moving.

Where was the truck? Where was Lonnie?

Kris seemed mesmerized and the cop repeated the move-on signal.

"Do what he says, Kris. We don't wanna get stopped and have to explain what we're doing out at this hour."

Kris gave it some gas and picked up the car phone. This time he got an answer and started babbling in foreignese.

Looked like it was Lonnie two, the Order zero. How the fuck had that happened? He'd been alone in that truck. How'd he flip the Jeep?

Who cared? The fact was he was running free and Reggie had two broke knees and was stuck with these sinister weirdos. Not fair. Not fucking fair at all.

Then again, on the plus side, this guy Lonnie had just earned himself a lot more enemies. And that could work for Reggie in a big way.

4

Jack made it to the Jersey City drop spot before dawn. He figured he'd have to wait for the Arabs to show, but they were ready and waiting. Bertel hadn't been kidding: These guys were hungry for ciggies.

As soon as the door rolled down and the unloading began, Jack retreated to a corner, the Ruger in his belt, his hand close to it. He didn't know if the Arabs had anything to do with the incident this morning, and none of them seemed to have the slightest interest in him, but he wasn't taking any chances.

He kept an eye out for the Mummy who'd been running the operation in the past. When Jack didn't see him, he motioned one of the unloaders over.

"Where's the man with the money?"

"Not here," the guy said, shaking his head. "Other man come soon."

"What's wrong? Is he sick?"

The guy shrugged. "Not here."

Not here . . . yeah, Jack could see that. But was his *not-here*-ness temporary or permanent? Bertel said he'd talked to him since the shoot-out, but had he? Had the Mummy been the guy in the limo the Mikulskis had blown away?

If so, that hinted at a possible link between Bertel and the sex-slave trade. It didn't mean Bertel was involved, or even knew about it, but it opened the unpleasant possibility.

Then the man himself appeared.

Bertel strolled in through the side door and stopped next to Jack.

"You made it on time," he said, nodding approval. "Good job."

"Also the last job."

Bertel's expression slackened with surprise. "What? Hey, now, you promised me three."

Jack crooked a finger and led him around to the driver's side. He pointed to the scraped and dented fender. Bertel stiffened, then stepped closer and ran a hand over the dents until he found a bullet hole. He jerked upright and faced Jack.

"What the—?"

Jack decided to play dumb about the real purpose behind the incident. "Somebody tried to hijack me."

"Come on!"

"I'm not imagining those bullet holes. They tried to shoot out my tires outside Salisbury."

"What happened?"

"I ran them off the road."

"No idea who they were?"

Jack shook his head. "And even less idea how they knew my route. Or that I was making a run. You and I knew it. So did Vern."

"Vern doesn't know the route."

"Who else then?"

"No one."

"Well, I sure as hell didn't set myself up."

Bertel stiffened when he caught Jack's stare. "Now wait a minute. You can't think—"

Jack didn't. Bertel was all about profit, and if he was going to set Jack up, it would not be while he was ferrying his precious cigarettes to a payday. But no reason not to let him feel a little heat.

"Just saying."

"Well, you can goddamn stop 'just saying' anything like that." His eyes narrowed. "When you brought that other cargo north . . . what route did you take?"

Hard to slip one past this buzzard.

"The same. And yeah, someone followed me then in another truck."

Reggie.

"And where is this someone now?"

"I don't know. But I saw the two guys in the car at a rest stop before they made their move and he wasn't one of them."

"But he could have been on watch along the route. He knows the type of truck you drive, and what you look like."

That seemed the only reasonable explanation.

A skinny guy in a skullcap emerged from the office and handed Bertel an envelope. No words were exchanged.

"Where's the Mummy?" Jack said.

Bertel shrugged as he thumbed through the bills in the envelope. "Told me he'd had a death in the family."

"A death, huh?"

Bertel looked at him. "Why're you suddenly so interested in our fat friend?"

Jack wondered who had died and if it might have been due to multiple lead projectiles acquired on Staten Island, but left the question unasked.

"Maybe I wanted to bid him au revoir."

"Yeah, right. The important thing is, the money's right." Instead of waiting until they were outside, Bertel paid Jack his cut now. "Sure this is your last trip?" he said as he pressed the bills into Jack's hand.

Probably thought the feel of the cash against his palm would be a potent persuader.

Not. At least not anymore.

Jack shook his head. "Sorry. You're a good boss but even without hijackers, the job's got far more exposure than I want."

"You got something better lined up?"

"No."

"You got *anything* lined up?"

"No."

"Then why not—?"

"I'll be keeping busy."

"Doing what?"

He opened the truck door and pointed out the Krispy Kreme box. "Delivering donuts to needy people."

"Cut the bullshit."

"I'm not kidding. You don't think Abe is needy?"

"Not in need of donuts." He sighed. "Ah, well. Take the truck back to where you got it." He stuck out his hand. "Hey, good luck. But if you ever change your mind, or you ever need anything . . ."

"Thanks. Hey, maybe you could help me with something I'm looking into."

"Shoot."

Jack had to smile at the unintentional irony of the expression.

"You know any hit men or enforcer types?"

He burst out laughing at Bertel's expression.

5

Ernst arrived early at Roman Trejador's suite. He knew what he was going to hear and wanted to get the bad news over with. Al-Thani let him in, then excused himself. The remains of lunch cluttered a table back by the floor-to-ceiling windows. The Spaniard sat on the couch in the front room, watching CNN.

"The swords are rattling louder and louder in the desert. War in the Middle East soon."

"That will be good for the One."

The One thrived on chaos.

"But over too quickly, I fear." He clicked off the TV and looked at Ernst. "Your men are dead."

Men? That meant both. Ernst already knew about one. Young Kristof had called with news of the crash, certain that one of the operatives was dead, and the other was either a prisoner, comatose, or dead.

These had been experienced men. But he maintained a placid exterior. "By what means?"

"Massive trauma due to an automobile accident. The police say their vehicle shows evidence of a recent collision which they believe caused them to lose control. The passenger wasn't wearing a seat belt and was thrown free. The driver suffered a broken neck."

"No gunplay?"

"Weapons were found at the scene, and one had been fired, but no wounds on your men."

"This is tragic. They were good men."

The Spaniard's eyebrows lifted. "Not good enough to stop a boy in a rental truck, apparently."

Very troubling, that. Kristof had reported that the driver was alone when the operatives gave chase. The slaver had identified him as the mysterious Lonnie.

Mysterious indeed. Ernst could not comprehend how a youth—assuming the description from their slave-running informant had been accurate—could have run two seasoned operatives off the road. Then again, no one knew for how long he had been a courier.

"He was probably just lucky."

"Well," said Trejador, "at least *someone* is having luck. Certainly not you."

Ernst stiffened at the tone. "As fellow actuators, striving to achieve the Order's goals, I would consider this a joint venture."

Trejador smiled. "So now it's a joint venture? Last I heard you were going to 'settle this affair.' Now two of your people are dead."

He's enjoying this, Ernst thought.

Well, were positions reversed, Ernst would be reveling in his discomfiture.

"We need to cooperate."

"Well, of course we do. But I'm of the school—perhaps you'd call it the 'old school'—that believes in *making* luck. And one accomplishes that by *being* there. But we've had this conversation before."

Yes, they had.

Ernst said, "How, pray tell, would my presence in the car have prevented it from running off the road, most likely killing me as well?"

The Spaniard allowed a brief smile that Ernst attributed to pleasant contemplation of such a possibility.

"Putting yourself in the same car? Absolutely not. An unthinkable redundancy. No, I would have been following behind in a second car, just in case something catastrophic—like being run off the road—or some mundane mishap—say, a flat tire—befell the first."

"And once the first car had stopped the truck, then what?"

"Stop the truck? Did I say anything about stopping the truck? That is cowboy stuff. I simply would follow at a discreet distance and find out where he made his delivery, and then follow him home from there."

Follow him home . . . what a simple solution. Why hadn't Ernst thought of that?

But Ernst knew his mind didn't work that way. He had a confrontational nature. He believed in facing problems head-on—gripping them by the throat and bending them to his will. But from a distance.

He'd approached the driver with that in mind: Capture him on a lonely road, take him to a secure location, and extract whatever he knew about the missing millions. Father had often warned Ernst about the use of force.

Father . . . ever the manipulator of men and circumstances. A whispered word, a planted suggestion . . . he hadn't needed to bend people and circumstances to his will . . . he merely paved a certain path, and people followed it of their own accord, thinking the choice of direction was theirs, when it was anything but.

Another question: If that would have been Trejador's course of action, why hadn't he suggested it? The obvious answer: He'd wanted Ernst to fail. No . . . too paranoid. Ernst sensed that Trejador perceived him—quite accurately—as a threat to his position. But despite his excesses, Trejador's loyalty to the Order was unquestioned.

"My dear Ernst," he said, waving a hand. "That is all water under the bridge, as they say. My latest interview with the slaver—conducted by phone only an hour ago—has convinced me that the driver you seek is clueless. He was there by happenstance, unwillingly recruited due to a mishap, and, according to the slaver, seemed genuinely afraid of whoever killed the Arabs. He is a dead end."

Ernst wasn't so sure about that. "The slaver says this Lonnie saw the killers. And he has a recollection of someone with Lonnie when he broke his knees. Where did he get help?"

"Certainly not from the gunmen who were out to kill him and his fellow driver. I think we should concentrate our efforts on finding those abducted girls. There are twenty-eight of them. Can someone move that many children around and leave no trace? Find the girls and we find the men who stole the money."

The logic was unassailable, but Ernst could not get past the feeling that this Lonnie was the weak link. The attack on the Arabs smacked of a certain level of professionalism. Stumble upon the perpetrators and one might fall into a snake pit. However, the driver was, by the slaver's account, a callow bumpkin. Ernst saw no downside to learning if he had indeed seen the killers. Should that turn out not to be the case, then only a little time and effort were at risk. However, if he possessed a single scrap of useful information . . .

He saw no point in arguing, however.

"Then we agree to concentrate our efforts on finding the girls?"

Ernst nodded but wasn't giving up on the driver. Not yet. He should have known Trejador would not give Ernst free rein in finding the money. This had become a contest between the Spaniard and himself, one he was determined to win.

SUNDAY

1

They lay gasping, tangled in each other's arms, until Cristin slid off and rolled onto her back beside him.

"You've improved since last week," she said.

She'd somehow managed to be even more voracious tonight than last Sunday.

"I have an excellent coach."

"Who hardly had to do a bit of coaching this time."

"I'm a quick study."

She pulled up the covers and snuggled beside him and they lay in silence for a while.

"What are you thinking?" she asked.

"About what an almost perfect night it's been."

She lifted her head. "Almost?"

"Well, dinner . . ."

"I loved it."

He shook his head. "I'm glad."

"You didn't?"

"Not my kind of food."

"You chose it."

"I know. I consider it a learning experience."

He'd heard Le Cirque mentioned on the radio and so he'd wrangled a reservation for two. He knew it would be expensive but that wasn't an issue. He'd wanted to treat Cristin to something really special—take her someplace she wouldn't take herself.

Maybe it was their young age, but when they arrived at the Mayfair Hotel, home of the restaurant, they were treated like second-class citizens. Despite their reservation, they were kept waiting for forty-five minutes. Cristin didn't seem to mind, but it rankled Jack. When they finally were seated the service was perfunctory and the food . . . well, Cristin enjoyed all the sauces and such, and the pinot noir was delicious, but Jack would have much preferred a cheesesteak and a good lager.

He left the restaurant hungry—for food and for Cristin. He delighted in her company and wanted to immerse himself in her. But she wanted to go to a place called Wetlands down on Hudson Street. Someone named Joan Osborne was singing there tonight and Cristin had heard she was good. Jack put on a brave face and hailed a cab.

Turned out she was very good. After the show they made a beeline for Cristin's apartment. No dancing around with Cuervo shooters and admiring her artwork this time. As soon as the door closed behind them they were ripping at each other's clothes and stumbling toward the bedroom.

"Well, I disagree with your 'almost,'" she said. "I don't see how it could be improved."

"Then my work here is done."

She gave him a gentle punch on the shoulder. "Hey! That's my line. And buster, you're not done yet."

He smiled. "I was hoping you'd say that."

She snaked a thigh across his pelvis. "What's your agenda for the coming week? No more hijacking attempts, I hope."

During the seemingly interminable wait for their reserved table, Cristin had questioned how he could afford Le Cirque on a deliveryman's earnings and he told her about a bonus for a special delivery—true in a way—and from there he'd slipped into a mention of the attempt. He skimmed the details, saying only that he'd managed to elude the would-be hijackers. He hadn't let on that the hijacking hadn't been random and that he rather than his cargo had been the target.

He hugged her closer. "Worried about me?"

"You're a friend. And I'm just now getting you properly trained. I don't want to have to start breaking in someone new."

He barked a laugh. "Now that's what I call concern for a lover."

"We aren't lovers, Jack," she said evenly. "We're friends—"

"—with benefits. Right. Is it okay if I love the benefits?"

"Perfectly okay. Just don't start attaching strings."

"Gotcha."

Right. No strings. The way he wanted it too. And yet . . . at a moment like this, as physically close as one could be to another person, feeling deliciously intimate, he could imagine how a string—just one, a little one—wouldn't seem so bad . . . wouldn't seem bad at all.

"So how about it?" she said. "What's in store for the week? Going home for Thanksgiving?"

T-Day was this Thursday, wasn't it. Where'd the time go?

And jeez, home would be the last place . . .

"No. You?"

"I wouldn't mind, but I'm running three parties."

"What happened to home cooking?"

"You get well-heeled families scattered all over the country and the world who want to fly everyone in for a holiday feast but don't want to do the legwork, who you gonna call? Moi."

"So no family turkey for you?"

She shook her head. "Nope. And no more driving for you, I hope."

"You got that right. Not worth the risk."

"Taking the week off then?"

"Not exactly." He hesitated, then decided to plunge ahead. "Looking for a way to con a con man."

He couldn't help it. It felt right telling her. It added a new layer of intimacy, and tonight, for some reason, he found himself craving intimacy.

"And what qualifies you for that?"

"Absolutely nothing. Well, I've gamed one or two people over the years with varying results."

She rose on one elbow and stared at him. "When?"

"High school . . . college."

"High school . . . you weren't behind that locker thing, were you?"

Jack knew exactly what she meant but kept his voice flat as he offered a puzzled expression.

"What locker thing?"

"Oh, come on! It was all anyone talked about for most of freshman year!"

He'd never told anyone that he'd been behind the pranks and wasn't about to start. It had ended in a death, after all.

"Oh, you mean with Oliver What's-his-name."

"It was Carson Toliver and you know it." She smiled. "I had the weirdest feeling it was you."

Jack felt his neck muscles bunch. "Me? Are you crazed? Me a frosh and him a senior, captain of the football team, no less. Where'd you get that idea?"

"Like I said, just a feeling. He started talking trash about your friend Weir—Weezy Connell and within a day or two all this weirdness starts coming down on him. And pretty soon no one's talking about Weezy anymore." She cocked her head and stared. "Funny thing about that."

"Pure coincidence."

He managed to return her stare, but it wasn't easy. It became harder as her slow smile spread to a grin.

"It *was* you!"

"No way."

"It was! How did you beat that lock—the one he'd glued and nailed? How did you get past that?"

"I don't know what you're talking about."

"You do! I've wanted to know for seven years now!"

"Seven years . . . has it been that long?"

Seemed like a lifetime.

"Yes! And you're going to tell me!"

"Can't tell you what I don't know."

"Oh, reeeeally? Vee haf vays of making you talk."

She slid her lips down his belly and began flicking her tongue against him. Immediately he hardened.

He laughed. "You don't really expect me to say, 'Oh, no, not that, anything but that, please stop, I'll tell you anything if only you'll stop,' do you?"

She ran her tongue up and down the underside of the shaft, sending a delicious shiver through him.

"Not yet, but you will when I don't let you come."

"What?"

"You heard me. You're going to get the worst case of blue balls you've ever had—epic blue balls. You're going to beg to come but I won't let you."

He laughed again.

She looked up at him, a challenge in her eyes. "You don't think I can?"

"Do your worst."

She bent to her work.

Eventually he told her everything.

MONDAY

1

Jack had wasted better than an hour following Vinny Donuts after his weekly payment pickup from Julio and learned nothing new. It looked like The Spot was the last stop on Mondays, after which Vinny drove his fellow hoods back to that appliance store and then took himself to the salvage yard.

Jack made a mental note to find out who owned that car cemetery, although he had no idea how to go about it. Maybe Abe would know.

He'd stopped for some bread and sliced ham at a mom-and-pop deli on West 21st and had just kicked his Harley to life again when a car screeched to a stop just ahead of him.

He heard "Jack!" followed by a stream of excited Spanish, then "Jack!" again. He looked up and saw a familiar face leaning out the window of a Plymouth Volare junker that had to be ten years old. Who—?

Oh, Christ—Ramon, one of the Dominicans from the landscaping crew.

Jack gunned the engine, wheeled around, and roared east, back toward Sixth Avenue. Had there been traffic coming he would have been running against it, since 21st was one-way westbound. He turned onto Sixth and raced uptown. Horns blared and tires screamed behind him. A glance in his left mirror showed the Plymouth reversing out of 21st the wrong way. It slewed to a stop, then, with Ramon still hanging out the window, waving his fist, it screeched toward him with smoking tires. The sun glaring off the windshield obscured other occupants in the car. Rico too?

Up ahead traffic had stopped at 23rd Street. Every eight or ten blocks or so, from the Village up to Central Park, New York enlarged one of its streets to accommodate two-way traffic, and 23rd was one of those.

Jack steered his bike between cars. No way the Plymouth could follow. He looked over his shoulder to see Ramon jumping out of the car.

Okay. If he wanted to go mano a mano right here, okay. Then he saw the machete in his hand.

"Oh, shit!"

He'd reached 23rd. Pedestrians and four lanes of crosstown traffic blocked his way.

Screw it. He gunned forward and, to a chorus of horns and angry shouts, wove his way through the slow-moving traffic. One lane, two lanes, three . . .

And then some belligerent taxi driver—yes, a redundancy in New York—pushed to get bumper to bumper with the car ahead to block Jack, as if it mattered one way or another to his life if Jack slipped past him. He half succeeded. Jack forced his way between the bumpers but had no room to squeeze his foot pegs through. Empty pavement waited less than two yards away.

He gave the cabbie a you-asshole look, then turned and saw Ramon a car length away, shouting something as he charged between the cars with the machete waving over his head. The cabbie spotted him too as the car ahead inched forward. Wide-eyed, he didn't push to close the space but waved Jack through.

Jack opened up the Harley and did a wheelie up Sixth Avenue. He passed his apartment and the garage where he kept the bike, and kept going.

Close. Way too close.

Maybe this was the city's way of telling him it was time to move out of the flower district and into a quieter neighborhood.

THANKSGIVING

1

Look at us, Roman thought as he turned away from the window and caught sight of the two other occupants of the room. What an unlikely trio.

Drexler sipping a Dutch pilsner, Nasser some club soda, and me swirling some Balvenie double wood around a single ice cube.

Drexler in that ridiculous white suit, Nasser in a thobe, and me looking oh-so-American in my flannel shirt and jeans.

Room service offered limited choices because of the holiday, and so they'd all decided to go their separate ways for dinner after the meeting.

How did we ever agree on a plan of action?

But somehow they had . . . up to a point.

"So, it's settled?"

Drexler sniffed. "I still think this Lonnie character knows more than you give him credit for, but I'm game for the sting—as the Americans would call it. It's all moot, of course, if you don't secure funding from the High Council."

"I will be at my most persuasive. Nasser?"

"I'm sure I can involve our young Palestinian friend. He had jihadist contacts at the refugee center and the mosque, plus he was friends with Tachus and I'm positive he wants some payback."

"The broken-kneed Reggie also wants payback," Drexler added.

"As do we." Roman took a dramatic sniff. "The air is redolent of revenge. That is good, as long as it is served cold. If we allow it to overheat our judgment, we will fail. We mustn't forget that we are dealing with bloodthirsty people."

Drexler raised a pedantic index finger. "But bloodthirsty people on a mission. Our advantage increases in proportion to their devotion to that mission. The more fanatical and emotionally involved they are, the better for us."

Roman could not disagree. "But we don't know their ideology or their religion. What is the threshold that will set them into motion? One child? Five? Ten?"

Nasser said, "I would say a single child would trigger them—*if* they know about it. But one child might well slip under their radar. We must assume they are not fools, so they must learn of the 'shipment' through their usual channels."

"Five then," said Drexler. "Boys? Girls? A mixture?"

It didn't matter, so Roman flipped a mental coin. "Let's make it boys, this time."

Nasser al-Thani frowned. "Assuming all goes according to plan, once we've captured our prey, what do we do with the children?"

Roman smiled. The answer was so obvious. "Capturing the killers is only step one. Our goal is the return of our investment. We will need a means to induce them to tell us where the money is. The children will make excellent persuaders."

"I agree," Drexler said, nodding. "But this will all take time to arrange, and I assume no one will object if I make use of the interval to track down the elusive Lonnie. Reggie is very motivated in that regard, and I've supplied him with his weapon of choice."

A waste of time, Roman knew, but let Drexler pursue his obsession with Lonnie. It would keep him out of Roman's hair.

2

Kadir Allawi and Mahmoud Abouhalima stepped out of the Al-Kifah Center and walked west along Atlantic Avenue. On a normal Thursday at this time, the streets would be jammed with traffic and pedestrians. Today, because of the American holiday, the two of them traveled unimpeded.

Both were fresh from prayers at the Al-Farouq mosque upstairs at the center where they'd listened to an enraged Sheikh Omar rail against their missing fellow Muslims who were home with their families. This was an American holiday, the blind cleric had shouted, where thanks were given to the Christian God and the Jewish God. No true follower of Islam should recognize this holiday. No such Holy Day—the origin of the English word "holiday"—existed in the Quran. Only the Quran could declare a Holy Day. This fourth Thursday in November had been declared a holiday by men, signed into law by infidels. Laws cannot come from men. All law comes from the Quran.

Sheikh Omar's lectures never failed to fill Kadir with holy purpose. But he had noticed a shift in the cleric's targets. Where Mubarak and Egypt's secular government had been his focus at first, jihad in America seemed his main concern now. For that reason—and that reason alone—Kadir was glad he was here in America, in the heart of the new jihad, instead of back in Palestine.

"Thanksgiving," Mahmoud said, speaking the English word then switching to Arabic. "It's not so bad, I think, if it leaves the streets to us."

"You have something to be thankful for—the FBI questioned you and then let you go."

"Yes, I thank Allah for that."

"And we can also be thankful that money has been promised for Sayyid's defense."

El Sayyid Nosair's picture had been all over the papers for a while after the assassination, but the furor seemed to have died down this past week. Word had come from Osama bin Laden that he was sending money for his defense.

"Yes, but it will go to a headline-hunting Jew."

Kadir had been shocked when a notorious lawyer named William Kuntsler, a Jew, announced that he would be defending Sayyid. He wasn't sure how he felt about that.

"I know Sayyid needs a defense, but a Jew?"

Mahmoud said, "Remember what Sheikh Omar says: We need not use pure Islamic methods in order to achieve a purer form of Islam. If our goal is pure, we may use whoever and whatever means to achieve our end. And if that includes using Zionist pigs to hasten their own destruction, so be it."

That lifted some of the guilt Kadir had felt about plotting to deliver those children into slavery. If it furthered jihad, it was all good.

"But what of Tachus?" he said. "Does no one care that he was shot down like a dog?"

"He was martyred in the cause of jihad and has gone to his reward. He is in Heaven with Allah and has seventy-two virgins to attend him. But those who attacked him also attacked jihad, because they stole funds that would further jihad. We shall deal with them—with all of them."

"How?"

"I will show you."

They continued along Atlantic Avenue at a quick pace. Kadir had to work to keep up with the taller Mahmoud's long strides.

"Where are we going?"

"Not much farther now."

They came to a point where they could see the harbor. Mahmoud pointed across the water to the lower end of Manhattan.

"Look at it, Kadir. Study the skyline."

Kadir did as he was bid. The sinking sun gleamed off the two gleaming fingers of the Trade Towers as they pointed skyward.

"Now close your eyes and imagine one tower toppling against the other, and the two of them crashing to earth in a pile of rubble."

Kadir closed his eyes and saw empty sky where steel and concrete and glass had risen, saw smoke rising to heaven from the ruins.

He opened his eyes. The Towers remained.

"A beautiful dream."

"Not a dream," Mahmoud said. "A plan. One you and I will make happen."

3

Neil Zalesky perched on a stool in The Main Event and watched the Lions crush the Broncos on the TV over the bar. The place was empty except for guys without families. His own was back in Toledo and he didn't miss them—couldn't even *remember* missing them, ever. Bunch of stiffs. On the rare occasions he'd go back home—only for funerals and only if someone really close had bought it—his mother would badger him with the traditional you-never-call-you-never-write shit. And what could he say? He never did. Out of sight, out of mind. As for the marriage thing—he'd tried it and look how that turned out. At least he didn't have kids tugging on his sleeve.

Marriage . . . the word triggered a memory cascade starting with Rosa, tumbling to Julio, and ending at the missing money.

Neil slammed his hand on the counter, knocking over his beer.

"Shit!"

He jumped and lifted his arm—his left arm—to keep from soaking the sleeve of his sweater. Wrong arm—pain shot through his broken humerus and into his shoulder—

"Shit!"

—causing him to twist off his stool. He shot his left foot out to keep from falling—the bad hip.

"Shit! Shit! Shit!"

Joe hurried over with a bar rag. "Neil, you okay?"

"Yeah. Just clumsy with this sling, is all."

But he wasn't okay. Nowhere fucking near okay. He hurt every minute of every day since the fall. He couldn't sleep. He couldn't work the old ladies. And he was out fifteen fucking grand!

All because of that greasy little spic.

Maybe not Julio directly . . . the lock on the apartment door had been picked and he couldn't see Julio being able to do that. Which meant the spic must have hired somebody. Sure as hell wasn't one of those two drunks at the bar all the time. Whoever it was, Neil had no doubt the same somebody had untied his knots at Rosa's. But how had the guy known he'd be at Rosa's—especially the second night in a row?

Only one way: He'd been followed.

The idea creeped him out. He stole a look around the bar. A couple of new faces, but that wasn't unusual. They came and went, but the regulars remained, well, regular.

He balled his fists—*shit!* Even *that* hurt.

Well, Julio was gonna feel some pain of his own when Neil bought The Spot. The place would already be his—or at least pretty damn close to his—if the owner wasn't in Saudi fucking Arabia. But his mother said he'd be home soon. Neil had always wanted to own a bar.

He'd control only ninety percent of it, but that was even better than owning it all. Because Julio would still hold ten percent, and ten percent wasn't dick. The spic would have no say. Neil was gonna make his life miserable. And once Neil turned the place around and got it back in the black, Julio would wait till hell froze over before he saw his cut.

Soon as he got control, he'd hire Joe to run the place.

Right after he kicked Julio out on his ass.

4

Vinny Donato leaned back on the couch and thought of that old Alka-Seltzer commercial he used to love as a kid: "*I can't believe I ate that whole thing.*" That was how he felt. He would have loved to loosen his belt and unbutton his pants, but he wasn't at home.

He remembered that particular commercial because it was playing all the time on TV when he was twelve, just around the time his father died. Dad had complained of indigestion, taken a couple of Alka-Seltzer, gone to bed, and woke up dead.

He wondered how his life would be now if the old man hadn't kicked off then.

Anyway, Mom was still around. He'd picked her up earlier today, around two or so, and driven her over here to Uncle Bill's place in Howard Beach. He was married to Mom's sister Marie and his real name was Biagio but people had called him Bill forever. Mom brought her revered veal-and-pork lasagna, and Vinny contributed some wine he and Aldo had lifted from the storeroom of a high-end liquor store in Forest Hills.

He and Mom had arrived just as Marie was setting out brimming antipasto trays: prosciutto, salami, and mortadella with provolone, Parmigiano-Reggiano, asiago, and gorgonzola, plus giant shrimp, the ever-present olives, along with sliced bread, breadsticks, and crackers.

The usual twenty or so aunts, uncles, nieces, and nephews had gathered for the annual feast. Between helping Bill with drinks, Vinny managed to inflict considerable damage on the antipasto. Then it was on to the serious food. Vinny poured the amarone and pinot grigio he'd contributed while

Marie put out platters of her huge homemade cheese ravioli swimming in red gravy.

The turkey followed, with Uncle Bill wielding the carving knife, but it was almost a side dish against Mom's lasagna, plus gnocchi pomodoro, and linguine con vongole.

Then fresh hot chestnuts, followed by a ricotta cheesecake, cannoli, a huge assortment of cookies. Plus Aunt Marie always set aside a couple of zeppole for Vinny.

No fucking way he could believe he ate the whole thing.

"Vinny?" Uncle Bill was leaning out of the kitchen, holding the phone receiver. "You got a call."

Vinny struggled off the couch. A call? Who'd be calling him today? Had to be important. Couldn't be family because all the family that mattered was here. Had to be business. But what?

"It's Tommy," Uncle Bill said, handing him the receiver. "He sounds funny."

Vinny jammed the receiver tight against his ear. "Yeah?"

"Yo, VinnAY!"

Christ, coked to the eyeballs.

"Tommy. How'd you know to call here?"

"'Cause you go to your uncle Bill's every Turkey Day."

No argument there.

"Well, Happy Thanksgiving, Tommy."

"Fuck Thanksgiving."

"Ay, don't say that."

"I hate Turkey Day. You know why? Because we don't do no collections on Turkey Day."

The ladies were busy all around him with the after-dinner cleanup. Vinny snaked through them and stretched the phone cord to the max—just enough to put him in Marie's laundry room by the back door.

"Nobody around to collect from, Tommy."

"Then we go to their homes and pull 'em out of their easy chairs and make 'em pay up on their front lawns."

Jesus, what had set him off? Had to be cash flow. More going up his nose than flowing into his pocket.

"But anyway, I didn't call to complain about this useless fucking holiday. I called to celebrate you and me goin' into business together."

Vinny felt a coolness trickle along his spine. "What business?"

"Salvage, man. That looks like a sweet deal you got going there. But I'm thinkin' it's too much for a guy who's never handled a business before. You need an experienced hand, so I'm gonna partner with you."

Vinny controlled his voice. "I'm doin' fine, Tommy." He wanted to add, *and the last thing I need is a fucked-up coke head snorting up all the profits.* But he held that back.

"But you could be doing so much better—and with my help, we'll both be doing better."

Over my fucking grave, Vinny thought. But he didn't want to get into an argument on the phone in his uncle's kitchen.

"I gotta go, Tommy."

"Yeah, I know. It's fuckin' Turkey Day. Tell your uncle I said hello. We'll talk about this tomorrow."

Vinny returned to the kitchen and with great effort replaced the wall phone on its cradle without smashing it. He turned to find his uncle staring at him.

"I don't know what you just heard, but that look on your face tells me it can't be good. Ain't I told you a million times—?"

Vinny waved him off. "It's all right. Nothing important."

Bill had a nine-to-five with the Transit Authority. Started as a conductor, moved up, but still brought home shit pay. When Vinny's dad died, Bill started with the father-figure thing, always warning him against getting involved with the "mooks." After Mom remarried, he backed off. And by the time Mom's second kicked the bucket, Vinny was out of the house, doing a little this and a little that and getting connected.

Bill gave him a long stare, then turned away. Vinny went and poured himself another glass of amarone.

Right now, all he could do was hope this scheme of Tommy's was pure coke talk and he'd forget it tomorrow. Otherwise, he had a problem. Tommy was Vinny's superior, but if push came to shove, Vinny would go over his head and appeal to Tony Cannon.

No fucking way was Tommy coming into the business.

5

Jack-Jack-Jack . . .

The name echoed through Rico's head as he limped along West 23rd Street, inspecting the faces of the passersby. The wind cut through his ratty hoodie.

"It's cold out here," Ramon said in Spanish as he walked beside him. He had his hands jammed into the pockets of his fatigue jacket. "And we ain't gonna find him today anyway."

Perhaps Thanksgiving wasn't the best day to be searching, but Rico had to do *something.*

"This is where you spotted the *maricón*, right?"

"Yeah—"

"And you said he had groceries like he was picking up food."

"Yeah."

"And where do you buy stuff like that? Where you live. He lives around here. I can smell him."

"Yeah, but—"

"But what?"

"It's been a long time."

"Long time? You think it's been a long time for you? How about for me? You said you chase him with your machete. Why—"

"I chased him, and I scared him, but I don't know if I could really cut him."

"Well, *I* can! It's been more than a month and my knee still ain't right! I can't take a deep breath without it still hurting. Bring him to me, and *I'll* cut him!"

He'd strapped his machete to his leg to act as a brace and to hide it. He'd made a slit in his jeans big enough to slip his hand through, so he could grab the handle and pull the blade free in a second.

He still could not work, and that humiliated him. He'd been reduced to taking money from his sister to pay the rent.

He knew what Ramon was thinking. He'd heard Carlos and Juan mention it: *Maybe Rico shouldn't have punched him.*

Easy to say now. And to tell the truth, Rico wished he hadn't. Jack had turned into an animal. But Rico had just been so pissed, him coming in and getting next to Giovanni, taking Rico's spot and all.

Jack-Jack-Jack . . .

He would find him, no matter how long it took. He patted the scabbard of his machete. And then . . .

6

Reggie wasn't used to shooting from a sitting position. Never tried it before. He was used to standing, and occasionally kneeling, but he couldn't stand yet, and sure as shit couldn't kneel, so he sat in his wheelchair and did his best.

Hard as hell.

But he wanted to get the feel of the new hunting bow. That weird dude Drexler had asked him his weapon of choice. Reggie had told him and the next day he'd found himself the owner of a PSE Infinity SR-1000. A *fine* bow.

He rolled his chair over to the target he'd set up on the far side of the basement. Drexler had moved him into the basement of this old stone building near Chinatown and the Manhattan Bridge. He called it a "Lodge," but what lodge it belonged to, Reggie didn't know. He hadn't recognized the big seal in the front foyer.

Whoever they were, they seemed to have bucks. Nobody had told him in so many words, but he could read between the lines and gathered that Drexler's people had funded the purchase of the girls; they'd been ripped off and wanted their bucks back.

Reggie was more than glad to help him.

He pulled his arrows from the seat cushion he'd propped on a chair. He'd attached a crude smiley face to the cushion and labeled it "Lonnie." His first shots had gone wide, some missing the paper entirely. But this last go-round had landed ten out of ten in the circular face.

He smiled at the grouping of punctures and began murmuring his Scottish grandmother's favorite song.

"*We'll meet again . . .*"

7

"So glum on such a festive day?"

Jack shook himself out of a reverie and looked at Abe, wedged into the other side of the diner booth. A steaming plate of sliced turkey, giblet gravy, mashed potatoes, cranberry sauce, and green beans sat before each of them.

Jack shrugged. "First time I've ever spent Thanksgiving alone."

"And I'm what? Chopped liver?"

Oh, hell.

"No, I didn't mean *alone* alone. I meant without my family."

"You're sad and lonely? Maybe you should go back."

"No way. I'm neither. Just seems strange, is all."

Would have seemed even more strange at home—the first Thanksgiving ever without his mother. He couldn't imagine the day without her. She'd always spent it in the background, bustling around the kitchen, with Kate acting as sous chef, while Jack and Tom and Dad watched football in the living room. Eventually Dad would get called away to carve the turkey. Then they'd gather around the loaded table and dig in.

A real Norman Rockwell scene.

He'd been trying to imagine what today was like in that house where he'd grown up. Had Kate taken over the cooking duties? Were tears flowing?

Would they find cooking dinner without Mom too painful and not even bother? Were they hunched over turkey dinners in a Marlton restaurant, just like Jack was here at the Highwater Diner?

He realized with a start that this wasn't just their first Thanksgiving ever without Mom, it was also their first T-Day ever without Jack. It bothered him that his absence probably magnified his father's and Kate's pain—he couldn't see Tom giving a damn. Were they thinking of him as he was thinking of them?

Moments like this made him question the course he'd set for himself.

He shook it off.

"How about you? No family?"

Abe shrugged as he shifted his portly frame on the bench. "None to speak of."

"What does that mean?"

"I should maybe say, None to speak *to*." He began spooning the gravy off the mashed potatoes and into his mouth. "Uncle Jake was the last to speak to me and he's gone."

Jack's old boss, Mr. Rosen. "Really? You know, when you think about it, it was his frail health started us on the twisty path to these two facing seats."

"How so?"

"Well, when did we meet?"

"First meet? In my uncle's shop, back in . . ."

"The fall of '83—October."

"If you say so."

"I do. Question is, why did you stop that particular day?"

Abe shrugged. "Let's see . . . I was on my way back from Atlantic City."

"Gambling?"

"I should gamble? Who has time? Send a check directly to Donald Trump would be better. Save us all a lot of effort. No, I was arranging the purchase of merchandise."

Jack smiled. "Sporting goods?"

"What else?"

"What made you stop?"

"I was on the Atlantic City Expressway, heading for the parkway, when I remembered that if I kept on the Expressway I'd cross 206, and 206 led to my dear uncle Jake. I hadn't seen him in a while and decided to drop in. Nothing 'twisty' about that."

"Yeah, but your uncle was sick that day, so he wasn't in the store. If he'd been in the store, he would have introduced me—'This is Jack'—and left me at the counter while you two gabbed."

"Instead I found you there alone."

"And you tried to get me to cheat your uncle."

Another shrug. "A test. You passed. Mazel tov. What's the point?"

"The point is, if your uncle had been feeling better or I'd flunked the test, you wouldn't have given me your card."

"And you wouldn't have looked me up."

"And we wouldn't be sitting here. Like I said: a twisty path."

Abe glanced down at his plate. "Gevalt! What's this? George!" he called, signaling to the owner who'd also served as their waiter—he and Abe apparently went back a ways. "A tragedy has befallen my mashed potatoes!"

Behind the chrome-trimmed Formica counter, George Kuropolis, fortyish, slender, turned their way. "What? You spill them? I swear, Abe—"

"No-no! Their gravy has disappeared and they're verklempt."

"Their gravy has—oh, I get it."

Half a minute later he was at their booth with a gravy boat in one hand and a bottle of white wine in the other. He proceeded to cover Abe's mound of mashed potatoes with another layer of gravy.

Abe beamed. "Such a mensch you are. They were waxing suicidal without their old friend, Gravy."

"Wouldn't want you eating waxy dead potatoes." He placed the gravy boat on the table. "I'll leave that here—to prevent another near tragedy." He went to pour more wine into Abe's glass but it was nearly full. "Hey, Abe—drink up. No charge. You buy the Thanksgiving platter, house wine is free."

Abe shrugged. "Why for I should drink? It takes up valuable space that could be used for food."

"I'll take his," Jack said.

George looked at Jack's empty glass, then at Jack. "You sure you're old enough to drink?"

"Barely," Abe said as he began skimming the gravy off his potatoes again. "But he's legal."

"How do you like the wine?" George said as he refilled the glass.

Jack didn't know wine but he knew terrible, and this stuff was it. He tried to get a look at the label. Really, was there a grape that tasted like Sour Patch Kids? But it contained alcohol and he needed some tonight.

"Very different. Did you make it yourself?"

He laughed. "Just a California Chablis I used to buy for my wife."

"And you're still married?" Abe said.

"I should say, my *ex*-wife."

And now we know why, Jack thought.

As George wandered away, Jack looked at Abe. "You were saying something about your family not speaking to you?"

"I have a very small family. One daughter, really. She's an academic and has no use for me. She speaks to me only when absolutely necessary and then very grudgingly. She lives in Queens, just across the river, but I haven't seen her since 1986. I suppose if I am thankful for anything, it's that."

"Not speaking to her?"

"She's a very unpleasant woman, a klogmuter, and we'll probably both die alone." Jack supposed he looked surprised because Abe shrugged and added, "You can't choose your kinder."

Jack was thinking that was how he felt about his brother Tom, and it was mutual—neither had any use for each other. But if Abe had a daughter, that meant he must have had—

"From finding a circumspect way to ask, I'll save you: I am a widower."

"Sorry."

"So am I," he said as he poured more gravy over his slowly shrinking mound of potato. "She was a beryah who kept guard over what landed on my plate, but she's gone."

"Can I ask how—?"

"She's gone. That's all that matters. A better subject is your twisty path. You want twisty? Twisty you'll get. Never mind that I gave you my card. You never would have used it if you hadn't moved to the city. And if a certain event hadn't occurred, you'd be having Thanksgiving dinner tonight with your family—your *whole* family."

Jack swallowed. "Yeah . . . 'a certain event' . . ."

The cinder block through the windshield . . . which led to another event . . . killing Ed . . . Jack hadn't told Abe that part.

"Which led to you dropping out of your old life and starting a new one here."

"All because of a homicidal asshole named Ed."

"This Ed? He was out to kill your mother?"

"No. It was random."

"You're so sure?"

"He was out to maim or kill somebody, anybody. My mother just happened to be in the wrong place at the wrong time."

"But why should he choose that moment to drop the block?"

Jack's turn to shrug. "No one was looking, I suppose."

"Exactly!" Abe said, pointing his fork at Jack's nose. "But what if someone had jogged by then, or walked their dachshund across the overpass then? He would have paused, and the block would have hit another car. Maybe our supposed jogger stopped to retie his shoe. If it hadn't come loose he would have reached the overpass about the same time as your family car; Ed would have waited for him to pass and the block would have hit another car traveling behind yours."

"Like I said—random victim."

"No!" Another jab of the fork. "All cause and effect. If the jogger had tied his shoe properly the first time, your mother would be alive."

Jack saw where he was going. "Or if Ed ran over a nail in the road and got a flat—same thing."

"Yes. A better outcome for your family."

"But maybe a car that cut him off on a traffic merge hit the nail and got the flat instead."

"Allowing Ed to arrive on time to cause the tragic outcome."

"Sounds like the theory about a butterfly flapping its wings in Ecuador—"

"—and causing a tornado in Kansas. The butterfly effect."

Jack was losing his appetite. "I can't go around wondering 'What if?' all the time."

"Of course not. Meshugge it will make you. One thing you do know: Like it or not, it all led to this dinner."

"And that's a good thing. But here's a thought: What if I'd lost your card? Seven years is a long time to keep a little piece of paper."

"Yet keep it you did."

"But if I hadn't, I wouldn't have called you back in June, and therefore wouldn't have met Bertel and gone to work for him."

"And thus wouldn't have been in a position to save those girls."

The girls . . . Bonita . . . he wondered where they were, *how* they were. Back with their families yet? He hoped so.

"Talk about a butterfly effect: If some lady hadn't called the ATF, I'd have made my usual cigarette run and the girls would have been delivered to those Arabs as slaves."

"Well, the Mikulskis would still have been there."

"But they wouldn't have been able to prevent Reggie from backing one of the trucks into the harbor. Strange to think how I never would have wound up in the Duck house if she hadn't made that call." He remembered another piece of the picture. "Hey, wait—if some dog hadn't run in front of the other truck that was supposed to ferry the girls, I would have driven away from the Duck house the next day no wiser about the girls."

Abe's eyebrows rose. "This dog was chasing a wing-flapping butterfly maybe?"

"Maybe. But as a result, I got dragooned into driving."

"So, in a way, the girls owe their futures to a busybody biddy and a jaywalking dog."

Jack thought of the attempted hijacking just days ago. "But you could also say that Tony's dead and I'm in trouble with those Arabs because of the biddy and the dog."

"Which brings us back already to Thanksgiving dinner together at the Highwater Diner."

"All because you gave me a business card."

"Which you saved instead of immediately throwing it away like any other teenager would do."

Jack shook his head. "The things lives hinge on. Almost seems like there's a plan."

"There is," Abe said, "but only the butterflies know what it is. They know just when to flap their wings. Unless you believe in God." He looked at Jack. "Do you believe in God?"

The question seemed out of left field.

"Why do you ask?"

"It's Thanksgiving. That is to whom we are supposed to be giving thanks."

"I've always seen it as more of a family day—a time for relatives to gather."

"It is. But that doesn't answer the question."

Jack thought about that cinder block coming through the windshield and crushing the life out of his mother. He remembered the assassination he'd almost witnessed just a few weeks ago, and what was going on in the Middle East with the Iraqis shooting up Kuwait, and all the people out of work here . . .

"Well, if there's a provident God, he seems asleep at the wheel."

Abe nodded. "Indeed he does."

"So can't we just be thankful?"

"We can."

Jack watched Abe attack the gravy again. With all the crap that had gone down this year, maybe he did have something to be thankful for: the guy across the table. Abe might not want to hear it, but Jack was thankful their lives had intersected. Thanksgiving was a family day and Abe just might be the first member of Jack's brand-new family.

He was also thankful that 1990 was edging to a close. What a crap year. He could only hope 1991 would be better. It couldn't be worse. Could it?

www.repairmanjack.com

THE SECRET HISTORY OF THE WORLD

The preponderance of my work deals with a history of the world that remains undiscovered, unexplored, and unknown to most of humanity. Some of this secret history has been revealed in the Adversary Cycle, some in the Repairman Jack novels, and bits and pieces in other, seemingly unconnected works. Taken together, even these millions of words barely scratch the surface of what has been going on behind the scenes, hidden from the workaday world. I've listed them below in chronological order.

Note: "Year Zero" is the end of civilization as we know it; "Year Zero Minus One" is the year preceding it, etc.

THE PAST

"Demonsong" (prehistory)
"Aryans and Absinthe"** (1923–1924)
Black Wind (1926–1945)
The Keep (1941)
Reborn (February–March 1968)
"Dat Tay Vao"*** (March 1968)
Jack: Secret Histories (1983)
Jack: Secret Circles (1983)
Jack: Secret Vengeance (1983)
"Faces"* (1988)
Cold City (1990)

YEAR ZERO MINUS THREE

Sibs (February)
The Tomb (summer)
"The Barrens"* (ends in September)
"A Day in the Life"* (October)
"The Long Way Home"****
Legacies (December)

YEAR ZERO MINUS TWO

"Interlude at Duane's"** (April)
Conspiracies (April) (includes "Home Repairs")

All the Rage (May) (includes "The Last Rakosh")
Hosts (June)
The Haunted Air (August)
Gateways (September)
Crisscross (November)
Infernal (December)

YEAR ZERO MINUS ONE

Harbingers (January)
Bloodline (April)
By the Sword (May)
Ground Zero (July)
The Touch (ends in August)
The Peabody-Ozymandias Traveling Circus & Oddity Emporium (ends in September)
"Tenants"*

YEAR ZERO

"Pelts"*
Reprisal (ends in February)
Fatal Error (February) (includes "The Wringer")
The Dark at the End (March)
Nightworld (May)

* available in *The Barrens and Others*
** available in *Aftershock & Others*
*** available in the 2009 reissue of *The Touch*
**** available in *Quick Fixes*